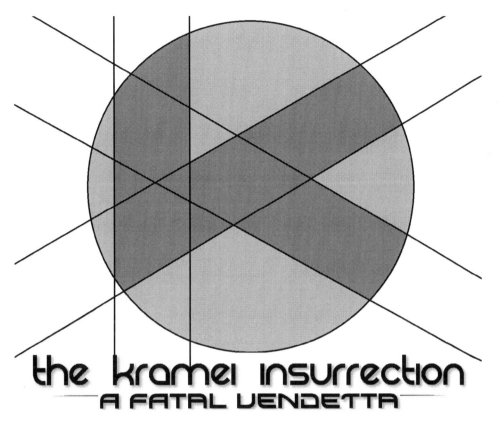

# the kramei insurrection
## A FATAL VENDETTA

BY JOHN HOUTZ III

The Kramei Insurrection - A Fatal Vendetta
Copyright © 2017 John Houtz III

First Edition

ISBN 9781549878749

# TABLE OF CONTENTS

*For Chris. I wouldn't have gotten far in this without him.*

# PROLOGUE

*This will be my final journal entry. It's been quite some time since I put my thoughts down to paper. That's to say I haven't had thoughts worthy of note? Maybe, but I write this journal not for myself, not for my fore-bearers, but to the new world order I leave behind. I begin this writing not even knowing if I will succeed, but the truth must be made available if I do not survive. I must take you back, though, to the beginning, for it was not The Kramei Insurrection. It was hundreds of years ago...*

There would be a coronation. The King would abdicate his throne to his son and heir. There were many whispers across the kingdom in regards to the power exchange. King Se'har had only ruled for a decade. He was in good health and surely had many years left to his reign. There were many rumors spoken amongst the people as to why he was stepping down. Some were logical explanations; others were ludicrous conspiracies. The recent political strife was one theory. The history books would paint him weak if he lost control of the colonists on Kramei. One theory, though rarely spoken aloud, questioned his mental state. Some felt he no longer possessed the will of mind to command the masses. The most popular, though, was the threat of patricide.

Not that it was ridiculous to think son wasn't capable of killing father; Xen-Que Poleb was as ruthless as they came. Whatever he lost in youth and arrogance he more than made up for in skill and ruthlessness. An accomplished warrior, Xen-Que had a military career not usually reserved for royalty. He wielded a power that was sinister and destructive. His father and brother's gifts were quite passive by comparison. The survivors of Old Moashei bestowed a powerful gift to every male member of the royal family. They had all proven their talent, for the most part. Xen-Que was no exception.

Xen-Que was a tall man, towering over most citizens in the kingdom. He was easily a head taller than his brother who was himself six feet tall. Modestly built, like his sibling, he never had to rely on brute strength in battle. Xen-Que's arms were much bulkier from wielding his mighty sword, *Solathros*. Until he had a son of his own, his brother would reclaim the great blade. His gray eyes were both beautiful and threatening. His hair was dark as a starless night and reached to the small of his back. There wasn't a single blemish on his entire body, save a sole exception. The palms of his hands looked scarred and callous. Despite living a life of privilege, he had insisted on preparing himself for the day's ceremony. His most loyal adviser never hesitated to enter the prince's private chambers, however.

"Your Benevolence," he said as he entered the room. In public, he would bow out of courtesy, but Xen-Que insisted against it in private. "I believe congratulations are in order. I hope to be among the first to say so. The youngest King in the history of the Crown. Perhaps the youngest ruler of any empire, even when counted amongst the Moaschen Emperors of yesteryear. Not that you needed any more accolades to secure your legacy. I mean no insolence in saying this, but the lack of a bride is the only thing that is missing from this glorious occasion. It is regrettable how this maiden has brought you such grief."

Xen-Que took up his sword from the fireplace mantel. This day was not just for Xen-Que, but his entire family. He would not detract from the day by having his fiancée present. Unfortunately, another loved the Crown Prince's betrothed. "It is fine, Javk. Today is a day for my brother as well, not just my own. I would not want to ruin this day for us by having my bride-to-be present at the proceedings today. It breaks my heart; it does. I know that he loves her, but love alone does not make a marriage. I hope he is wise enough to see that."

"Of course, your Benevolence. But I can't help but ask if you have any reservations to this union? Knowing how the prince feels, did you ever think of declining?"

The Kramei Insurrection

Xen-Que opened his mouth as if to speak, but he faltered in his response. It was a fair question, though not his adviser's place to ask it. He didn't have a genuine answer. "No," he finally announced. "This wedding is as important to the future of this kingdom as my ascension. The Old Family tutors us, but that was the price they agreed to for their kind to survive. If we do not want to suffer the same fate of those they betrayed, we must unite in marriage. Unite in blood."

There was obviously a reason Javk wanted to talk about this, but whatever it was, he felt best to abandon the conversation. "May I suggest the navy suit Lord von Breischa had made for you?"

"I do appreciate your advice, dear Javk, but I would prefer my uniform." Xen-Que was still very much a brat and stuck in his ways. His chosen attire was also dark blue. The suit offered was a gift just for this occasion. The Crown Prince still felt the need to put his tastes and opinions over those of others, including (and especially) his most honored adviser.

Xen-Que's uniform was exclusive to him; no one else in the military wore it. His trousers were dark green and otherwise dull. Gold fasteners adorned the top and ranged from his thigh to his neck. The buttons were off-center toward the left side of the shirt. He wore a pair of tightly laced brown boots. There was a dark green armband on his right arm that bore his royal seal. The insignia was a lighter shade of blue. He had earned many accommodations, but he chose to wear only two. The King's Cross was his reward for his actions on Moaschen. He saved his entire battalion from an ambush and captured the pirates that wrought havoc on trade ships. The annual games from earlier in the year is where he earned the second medal. He bested his brother in a duel which headlined the event. Some claimed that Xen-Que cheated. His father asserted that the now Crown Prince acted quickly and creatively. He demonstrated that he would do whatever was necessary to win; an attribute his brother, the heir-apparent at the time, lacked.

Next was his aiguillette, which signified his high standing. There were multiple small ropes intertwined with four tips visible. One pair swayed freely under his armpit. Studs near his collar attached the ends of the other two. He completed the outfit with a custom sword belt. The standard balteus would not be suited for holding *Aldring*. He set his hair band next.

It was a gold rim that traveled behind his head and was mostly concealed by his long hair. A circlet pulled back his mane to emphasize the sharp features of his face. Long and regal, his visage displayed the wisdom and experience of a man twice his age. Attached to his headdress were two golden plates which concealed his sideburns. He kept the rest of his face shaved clean. He forewent the cape typically worn by princes and other high-ranking officers. His gloves were all that remained. He let them rest on the table in front of him.

"Javk," he beckoned, "my medicine, please." His counselor made haste to a refrigerated container by Xen-Que's lavish bed. He retrieved a vial containing a blue liquid, then the injection device from a nearby drawer. He broke the seal on the bottle and quickly slid it into the delivery apparatus. With the seal broken, the liquid began to glow with a faint light. Xen-Que took the needle and shoved into his neck. He simultaneously pressed in the pressurized plunger on the opposite end. He grunted in pain as he pulled out the needle. Strained gasps accompanied the next several moments. A slight bit of smoke drifted from the insertion site.

Javk was visibly disturbed by the sight of his prince's need to do this each day. "My prince, if this drug is so painful to imbibe, why keep taking it?"

Xen-Que ejected the empty vial and discarded the needle. He took a deep breath and turned his entire body to face his friend. "Have you ever been burned, Javk? I mean not plucking up a blazing pot that you treat with some cold cream or accidentally dropping your lit pipe onto your lap. A scalding so harsh you felt your skin bubble and flee. A feeling so hot that it's almost cold. So intense a scorching that it was killing you. Have you been burned?"

Javk averted his look from Xen-Que. "No, my Lord, I haven't. My apologies, that was inconsiderate of me."

Xen-Que politely smiled. "Do not be absurd. I understand that you only fret for my well-being. Though the sting seems to have increased over the past several weeks, it is more palatable than the alternative. It is a straightforward and concise solution to a strange side-effect." He grabbed the gauntlets from the table and slipped his hands inside.

"Perhaps you should do without the gloves," Javk suggested. "Surely they are getting expensive. I wager that you intend on making a demonstration of your piety."

Xen-Que chuckled. "A bet you would lose, friend. Your absence during my coronation is a great shame. I appreciate your counsel this day, but I cannot linger any longer. May history smile upon this day. I shall see you again soon." He turned from Javk and walked briskly from the room.

Javk walked up to the door and closed it behind his prince, "Not to worry my Lord," he whispered. "I will be there." He walked toward his prince's mattress. He picked up the cooler of medicine and placed it on top of the bedding. He opened the lid and stared at the remaining vials.

"Have you done your duty, Mr. Gie?"

He looked up to see another man standing in front of him. His hair had turned gray in such few years. This man had one telling feature. A scar that traveled across the bridge of his nose to his left jaw. Covered in rags, the sight of him brought Javk some guilt. "Daben. Give me one moment of peace, won't you? How did you even get in here?"

His co-conspirator clicked his tongue. "Surely these not be the wasted days. Please, someone, save us from our decrepit ways. And the hour too is drawing near, that our fates be decided 'ere. To ruin and to fear — the end of all things." He couldn't help but grin after quoting part of the old prophecy. "Do not forget what we are up against, Javk!"

The words of The Unknown Council rang cold in Javk's ears as he heard them spoken. He knew his partner was right. He bore no love to the monarchy itself, but he had come to know the two princes. He had learned to admire them. Even trust them. He asked himself if the children had to suffer for the sins of their parents. "Must they be executed? Xen-Que and h—"

"No!" Daben pushed Javk away from the bed. "What would you do? Put them in a cage? One lined with lead and the other with what, exactly? You know as well as I do this only succeeds if they all die. Even one left standing might not undo our work, but I can assure you that neither of us would live to see its fruit. The elder will turn all to ash while his junior provides an iron cloak. It is our good fortune that a lady has come between them. If they were to combine their efforts, they would be unstoppable.

Their amiable truce will only get stronger. They must be divided. They must be conquered."

Javk knew that Daben was right. It was, after all, why they had started this whole thing. He recognized from the beginning what the realization of their goals would cost. "I have no argument, Daben. Truly, I don't. It must be done. It's a shame that I've gotten close to them. But there is no other way. Tonight the blood of the Regal will be spent. The nobles will all be wasted. I will be one of the few left in this world to mourn them sincerely."

The palace had swelled quickly. The central chamber was the first to reach capacity. Xen-Que's friends and those chosen for knighthood occupied the first row of seats. The room was only briefly silent when the King approached his throne. Se'har's subjects were respectful to a degree. To describe them as courteous would be an exaggeration. Only those yet fearful of him bowed or did anything of the sort. He had lost the respect of his subjects. He sat on his throne next to his queen. He didn't bother to engage with the mob before him. He was clearly eager to conclude the day quickly.

The ceremony started immediately. Xen-Que climbed the stairs to the platform under the throne. His father stood in front of his seat, waiting to end this chapter of his life. "Kneel, my son and heir, Lord Suzerain and Crown Prince of Damos." Xen-Que fought away a grin as he obliged. He tried to remember the last time he knelt. Not as long as the wait would be for the next occasion. He knew that he would never bow again. "You are my heir to the Kingdom of Damos and all her colonies. Many a year have I ruled her, bringing prosperity, justice, and health to those who need it. Punishment, vengeance, and death to those who deserve it. I have sent men to live or perish in her defense. I have rewarded those who have done her glory and condemned those who do her wrong. Do you swear to do all these and more in her defense?"

Xen-Que nodded. "Yes... I do."

The King grabbed hold of a dagger, or rather what appeared as a dagger. As he tugged the blade free, it continued to grow. It was somehow much longer than the sheath that housed it. The sword's length nearly matched Xen-Que in height. "You will cast aside the family surname of Poleb. Kings only have the need for one title. I, Se'har the Second, name thee, Xen'que the First." He tapped his son on the left shoulder. "Sovereign of the Moaschen Empire," he touched the right shoulder, "King of the Damosi and Old Iedenia." He stepped away and offered his son the handle of the sword. "Take *Aldring*, the anchor of *Narthalos*, and be recognized as King."

Xen'que stood up and accepted the sword. "Thank you, father. I humbly thank you for all your years of service. Damos will not forget the grace of your rule. Enjoy your time away."

His father grabbed his son's shoulder. Xen'que became visibly angered by this, though he tried his best to hide it. "Be careful, my son." He then abruptly turned and left, followed promptly by his queen. His sudden departure was odd, but no one bothered to follow.

The former King burst through door after door. The coronation exhausted the last of his composure. He frantically moved about the halls, his stupor frightening. A locked door impeded his escape. "Why is it locked?" He cursed. Se'har had done well to make sure nothing would hinder his escape. He did have the key for this door, but his maddening recoil made it nearly impossible to unlock, as he fumbled with the key. He stabbed at the keyhole many times before eventually dropping it on the floor. He cursed at the key as he picked it up, and finally jammed it in the lock. He turned the tumbler and slammed the door open. It was at that moment he locked eyes with his enemy.

Daben kicked him in the chest, the force of the strike put him on the ground. Se'har pulled a knife from his robe, but Javk's spear quickly disarmed him. The queen attempted to double back to the throne room. She quickly found herself on the floor with a spearhead in her back. She began to bawl from pain and distress. Daben approached her with evil intent. He violently ripped the spear from her and turned her over with his foot. He swiftly came down on her throat with his sword, silencing her forever.

A Fatal Vendetta

Javk unsheathed a dagger in his possession and stabbed the former king in the thigh. He grabbed the bloodied mess by the collar and shoved him up against the wall. "*Yahda* has quite the potent elixir within the core of its blade. You would do well not to have it inside you for too long without counteracting the toxins."

"You will not get away with this, traitor! Xen'que will make you wish you had never been born!"

Se'har's threats fell on deaf ears. Javk pressed the dagger deeper into the flesh. "You have a limited foresight, my lord. There's something I don't quite understand regarding our current predicament. If you know what we plan to do here today, why flee? Why not fight? Why save your self and forsake your sons? Why should they suffer for your sins?"

"That doesn't matter," Daben interjected. "King Xen'que requires a daily injection of *flammasedodoxicrine* to use his power unrestrained. Now, we have been trying to synthesize a counter toxin not to dull the pain he experiences, but rather increase it. We've been unsuccessful in that venture. Javk has managed to discreetly crack the seal on the vials before injection, compromising its potency. We anticipate that the blood-rage Xen'que will suffer from the events of today will make this a non-issue, as he will be blind to the painful application of his gift. Prolonged use will also make blind his hand, though. Now, in the unlikely event he makes ready his escape, I need to know where his medicine is stored so that it can be destroyed. That way, his threat to our new world order will be small. With injections withheld from him for an extended period, his powers will control him. Now, where is it?"

The old king sat silent. Daben looked to Javk and nodded. Javk pulled the dagger from Se'har's thigh and thrust it into the armpit above. The old man winced in pain. Javk leaned in close so that he could hear. "You aren't in a strong negotiating position, my lord. The more points of entry, the faster the poison will filter your system. The harder it will be to be cured."

Javk backed away. "Now," Daben resumed, "where?"

The old man took a deep breath. "You think you have already won. You think I am allowing your victory, which I run to save myself? Maybe my visions showed me that I must sacrifice myself for my kingdom to survive. Maybe I am drawing you away to afford my sons' time to react. Maybe I

17

give up my throne because it has better hopes of enduring with Xen'que seated there." He headbutted Javk in the nose.

He tried to flee, but Daben reacted quickly. He took the spear and buried it in Se'har's neck. The former king collapsed. He soon stopped moving. Javk used a handkerchief to stop the blood flowing out of his face. "Damn you, Daben. We needed him alive!"

"What's done is done," his partner replied. "Our fates are sealed. Whether we triumph or perish, we must continue. History will remember us as heroes this day. Make your way to the stables. Be diligent and wait. I have an appointment with our new King; I must save him from his company. So many nobles have come to one room to kiss his ass. I must do something!"

Javk didn't appreciate Daben's humor. He watched his associate make his way toward the main entrance of the throne room. Grenade in one hand and a pistol in the other. "How did it come to this," he wondered to himself. "How did it ever come to this?" Javk hid the bodies. He then gathered his things and made the long stride to the courtyard. He did not stop or treat with anyone that called out to him. He walked over the stone path and avoided the eyes of those he passed. He knew the eyes of loyalists from the eyes of freedom fighters. Could those eyes see which he was? He escaped the gaze of anyone who might spy on him. He entered the stables and hid amongst the horses. Here he would wait for the battle to begin. He wondered what would come to an end today, the demise of the monarchy or his own. He could only wonder.

*The new King of Damos put up quite a good fight. He managed to survive the ambush in his throne room, though most of his captains did not survive the initial salvo. The conspirators tried to contain the battle to the walls of the palace, but it quickly spilled outside. Xen'que's brutal efficiency was all that matched his rage in combat. Man after woefully inept man fell to his blade. Entire squadrons went up in smoke from one flick of his wrist. It was only when his closest ally, his enemy in disguise, alerted him to an invisible threat, did he falter. King Xen'que felt a knife in his back when he lowered his guard. His Benevolence and all his men suffered a quick drop and a sudden stop.*

# 1. THE MASTER

The darkness of night had fallen over the land. The world had been without a king for nearly five-hundred years. In its place was a democratic society which had flourished with relative peace. The more things changed, the more they stayed the same. No longer the homeland of an empire, the planet Damos was now the seat of a republic. Officially named the Valabrei Republic and informally as the Republic of Damos. Legally speaking, parliament acted as the King in his absence. With the death of the entire Poleb family, there were no living heirs to the crown. Many citizens were furious, particularly the Iedenian Guard. The private army of the King attempted to seize control from Javk Gie (who tried to declare himself as Suzerain with minimal support). An executive would be needed to govern parliament. A president was the accepted solution to prevent civil war. The Iedenian Guard agreed to maintain peace, but would not subject itself to direct obedience.

Moaschen would have been the largest planet in the sky had it not been mostly destroyed. The surface was mostly uninhabitable; the Great Brace of Moashei contained the bulk of its population. In modern days it served as the harbor for the Damosi Navy, headquartered at the West Fork. Legend claimed the old empire that preceded the Damic Kingdom built the brace. An asteroid belt separated Moaschen from the other planets and contributed to the rampant piracy in the area. President Evan Gie had recently tried to expand the Republic's control over the field of rocks. A majority vote from Parliament and objections from the Guard blocked the legislation.

# A Fatal Vendetta

The jewel of the system was Iedin. The world was a visual paradise. Every aspect of its terrain was beautiful to witness. The vast mountain range was the only exception to the ideal climate. Water covered three-fifths of the surface, much of it drinkable. There was no great expanse of water in any one place. There were as many beaches as there were green-land. The Hotel Iedenia was the most pleasurable travel destination to visit. Se'har ordered its construction for the king to reside when visiting. The last king, Xen'que, didn't live to see construction finished. It found a different life as a resort. The Iedenian Guard generally banned any members of the Republic government vacancy (though there were a few rare exceptions).

There were some disputes when it came to some territories. The Moashei asteroid field was never formally a part of the kingdom, nor were the Brescha Masses (the heavenly bodies that nearly destroyed Moaschen, if you believed the stories). The only remaining world was Kramei. There was supposedly unrest amongst the Krameian citizens during the last days of the kingdom, but nothing near the current political climate. The planet was never as beautiful as Iedin, but the landscape had suffered greatly in the past few decades. The most recent natural disaster was when Braeden Almasy's warship crash landed in the Plains of Harvest. The vast vegetation of the area had mostly turned into a desert in the following years. The unrest began around eight years ago. The political party that opposed Republic rule was the current majority. A single man managed the charge.

Daben Celt shared his name with one of the conspirators that toppled the monarchy. His goal was also to topple a dynasty. He often asked his followers to define him in one word. He wasn't a pirate nor a mercenary. Those faithful to him described him as a visionary. In his mind, he was simply the best. The best at what? No one had quite the word for that. Whatever that word might have been, he was the best at it. A man who had seen his fair share of harvests, Daben was still in the prime of his life. His hair was as black as the old kings. He would have looked regal was it not for his rough edges. He bore a scar on his left cheek, running nearly parallel to his sideburns. He refused to speak about how he received it. Tall and muscular, he towered over, and intimidated, most men. Though the number had dwindled in recent years, there were still those who did not fear him. He worried about one man in particular. One person who made Daben uncertain about the success of his grand schemes.

He heard footsteps. His lieutenant was approaching. With care, he locked the clasp on the binding of his journal. It was a copy of the original Daben Celt's confessions. He had taken to chronicling his struggle alongside his namesake's. He placed his musings into the bag resting at his feet. He leaned back in his chair and removed a handgun from its holster. One of a pair, he owned the finest pistols money could buy. Or the best quick hands could steal, in this case. He took great care their maintenance. There were some who might suggest he cared more about these instruments of death then he did his own children. He had recently modified them both. He grabbed the barrel and rotated it upside-down to load a distinctive slug.

His firearm found itself pointed at the head of the statue towering over him. Javk Gie, co-founder of the Republic. It lumbered over the land as the regretful conqueror of its likeness. The king's murder occurred on this very spot, according to legend. This effigy stood at the heart of the Old City. Erected to commemorate The Battle of Monarch Fall and to those who died. Javk's likeness served as a reminder that freedom would always triumph over tyranny. It was illegal for citizens to enter the estate of the old kings, so most never saw it in person. One shot from his handgun shattered the bust. The entry point smoldered in the rock. The dead foliage at the base slowly burned away. He heard the footsteps stop. "You had better have a good reason for disturbing me. I gave strict orders that I wanted my privacy."

"Ljero Liachem reporting for duty as Lieutenant of Damos Operations, sir." The man resumed his approach once Daben lowered his sidearm. The young man walked into his commander's line of sight to present himself.

Daben was less than pleased. Not only that, but hints of rage were noticeable in his green eyes. "Where is the Fury? I was very clear that I wanted him heading this operation."

Ljero handed Daben a letter. The general of his militia sent his regrets. The situation on Kramei had escalated. He had to plan a counter assault to stop a preliminary strike. "He also apologizes that these efforts keep him from here," he explained. "The defense of our homeworld is paramount.

He believes the protection of our people is a high priority. Perhaps even more-so than one man."

Daben read the rest of the letter. A Damosi garrison had arrived. Their military occupation of TAC-OPS was in jeopardy. "I do not require Cineon to coordinate the defenses on Kramei! I told him I would send Areka for that. My need for him is on Damos!" He threw the note into the fire that fought for life. He stroked his face. He looked upon the messenger. "And he sends you in his stead. I know you are talented, Ljero. I have trusted you in many things. You've done well to help sow distrust in Vardos. You are as good as anyone in our effort. But let me ask you something. Do you think you are as good as my right hand? Do you think that you have what it takes to apprehend this asset? Can you catch the Son of Eidolas?"

Ljero's face grew pale. He would have been quick to tell Daben he was that good, if only he had convinced himself of it. "What? We're hunting down the Praesage?"

Daben chuckled from delirious rage. "Maybe, maybe it is for the best. After all, Cineon is the one that allowed him to get away in the first place."

"Sir, you can't honestly suggest Cineon was to blame for what—"

"He didn't escape on his own," Daben interjected. "Cineon showed a rare moment of pity, and a displayed a shocking lapse of judgment. If you want this task, you had better not fail me. You had better bring back my once brother-in-arms. The castle is our extraction point. Be cautious, Mr. Liachem. If Gie learns of our presence, then they may look for us here. Once you have succeeded, we will enter the third phase of our operation." Daben picked up his coat and turned toward the abandoned palace.

"Cineon gave me his actual name, but not much else," Ljero explained. "Is there any other information you can give me that might assist in the success of my mission."

Daben turned back to face his lieutenant. He almost looked angry. "When my old partner left, he compromised plans for my original design. Details I had to purge. That is why I have compartmentalized the command structure. Lieutenants only know enough to get their specific roles done. Cineon is my top man. If there is anyone that knows more about our plans than me, it is Cineon. Because I trust him. Irrevocably. He has acted well to be deserving of that trust. You have not. You have clearance to use any non-lethal measures to ready the Praesage's capture. Be warned; I will not tolerate you exposing our presence here. Throw as many men into his blade as it takes, but you take him down. You cover your tracks. He'll know who you are if he spots you. So as long as there aren't any witnesses, you shouldn't be bothered by law enforcement. But I want him alive. Do you understand?"

Ljero nodded. "Sir, yes sir. I have four squads at my disposal. Cineon's briefing tells me that he has lived in the capital for two years now. Probably to deter any attempts to capture him. He will know all the exits. He is likely to be armed. We are unsure how tactical his defense may be if he's placed any. Our reconnaissance has no reason to believe he would have any plans to defend from a public place."

Daben smiled. "Splendid. When you engage him, be sure he is away from a crowd. Do not leave any witnesses. Bring along any companions that may be in his company. He will not just drop his arms and aid us; we can use loved ones as leverage to deputize him." Ljero shook hands with Daben. He tried to pull his hand away, but Daben tightened his grip and pulled him close. "Do not fail me, Ljero."

Ljero freed his hand. "Sir. I won't."

Daben turned away again. He twisted the barrel of his gun to the default position. He made his way back to his base inside the palace. Ljero saw a flash of light inside the castle. Daben was up to something else. "More secrets that you don't trust your captains with, I assume," he muttered. He looked at his watch. It was time to meet up with his team.

# 2. PREGAME

*For you see, war is purely a human concept. Animals do not engage in war, but war turns people into animals. When allowed to roam, animals that escape the violence of the world become docile. Free to be kind, gentle, loving. They take for themselves things they could never have before. A life. But once a killer, well, it's only a matter of time.*

Conditions on Kramei had only gotten worse in the years that followed the failed Moaschen uprising. Half a decade had passed since the Kramei Independence, and Liaison Lobby for Ending Radicalism came into existence. In the last several months they had become more aggressive in their tactics. Events on the surface produced hours of news coverage every day. The public had many questions. What hostilities, if any, were taking place? Was the government acting accordingly? Would it come to war? Krameian sympathizers accused the Damosi Network Consortium of doctoring the reports. Portrayed as outright villains, members of the Lobby had no voice to defend themselves. The Republic argued their actions spoke louder than words ever could. Some suggested the government wasn't showing both sides to the story. The DNC vehemently denied such allegations. They asserted that the entire population did not represent the extremism of the Lobby. A special news report explained the current state of things. "Referred to as the Fury of Kramei, Cineon, surname unknown, continues to evade Republic authorities. The central DNC hub on Kramei is his last confirmed sighting.

General Greene had no comment on what Cineon's intentions might have been."

Senjek Bohmet peered out his window and watched the rain trickle down the glass. He wasn't originally from Damos. After being born on Iedin, his family moved to Kramei when he was still a toddler. He moved to Damos a few years ago; he feared getting stuck there amongst the growing violence. The Republic continued to insist it wouldn't turn to war. He wasn't convinced. Diplomacy had so far failed to resolve tensions. The situation only grew worse, despite what news reports would say.

He abandoned the view of his window. His brown eyes showed the exhaustion he suffered from his day at work. He sat down in his armchair. He ran his hand through his red hair. It was short on the sides and the back, but there was enough on top to grab hold of his locks. He was glad of the safety here, but Damos was very different from Kramei. He felt restless on most days. Survival was a regular day-to-day routine when he grew up. To get noticed here may have meant ridicule or recognition. If you ran into the wrong people on Kramei, it led to being drafted or killed in recent years.

The government employed him as a private defense contractor. The government didn't find him; he sought them out, but they initially turned him away. That was until the day he met Dak Johnsen in a restaurant. The captain wasn't in uniform, so there was no way for Senjek to know who he was. They talked for nearly an hour that afternoon. Dak felt that Senjek would be a valuable asset. His town was one of the first targets of the Lobby's growing militia. Senjek stunted the extremists' attack and gave people the chance to evacuate. Anyone that was able to escape the clutches of the Praesage, however brief, was someone worth having on the Republic's side. He immediately sent a message to President Gie. He reasoned that such first-hand experience would be invaluable in training counterinsurgency squads. Senjek was soon contracted to teach survival skills and introductory hand-to-hand combat.

Senjek wore a pair of plain blue jeans and button-up white collared shirt. With the sleeves of his shirt rolled up, the tone and definition of his arms were easy to see. The shirt had the top three buttons undone. He had his own sense of fashion and refused to compromise for the sake of others.

He had a watch for formal occasions and didn't wear it day-to-day. He had a pair of black boots that seen better days. He refused to part with them, though. The footwear was the only thing he had left from his old life.

He knew the night would be awkward to some degree. He invited Dak to meet him for dinner and drinks. Their relationship had evolved from strictly business to an actual friendship outside of work. They had gone out for drinks a few times with trainees, but a few weeks ago they went with just another instructor. Dak confessed to his two teachers that his wife planned to file for divorce. He wanted them ready in case he wasn't around so much. He laughed after saying that. He said it was ironic. Him spending too much time in his work was one of the issues his wife cited in their differences. She finally got him to spend a wealth of time dedicated to her. He feared the divorce would compromise his involvement in the training of counter-insurgents.

Dak resigned himself to the outcome. Senjek had asked his girlfriend to join them tonight. He hoped that seeing another healthy relationship might get Dak to fight for his marriage. Dak and Farraeh grew up together but didn't talk until high school. It was a spark of young love that had only recently started to flicker. For whatever reason, they had fallen out of love with each other. Senjek couldn't imagine falling out of love with Treistina. He smiled at the thought of her. He had never met a more beautiful girl. Of course, generally speaking, the women of Kramei were much different from those of Damos. Not very posh or refined, but the two societies were very different between the two planets.

Treistina was a blonde, an apparent weakness of Senjek's. He suspected it wasn't her natural hair color, though. So far it was a novel romance. Boy meets girl; boy falls in love with the girl. That's how far along the story was at the moment. They had been together for most of the two years he had lived on Damos. They were practically living together at this point. More and more of Treistina's possessions found their way into Senjek's home (despite the fact she had her own apartment). His place wasn't as lavish as her flat, but it was bigger than hers, so there was at least some sense to it.

He wasn't overly enthused about it, though. Not that he didn't want to live together, he just had some concerns about what it would mean. Treistina had subtly mentioned marriage a few times in passing in the past

27

few months. He feared the subject might arise more often and with more urgency if they lived together. The very idea made him uneasy. It wasn't hard to imagine spending the rest of his life with this woman, but an engagement was a significant commitment. He was happy with the way things were now. If he needed convincing not to do it, he had to look no further than Dak. He married his college sweetheart. Even though he was rarely home, Captain Johnsen always talked about Mrs. Johnsen. It was evident that they were truly in love at some point. How that managed to fall apart frightened him.

It had been a long time since he let himself get attached to anyone. He had suffered some traumatic losses of loved ones. Past casualties combined with a childhood on Kramei was a standard recipe to spawn the emotionally distant. He wasn't proud of everything he had done in his former life. There were parts of himself that he kept for himself. He was in an increasingly serious relationship, and he wondered how long he could hide the pains of his past from her.

He poured himself a glass of whiskey. He enjoyed a small drink before having dinner. It was an effort to appear classier. One attempt on his part to reach out, he mused. He put the glass to his mouth when there was a knock on the door. He stood from the chair and walked to the door. He ran his hand through his hair again to make sure nothing was sticking out. He already had a smile on his face. "Hey babe, I thought you said you were going to be a while?" he inquired as he opened the door.

"I never said that, Bohmet. And don't call me baby," Dak said condescendingly. Senjek was speechless. "I hope I didn't give you the wrong idea. We work as colleagues, but I'm not looking for that kind of relationship. Oh! Thanks for the drink, though!" He took the glass from Senjek's hand. Too embarrassed to answer, he watched Dak sip the alcohol. Dak surveyed the living room. "Nice windows. I would have thought floor-to-ceiling would be a little the way of Iedenia for you, but what do I know?" A bewildered Senjek tried to explain himself, but Dak cut him off. "You were born on Iedin, Bohmet. That doesn't make you Iedenian. Do you try to butter the ladies up with this little half-truth? Your wardrobe doesn't exactly lend credence to your heritage."

"Ouch," Senjek replied. "I suppose there's a limit on how much a guy can cover up his harsh Kramei upbringing."

28

Dak shrugged. "Your sarcasm is wasted on me, Senjek."

"Sarcasm?"

"Yeah, that was your sarcastic voice." Senjek's reply was without words. He just stood there confused. "OK, whatever. So much for having you figured out."

"Don't take it personally, Dak. People surprise you every day. It can't always be Lobby movements. We don't want our personal lives to lose out on the excitement of life, do we?"

Dak scoffed. "Yeah, I guess not. Speaking of the Lobby and our personal lives, and I hope you don't mind, but I asked a mutual friend to join us tonight."

"You're pulling my leg. Evan Gie is going to come out of his shell?" Dak didn't answer him directly. Instead, he only shrugged ambiguously. "Well, if it's true, good for him. I don't think that man's had a day off in three years. He hasn't even left the office to mourn his brother or wife. Shit, after that little scare with Eve on Iedin, you'd think he'd spend some more time with her. I hate to think what he'd become if he lost her."

"Yeah," Dak replied. He poured another glass for Senjek. "That's not entirely accurate, though. After the thing with Eve, parliament mandated he take a leave of absence. Not sure how much good it did. Of course, he declined my offer to inspect the nightlife. I understand that he's busy and maybe wouldn't want to spend time with grunts like us, but…"

"When is he going to live his life?" Senjek's remark echoed the sentiment of other military members. "Maybe the land's highest office has some crazy rules. Maybe he doesn't come because he can't?"

"I don't know about all that. I mean, why not? I don't see what part of being president says you can't drink anymore. Hell, Baron says he works too much. If a von Breischa says that, you know you must be doing some serious overtime."

"General von Breischa? He's made contact?" Senjek asked with great interest; the General of the Armies of Damos had been silent for over a month during a special op.

Dak shook his head. "So far as anyone's said, the operation calls for Network silence."

Senjek couldn't believe what he had just heard. "I'm going to stop you right there. You're telling me that his mission statement includes intentionally withholding Network access to his operation? Isn't that illegal?"

Dak was known for his asinine grin, and he suddenly displayed it. "Yeah, well, that's why you didn't hear it from me. You can have your black ops, just keep it away from me."

Senjek clinked glasses with Dak in agreement. "Enough about Baron von Breischa. You know Evan," Dak took a sip of his drink, mid-sentence, "Evan told me something the other day that I was not expecting to hear. I told him you were introducing me to Treistina and you know what he said?"

"I don't know. 'Why are you telling me about some woman I've never heard of before? Is that Senjek's girlfriend or something? Why are you in my bathroom?'"

"Ha ha, hysterical, shut up. Here's a story that will get you real good. So I tell him you're introducing me to Treistina and he says, 'Treistina Yahn?' I said 'Yeah, why?' He tells me that Treistina was friends with his sister."

Senjek coughed. He stopped swallowing his drink, and some got stuck in his throat for a moment. He regained his composure. "Wait, this is news to me. Treistina is friends with Eve Gie? She's never once mentioned anything like that."

Dak quickly finished his drink. "Yeah, well, I don't know about that. Friends might be a bit of a stretch at this point. I don't think it's quite on their terms, but they haven't talked in a while."

"Doesn't explain why my girlfriend of two years has kept me in the dark that she's friends with the second most influential person in the Republic."

"Maybe in rank, but I don't think she's the second most powerful person." Dak's face got noticeably paler. "Senjek, uh, from what I've dug up, I don't blame her. Eve didn't win the contest for an expense paid trip to Hotel Iedenia."

"What are you talking about? What contest?"

"Every year, up until the year the bomb went off, the DNC had a competition to send two people to the Hotel for two days. The Hotel is part of an anti-trust between the government and the public shareholders of the Consortium. Diplomat, military, whatever. Anyone associated with the official government isn't allowed to go there. Well, they say it's because of anti-trust with the DNC; we know the real reason they aren't allowed in."

Senjek nodded as if he understood, but he clearly didn't. "OK. What does this have to do with Eve and Treistina knowing each other?"

"Being born in the Gie family, Eve has been involved in some sort of politics since she was a girl. She had always wanted to go. Treistina won the contest. She selected Eve as her plus one. Found a loophole, but Treistina had to back out at the eleventh hour. Something about her passport not aligning with Network quota or some nonsense."

"No, I had the same problem when I tried taking her to Iedin. Her credentials were invalid. It took me a few days to get it sorted out." Senjek sank into his chair. "Shit. I never knew. I can't believe she's never told me this," he declared in spite of the fact he wasn't entirely forthcoming when it came to his past.

"Well, as I like to say, you didn't hear this from me. Your girl may feel guilty about it. She's not the only one that feels that way, either. After his wife and brother, Evan's been seeing ghosts. He got suspicious. Started investigating into it. Told Treistina they couldn't speak to each other anymore."

"Holy shit. That's insane. Maybe I can say something to Evan? Get him to come around?"

Dak scoffed. "Try if you like, dude. That man needs some serious head shrinking. He hides it well, but I'm starting to see the scars. A lot of us are starting to see the scars."

"Anyway, I brought you over for a night on the town," Senjek said, changing the subject. "Here we are talking about work. I don't want Treistina to think you're some stick in the mud."

"I don't know about that," he replied with his classic smarmy tone. "I think Ms. Yahn will find it hard to think poorly of me with you wearing that shirt."

Senjek looked down at his shirt, then back at Dak. "What's wrong with my shirt?"

"Nothing. It just so happens to be the exact same shirt I'm wearing."

"Yeah, of course it is, because you shop at Sue's!" Senjek laughed at the mere thought of the statement, but Dak's face told a different story. "Yeah, OK. You shop at Sue's. Good one."

Dak merely shrugged, ambiguously as he was known to do. Upon further inspection, the two shirts did look a lot alike. "At least now my tastes are a little the way of Iedenia," he said sarcastically.

# 3. A GIRL NAMED TREISTINA YAHN

Based on her material possessions, Senjek assumed Treistina enjoyed the finer things in life. She wondered if he felt compelled to provide her with a similar level of comfort. Maybe that was why he started working with the government. She knew he had other reasons, though. The woman had her fair share of tragedy, but it didn't haunt her the way it haunted him. Senjek offered his condolences when she told him her mother had died. "Don't be, she wasn't a good person," she said to him. Senjek tried to convince her that she shouldn't hold onto such hate. She didn't want to speak of her at all, though, so Senjek let it be. Treistina hadn't talked to her brother in many years. Again, her boyfriend insisted she should try to make contact. Unfortunately, Xander was a member of the Kramei Lobby so a family reunion would be impossible. She did not let these things rule her life. In fact, she did quite well for herself. She didn't currently have a job, but she had some money. She had relied solely on a trust fund in the last year. Her father set it up after she and her brother were born. She was the only one using the money since Xander was on Kramei.

She was no stranger to the advances of men. She had heard many pick-up lines; once a man accused her of being a model. She was in excellent shape, despite her upbringing. She maintained a strict personal fitness regiment for herself. She exercised on a regular basis and did not stray from her diet. She was shorter than most of her girlfriends, standing near five feet and nine inches. Born with dark hair, she had died it blonde years ago. Her skin was smooth and without any blemishes (except the freckles

33

on her back). What enchanted most men was her emerald-green eyes. It wasn't uncommon for Senjek to compare them to something extravagant. He once brought her to a cavern filled with green gemstones. The sight and the gesture greatly moved her. Senjek told her he wanted her to see what he saw every time he looked into her eyes. She bore a mischievous grin just thinking about their visit to Jade Peak on Iedin. It was a memory she would cherish for the rest of her life. It was that night she realized she was in love with him.

She slid into a green sweater to compliment her eyes, though pale in comparison. It was a tight fit to her lines and brought out her bust, which, while modest, was also a feature that Senjek admired. Whenever doing her makeup, she always paid particular attention to her eyes. Senjek could probably stare at them for hours if neither of them had anything else to do. She mostly relied on eyeliner to bring out the shamrock hue. Anything more would detract from their natural beauty. She struggled with what lipstick she was going to wear. She eventually decided on burnt-orange. White slacks and a tan sash tied around her waist accentuated her curves. She pulled on sand-colored boots that nearly reached her knee. She usually didn't wear hooped earrings but wanted to leave a good impression with Senjek's friend.

Her mobile started to ring. She glanced quickly to see who was calling. It was her father. "It can wait," she said to herself. After the lip gloss, she directed her attention to her eyelashes. She gently brushed each lash, alternating from left to right. She smiled in the mirror. It was hardly her number one feature, but Senjek once told her that her beauty would just not be the same if it weren't for that smile.

Finished with her make-up, she let down her hair, which tumbled gracefully over her shirt. She took a brush and combed out any knots. Her hair nearly reached her buttocks. "Maybe after tonight I'll get a haircut," she mused. She walked in front of her mirror, hoping she liked this outfit. It was already the third one she tried on. "I think that will do," she said, satisfied.

She went into the kitchen and pulled a pint of ice cream out of the freezer. She pried the lid off and saw that it was nearly empty. It had lasted for over a month as she didn't indulge often. She grabbed a spoon and disposed of the lid. She didn't let the small portion of the treat bother

her. Instead, she thought it convenient that she didn't need to get a bowl. She sucked on the edge of the spoon after taking a bite, deep in thought.

She wandered aimlessly around the room before realizing she had dazed out. When she regained her bearing, she looked at a picture of herself and Senjek on her vanity. For some reason, she remembered the first time she saw Senjek. Her smile subsided. It was not something she was proud of to this day. As far as she knew at the time, he was just another guy. If she didn't become involved with him would she feel guilty now? What if she met him under better circumstances? Would she still have fallen in love with him? Her family didn't exactly approve of her dating him, either. Just because she had an easier life than most on Kramei, somehow Senjek wasn't good enough. True, he wasn't as polished as other men were, but he was plenty a gentlemen for her. He took her to dinner when he could, sometimes to very nice places. She didn't care where he came from; she knew where he was now. With her – and that was all that mattered.

Her phone started to ring again. "Enough with the calling," she exasperated. She answered the phone. "Hello?" she barked. "Hi. Sorry, Demarcus, this isn't the best time." She turned around and walked away from her vanity. "No, I'm not avoiding your calls. I've just been busy. I'm actually about to go meet up with Senjek. Yeah, I know. I know! You're not listening. I think I love him. Like really love him." She listened to the other person rant for a few minutes. "I think I don't care what you think about it." She walked into her closet, looking for a coat to wear. "No, I'm not just going to let this go. I am your daughter. Maybe instead of trying to control my life, you should let me live it for myself."

She grabbed her brown coat and stormed out of the closet. "Stop calling him that!" She did nothing to hide her emotions. Her father had pissed her off. "I don't care. He doesn't care either! I know you have this idea of who he is built up in your head, but he's not that person!" Treistina fumbled with the phone as she tried putting on her coat without losing any of the conversation. "I don't need your money. Maybe I'll get a job somewhere. Do whatever you want, Senjek and I can survive. All we need is each other."

She picked up her keys to her car and was about to hang up before she heard one final word of protest. "It's stronger than anything you've ever believed in. You can do what you want. I honestly don't care anymore."

There was further dissent in his words. "No, because I don't understand why you just can't be happy for me. Just because you're a widower no one else is allowed to fall in love? I'm done. I don't ever want to see you again. Stay out of my life. Don't try to see me. Don't call me ever again." She emphatically pressed her thumb to the phone's screen, ending the call. She immediately blocked the contact in her phone. She blacked out she was so rattled. She suddenly found herself driving her car. "Just take a few deep breaths and take in the sights," she whispered to herself.

She looked forward to visiting the future capital city. Named after the last King of Damos, though an obvious bastardization, New Xenue would one day replace Gie City. President Gie strongly pushed for the moving of the nation's capital closer to the original seat of the monarchy, but Parliament opposed to naming it New Gie. The name honored the history of Damos, with a name that evoked their rich history, but careful not to acknowledge the monarchy specifically.

The old castle would find new life as the presidential mansion. However, current laws prohibited any activity inside of the Royal Estate. Javk Gie's grandson made the mandate in the early days of Republic. 'None shall trespass the grounds of Monarch Fall. It shall be a monument to the sins of the Royal Family and the crimes charged onto them by the Chamberlain of Damos', an office that became the modern presidency.

New legislation was currently underway to undo this line in the Republic's constitution, though it wasn't without its opposition. There were those who felt Monarch Fall was a necropolis and to assume regular activity there would be a disrespect to the people who died there. Many felt it should forever serve as a reminder of the oppression the people of Damos once endured. In the meantime, construction began in the outlying areas. Senjek's apartment building was only a part of a complex and genius urban plan. Started years ago, most of the completed work lied in transportation. Roads, transit rails, and non-motorized pathways were leagues ahead in development in comparison to other aspects of New Xenue.

The infrastructure of roads surrounded the lands of the old monarchy. The paths that crossed into this territory were the only ones unfinished. To the north of the new capital was the space elevator reverse-engineered from technology left behind by the original Moashei colonizers. In service for over one-hundred years now, the manufacturing origin remained classified by the office of naval intelligence. Its function, however, was a matter of public record. It provided transport from the planet's surface to Moashei I, an asteroid culled from the Moashei Field. The asteroid's primary purpose was a counterweight to counteract the globe's gravity and keep the tether tight. The government alone monitored and controlled this area of space. Most of the traffic on the elevator was for the dock, though occasionally it would be used for maintenance of the Network.

The Damos Network was the single largest communication network ever to be created. It was responsible for every type of telecommunication: television, phone, data, networking and audio. While establishments on Kramei, for instance, had separate services for TV and cellular telephony, all of this information was from one source on Damos. Jointly owned by a consortium of businesses, its chief shareholder was the Damos government. Its creation helped facilitate an increase in privacy and security while nearly eliminating piracy and other illegal activity. Older communication lines, such as electromagnetic radio, were illegal due to their lower security. The Network helped to curb illegal activity. Detection of older bands was relatively easy to detect due to The Network's bandwidth being exponentially smaller than even its closest peer. Members of the Lobby claimed they had hacked Network communications without detection. Parliament denied such allegations. The Damos Network Consortium, or DNC, claimed it was impossible to hack the system without being noticed.

The DNC's headquarters resided south of the space elevator on the very edge of space north of Monarch Fall. It was the closest inhabitance to the old city. The military housing that contained Senjek's living quarters stood on the opposite end of the king's estate. He lived in a relatively upscale unit reserved for private contractors. As he lived on the top floor, you could nearly see the castle in the distance. Senjek would look out his window and admire the intricate web of roads. Multiple lanes for each direction with burrows and bridges to reduce congestion caused by cross traffic. Parking lots and garages were all one side of the road, indiscriminate of whether or not the facilities they would serve would be on that side. Canopied walkways extended over the traffic. The military housing was relatively close to a proposed recreational district which would include shopping malls and restaurants. They would not be going to this area for dinner, however. There was a connecting highway from New Xenue that went into Gie City. Treistina imagined a perfect night in her head. Senjek didn't have any family, so meeting his friends was the most acceptance she could achieve. She just hoped Dak approved.

# 4. THE KRAMEI INSURRECTION

"Charge!" shouted a Sergeant of the Damosi 117th Infantry. He held his sword high as a beacon for those under his command to follow. "Re-take the Repulsor!" Cannons roared to life from both sides. Missiles whined overhead. Man bloodied man as the once-forested landscape of Kramei became even more barren. A grenade landed next to his fire team. With a fierce roar, he used his sword to drive the explosive away. It turned into a ball of fire seconds afterward but provided enough to force to knock down members of the neighboring squads. The commander removed his helmet. The ringing of the explosion had echoed inside his headgear. He looked up and saw his men rallying under his example, moving ahead during his brief collapse. His corporal helped him to his feet. When he realized the sergeant wasn't injured he continued forward to lead the assault. He picked up his helmet and continued onward, now nearing the rear of his formation. He put away his sword. Though capable of battle, guns were still the prevalent form of violence (at least for now). His squad approached an abandoned trench from the enemy. His corporal had already taken up possession inside, allowing further advancement from the Damosi side. He slid into the ditch and ran up to his man in charge. "Report! What's going on up here, Veian? Where the fuck is Sehar Company? Where's our support?"

Corporal Grebllyh got off a few more shots with his rifle before answering the Sergeant. "Always told those boys it was a bad company to be in. Bad luck! The whole company is KIA, sir!"

"Bullshit! No way they took out that many men that quickly!"

Grebllyh ducked down into the recesses of their cover when a bullet whizzed past his ear. He looked over to his commander. "Sir! We have hostile infantry scattered all over the Plains. We're pinned down. Radio says the Kramei Militia has rearmed the Repulsor half a klick northwest to our location. Sounds like bullshit, but it's the best recon we have."

"Damn it," the Sergeant cursed under his breath. "Sehar Company was packing heavy ordinances. If that Repulsor is online, they may have been inside the Radius Effect when they launched their offensive. They didn't stand a chance. We need to get the word out to Forward Command about this development."

"Negative. Contact with Forward Command is without secure channels and not recommended. We believe we've relayed essential information to our predicament, but we're unclear of Command's official position."

The Sergeant nodded. "Secure or not, I want our men to know the Radius Effect is coming back online. Heavy ordinance needs to cease. Holster all sidearms. I don't want anyone using a weapon that can achieve entrance velocity. Do we have any intelligence that can suggest what prompted this offensive?"

"No, sir," Veian replied. "Our latest field briefing indicated that negotiations were still ongoing and that any military threats were 'unjustified.'"

"Right," the Sergeant said in a tone that failed to convince himself. "Hostilities unlikely, my ass." He emptied the clip from his rifle and loaded a fresh magazine. He turned on the safety and wrapped it behind his back. "All right, men, listen up. Here's the spread. If negotiations are still forth-going, then we can assume Command has declared Hermetic Contingency."

"For you army brats who didn't pass your intro to martial law, that means any uplink data of this skirmish to the Network is classified," the corporal interjected. "Any evidence of hostilities is compromising of national security. Sergeant, I recommend immediate quelling of the conflict by any means necessary."

The sergeant nodded. "Agreed. We're in a shit-storm, fellas. I'm issuing a standing order that this is our primary objective. They opened fire on us, but there's no happy ending if word of this gets out. Weapons free. I don't want things getting any more fucked than they already are. If this doesn't end here we might be looking at full-on war, gentlemen. If a declaration hasn't already been made." A mortar rattled the entrenched band of soldiers. A few grunts lifted their guns above their cover and fired blindly ahead, warning off enemy troops.

Veian immediately scolded them for opening fire. "Do you not know what a Repulsor does? Holster those firearms!" He waited until every last man did as he commanded. "OK. This is how we're going to play it. If my intel is good, the first order of business is that Repulsor. The Radius Effect will only increase over time. This plays right into Cineon's hand, and we do not want that. Cineon's men are better trained for cold combat, and we don't have time to wait them out. What's the plan, boss?"

"Alpha and Bravo squads are going to be bait. Their job is to draw enemy fire away from Fire Squad Omega, which will consist of myself, Corporal Grebllyh, Specialist Deem, and Private Feathers. Omega's objective will be to disable or destroy the Harvest Repulsor. Fire Squad Alpha will synchronize behind us by four minutes. Alpha will back up our retreat and will halt their advance five-hundred yards to the target."

"By the way, Network comms are down. That means we'll be running silent, so watch your six. We will not be broadcasting because they can monitor our backup channels," Grebllyh added.

"Well said, Corporal. If a cease-fire is announced, it is Alpha's responsibility to recommend Omega an immediate mission abort. If not, once the Repulsor is down, Omega will be allowed two minutes to get our asses the hell out of dodge. The Repulsor off-lining should re-establish secure comms with Forward Command. After two minutes Alpha is to contact Command and authorize immediate surgical bombardment of hostile targets on my order."

The Corporal refreshed the shells in his shotgun, though he had no intent to use it. "We don't have to kill them; we just need to box 'em in and get a lid on this. The two minutes is a luxury afforded for Omega; bombardment is to commence regardless of our extraction. Any questions?"

"Are we really prepared to destroy one of the most expensive pieces of equipment in the Republic?" one soldier asked. "Why can't we start bombardment with the Repulsor online?"

"Fucking A, do any of you army kids pay attention in class?" the Corporal answered, clearly agitated. "That's why you're on Bravo squad. To shut your mouth and do what you're told. Because you clearly can't think for yourself. Now! Does anyone else have any suggestions on how to kill everyone from here to the Hub?" The corporal looked around, waiting to see if someone answered. "Yeah, didn't think so."

"Enough! Alpha and Bravo, travel further up this trench and link up with Corporal Grebllyh's marine unit for support. Everyone else will hold this position and provide us covering fire as we advance to the next trench. Good luck gentlemen."

With a non-verbal cue from the Sergeant, Alpha and Omega strapped on their helmets and freed their weapons. They put their backs up against the wall of sand and kept their blades close. Alpha and Bravo squad moved up the trench toward the marine units.

Veian looked side-to-side, assessing the members of the task force. "This is what we signed up for, men. The chance to defend brother and country. I know none of us want to be in the shit, but we are now. Alpha, keep your heads down. Omega, you're in good hands. It's our mission to guarantee Damosi interests here. And we will do exactly that. And do you know why?"

"Sir, no, sir," the squad replied, allowing the Corporal to say what everyone knew he would.

"Because we're that damn good! Hooah!"

"Hooah!" the commander echoed with the rest of the squad. "As some of you may know, Mr. Grebllyh is here because this First Strike unit was his idea. He might not be wearing our color of fatigues, but we're all brothers. Our fraternity will be a lasting bond with the success of this mission. I wouldn't have any of you with us if I didn't personally think that you were up to the task. We will not leave a man behind. We will not fail our mission. KILLER has wasted many innocents to forge their messianic message to the people of Kramei. We will avenge those lives. We will shatter the cloak of deceit brought forth by Daben Celt or my name isn't Besen Gie!"

The two officers quickly managed to get past the fighting and had quietly hiked up to the Repulsor. Veian went ahead and ducked behind a cannon. He peered over the equipment and saw two men guarding the entrance to the core. He tightened his form and signaled back to his sergeant. Besen nodded to relay that he understood the situation. He turned to the other two members of his fire squad.

"OK, this is it, boys," he said in a hushed voice. "Mr. Grebllyh has identified two troops guarding the entry to the Repulsor's gravity core. Ranged weapons will be useless now that we're inside the Radius Effect. Avoid using combustive-accelerated weapons at all. While shotguns have sometimes remained productive inside the broadcast of the Repulsor, we are now in the Eye of the Radius. Bullets, rockets, laser-guided systems, you name it. If you fire anything that can achieve entrance velocity, it won't repel by any defined algorithm. There is no telling where your bullets may stray. Veian's shotgun, should he be forced to use it, could have its rounds flip around and hit him in the back. There's just no telling what will happen." He handed his rifle to Private Feathers. "Swords. Rocks. Anything savage. Anything by the force of your arm. Veian will ambush anyone who pursues our exit. Specialist Deem will support me from the outside with his throwing knives should anything go wrong. Feathers you back up Deem or Mr. Grebllyh should anything happen to either of them. I will infiltrate the core. The longer the Repulsor remains active, the more potent the Radius Effect will become. Keep good care of my gun, Feathers. I'm going to want it back."

Besen pulled his combat sword from his balteus and darted to a cannon opposite of Veian. Veian had been monitoring the patrol of the two guards, determining the precise moment to take them down. Veian signaled that he would take the guard on the right and Besen the guard on the left – they would be taking the guard opposite the side of the field they each stood. Veian positioned himself to move. He mouthed the following, "One… two… three!"

Veian turned to his target and darted toward him. He kept the muzzle of his gun close to the ground. As Besen illustrated to the other members of the fire team, if Veian misfired, it could prove fatal. The other guard saw Veian dart toward the Repulsor entrance. He reached for a crossbow on his back, but Besen's sword slashed his wrist. Before he could cry in pain, Besen cut his throat. He finished him off with a thrusting stab into the stomach.

The gurgling blood from his throat and mouth did not go unnoticed. The first guard turned to see what had happened, but he quickly felt Veian's shotgun in his chest. Point-blank-range was the only safe shot the corporal would have in this proximity. With the enemy quickly eliminated, Veian ran up to the entrance and stood opposite of Besen. The sergeant peaked inside and saw nothing. "All right, Mr. Grebllyh. I'll take it from here. Be careful."

With a quick nod from Veian, Besen turned the corner and ran inside. He held the guard of his blade close to his face. He would be quick, quiet, and ready. He soon entered the gravity core. The design of the core was both dangerous and efficient. The round atrium was meant to allow the repulsing gravity wave to expand spherically. The room itself was enormous. If walking at a relaxed pace, one could reach the center in about five minutes.

The room was a dark blue, but not necessarily dark itself. The blue color came from the center. The cobalt light was the only visible sign of the Radius Effect. It was only visible inside the atrium. There were many ways to disable such a priceless machine. Some were more effective than others. They could compromise the outer framework; the Radius Effect would lose momentum and flatline. The mass inside the core could be increased and stop the snowball effect. This action would cause the wave to collapse on itself slowly. The safest way to immediately sever the effects of the Repulsor was to eject the core or destroy it outright.

This piece of equipment was still valuable government property. Besen would salvage whatever possible. This particular Repulsor was the first working model of its kind, so historically it was also significant. He would only destroy the core as a last resort. Ejecting the nucleus carried risk as well. Assuming Besen would be unharmed by the eject sequence, he would have to escort the core back with him. It would be hefty and difficult to drag. Removing the core and leaving it there was not an option. Though it would serve his immediate goal, the reintegration of the core would restore the Radius Effect. There was peril involved even getting to the housing. There was no decent crosswalk to the center. The design required as little architecture inside as possible to facilitate its function. From the two entrances, one at each polar end, two catwalks were leading to the center. That was it.

Besen attached a rappelling line to the railing of the crosswalk. If he fell into the core, it would take some time to get back up to the top. Paranoid of discovery at any moment, Besen slowly made his way across, sword in hand. He eventually made his way to the center and detached his safety harness and approached the central terminal. He typed the following:

>>*Priority access…*

>>*clearance level_Military contingency…*

>>*define_Hotel…*

>>*authorization code required_112032434866…*

>>*…*

>>*accepted…*

>>*fail-safe measure_Core ejection…*

>>*eject core y/n_Y…*

The latch on the core's cell hissed. The computer inside the facility had done all it could for this task. Besen needed to complete the process manually. He reached for the door that shielded the core, but a stray blade swung at his head. He jumped back, startled. It wasn't a warning strike. Where the intruder came from was a mystery to Besen. He felt his heart pound in terror from the sudden attack. His eyes didn't wander from the Lobby member. "What's this? Some kind of trap?"

The man laughed. "I must say, you took out my guards with near perfect execution. And they say you are measured by the strength of your enemies. You've done well so far, Besen. But now I have you right where I want you."

The man held a gun-blade in his hand. Simply put, depending on the model, it was a sword with a gun for a handle. The pistol vibrated the blade to create more severe wounds. Not necessarily a safe weapon to use in the current environment, even for its wielder.

Besen didn't question how the man knew his name. There was something even stranger than that. "Your voice," he whispered, "your voice. It sounds familiar. Do I know you?"

"Never one good with names, I see. You forget the men just as readily as the women." He pulled back his hood to reveal his face. It was one Gie recognized. Evan didn't know many bald men. His blue eyes were indistinguishable in the light of the Repulsor. "I am Commodore Amon Veise, Lieutenant of Infantry. I am Cineon's man on the ground. And I'm afraid I can't have you ruining our fun already."

Veise struck for Besen's mid-section, but a quick pivot of his foot and the Sergeant was away from the blade. A swift and sharp thrust to his chest across both shoulders was next, but Besen brought his hands to his waist and flipped the tip of his sword upward. He used his center of gravity for leverage. The enemy blade was inches away from piercing his neck. "You can't be," Evan muttered. "You're dead!"

Veise grinned as their swords clashed. "I was hoping to say the same about you. I guess this won't be easy." He grabbed Besen's cross-guard with his free hand. He fell to his back and flipped Besen over his head. Gie dropped his sword as he crashed into the cold metal floor. Veise was quick to his feet. He used his foot to kick Besen's blade into his own hand. Besen was quick to his feet. He reeled back, seemingly unarmed. Veise brashly went for a killing stroke. Unbalanced with another sword, Besen was able to evade the strike. He revealed a dagger, and during mid-stroke, Besen sliced into the barrel of Veise's gun-blade.

Deep inside the Repulsor, the barrel exploded violently. Veise crashed against the wall. Besen held on dearly to the edge of the platform, trying desperately not to succumb to a fall that would injure him greatly. His opponent quickly recovered. The gun-blade's firearm function was irreparably damaged, but Veise was still able to use it as a sword. The dagger was still in Besen's hand, but it was too short a weapon to fight with when hanging for dear life.

"Looks like I'll be living to fight another day," Veise touted. He approached ominously. Besen threw his blade at Veise, but he missed. The dagger had lodged itself into the framework. The Commodore laughed and turned his attention to the blade. "Wow! Really? I don't see how Damos expects to win when their own commanders can't hit a target from such a short distance."

Besen didn't miss, though. His action was deliberate. With Amon distracted, he grabbed the edge of his sword and pulled Veise over the brink of the catwalk. With Veise gone he called for Veian to come in after him. He ripped part of his shirt off and applied pressure to his hand since he cut it during his stunt. Veian entered the atrium and surveyed the area with his shotgun.

"Mr. Grebllyh," Besen shouted, "don't you fucking even think of firing that thing at all in here. I need a field dressing."

Veian rushed over to Besen. He wasn't a medic, but he could help some. He wrapped Besen's hand with a bandage. "It doesn't look like the wound is that deep, but we need to hurry up and get out of here. Who knows what reinforcements might be on their way."

Besen got to his feet and walked over to the core's latch. "Agreed. Can you get my knife out of the wall while I finish here? Go ahead and hold onto it, you need something closer range than that shotgun. There's a button underneath the hand guard, make sure you aren't pointing the blade at your face if you hit it."

Veian scoffed. "Right, whatever." Veian jumped up to reach the dagger and yanked it out. He pushed the button right away and was promptly startled as the blade expanded in front of him. "I bet this doesn't hold up to a whole hell of a lot."

Besen chuckled. "You'd be surprised what it holds up to. It's old too – an heirloom. Evan gave it to me at my dad's funeral. The same button retracts it."

Veian pushed the button again, and sure enough, it reduced its form back to a dagger again. "I'll die before I give this up, then. What happened to the guy in here with you?"

Besen cracked the latch on the core. "Amon Veise. He fell to the bottom of the atrium. I wouldn't worry about him; a fall that far would knock something loose. Probably broke a leg as soon as he hit. Here we go." He pulled the core's cell out of the Repulsor, disabling the Radius Effect immediately.

"I thought Commodore Veise was declared dead?" Veian asked. The look on his sergeant's face made it clear he didn't want to discuss that. Grebllyh nodded. "As soon as we get comms back up we got two minutes to make like a tree." He grabbed the other end of the core and helped Veian walk it out. "This thing is pretty heavy. Difficult to imagine one person carrying it down."

Some mechanical whirring sounded, and the core suddenly dropped to the ground. Veian and Besen tried to lift it back up again, but it wouldn't budge. "What the," Besen muttered as they sought to move it again. "What the fuck? We almost have it out!"

Veian looked at his wrist-comm. "Two minutes have started. What the hell is holding this down?"

"It's called a magnet, asshole," said another voice.

Veian and Besen turned around and saw Amon Veise ascend the atrium. He held onto a chain that moved upward, a third-party mechanism inside. A clear backup plan in case someone tried to offline the Repulsor. The corporal reached for his shotgun, but Veise drew faster. He fired a spear-gun at his chest and sent Grebllyh flying outside of the atrium.

Veise fell from the chain and landed on the platform again. "We'll be quite safe in here from any bombing runs, I assure you, Mr. Gie. I'm not so sure about your friend, though." He pushed a button on his wrist, and the entrances sealed shut. Veian was now trapped outside. Besen looked around for another way out, but there was none. He looked over to Veise, nostrils flared.

Veise probably never smiled so wide before in his life. "Now," he taunted, "where were we?"

# 5. CROSSROADS

Senjek changed to a black dress shirt and rolled the sleeves up to his elbows. He fastened every button except the top two. Treistina had suggested more than once that he get tailored for his nicer clothes. He was against the idea, content to get clothing off the rack. He sat down on his bed. He preferred a more casual look and decided not to tuck the shirt in. With a blank mind, he stared at the floor for a few minutes. Dak could be heard pacing in the other room. They hadn't been friends for that long, but Senjek felt sorry for the man. His marriage was falling apart, whereas Senjek believed he found the love of his life.

He couldn't help but feel he was reaching out to Dak for selfish reasons. He knew he loved Treistina. At least he thought he knew. There was some lingering doubt in his mind somewhere. Had he pulled Dak's spiraling life into his own madness to reassure his own feelings? Senjek didn't have any family anymore. Did he just need a friend to tell him she was the one? Could he even really trust what Dak's opinion one way or the other? Senjek had been through his fair share of heartbreak. He feared he lacked the capacity to love this girl truly.

He fondly reminisced about the first vacation they took together. Treistina told him she loved him for the first time. She wasn't eager to go in the first place, but he convinced her. He wasn't sure if she had ever been camping, but it was evident that she had never done so in such conditions. There was a two-week break between the classes he taught. He was able to secure an expenses-paid trip to Iedin for five days (the perks of being a military contractor). This initially excited Treistina, the beaches of Iedin were famous for their luxury and extravagance. Though the government would pay the tab for the trip and certain expenses, Senjek wasn't that valuable an asset. Treistina poorly masked her disappointment when they arrived at Jade Peak. The mountain range was as beautiful as the coast, but the conditions were not as welcoming. Exploration of the caverns was mostly limited to guided tours. Senjek managed to pull some strings and gained permission to spelunk unsupervised. The mouth of the cave was easy enough to reach. A child could navigate the paths easily, so there was no danger in scaling the mountain.

"You really have a thing for secluded getaways, don't you?" he remembered her asking. A fair observation. Senjek considered himself a romantic at heart, but he never had much time in his life for women. Treistina was a remarkable woman, and he knew that he would have to do something special. Something no guy probably ever tried doing for her. Something she'd never forget. Her attitude changed once they entered the caverns. The bluffs were awe-inspiring to behold, but inside was where the real beauty lied. The walls were lit up by the gemstones inside. When the mountains were active volcanoes, the eruptions from the planet's core expunged certain radioactive vapors. The fumes were deadly to life underground. Once they left the planet and made contact with the surface air, the toxicity abated in a few of years. The gas chemically altered the face of the mountain. The exterior had a slight green hue due to greater exposure to winds which carried the vapors away faster. The further one burrowed, the more vivid the display became.

Treistina clutched his arm for warmth as they went deeper inside. She was too awestruck by her surroundings to notice it became warmer the deeper they got. Senjek led her down a slope off the main footpath to a hot spring. The area wasn't part of the tours; the innkeeper entrusted Senjek with the location. Treistina had expected to spend the night in their cabin, but Senjek had set up camp inside the mountain.

"What do you think?" he asked. He paced around the enclosure. "I was up here yesterday while you were having one of those marathon phone calls with your mom. I knew I had to bring you here as soon as found about this place."

He took a few moments to admire the scenery. The reaction he witnessed was not what he had expected. He saw a tear form in Treistina's eye. "Senjek…" she cooed.

He got close to embrace her, but she fell to her knees. He knelt next to her. "What is it? What's wrong?"

She looked into his eyes. Treistina hadn't taken much notice of them before, not like this. She could tell he wasn't in deeply love, not really. There was something she hadn't seen in him before, something she hadn't expected to see. Deep inside of those brown eyes. It was at that moment that she knew. After a few weeks, she already knew. All she had to do was decide. "It's beautiful," she finally managed to reply. "No one's ever done anything like this for me. And I didn't even want to come."

He wrapped his arms around her. "Well, don't cry!" he said faking a laugh. "It's just a hot spring, you know? There's probably tons of them." To this day he didn't know why he tried to downplay the moment. Her reaction was undoubtedly odd. He felt confident their excursion would end in one of two ways. They would leave after they had explored or they would have a swim. The latter seemed less likely than what he anticipated when he planned the trip. "There's other parts of the mountain to visit. We can always go back to the cabin." He convinced himself that he blew it.

She brought herself eye level with him. He felt the smooth touch of her hand on his left cheek. "I wish we never had to leave. I wish the whole world were in here."

He hadn't anticipated that reaction. He also wasn't prepared for Treistina to place her hand on the inside of his leg. He barely had time to react to that as she kissed him. He wasn't unprepared for this, but he didn't expect it here or soon. He gently lifted her up and laid her down under the tent. He brushed the hair away from her face. "Your eyes remind me so much of these lights in here. I wanted you to see the beauty I see in you."

She grabbed a fistful of hair on the back of his head and pulled him closer. She bit his ear lightly before whispering something. "Senjek, you can stop talking now."

There was a knock at the door. Senjek snapped out of his daydream. He looked up and saw Dak peering through the cracked door. "Sorry to disturb you from your reminiscing, but some of us have to be up very early in the morning. Some of us would like for things to wrap up sooner because we didn't start later." Dak walked over toward the nightstand and motioned the phone that rested there. "Want to give her a call and see where she is?" He lifted up Senjek's mobile and shook it in his hand.

Senjek ripped the phone from Dak's grasp, obviously annoyed. Dak didn't care, though. Senjek turned away from his friend and activated the phone's screen. He began to enter her Network information. "Wait a minute," Dak interrupted, "are you manually typing her number?"

Senjek looked over his shoulder at Dak, apparently confused. "Yes? Why?"

Dak scoffed. "Wow. I just assumed you'd have her contact info saved. You have that number memorized?"

"Obviously I do, Dak. It may be hard for you to grasp, but technology, where I come from, isn't always caught up with the cutting edge on Damos. This is how I went about calling people. I guess I'm just stuck in my ways." He heard her voice on the other end of the call. "Hey baby, I —" he stopped when he heard her start speaking again. It was her voice mail. He ended the call. "No answer."

Dak took the phone away. "Allow me to put this back." He browsed through the contacts saved to the phone as he walked away. "You have me in here. General Raines, General von Breischa's office, and you even have Evan's private line. There are many important numbers in here, and I know you aren't calling at least one of them."

Senjek walked over to Dak reclaimed his mobile. He shoved it into the charging dock. He bit his lower lip and turned around to face his colleague. "What's your point, Dak?"

Dak shrugged. "I don't know anything about this girl, Senjek. So why are you dragging me out to meet her?"

"I thought the answer to that question would be obvious. We're friends; I'd like you to meet her."

"Don't play stupid with me, Senjek. I know why you have me here. We aren't that close. Yeah, we're friends, but we're work friends. Exposing me to the intimacies of your personal life? You're afraid. You want someone to tell you how you feel. I know what this is all about, so before she gets here before we get out there, tell me what I'm doing."

Senjek looked down to the ground. "I'm still not sure how I really feel about her. If this is something that can go the distance. I'm asking you, as my friend, just to help me."

"You are such a fucking idiot, Bohmet, I tell you." Not exactly the response Senjek was expecting. "I wish you could hear yourself. Let's look at the facts. You've been with this girl for two years now. Fact. You just blacked out thinking about her. Fact. She's one of the few things you discuss at work. Fact."

"That's just great. You think you know everything. You think I'm an open book. Well, I'm not. There's a lot about me you don't know. There's a lot she doesn't know about me. I want to know if I can trust someone with my secrets. Do you wanna talk facts? Here's a fact for you! She and I have been utterly incapable of talking about our families. How can we be this far along and can't talk about that?"

"You're freaking out, man, that's all this is. You need to chill out!"

"I'm sorry, Dak, but I can't just ignore it! How can I ever love this girl if I can't trust her?"

Dak didn't know how to respond. What he said next would have long-term repercussions on Senjek's life. Dak let go of his anger. "Dude, just listen to me. I might be losing it myself, but I know the look in a man's eye when he sees the most important thing in his life. You're not sure if you can trust her with everything? You know, some things are just harder to talk about than others. I can't talk to you about my wife. Doesn't mean I don't trust you."

"Dak, it's not the same thing," Senjek replied.

"Just because you don't want it to be doesn't mean it's not. You say you don't know how you feel about her. I look in your phonebook, and you have confidential contacts listed in it. Even the President's personal line; going to ignore the fact that you even have that. But all these different numbers and there's only one that you have dedicated to memory?"

There was a knock at the front door. Dak immediately knew who it was. Someone he had never even seen in a photograph. Senjek looked over to the door, then back again to Dak. "What are you saying?"

Dak's phone began to ring. He sighed and pulled it from his pocket. A restricted Network call. Something was going on at his office, probably important. Dak averted his gaze from his caller ID and looked at Senjek.

He declined the request and returned the mobile to his pocket. "I'll run with you tonight, is what I'm saying. I'll be your wingman, and I'll laugh at your fucking jokes. But I'm not going to tell you how to feel. You're a smart guy. One of the brightest guys we got training our troops; kids that are touching boots on the Plains of Harvest. But if you can't see what it took me less than five minutes to find out for myself? You shouldn't be teaching anyone anything. It's written all over you, man. Why are you fighting it?"

Senjek looked embarrassed. "Sorry, Dak. Maybe you were right. Maybe I was just freaking out. Maybe I'm afraid. I've lost so much in the past; I decided it was better not to let myself get attached. Someone can only hurt you if you give them that power, you know? I can't believe you, and I are even talking about this."

There was another knock on the door, this one more forceful. Dak looked back at the door, then back to his friend. "Maybe I'm the friend you always needed. That you never had. And you mine. I'm sorry too. You're right. Treistina should know more of your buddies."

# 6. REPULSOR EVAC

Mortars flew overhead, and missiles whined as they pierced through the sky. The light was bright, and the ground shook. Veian finally started to retain some understanding of himself. He soon began to recall where he was and what he was doing. His body continued to shake. He felt his body shift, but he couldn't move. There was a breathing apparatus on his face. He was on a gurney. He tried to move his head, but his neck was held in place so he couldn't move his spine. He pulled the mask away from his mouth. "Where's Besen?" he finally whispered, thinking past whatever was wrong with him. A whisper to him, he was speaking regularly. In fact, he was loud enough for someone to hear him in the hostile environment.

"Try to be still, sir," Feathers replied. "You took a pretty nasty fall, and we don't know how much damage that spear has done."

A nearby explosion rattled Omega squad. Veian hurtled to the ground from his gurney. The restraints came loose, and he tumbled violently to the ground. Still rattled, the corporal scoped the battlefield with his rifle. Images blurred in the distance. It was if he saw everything through milky glass. His hand slowly wandered up to his neck and ripped off the brace that bound it.

He suddenly remembered his shotgun. The groggy marine looked for his firearm. He heard a roar, but couldn't discern from which direction. The glare in his vision cleared when an enemy soldier suddenly stood in front of him with a javelin. The man flipped the primitive weapon to point the tip at Veian's gut. He hefted it upward as to impale the wounded marine. Veian pulled out Besen's dagger, expanded the blade, and stabbed him in the kidney. He grabbed the javelin and pulled the man down to the ground. He found his own face in the soil. He pulled himself up enough to breathe. Blood and earth caked the inside of his mouth. He extended his lower lip and tried to blow the dirt out of his eyes as best he could. He looked to his left and there it was. He could see his shotgun.

He reached out plucked his weapon from the land. He rolled to his back and loaded a shell into the chamber. He saw another hostile approach him with a mace. Veian pointed his shotgun at his enemy (who did not as much as flinch to the prospect of being at gunpoint). He almost pitied the men of Kramei in this conflict. He had no doubt they knew about Repulsors and the dangers of using ordinance inside the Radius Effect. This poor soul had no idea it was no longer active. The assailant shifted his weight to ready his killing blow.

The boy was soon on his back, his chest littered with metal. Veian didn't hear the man scream. He didn't die instantly, and Veian could see him writhing in pain. The only sound the marine heeded was the sliding metal of his shotgun as he loaded the next shell. He slowly got to his feet, the effects of his fall still in his bones. He ended the man's misery and dragged Besen's dagger across his throat.

Veian looked down and saw a spear stuck in his chest. "Veise," he muttered. He grabbed the spear as closely to his chest as he could. With his other hand, he grabbed the blunt edge of the spear. He closed his eyes and snapped the handle from the head. The weapon was still inside him, but he had improved his mobility. He tried to quell his rage. The blow should have killed him. He tried to think rationally. He suffered a devastating blow from what to have been one of Cineon's top men. He didn't know how he was still alive. "Besen," he grumbled. He briefly forgot about his friend during his own imminent danger. He turned around toward what he thought was the entrance. A hostile rushed toward him with an ax. He raised his shotgun to fire, but the ax was well on its way and knocked it loose. Veian squatted and dodged the follow-up strike. In the same motion, he stabbed the man in the back of the leg.

Veian dodged another swing. The fell to one knee as he tried to stand. He expanded the blade, ready for the next assault. No further aggression came. His foe fell victim to incoming fire. Veian had caught a glimpse of Alpha squad before he fell into a nearby trench. He could hear a mortar hit the ground moments after he was safe in the trough. He propped himself against the wall of the entrenchment. Gunfire drowned out the voices. He collapsed the blade of Besen's dagger and sat it down next to his shotgun. The bright lights around him began to dim. "Just like a bad trip," he said to himself. He hoped his dry humor would dull the shock of what was going on. He steadily readjusted to his surroundings. He picked up a canteen and drenched his blonde hair with water. He tried to get some in his mouth, but just as much splashed against his chest. A medic quickly approached the injured marine. "Where's Besen?" he asked again.

Feathers jumped into the trench. He grabbed the Network comm and barked into it. "Mayday, mayday, mayday, this is Feathers! I repeat, this is Private Feathers. I'm half a klick southeast of the Harvest Repulsor. I am under fire and surrounded by hostiles. Bombing run was ineffective. I repeat, the orbital strike was unsuccessful. Enemy armaments are more vast than previously believed. I'm with Alpha and Grebllyh, requiring immediate extraction!"

A response came promptly. "This is General Greene, Feathers, we read you. Where is the rest of your squad?"

"Wasted. We loaded the corporal on a stretcher and was hit with a grenade during our retreat. We did what we could for Deem, but," he paused and choked down his remorse. He closed his eyes tight to stay his tears. "We couldn't save him, sir. Gie fell behind. We believe he's still inside the Target, so he should have survived the bombardment. Grebllyh is wounded with numerous lacerations."

The last statement shocked Veian. He looked at himself. He hadn't realized the full extent of his injuries. He didn't think his encounters had yielded any hits. He must have rolled through glass or shrapnel (or both). He refused to think of himself. One of his brothers, and he considered these men exactly as such, had fallen behind. The marine tried to rally for the radio. He didn't know what he would accomplish. Scream at the top of his lungs that they had to go back? Rush back into danger for one man? His squad restrained him well before he could even reach Feathers.

"Roger that, Feathers. We will be bringing in extraction for your wounded, but your men are staying on the ground. We're bringing in reinforcements to contain this skirmish. The control of information is paramount. We cannot afford for word of this to get out. Eliminate or capture as many enemy units as possible. Put Grebllyh on the line."

Feathers nodded for his men to relent and they released the marine. He took the radio, "Sir, we need to go back for Besen!"

"Sergeant Gie is still considered a priority, Corporal, I assure you. We're receiving bio-comm data on you, and we're getting you out of there. You're hurt badly. You might not know it, but trust us, you're not in a good way. We're field promoting Feathers to corporal, and he will be assuming control of the rescue op. You're done here, Mr. Grebllyh."

Veian's grip on the field comm tightened. "Sir, with all due respect, this is not your call. This is my op. I'm not leaving a man behind!"

"Now you listen to me, marine," Greene shouted. "You are going to die if we don't get you looked at. If you don't want your op to leave with a man in enemy hands, then I suggest you give Mr. Feathers your blessing in moving forward in your stead. Need I repeat myself again, Corporal?"

Veian nearly broke the radio in disgust. It was his fault Besen was out there. It was his plan. His team that he personally trained. A man who sat behind a desk had benched him. An officer that partied for four years just to tell soldiers they couldn't do their job. "Sir," he finally replied, "no, sir." He could feel his emotions boil in his stomach. He felt his head get heavy. Everything started to grow dark. He fell forward. He kept his face from bouncing off the ground with his left hand. He spat blood and snot from his mouth.

The field medic rolled Veian on his side and restrained him. A field analgesic was quickly applied. "Hang in there sir, a friendly bird is on the way."

Veian lifted his hand and wearily pointed to his firearm. Feathers picked it up and wrapped Veian's fingers around it. "They're going to have to pry it, sir," he said, visibly shaken by the death and violence. A tear came from his right eye as he held Veian's hand around the shotgun. "You're going to be just fine, sir. So is Besen. We're gonna get him out, and the two of you are going come back and kick our asses for stopping this war before you even got a chance to fight in it. I'll get him back. You have my word."

Veian lifted his other hand and pointed. Feathers turned his head and saw Besen's dagger. He picked it up and put it in Veian's other hand. Veian shook his head. "No," he said, his voice grew quiet. "I'm not doing anything of the sort. I'm not coming back because I'm not leaving. When I see Besen, I'm going to kick his ass for finishing this without me." He feigned laughter. Tears began to roll freely from his eyes. He pushed the dagger's handle back into Feather's hand. "But he's not doing it without this. You find him. He's going to want this back."

"Don't talk like that sir; you're going to be fine. We're gonna get you out of here and you—"

"Promise!" Veian shouted. He sniffed back his tears. "You promise me! No matter what. You find him. You go ahead for me. You find him.

Feathers took the dagger and shoved it inside his boot. He wiped the tears from his eyes with his arm. "You got it, corporal," he replied.

# 7. A NIGHT ON THE TOWN

Dak had never been to a diner the caliber of the one he would attend tonight. He'd been to nice restaurants, but never one that required a reservation. It wasn't merely the price that had deterred him in the past. He was more impulsive and never planned social events in advance. The restaurant had a rather large dining room, the tables graciously spaced apart. There were a few white stone pillars that dotted the room. The columns reached from floor to ceiling but were more for appearance than support. The floor was some synthetic substance, silver and polished; it didn't smear or get dirty easily. If you looked down, you could see your distorted reflection.

The roof was a dozen and a half feet high. The ceiling was ebony and dark green with elaborate displays carved into the plaster. The entire outer wall was red-gray brick, save a single window. The glass was as tall as a person. The pane was a single piece that wrapped around the entire west side of the establishment. A thick milky glass separated the kitchen from the dining room. It wasn't possible to see much except roaring flames and silhouettes of the cooks. Above the kitchen was another floor which contained private balconies that provided more private (and expensive) dining.

A light dinner was only the first part of the night's itinerary. There was an attached bar beyond the gallery. The pub served diners but also allowed walk-in patrons for drinks only. They would all go there for drinks after dinner, but Senjek had already ordered a beverage. He claimed it was to whet his appetite. Dak wasn't sure if he believed that. He sat down at their table. Treistina had visited the washroom, so it was just the two of them for the moment. "Slow down, buddy. Last I checked, this isn't a party. This is a social date. You don't want me to have to carry you back, do you?"

That did nothing to discourage Senjek. "I don't plan on drinking much after this. Somebody has to drive, and I don't like taking cabs. Besides, I've been told that if I ever got a reservation at this place, that I had to try a Damosi Waterfall."

"Fine," Dak relented, "how is your fancy drink?" Senjek didn't answer. His facial expression suggested that it wasn't something he was likely to try again. "What? It can't be that bad. What's in it?"

"Tastes like a lot of different things. I'm not sure exactly, I was just told to ask for it," Senjek admitted.

"By who?"

Senjek forced another gulp of the liquid in his glass. "Besen," he muttered under his breath. Dak couldn't help but laugh. "Yeah, he's quite the joker, isn't he? But forget that, tell me what you think so far."

"A quality establishment. Seems a little expensive for an occasion such as this."

Senjek nodded. "You won't see me arguing that. I try not taking her to places that she has to pay for, especially for something like this, but she insisted. But I wasn't asking about the restaurant."

Dak had to think about that question. There was a brief introduction before the group left Senjek's flat. Dak remained mostly quiet during the car ride. Senjek tried directing conversation toward Dak, but Dak only said enough to get Senjek to talk about something else. He hadn't been around Treistina long enough to form any real opinion. "She seems like a sweet girl," he finally replied. That answer visibly underwhelmed Senjek. "Give me a break, man. I literally just met her. I'm not going to be able to give you her life's story. Be glad I've agreed to do this at all." Dak's phone started to ring again. He pulled it out to see who was calling now. Same as before. Restricted Network Call.

"You can go ahead and answer that," Senjek suggested. "I don't think Treistina would mind; she already excused herself. Besides, our appetizers aren't ready yet."

Dak declined the call again. "No, odds are this phone call ends with me having to leave. Someone probably wants me to come in for some stupid counter-insurgency meeting that can wait until morning. Maybe there's another power failure at West Fork. Hell, maybe the Lobby took Forward Command, and we're about to go to war."

Senjek was unsure how to respond. He feared his friend might be serious. "That last one sounds like a bit of stretch. But what do I know, you're better briefed about the logistics than I do. I'm just your introductory course adviser; I don't have the pleasure of knowing details of what's going on at Harvest."

"I wish I could say the same. You don't even want to know. The reports coming out of there each day. A bunch of bullshit is what it is," he put bluntly.

"Is that any way to talk in front of a lady in a nice restaurant?" Dak heard the voice from behind him. He squeezed his eyes shut in embarrassment. The first candid thing he had said all night, and he was already cursing.

Senjek smiled at Treistina as he saw her return from the restroom. He directed his attention back to his friend. "Dude, what are you doing? You said you'd tone down the sailor talk."

Dak didn't get an opportunity to reply as Treistina had already taken her seat. "Don't lose sleep over it, darling. I suppose if I were a real lady, my lovely boyfriend would have pulled my chair out for me." She turned her back toward Dak to face Senjek.

Dak's visage had started to turn red. "Come on guys. This is a really nice restaurant, let's not get all wound up, huh," he said nervously.

Treistina put her hand up. She turned away from Senjek. "I'm sorry, Dak, is it? I know that Senjek brought you out because he wants me to meet more of his friends. And I'm glad that you've finally decided to add to the conversation, but whatever you want to say can wait a minute." She looked back over to Senjek. "Do all of your friends lack manners? Is this the kind of people you hang out with?"

"You know I mostly hang out with military guys," Senjek replied in a hushed voice. "I said he might be a little rough around the edges. He's a real nice guy when you get to know him."

"You also said that he knew how to behave," she shot back in an even lower tone. "Did you let him borrow that shirt I bought you so maybe I'd look past his filth?"

"The filth is right across the table. I can still hear both of you," Dak muttered with increased uneasiness.

Treistina looked at him again. "I'm sorry, Dak. I don't mean it personally when I say this, but we're just fucking with you."

"Don't take it… wait, what?"

Senjek burst with laughter. "Dude, I can't believe we got you! I don't think I've ever seen her go that long without so much as grinning."

"Serves you right, Mr. Johnsen," Treistina added, trying to contain her laughter. "You were so quiet during the car ride. I knew I had to do something to get you out of your cage."

Dak sat there for a few moments. He couldn't decide if he was embarrassed or annoyed. "I have to hand it to you. You got me," he admitted.

"I'm sorry, Dak. I didn't mean to make you uncomfortable. Please, be yourself. I'd really like to get to know the man who can stand to be a friend of Senjek Bohmet's."

"Not much to tell, actually," he stuttered. "Career naval officer. I suppose I could use some more posh, but next to Senjek, who could tell?"

"Hey," Senjek interrupted, "I am very sophisticated in my own way."

"As much as it might turn a girl on," Treistina interjected, "being a romantic doesn't make you a gentleman."

"I couldn't agree more," Dak declared, eager to keep the heat off himself. "Picnics at satellite-rise might get you far with a girl, but if you want to be a gentleman, maybe rent a tuxedo."

Senjek chuckled. It took a bit of prying, but Dak was finally behaving like himself. "You going to let me borrow your car to drive around in if I do?"

"Only if I help you get your Class V license so you can drive more than ten feet without getting pulled over."

"OK, boys, put them away." Treistina intervened. "We're here so I can get to know Dak a little better. Senjek mentioned that you're married. Could your wife not make it?"

The Kramei Insurrection

The smile on Dak's face froze. He looked over to Senjek, who was no longer smiling either. Dak could hardly hide his disdain. He would have thought Senjek would have mentioned this to Treistina beforehand. "She's coming back from Iedin tonight," he replied after a short, but noticeable pause. "She needed some space. We haven't talked in a few weeks."

Treistina looked away from Dak. "Oh. I'm sorry to hear that. Is everything OK?"

Dak scratched the back of his head. "Yeah, it's just, you know, something married people go through. Just a little rough patch."

"Aw," she whimpered. "I'm sorry, I didn't know."

"No, it's OK. I doubt we could have gone the whole night without talking about it. Might as well get it out-of-the-way early. It was my ONI promotion, I think, where it all started."

Senjek could tell by her expression that she didn't understand. "Working in intelligence is a little different from being a regular officer. Longer hours. Less time at home. More secrets. I'm telling you, man; I think she's worried about her daughter."

"Our daughter," Dak replied, unappreciative of the way Senjek phrased it. "I'm trying to balance everything as best I can. I want to spend as much time with her as I can, but I don't want to lose everything else in my life too. There's a part of me that I can't express at work or home. Going out with the guys, or even just doing something alone. She just doesn't understand."

"Don't worry, Dak. You seem like a really nice guy. We're only human. Hopefully, you can both see that and find a way to get past this."

"Thank you," Dak said in return, "but enough about me. How did you two meet?"

Senjek started to speak, but Treistina cut him off. "It's a funny story," she began, "I think the first time we saw each other, he had given up his cab for me. If I'm not mistaken."

"Yeah," Senjek agreed, "it was when I first came to Damos from Kramei, and I had just left the immigration center. I had just got past the door, and it started to pour down raining. I was stepping into the taxi when I see this girl in the corner of my eye. She was rushing to the curb, carrying all sorts of boxes. I looked around and didn't see any other cars

64

coming. I called out to her and told her to take mine. She thanked me, got in, and that was that. Very gentleman-like, if you ask me."

Treistina smiled at that. "Yes, it was! He probably thought he'd never see me again, but I lived in the same housing unit back then. I wasn't on that good of terms with my father at the time, so he cut me off, and I had to get my own place. Senjek got there as I was struggling to climb the stairs. He even offered to help me carry my things. I don't think he was expecting anything in return; he was just happy to help someone out."

"I didn't see her again for about two months after that, I think," Senjek recalled. "She was actually on the top floor, and I was on the bottom, so it's not like we were going to run into each other every day. I ran into her at Sue's while I was trying to find something to wear for a job interview. She didn't quite recognize me, but after I had talked to her for a while, she remembered me. Once the ball got rolling, I asked her if she'd like to go out sometime. She, of course, turned me down." The waiter returned and brought Treistina and Senjek the salads they had ordered, as well as a glass of water for Senjek. He continued to talk while he mixed his greens. "A week after that we cross paths at the housing unit, and I try to get her to reconsider. At this point, she's past letting me down easy. She tells me that I seem like a nice guy and all, but 'we are from two separate worlds.'"

Treistina swallowed the bit of salad she was eating and interrupted, "I still feel terrible for saying that. I showed up to his room the next day to apologize. He said he'd accept my apology if he could take me out, and I agreed."

Dak tried to appear interested in the story, but he wasn't exactly at a point in his life where he wanted to hear about such things, especially with his own love life in turmoil. "So," he said, "where did you go on the first date?"

Senjek scoffed at that. "Not exactly the best idea, in hindsight. Remember when they quarantined Sehar Island because the Kramei Lobby made a bomb threat on the bridge?"

"Yeah, I remember," Dak snickered. "Is that where you went?"

Treistina continued the story. "He brought me to the bowling alley, right in the center of the island! So when the threat was made, they started sending people there for shelter. There were so many people there you couldn't move. Luckily, Senjek managed to sneak us into some utility room where it wasn't so crowded. Just the two of us."

"Yeah," Senjek bellowed. "We were there for hours waiting for the threat to be cleared. We just stayed there and talked until things died down. We really got to know each other that day, I think. I'm not sure if we would have gone out again if that hadn't happened because Treistina seemed hesitant about the whole thing."

"Well, I'm glad it did happen and that we're here together now because I couldn't imagine you not in my life." She took Senjek's hand in hers. "Our second date was much more without consequence. Well, mostly," she retracted, with a sly grin. "I think he was just making sure I didn't bail when he brought out his more elaborate displays of affection."

The waiter returned again, this time with much more food. "Who had the steak and lump cake?"

"Uh, that would be me," Dak answered, helping the waiter by grabbing the plate and setting it down himself. He still felt a little ashamed for getting something so expensive when Treistina was the one paying the bill.

"OK, if I remember correctly, the lady had the soup and the baked potato?" Treistina confirmed this with a cheeky nod. "And this must be you, then," placing the remaining plate in front of Senjek. "Were you done with your salad?"

Senjek picked up the bowl to hand it to the boy, "Yes, thank you." The waiter took the dish and asked if anyone else needed anything. After assuring him they were fine for the time being he left, assuring the group that if there were anything else they needed that he was in earshot.

Senjek cleared his throat. "Right, now where were we?"

Dinner had concluded without much conversation. Senjek tried to pay for the bill, but Treistina managed to grab the check before he could. This didn't strike Dak as odd. Senjek mentioned that it was Treistina's idea to come here, that he wouldn't have spent the money on such an occasion. Of course, he played the part of the gentleman and tried to pick up the cost; even if he could barely afford it.

Dak looked across the floor toward the bar as Treistina left to get a round of drinks. For the most part, he had started to like the girl. "Dinner and drinks. I have to admit, now that we're here, doesn't seem like too horrible an idea. Everyone finds out a little something about everyone; then we have some fun."

"Some people just have a knack for these things," Senjek replied, sounding quite proud of himself. "So, what do you think about her so far?"

Dak shrugged. "Honestly? I don't know how you pulled in a catch like her. She seems way out of your league – no offense."

"None taken," was what Senjek said, but his tone of voice was very contradicting to his words.

"What I'm trying to say," he continued, "is that you guys are from two different worlds. Just like what Treistina said to you when you guys first met. You guys couldn't have come from further walks of life. If you guys weren't displaying all the little nuances of a serious relationship, I'd say she was slumming it with you." Senjek gave a cold stare to Dak. "What? You asked, man. Just saying."

"Well, you don't 'slum it' with someone for two years, Dak. I have a key to her apartment. If I weren't stuck in military housing right now, she'd have a key to my place."

Dak sighed. "Look, forget I said it. It's obvious to me that you are important to her. There's just something about her that I can't put my finger on. I don't know."

Treistina approached the two, drinks in tow. "Here you go, Captain," she teased, handing Dak his drink. She took a sip of what she certainly considered a much more sophisticated drink. Dak accepted the glass and raised it, metaphorically to toast, but Treistina took her sip, seemingly unaware of Dak's gesture. He rolled his eyes and followed her lead.

Treistina held Senjek's hand as they leaned up against the bar. "What do you think about moving in together?"

Surprised at what he heard, Dak began to cough, as he didn't swallow his drink completely. Senjek looked over to Treistina, surprised himself. "What?"

Treistina shrugged. "I don't know, just something I've been thinking about lately. I think we're in a pretty serious relationship and it doesn't make sense for us to be living separately. You wouldn't have to stretch yourself thin trying to pamper me like this."

Senjek tried to feign ignorance. "What do you mean? You said you wanted to know some of my friends. This is what we're doing. I wanted to present a good first impression of you to Dak."

"I'm sold, by the way," Dak said, trying to ease the tension.

"We've been together for about two years. Don't you think it's time?" Treistina said. She either hear Dak or ignored his comment.

Senjek took a deep breath. "I don't know. I wasn't really prepared to talk about this sort of thing when out-and-about with a friend."

Treistina smiled and looked over to Dak. "What do you think Dak? As Senjek's friend, do you think he should move in with his girlfriend?"

Senjek glared at Dak. "Uh," Dak stammered. He looked aimlessly around the room, trying to think of an answer. He looked back over to Senjek, whose expression hadn't changed. He returned his eyes to Treistina, who was still waiting for a reply. "Financially, it makes sense, I guess. Once his lease his up, that is."

Treistina wrapped her arms around Senjek's waist. Her smile disappeared, apparently upset now. "It's just that you're at your new job a lot now. I don't get to see you as much, and I want to spend more time with you. I was hoping that we were serious enough that we could weather such a big step."

Senjek sighed. He wrapped his arm around her and held her. "You know I love you. I know I don't say it enough, but I do. I love you. I always will. I just… I don't know. I don't know what to think about it, and I need to think about it."

Treistina nodded, with her head buried in his chest. "I love you too."

Dak finished his drink. "And I… am getting another drink. I'll be back."

Dak left the display of affection and approached the bar. He ordered another rum and cola. "Dark this time, please," he quickly added, as Treistina had ordered one with light liquor.

"Sure thing, sir," the beekeeper responded. He poured the two ingredients concurrently, which led him to stir it hardly at all. He handed the glass to Dak, who thanked him for the speedy service.

Dak turned, but not to walk back over to Senjek and Treistina. He had begun to feel uncomfortable around their blatant assurances of love. He didn't know if it was because it was humble or if because it evoked memories of his own failing marriage. He started to walk back over nonetheless but bumped into someone.

"Oh, excuse me, I didn't see you there, sir," said the man. "Looks like you spilled your drink. I am sorry about that."

Dak quickly took note of his soaked garments before he looked at the man. It was obvious by the tone in his voice that he was insincere. "It's fine," he merely said, trying to avoid a confrontation.

"No it isn't, I'd like to buy you another, what were you having?" Dak opened his mouth to respond, but the other patron cut him off. "Wait a minute. I know you, don't I?"

Dak shook his head. He had never seen this stranger before. "No, I don't believe we've met."

The man smiled. "Ah, you may not know me, but I know you. You're Captain Dak Johnsen, aren't you? Let me get you a drink."

Dak stood between the man and the bar. "It's fine. I wouldn't call myself famous, how exactly do you know me?"

The man laughed. "Everyone knows who you are where I come from. We're briefed quite thoroughly."

Senjek and Treistina had noticed the incident and approached the pair. Senjek was afraid that trouble was on the horizon. "What's going on, Dak?"

"Your friend here was just turning down my generous offer for a drink," the man explained. He turned to face Senjek and saw Treistina. "Well, hello. I'm Kentidu, could I get you a drink, perhaps?"

The apparently named Kentidu started to get closer to her, but Senjek put his arm in the man's path. "She has her drink, thanks, though."

Kentidu pushed Senjek's arm away, ignoring him. "Certainly you could use another soon, I'm sure."

Senjek put his hand on the man's shoulder, pushing him away and stepping in front of Treistina. "I said she's good, buddy."

"Senjek, it's fine," she said, trying to stifle Senjek's bravado. "He's right, though, this will probably be my last drink here."

Senjek had turned his head toward Treistina while she spoke, but when he directed his attention back to the intruder, there was a smug look on his face.

The Kramei Insurrection

"You see, Senjek? She's done drinking. Here. Why don't you just take a walk?" Kentidu taunted. Senjek pushed the man in the chest, this time much more forcefully. "Oh, kitty has claws. You wanna go, princess?"

Dak put his hand Kentidu's shoulder and pulled him back. "That's her boyfriend dude, just move on before you embarrass yourself."

Kentidu lashed back at Dak, knocking him down. "Hey, fuck off pig! This ain't any of your business."

Kentidu turned his attention back to Treistina, but the only thing he saw was Senjek's fist. Senjek winced in pain and began to shake his hand. Senjek came to the defense of his friend, but it was not a good idea, as Kentidu had friends too. Senjek soon found himself on the ground.

"That's what you fucking get, asshole," Kentidu spouted, as we wiped from his cracked lip.

Dak broke his glass over the man's head. "Treistina! Get out of here." Kentidu had half a dozen friends with him. They didn't let Dak say anything else as they jumped the young captain.

Senjek got up and swung on one of them, but missed. He felt a sharp blow to his stomach. He stumbled back a bit but regained his composure quickly. He leaned forward with a follow-up swing. He tried again with his left, but his offense failed to make contact. Senjek crashed to the floor after a punch in the face.

Dak had already knocked one of the assailants unconscious. He found himself being held by one while another pummeled his chest. Dak headbutted the one hitting him to stop the barrage of fists. He wrenched his arms loose and landed an elbow to the other man's temple.

Kentidu had recovered and punched the captain in the face before he could see it coming. Dak remained on his feet but took a step back to catch himself. Kentidu swung again, but Dak grabbed him by the wrist. In a quick motion, he broke the wrist.

The fight stopped abruptly when the bartender produced a shotgun and loaded a shell. "That's enough!" he shouted. "You there drinking the rum and cola. You and the guy with my glass broken over his head are staying here until the authorities get here. Have a seat."

Dak sighed. "Sir, I'm an officer in the Damosi Navy, I assure you—"

"Do I look like someone who gives a shit? You get into a fight and start destroying my bar? I don't care if you're the Commandant of the Iedenian Guard. You aren't going anywhere."

"Shit," Dak muttered under his breath. He walked over to Senjek and helped him to his feet. "You okay, man?"

Senjek rubbed his jaw. "Yeah, I think so. What the hell was that all about?"

Dak shrugged. "I don't know. All those years surviving on Kramei… you didn't get into many fights, did you?"

Senjek accepted a bag of ice from one of the bar workers, who could tell that Senjek's face had started to swell. "Thank you," he replied, placing the ice up against his face. "What's that supposed to mean?"

Dak chortled. "I'm saying you aren't very good in a fight. For someone whose job is about teaching people how to survive in hostile environments, you don't exactly practice what you preach."

Senjek rolled his eyes. "Well, you know what they say about those who can't. They teach." He closed his eyes briefly in an attempt to manage the pain. "Where's Treistina?"

"I saw her run to the exit. You go on ahead make sure she's good. I'll get this swept under the rug. You don't need this now. Go home and start packing for your move." Even after a fight, Dak couldn't resist a jab at his friend.

Senjek laughed sardonically. "Hysterical, that one." He placed the bag of ice on the bar. He couldn't refuse his friend's help. "You're right about one thing, though. I don't have the clout with the police that you'll have. Thanks for taking the heat. Thanks for coming out tonight, too. Hopefully, it goes better if there's a next time."

Dak patted Senjek on the back and walked back over to the bar. "Can I at least get another drink while we wait?" he jested.

# 8. THE FURY

"Now, where were we?" Besen recoiled. He didn't have his sword or a gun. Veian was outside injured. "Oh, that's right," Veise continued. "Magnets." He pushed another button on his wrist, and the Repulsor core began to float toward the ceiling. Besen's eyes widened. He had a terrible feeling about this. Impossible, though it may have seemed, Veise's smile got wider. "Just point-and-shoot, really." With his digits still pressed to his wrist, Amon slid his index and middle fingers toward Besen. The core flew violently into the sergeant's chest. Besen rolled to his stomach and writhed in pain. He couldn't tell how badly he was hurt, but he had a strong feeling he had internal bleeding as he started to cough blood.

"Did you really think that Cineon would entrust the defense of this facility to someone who was ill-prepared for such a task?" Besen pulled out his radio, but Veise quickly kicked it away. "Don't worry, Sergeant, our time together will be uninterrupted as the seemingly unprovoked bombing of Krameian civilians will supply us with enough propaganda to fill the Lobby's ranks."

Besen felt his consciousness falter. He wasn't sure if he understood his foe. "Unprovoked?" There was a loud bang outside the Repulsor. The aforementioned bombing run that Besen himself had authorized had started.

Veise's grin turned to malice. He slowly got closer to Besen, unmoved by the explosions outside. "Yes. The Damosi regime has attempted to snuff out our rebellion, which has largely been political, with excessive force. You may be able to chalk up a few random acts of vandalism to the Lobby, sure. Our more sinister deeds have either been unproven or covered up by the Republic herself. Public support from Damos in the coming war will divide a nation as Kramei recoils to defend itself."

Besen continued to distance himself from Veise, desperate to reach a weapon without being noticed. However, there were words spoken that halted Besen in his tracks. He felt his heart drop into his gut. He must have misheard Veise. "What do you mean, war?"

"Only the most appropriate response to such a heinous act by the Damosi military. We will declare war on the state of Damos, and to any other states that choose to join with her. You'll find that our impending transmission over the Network, depicting the events happening now, will be shown in a light that will discourage aid from the Iedenian Guard and any mercenaries on Moaschen."

Besen was finally able to grab hold of the firearm Veise dropped in their first scuffle. It did more harm than good. Veise continued to manipulate the magnetism in the room and pulled Besen up into the air. Surprised by the sudden ascent, Besen lost his grip on the gun and tumbled back down to the platform. He barely managed to get a hold of the railing or else he would have rolled off the edge.

"Sergeant, you just aren't going to play nice, are you?" Amon walked over to the Repulsor core and lifted it up by himself. The Commodore was incredibly strong. He waddled over to the cell latch and reinserted the core. A few simple keystrokes later and the system started to reboot. "A valiant effort, of course. Unfortunately, you played right into our hands and did precisely what we wanted you to." Veise picked up his sword and shoved it into the central panel. The boot sequence continued. Without a physical input device, there would be no hope of any soldier getting the core back out safely. "We don't even need to make lies to our own troops. Your actions here today will reassure the resolve of all." He grabbed Besen by the collar, lifted him into the air, and slammed him into the core's outer casing.

Besen bounced off the metal housing. He tried to defend himself, but his haymaker narrowly missed his opponent's jaw. He felt a knee in his

73

gut. Veise punched him again in the face, sending him to the cold grate walkway again. "Give it up, Besen. You're finished."

The villain proceeded to kick Besen in the face, but the sergeant caught the errant leg. The Commodore quickly tried to free himself but to no avail. Besen tugged on the limb and butted heads with his saboteur. With them both on the floor, Besen grabbed Veise by his hair. He smashed the commodore's head into the unforgiving metal beneath them. Gie feared for his life if he couldn't escape. He feared a public execution like his father had suffered. Besen crawled back to his radio. "This is Sergeant Gie request—" he stopped speaking and quickly turned the radio off. Something caused the radio to create ear-piercing feedback. He looked up to the core and finally noticed that Veise restored power to the Repulsor. No more communications. No more guns. There was another booming ruckus. He looked around and saw the doors unlatch. He turned to see Veise, who had recovered to his feet.

The Commodore laughed. "Go ahead. Leave. You won't make it far. The pieces are in play. Even if you warn Evan of our grand design, it'll be too late."

Besen continued to crawl, desperate to escape. He had no doubt Amon believed the words he spoke, but Besen had faith himself. "You're wrong. We'll stop you. We'll defeat your army. We'll make the Master, the Fury and the Praesage of KILLER pay for their crimes."

Amon couldn't help but be amused. "Cute. I'd like to know how exactly you plan on doing that when both of those men are safely on Damos."

Besen continued to retreat to the exit. He was barely able to comprehend what he had just heard. "It doesn't matter where. You'll never get away with this," he warned.

"No, he won't."

A sudden flood of relief came over Besen. His team had come back for him, despite giving expressed orders not to do so. The blatant defiance to Veise's claims was a giant weight lifted from his shoulders.

"Cineon!?" Veise blurted in disbelief.

Despair supplanted Besen's relief. He turned around and saw not reinforcements, but Daben's general standing right behind him, the Fury himself.

74

"No, we can hardly allow Amon to 'get away' with delivering aspects of Daben's masterstroke to the enemy. Wouldn't you agree, Besen?"

Besen reeled in shock and fear, but it was too late. Cineon pulled his bow from his back and slammed the limb into Besen's neck. The sergeant felt his windpipe collapse as he clutched his throat. Amon started to back away as well, suddenly afraid. "Sir, he was never going to be a threat. What is the harm in demoralizing one of their pitiful soldiers before ending him? Even if he made it back to his side, they could do nothing to stop us."

Cineon produced a throwing star from his belt. Veise clutched at own throat where the projectile landed. He didn't sever any major blood vessels. Not enough to kill, but enough to bring a fair amount of pain. Cineon put the star exactly where he wanted it.

"Please! Sir, please! I made a mistake. I realize that now. I'm still valuable to Daben. I can still lead in battle."

Cineon ignored the commodore's pleas for mercy. There was no sign of hesitation as he continued to stalk toward Amon Veise. "You told him that Daben was on Damos!" he shouted in rage. He looked over at Besen, who wheezed for breath as he tried to make his escape. How he was still moving after so much was a mystery to Cineon. The sergeant wouldn't move for much longer without medical help.

Amon looked on helplessly as Cineon pulled out his blade. The handle was not that of an ordinary sword, but a pistol. Each member of the Lobby Triumvirate supposedly carried one. Veise had only ever seen The Praesage wield one, though. Cineon grabbed Amon by the left wrist and held him up. He slashed Veise in the belly and pushed him to the ground. He didn't pull the trigger; he only used the blade to incite fear before he attacked. Cineon stood over the Commodore, waiting for his last pathetic cry for mercy.

Veise knew he reached his end. "You are a blind fool, sir. You would so willingly discard one of your best men for this so-called 'betrayal.' So confident you are in Daben's asset. Know this: your gun-blade wielding Messiah will never again carry the Lobby's colors. He would rather kill you all or himself! You know that better than most!"

One sudden drop of Cineon's blade silenced the Commodore for good. He dropped to one knee and took a hard look at the weapon. He was a skilled warrior, but not with the favored weapon of the Praesage. He and Daben only carried them for show. "I am sorry, Amon. I truly am. I wish you could realize my actions are for the greater good."

"Freeze!" shouted a voice from outside of the Repulsor. Cineon turned around to see an entire squadron of Damosi soldiers.

He turned his attention back to the recently fallen Amon Veise. He pulled his tools of destruction from the body. He wiped the blood from the fuller and replaced them on his person.

"I said, freeze, asshole!" Feathers repeated.

Cineon let loose an exasperated sigh. He stood up and began to walk toward the enemy troops. Besen started to wheeze, seemingly in protest, but without being able to speak, Feathers had no idea what was about to happen.

Feathers pulled back the hammer on his sidearm, letting Cineon know that he meant what he said. "I'm not going to tell you again, Fury!"

Cineon continued his march forward, unafraid. He brandished his gun-blade menacingly before restoring it to the holster on his back.

Feathers chuckled. "The great and powerful Cineon thinks so much of himself in battle. How arrogant that he can think he can just walk against anyone, no matter how outmatched. You expect us to cower in fear of your reputation? I have you in my sights. With a gun. Fucking stand down!" Feathers delirium over Cineon's bold advance turned to anger as he continued. "I think I might enjoy this more than all the people you've killed in your career, fucker."

Besen stretched out his hand, desperate to get Feathers' attention. "No," he croaked. His cries of protest were useless; the mechanisms of the Repulsor drowned him out.

Cineon smiled. "I very much doubt that."

Feathers saw Cineon reach for an arrow. His pride blinded him to the fact that Cineon wanted him to notice. Feathers made his move and pulled the trigger, completely unaware that the Repulsor was active. The bullet flew from the pistol and became trapped in the Radius Effect. Despite quickly getting caught in the wave, the shot managed to graze Cineon's hip. At least he had met his goal of shooting the man.

Feathers would not fare so well. The gun exploded in his hand and split his palm open. The shards flew backward into his eyes and face. The remaining members of his squad quickly realized his folly. They took their fingers off the triggers of their guns. Unfortunately, most of them didn't bring another weapon. Feathers reached for Besen's dagger in his boot. Blinded by shrapnel, his hand wandered clumsily. He accidentally hit the button on the hand-guard. He screamed in pain as the blade extended into his heel.

With their squad leader completely incapacitated it was easy pickings for Cineon. He had his arrow set on his bow and had singled out the nearest threat. One of the troops relieved a fallen Lobby soldier of his crossbow. Probably the only immediate danger, but still no match against Cineon with his bow. A single arrow in the head ended the threat. Cineon stepped forward and rotated his body in a circle. He did this to put his entire body weight into his strike. The limbs on his bow had spikes at the edge with fullers. He used these grooves to line up shots in multiple directions at once, but he also used the spikes as a close-quarter weapon. Perhaps less significantly, and entirely by accident, it created a silhouette of the bow that created the shape of the letter K, symbolizing Kramei.

There was one other person that possessed something besides a gun, and he now had two metal spikes in his chest. He fell to the ground with the bow stuck in his body. A gun could still be used as a blunt weapon, though. The next soldier advanced on Cineon directly. He swung the butt of his rifle at the general's head. Cineon dodged the strike, grabbed a knife from his belt, and slit the assailant's throat in one fluid motion. Cineon reassessed his surroundings. He had two men coming at him at once now. In the blink of an eye, he threw the knife in his hand. The flying piece of steel curved through the air with mathematical accuracy. It went outward and came back in, hitting the trigger on one of his assailant's rifles. The explosion that followed incapacitated them both.

This time the bullet didn't hit Cineon; it struck another member of the rescue squad. Cineon jumped into the midst of the group and pulled his bow from the limp body on the ground. Besen tried to help, but he was no match for the Fury. Cineon brought the bow over Besen's head, with the limbs behind the Sergeant's head and the string in his line of sight. Cineon pulled back the string and let it snap into the sergeant's eyes and nose.

He holstered the bow to his back and rolled over to Feathers. Cineon pulled the expanded blade from the poor man's heel and slit his throat. He retracted the blade as a bayonet tried to make contact. The blade moved out-of-the-way impossibly fast, and the attacker became unbalanced and hit nothing. A kick in the back sent the soldier to the bottom of the atrium. Even with the intense noise of the Repulsor, Cineon could hear the body break beneath him.

Only one remained. A private who hadn't fully recovered from the rifle that exploded. Cineon lunged toward the boy and stabbed him in the heart with the dagger. Blood splashed Cineon's shirt as he pulled the blade from the fresh corpse. The Fury took a moment to gather himself. He looked around and saw nothing else move. Cineon heard wheezing at his feet. It was the only other sign of life in the atrium. He threw Besen over his shoulder before the man fell unconscious.

# 9. RECOVERING AN ASSET

*He will not come quietly. We are unsure if he will put civilians in danger. If he'll put his 'friends' in harm's way, or risk blowing the whistle on the Lobby's presence on Damos. He hides behind a military career, trying to forget his past. No one could forget what he has done. He certainly can't. This makes him vulnerable, and if anything, a reliable target. We know how to turn his strengths into weaknesses. We are aware how ruthlessly and efficiently he will react, and we can use that to our advantage. But he will not come quietly.*

"Guessing you got a cab home. I'm sorry about what happened. I hope you're okay. I'll try again when I get to my apartment. I'd like to swing over to your place so we can talk. Love you." Treistina didn't answer when he called, so he left a message. He tried to think if there was a way the evening could have ended any worse. Senjek hung up his phone and put it in his pocket. He heard someone approach him but hoped they would walk past him.

"She sure did get out of there in a hurry." Senjek ran his hands through his hair, disgruntled. What now? Was someone else looking for a fight? He pretended that he didn't hear anything and continued to walk. He hoped the man was speaking to someone else. "It's not like you to lose a fight, sir. I must say, bravo. That was one hell of an act." Senjek turned upon hearing that. There was no else the around. "Ooh. That looks bad. You might want to see a doctor, sir."

Senjek felt a lump in his throat. This wasn't possible. He didn't recognize this man, but he knew why he was there. Senjek knew what he wanted. "What are you doing here? Who are you?" He demanded to know.

"Oh, where are my manners? Ljero Liachem, Lieutenant of Damos operations and interests." Ljero offered his hand, as to shake, but Senjek rejected the offer. "Very well, then. Mr. Celt would like to have a word with you."

The remark amused Senjek. "Daben Celt. Wants to talk to me? Is he close?"

Ljero smiled. "Maybe."

"Of course," Senjek replied. "And what makes Daben think I want to talk to him?"

"General, please—"

"Don't call me that!" Senjek shouted.

Ljero took a step back. "Sorry. Let's try to keep this civil. We don't want the arriving authorities to find out about any of the past political affiliations either of us may have had. Or have, in my case."

"Then make it quick."

"As you wish. You must know why I'm here, Senjek. The time is upon us, the realization of a dream. Everything that you created has grown. Everything you had planned, all your hopes and dreams for Kramei are happening now. The Lobby's endgame is fast approaching. Though Daben is aware of the rift between you and him, the man is quite eager to have you return so that you can enjoy the fruit of your work. Simply put."

Senjek laughed out loud, stunned by the proposition Ljero offered. "Daben wants me to come in? You're shitting me."

"I assure you his offer is quite legitimate. What's happening now is only possible because of your vision, Senjek," Ljero added.

Senjek got in Ljero's face, visibly angered. "What Daben is doing is not my plan. I wanted to improve the state of Kramei, not to be the leader of a new world order. Don't you understand that he's lying to you?"

Ljero shook his head. "Senjek, even if I were brainwashed and disillusioned as you claim, what reasoning could you introduce to alter my position? It would be futile. Nearly by your own admission, the only one that is crazy, is you."

A Fatal Vendetta

The conversation only further frustrated Senjek. He backed up and started to pace in order to calm down. "What makes Daben think I'm going to come back into the fold after what he did?"

"Like I said, the Lobby is as much your baby as it is his. You should be with us for our success. Do not allow your personal losses interfere with your responsibilities to the Lobby." Ljero tried his best to sound reasonable.

"I don't have any responsibilities to the Lobby!" Senjek yelled. "I would rather kill every single one of you than lift a single finger to help you!"

Ljero chuckled. "Well, that's the problem, isn't it? You're not a killer, are you? Not anymore?"

Senjek stepped closer to Ljero, his face a breath away from Daben's agent. "I'll tell you this. You report back to Daben. You tell him the best way I can help him is if he kills me. Because I will work at every turn to destroy everything he's created. I will try to stop him until my final breath. You can count on that."

Ljero closed the small distance left between them. "Well, you know this, Senjek. Daben is not stupid. You founded the Lobby with Daben. He's tried to phase out aspects of our grand design that you can compromise, but there's only so much he can weed out. He's also sure that upon your untimely demise, information about our plans will become available, and we can't have that. Trust me, if it weren't the case, you would have been long dead." Senjek backed away. It was evident his adversary intended to back him into a corner. "Of course," Ljero continued, "Daben has information about you that would compromise your entire life here. We could expose you. Daben is untouchable to the Damos government. They want someone to blame. That's you. The man who founded the organization that has committed so many atrocities in the name of Kramei's independence. Evan Gie will destroy you. But if you come with us, you can have everything."

"Except my soul. I'm surprised Daben just didn't order you to kidnap me."

"My orders are to take you by force, if necessary. I thought I'd ask you first. As a courtesy. Maybe make this transition easy. I think you'll find that you're coming with us in any case."

"If you come after me," Senjek warned, "somebody's going to get hurt. Tell Daben to drop it." He put his back to Ljero and stormed off.

"I'll relay your message," Ljero replied, but Senjek continued to walk away. His stubbornness infuriated Ljero. "People *will* get hurt, though! How many bystanders are you willing to hurt? How many of my men are you prepared to kill, General Bohmet!?" Senjek still refused to break his stride. "Let us hope that you can keep everyone safe. Including that precious girlfriend! I hope nothing happens to her! You probably shouldn't go home, either! We'll be waiting!"

# 10. DEPLOYMENT ORDERS

"This is behavior unbecoming of an officer, Mr. Johnsen. I cannot stress my disappointment enough." Dak lowered his head in shame. The local police arrested him after they responded to the scene. They turned him over to Zebediah Lissette after they discovered his rank in the military. The Admiral was the highest ranking person in the Office of Naval Intelligence. The physical office was inside the presidential mansion. Despite the president's wishes, it wasn't the official headquarters of ONI. Parliament was against having military offices inside an administrative building, so the transition was not official. The Admiral himself had not taken a side in the debate, but the president insisted he present during Dak's disciplinary hearing.

"I regret getting into a fight at a bar, sir, but they swung on a friend of mine first. He's not too good in a fight it seems. I had little choice in my actions."

The Admiral lit a cigar as he lounged back in his chair. "When you picked up this habit for drunken brawls, did you also develop a penchant for not addressing a superior officer when being addressed?" Dak bit his lower lip and closed his eyes in embarrassment. He let out a short breath before he opened his eyes. He lifted his head, stood at attention, and stared ahead in the Admiral's direction. "Good. At ease, Captain." Zebediah spread out a number of documents on his desk. Reports of the incident at the restaurant. Dak was the only suspect detained from the alleged brawl. There were other things to address besides the charges brought forth by the police. He read them out loud. "Fraternizing with a private contractor of the state, behavior detrimental to a service member of the Damosi Navy, and being under the influence in the course of duty."

Dak had an issue with the last charge. "Sir, if I may, I won't deny to having a few drinks, but I was not on duty." The Admiral placed another document on his desk. The Hera von Breischa Act. A controversial executive order to this day; Dak never anticipated its citation in such a petty fashion. He couldn't help but chuckle. "I now see the error of my ways; I didn't realize General Vardos was conspiring to commit treason, sir."

The Admiral took another puff from his cigar. To say there was disappointment in his eyes may not have been the correct word. "Sarcasm is your least appealing trait, Captain. The Iedenian Guard is a valuable and trusted branch of our military. The circumstances that create law, regardless of their current relevance, does not permit you to disregard them. As a member of military intelligence you are expected, and in fact required, to maintain the standards of behavior expected of a service member. At all times."

It was after that statement when Evan Gie stormed into the room. "Dak, what the hell were you thinking?" Both Dak and Zebediah stood at attention upon the president entering the room. Dak felt more uncomfortable with every second the review progressed. A young rising political figure, Evan got elected to office when he promised to restore order to Damos like his ancestor once did. Unfortunately, the major hostilities of the Kramei Lobby only began to occur after his inauguration. He discreetly scanned the room, but what for was anyone's guess. He looked at the two soldiers as they made their best impression of a pillar. "Right, at ease. Both of you."

Dak decided it was best not to let his superior officer speak first. "Evan, Senjek was introducing me to Treistina. Some drunk guy tried hitting on her, Senjek told him to back off, he started swinging. I swung back."

"Are you in a fighting mood? Is that why you're in bars fraternizing with a private contractor in the first place? Captain?" Evan made it clear with that statement that he would not allow their friendship to play a part in this hearing. "Attacking a civilian in a public place with dozens of witnesses. I suppose you decided that Celt's propaganda machine needed help antagonizing us. Enough people saw it that if the Network *doesn't* report it, we'll just be adding fuel to the fire. And speaking of fires, I told you that you can't fucking smoke in here!" He suddenly turned his attention to Zebediah and plucked the cigar right from his lips. Evan extinguished the smoldering tobacco in his fist as he threw it into a nearby garbage pail. The Admiral said nothing. Evan smiled. "And you, Mr. Lissette. I also told you that you were not to start this review until I got here."

"With all due respect,"

"If the next words out of your mouth are 'Mr. President' I will drag Senjek Bohmet down here and have him pummel you until he learns how to throw a decent punch. Then Mr. Johnsen won't be the only disgraced naval officer in the room!"

The Admiral tried his best to keep his composure. "Evan. I wanted to make sure that Mr. Johnsen is afforded the ability to understand the seriousness of his actions without any... bias."

Evan nodded. It was a fair enough statement. It wasn't a secret that Evan had developed a friendship with Dak and Senjek. Evan firmly believed that he was above allowing such things to interfere with the duties of his office. He couldn't fault others for thinking otherwise, though. He motioned for the Admiral to take his seat. Evan sat down beside him and instructed Dak to sit as well.

"So you were only defending Senjek and his girlfriend? Are things that bad between you and Farraeah, or was she not there?"

Zed's eyes widened. He had glanced toward Evan before he looked over to Dak. The captain kept his eyes fixed on the floor. The Admiral feared Evan might allow his personal relationship with the captain to influence him, but not like this. "Mr. President, I don't think it's appropriate to bring Mr. Johnsen's marital strife into this."

"When Dak allowed his personal relationship with Senjek to interfere with his duties to the Republic he opened every aspect of his personal life to be scrutinized. Well?" Dak didn't answer. Evan nodded to himself. "That's what I thought. I take no joy in salting a fresh wound, but you brought this on yourself. I wish things were better at home, Dak. I do. You and your wife are going through a rough patch, and I don't blame you for wanting to fight. If you want to brawl, I suggest you start taking swings at the Lobby."

Dak's eyes darted up to Evan. He wasn't sure what to make of what he had just heard. "What? Why do you say that?"

"You heard me," Evan said, "you're going to Kramei. I need someone there I can trust on the ground in case things go south. You're the only person I trust to call the shots on the field if it comes to war."

Zebediah was just as surprised as Dak. "War? Let's take a step back. Nobody on either side is talking about war. And let's not ignore the fact that General Greene is the commander of ground assets on Kramei."

"Admiral, there are already battles happening on the Plains of Harvest that I'm trying to keep under wraps. Their general, Cineon, has taken control of our Repulsor. We infiltrated and took it offline to make a bombing run to isolate the incident. It currently isn't going to plan. General Greene doesn't seem prepared, or willing, to go all in."

"Why do you need me on the ground? Besen can do a much better job than I could leading troops," Dak reasoned.

"Besen is good at following orders, but not giving them," Evan responded. "He was leading the op to take down the Repulsor and hasn't been heard from since. At this moment we believe him to be held captive by the Lobby. Cineon has to know the consequences of taking a high ranking officer prisoner."

The Admiral wasn't happy with that answer. "That doesn't mean that war is inevitable, Mr. President. Proximity to Repulsors have effects on transmissions; there may be a less malevolent explanation. I wouldn't fear the worse for your nephew."

"If you want peace, prepare for war, Mr. Lissette. I want to be ready. We need the appropriate personnel on hand at the Harvest Forward Command Center. If Daben or Cineon declares war, Harvest will be the first bastion," Evan stated.

The Admiral picked up his hat, which had sat idly on the edge of the desk. "Well, I'll take my leave, then, Mr. President. I won't offer my opinions; it seems as though you've already made up your mind."

Dak stood to attention and traded salutes with the Admiral. He watched as he left the room. Evan said nothing to stop him. Dak also kept silent as he looked to his president. He wasn't necessarily thrilled about going to Kramei.

"Dak, we can't afford to lose the Forward Command Center. If that outpost is lost, we can't defend the space elevator. Cineon is taking more ground every day. Little by little."

Dak sat down. The news shocked him. "What? I thought they were just trying to raid our bunkers."

Evan shook his head. "No. They seized TAC-OPS at the base of Mount Fong and have slowly been advancing their line. It has been a steady advancement, and we've done little to slow it down. We have the surrounding terrain locked up, so they have their backs against the wall. The most we've done is prevent them from leaking word on events, but at the current pace they'll be attacking Forward Command within 92 hours."

Dak sighed. "What about Besen? Do you think something has happened to him? Is that why you're sending me in now?"

"I'd rather not think like that right now, my friend. I don't need you on the front lines. Right now I need you heading up things at Forward Command. Make sure things are ready for a major offensive. Cineon is unrelenting and without mercy. If Forward Command is his target, I assure you that he'll have it if we don't put up a fight."

"I'm flattered in your confidence in me, but what about General von Breischa? Wouldn't he be better qualified? Have we heard anything from him yet?"

Evan, again, replied in the negative. "Don't you worry about Baron. Besides, it's classified. Not the kind of operation he would come up with, but who am I to judge the greatest military mind in Republic history? I would be much more at ease if he were here to lead the counter-assault, but I trust you as well, Dak."

The president handed Dak a folder that contained classified materials. "You no longer report to ONI, Captain," Evan continued. "You report to my office, now. I have no choice but to declare General Baron von Breischa as missing in action. Though you are a commissioned officer in the Navy, I am appointing you as the acting General of the Armies of Damos."

Dak stared at the folder in shock. He looked up at Evan. "Sir, I'm honored, but what about my ship? Her retrofit is scheduled to be completed soon. If I'm on Kramei, who will command the navy's flagship?"

"Don't you worry about who will captain *Hieprida*. We will cross that bridge when we come to it. Please keep this to yourself for now; I have not yet informed parliament of this. I don't want the Lobby to know we are preparing for the worst. The last thing I want to do is inadvertently force Daben's hand."

Dak got to his feet. "Yes, sir. I understand."

"Dak, please. It's Evan. Now, go to the Harvest Forward Command Center and report to General Greene, as his relief. Ready your defenses as quickly and as discreetly as possible. Don't give Cineon anything." He saw the protest in Dak's eyes but knew the man well enough to know he wouldn't disobey a direct order.

# 11. LAST NIGHT

Senjek didn't go to his flat. He proceeded directly to Treistina's apartment. Not that he would be safer there. If Ljero were a disciple of Daben and Cineon, Treistina would be the best way to get to him. Senjek would have done the same thing. It had been years since he was in league with the sinister duo, but the killer instinct quickly returned to him. He viewed all the pieces as one big picture. The need to stay two steps ahead at all times. It was as if he never left the Lobby.

His emotions had not yet completely consumed his judgment. His first instinct was to storm into Treistina's apartment, guns blazing. He knew that if it were a trap, he would be no help to either of them. He had to maintain some semblance of patience.

He parked his car near an EMT station two streets away. If this were a trap, Ljero would have the apartment under surveillance. Senjek had to be realistic, though. He was less prepared, under-equipped and outnumbered. He could park further outside of Ljero's surveillance range, but could Senjek successfully sneak in and back out with Treistina in tow? He would have to place faith in the fact that Ljero wouldn't come for him here – at least not yet. His car would be safe. The Lobby wouldn't risk exposure near emergency vehicles. Senjek realized that Daben's plan was at a stage that required either Senjek's elimination or reassimilation. That meant that if exposed, KILLER would have substantial problems on Damos if discovered. He had to play on this knowledge and use it to his advantage.

# The Kramei Insurrection

It was for this reason that Senjek believed that Ljero made an error. The Lieutenant mentioned that he was under orders from Daben to take Senjek by force. Undoubtedly Daben intended to take Senjek by surprise. For the time being, Senjek would have to hide in plain sight. He would have to risk being seen by his enemy for now but could put himself in a position that made an assault implausible. It was a game of chess, now. Ljero moved first and tried to scare Senjek into submission. Senjek would not yield so easily. It was a mystery to him why Cineon wasn't there to lead the mission.

Ljero had already unwittingly given Senjek considerable insight to his inexperience. The threats to Treistina and his other loved ones was obviously dubious. He was bluffing. Daben would most certainly use anyone close to Senjek as leverage. Though this may have meant no harm might come to them, it didn't make them safe.

He stepped out of the parking lot and into the street. A few dozen people walked about the area. Were any of them members of the Lobby? There was no way to know for sure. He hoped that he was too exposed for KILLER to risk showing themselves in the middle of the city.

Senjek made his way across the street and onto the sidewalk. Everyone he passed was potentially an uncover agent of the Lobby. He was suspicious of anyone that looked his way. He was exposed and couldn't shake the feeling of being watched. He firmly believed his enemy wouldn't approach him right now, but paranoia overcame him.

He bumped shoulders with someone as he made his way to Treistina's complex. He quickly ran his hand through his hair, unable to completely repress the urge to strike the man. He apologized to the stranger and continued to walk down the side of the street as if nothing had happened.

Next, he heard a loud series of banging noises. He flinched as if he was under fire. He quickly regained his composure, though. He nonchalantly looked around for the source. There were a handful of kids playing with firecrackers on the other side of the road. Senjek quickened his pace.

He made it to Treistina's apartment complex unscathed. Maybe Ljero was bluffing. Maybe he was alone. Maybe the cavalry wasn't coming. He pressed Treistina's apartment number on the panel. He looked over his shoulder to see if anyone was coming. The street had all but cleared. He turned back to the panel. No answer. He pushed the button again. He became worried when she didn't answer. It hadn't been that long, but a mounting fear grew in his mind that something had happened. He pressed it a third time.

Still no answer. Senjek firmly planted his feet to break the door down. He stopped himself. "She might not be home," he assured himself. Senjek reached into his pocket for his phone. He pulled it out of his pocket, but it slipped from his grip. The mobile device landed on the pavement beneath him. It made a huge raucous, or it least so it seemed to Senjek. He looked around with the expectation that a chorus of bystanders would be staring at him.

He didn't see that. The impact of his phone hitting the ground went unnoticed. The street didn't suddenly fill with bodies. It was a big city, and no one would notice such a small thing. He quickly picked it up and began to dial her number.

Suddenly, there was a voice that rang through the panel. It asked who was there. Senjek was relieved to hear her voice. "Baby, it's me. Can you buzz me in?" He tried to sound calm and collected, but he could sense that there was some urgency in his voice.

"Senjek?" she answered back. "I thought you'd still be tied up with your friend at the club. Is everything okay?"

Senjek nodded. He looked over his shoulder to make sure no one else was coming. "Yeah, everything is fine. Can you just let me in?"

"Sure can!" she replied. There was excitement in her voice. She was happy to hear from him. The door had made an audible buzz before it unlocked. He opened the door and afforded himself one last sweep of the street to see if anyone followed. Still nothing. He stepped inside and made certain he firmly closed the door behind him. He made sure it locked in case anyone tried to rush the entrance.

He let loose a sigh of relief. He looked up the stairs to see if anyone loitered above. There was no one from what he could see. He quickly made his way up to her room and knocked on the door. With the undoing of a chain lock, Treistina opened the door to her apartment to let Senjek in. "Hey, baby!" she exclaimed. Treistina immediately hugged him once he stepped inside. She planted a quick peck on his cheek and draped her arms around his shoulders. "Are you OK?"

Senjek cracked a smile. "Yeah. Of course. Why wouldn't I be?"

The Kramei Insurrection

Treistina averted her gaze as if she was surprised to hear that. "Uhm, because you and your friend just got into a fight at the club." She looked into his eyes with a smile. "I've never seen boys fighting over me. It was a little sexy." She bit his bottom lip as she kissed him.

"Right, that," he replied sheepishly. He closed the door behind him and replaced the chain lock. He locked the deadbolt as well as the tumbler in the door knob. He followed Treistina into her living room and sat down next to her on the sofa. "How are you feeling?"

"I'm a little shell-shocked, I guess. I don't think I've ever seen a fight before. Not up close, anyway. How's your friend Dan?"

Senjek chuckled. "It's Dak, actually. His name is Dak. He said he was going to stay behind and take the heat for it, but he should be able to stay out of trouble. He's got friends in high places. I thought I'd come over and make sure that you were okay."

Treistina smiled. At that moment Senjek remembered that the life he left behind was all made worth it, if only for that smile. He might have given up on himself were not for that smile. So many things could be wrong in the world, but just seeing Treistina's happy face was enough to let all of his past demons sleep.

"It's sweet, that you're worried about me, Senjek. But you might want to worry about yourself a little bit sometimes, too."

Senjek was taken aback by that response. "What do you mean? I'm all right."

"Sweetie, you're bleeding," Treistina replied bluntly since the extent of his injuries was oblivious to him. He had forgotten. He touched his lip, and it was wet. He looked at his finger, and there was indeed blood. "You must have been really worried about me if you didn't even realize you were hurt," she teased.

"What can I say? You might be the most important thing in my life right now."

Treistina started to blush. She leaned in close to him and wrapped her arms around him. "You're sweet. You might want to see a doctor about that lip, though."

Senjek had his right arm around her now and put his left hand over hers. "I'll be okay. I just wanted to make sure you're safe. I don't ever want anything to happen to you. I love you. Very much."

92

Treistina pulled away. She sensed that something was wrong. "Is there something you aren't telling me?"

He shook his head. "No. Things couldn't be better. I'm just sorry I brought you out to meet my friend and things ended so badly."

Treistina wasn't convinced. "Senjek, just tell me. We've been going out for how long now? Can't you just be honest with me? Tell me what's going on."

"I want you to move in with me," he blurted.

She lifted herself up off the couch and pulled her hand away from his. This was a genuine shock to her. "You what?"

Senjek smiled. "After what happened tonight I realized that I don't want to take life for granted, or what I have for granted. I've been so blessed since I came to Damos and I've been afraid to have anything for myself. To let myself get close to anyone. I had an epiphany, though. Like I could finally see everything clearly all of a sudden. Some things in life are worth having and that I can have those things. And I don't want to lose them once I have them. I don't get to see you as much as I'd like and I want to spend more time with you. I've been afraid to let you in, but you're my everything. I can't stand the thought of not being with you. I love you, with all my heart, Treistina, and I'm ready to take the next step."

A single tear trickled from Treistina's eye. She sniffled and wiped it away. "Really? You mean it?"

Senjek leaned in and placed his lips on hers. He grabbed her leg while he parted her lips, enveloping the bottom of her smile with his. His every kiss returned in kind, every part of Treistina seemed to be rejoiced by Senjek's sudden offer. He pulled away slowly, but not far. He could still feel Treistina's soft breathing on his lips. His eyes were still closed, savoring her passion. He beamed; not feigned as he often did, but truly. He opened his eyes, his smile all the more heartfelt at the sight of Treistina's joyous expression. "I know it might seem a little sudden, but what do you say?"

"Well, Mr. Bohmet," she replied, as she rose from the sofa, "if you really want me to believe you, I'm going to need a little more convincing," she teased. She ran her fingers along his back as she walked around the back of the couch. She slowly walked toward her bedroom.

"You go ahead," he called out, "I'll be there in a few minutes."

# The Kramei Insurrection

He walked over to the sliding door that led to the balcony. He unbuttoned his shirt about halfway when he suddenly stopped. There was a car sitting across the street. There was someone in the driver's seat, but the car wasn't on. It was just sitting there. He knelt down and pulled up one of the floorboards and reached down inside. His fingers closed around the handle of the gun he planted there. He was about to bring the driver into his sights when he suddenly let go of the pistol. The car's engine turned over as a woman began walking towards it, holding a small child. He was curious as to why a family would be leaving this late at night, but it wasn't anything to do with the Lobby.

He closed the door behind him as he went inside. He would have locked the door if he could. He walked into the spare bedroom and closed the door. He placed his phone on the dresser and put his hand on top of it. "Fury. Praesage. Master. Killer." The phone reacted to the phrase and scanned his hand. His biometrics were confirmed which granted him access to an encrypted partition. A series of holographic displays covered the walls. "OK, Phyllis. Monitor all activity and alert me of any hostile or suspicious activity." He looked at the screens to gauge the response. He pulled out a pneumatic syringe and injected something into his skin. "OK, Phyllis. Monitor my location and have Transport One ready to intercept my position if necessary." He surveyed the screen to ensure the process successfully executed. "OK, Phyllis. Secure partition." The system chimed, and the holographic displays disappeared.

Senjek walked into the living room and finished unbuttoning his shirt. Sleep would be hard tonight. He hoped Treistina would be able to get some rest. If they had to go on the run, he couldn't afford her being drowsy. He ran scenario after scenario through his head. He fantasized how KILLER might strike. He had hope that he could get away with one night here. He decided that Ljero would be too brazen to stake out such an obvious hideout.

He stood near a window behind the balcony. It had started to rain; his toned chest left exposed as his shirt buttons were all undone. His usually clean shaven face showed signs of stubble and stress. There was a small clatter in the next room. His senses raced, but he kept his outward appearance composed. He turned to see what it was.

"Baby, it's getting late. I thought you were coming to bed," a familiar and angelic voice softly spoke from the darkness.

"In a minute," Senjek replied, "I'm just trying to clear my head. Gather my thoughts."

"Thinking about what we talked about tonight?" Treistina inquired. "Are you having second thoughts?"

Senjek looked over toward her. "No," he said. "No, it's not that. I just got a lot on my mind right now."

The young woman emerged from the darkness. She was in her nightgown. It was entirely white and nearly reached down to her ankles. It covered her figure completely, but it didn't necessarily leave everything to the imagination.

He found himself staring, awestruck at her beauty. She just wasn't conventionally attractive, either, she was gorgeous to his eyes in ways that other men simply couldn't see. Her face grew red; she realized that Senjek was staring at her. She walked over to him as she rubbed her eyes. She might not necessarily agree with him in her current state. She was her own biggest critic, and rarely let herself be without any makeup.

She leaned up against him and closed her eyes. She buried her head in his chest, clearly exhausted. She yawned. She only fought the urge to sleep because Senjek wasn't in her bedroom. "We can talk more about it later. Leave tomorrow's worries for tomorrow. Come to bed."

Senjek rested his chin on her crown. Her hair was soft and reminded him quickly of the warm confines of her mattress. It was evident she wanted him to return to that bed.

"I thought about getting breakfast in the morning," he said, abruptly. "I figure a nice warm meal would be a good way to start the day."

"Mhmm," she mused, "maybe if you bring it to me in bed."

Senjek chuckled, amused by her one-track mind. He wrapped his arms around her and hoisted her into the air. "I'm already bringing you to bed. A little selfish, aren't we?"

She closed her eyes and leaned her head against his chest. He looked at her smile as he walked her into the bedroom. That smile served as a reminder of everything for which he fought.

# 12. CHANGING OF THE GUARD

"Welcome to the Harvest Forward Command Center, Captain Johnsen" Dak shook hands with the officer that had greeted him. He had never met Admiral Kinem before. He wished it was under better circumstances. "It is my understanding that you have been promoted to Acting General of the Armies of Damos. I hope that I'm one of the first to congratulate you. I'm sure you're up to the task, but I'm sure being personal friends with the president doesn't hurt, either. It's not what you know…"

Dak forced a laugh in an attempt to add levity. He didn't appreciate the Admiral's crude implication. "I assure you, sir, Evan wouldn't put me in charge unless he felt I was the man for the job."

"Dak, please. Call me Kin. I think we're going to be working very closely with each other, unfortunately. Unfortunate in such circumstances, that is. Not unfortunate that we'll be working together. I hope that we can speak to each other candidly, as you do with President Gie."

Dak looked around. He noticed a group soldiers pass by, no doubt trying to eavesdrop on their conversation. He looked back at the Admiral. "Sorry. It's been a while since my first tour on Kramei. I would like that very much, Kin."

Kin chuckled. "Good to hear! I'm just pulling your chain, Captain. Is it Captain? Or should I address you as General?"

Dak bit back his growing smirk. "I would prefer Captain for the time being, if it's all the same to you, sir."

"Ah, 'sir,' again! What did I say? I think we can operate on a first name basis. General von Breischa and I were able to do so. We're peers now, you and I. I trust President Gie has gotten you up to speed on things on the ground?" Kin motioned with his hand up the hall. Dak nodded and began to walk with the Admiral.

"We've lost contact with Sergeant Gie in his, as of now, apparent failed attempt to retake the Harvest Repulsor. Intel is scarce due to a lack of transmissions from the ground, but we're hoping for the best," Dak summarized.

"Things are a little more fucked down here than what you've been briefed on, Dak. We have numerous confirmed casualties on our side. Besen has been declared as missing in action. The Lobby has the Repulsor for now, but that's not our primary concern. Current intelligence reports state that The Fury has secured a Network transmission hub. He's theoretically capable of making unauthorized uploads to the data stream."

Dak stopped dead in his tracks. "They've hacked the Network?"

The Admiral continued to walk and signaled Dak keep up. "Of course not. The Network is nigh uncrackable. Even if Cineon gains access to the system here, it doesn't mean shit. We've already reported an asset loss to the DNC, and they've orphaned existing security exchanges. Until the Consortium gets a triple-confirmed green light from HFCC, Cineon won't be able to authenticate his server to the uplink."

Dak pushed opened a door, leading into what he might call the bridge of the facility (being a navy man, after all). "I don't understand… Kin, if he can't make any transmissions, then why is the Network hub a priority over the Repulsor?"

"One word, Captain: propaganda. With control over the hub, Cineon has access to Network assets. Can you imagine what damage the Lobby can do with that? Cineon now has photographic proof of ground hostilities. Troop movements from both sides that we've been trying to keep a lid on. He has evidence of strategic military strikes from both sides, data he'll manipulate to antagonize the Damosi government further."

Dak sat down in a chair that overlooked a map of current troop movements. The fact the Lobby managed to get anywhere near the Repulsor in the first place shocked him. "OK, even without the Network supplied data, we'll still have access to the same footage. We can just release the unaltered content in retaliation if it comes to that."

Kin sat down next to Dak. "I'm afraid it's not that simple. Our plan to disable the Repulsor was so that we could launch a strategic bombing of the area. To cut off their bulk ground troops and capture them. Stop this war before it begins. Cineon apparently either anticipated this or purposefully allowed us to do it. We took down the Repulsor, and the bombing run commenced. Unfortunately, the Repulsor went back online shortly after that. More Lobby and Kramei troops appeared after the bombing run, catching us off guard. Previous intel on the size of their numbers has proven false. With these additional forces coming out of nowhere, we're preparing for the possibility that they have even more in waiting."

"So, Daben has Network definition video of the Damos military invading a Krameian controlled structure. The public won't see that it was taken from us by force. Then, once we regained control, we disabled it. We bomb Krameian and Lobby troops, seemingly without provocation. And that's how the Lobby will paint the chain of events. That about right?"

"Almost," Kin answered. "The Fury has Network definition video of events. Not Daben Celt. This is why the Network hub is a priority target. The definition is too high and encrypted for Cineon to move by any other means than the Network itself – as of now, at least. He can lower the quality, but then the legitimacy of the video can be questioned. Given enough time, Cineon can make a physical backup and smuggle it off planet to Moaschen or Iedin. Then he could leak it to third parties that might be able to use legitimate Network contacts to broadcast it. We still have time to retake the hub and stop that from happening. This is where you come in."

Dak listened to the Admiral with all of his attention, but he was certain that he must have misheard the last remark. "This is where I come in? How do you mean?"

"General Greene plans to send a demo team to take the Repulsor down for good. It's risky at this point, but the pros outweigh the cons. You're a little too green to be leading the Armies of Damos. What better way than to have you lead a detachment of soldiers to deal with the immediate problem?"

"Sir… Kin, I don't think this is a proper use of my skills," Dak protested.

"Maybe not, but we need to know you can lead from the front, and the army brass only agreed to allow your appointment if Evan agreed to this assignment. We have no reason to believe that Cineon will be there. The hub is vulnerable to counter-attack, and he knows this. Blow the whole place up if you have to, we don't care. Just don't let KILLER get away with proof of what's going on here or we're going to be stuck on this rock for a long time."

The Plains of Harvest were once a modest jewel of Kramei's former beauty. One could see grassland as far as the eye could see. Unless, of course, fields of corn or other vegetation didn't block your view. The region was named Harvest because the monarchy utilized this area to create a significant amount of the food supply for the kingdom. The ecosystem flourished for hundreds of years under both the autocracy and the Republic. This area was the first to decline among the many green places that once dotted the surface of the planet.

It was subtle, but members of the Lobby made claims that there were signs of degradation as early as thirty years ago. Crops no longer grew as abundantly. Over the years the ground became hard and wouldn't take seeds. The blame was initially thought to be sabotage from local terrorists. Allegations of Republic incompetence quickly overtook such claims. Citizens asserted that Damosi planting and gathering was too aggressive.

Evan Gie and the rest of the government didn't feel the same as the Lobby, however, and disavowed responsibility for the physical state of the planet. Damos made several restoration efforts, but these attempts were either ineffective or lacked the resources to make it an earnest venture.

The inhabitants quickly grew impatient and frustrated. Soon they became violent. A group intent on ridding this cancer from the planet soon began to make headlines. A champion for the peoples of Kramei that would kill this threat to their continued existence. Their message was clear – self-rule independent of Damos. The degradation of the planet's surface was reason enough to secede. Their tactics weren't the most diplomatic, though. The group asserted that it was Damosi indifference that saw the total loss of Harvest as a natural resource.

The Lobby did not begin as a purely a peaceful protest, however. Some of their members were prone to taking far more extreme actions to achieve their goals. Dubbed as The Triumvirate of Terror, the three most antagonized members of KILLER were Cineon (the Fury), Daben (the Master), and The Praesage. The last was an unidentified figure, having never shown his/her face. This anonymity enabled other people to assume the persona, but it was common belief that it was one man. The most wanted of the three, though the whole Triumvirate topped the Republic's Most Wanted list.

Two of those men were either missing or dead. Dak only knew the location of one of these men and this place was somewhere on the Plains of Harvest. After displaying his credentials, Dak was allowed beyond the Forward Command Center and into the war-zone. The large blast door opened and General Greene greeted him on the other side.

"I know why you are here and I must let you know I do not agree with the President's wishes," the General said in response to Dak's arrival.

"Captain Dakren Johnsen, reporting for duty. I relieve you, sir."

General Greene sighed. He didn't know if Dak was pleased to advance his career or begrudgingly followed the orders of his reassignment. "Well, let's get you briefed, then. It's not looking good. Besen and the Marine assigned to his unit for Advanced Tactics lead an operation to take the Harvest Repulsor offline. They were successful, albeit briefly. We were only allowed enough time for the initial bombing." Dak and Greene briskly walked from the entrance of the Forward Command Center to the Advanced Tactics Outpost. "No significant damage came to our foes, but they were prepared with a counter-strike," Greene continued. "With Besen captured, a wounded Grebllyh sent the rest of the team on a rescue mission. A mission the rescue squad died attempting. We currently believe that Besen is still alive and that the rescue attempt was foiled by Cineon personally."

Dak sat down in Veian's chair, stunned. He looked around at his surroundings. The ATO was in the shadow of HFCC, but it was nowhere near as fortified as their main command post. Advanced Tactics wouldn't stand up to an intense sandstorm, let alone a full Lobby assault. The outpost was mostly an array of tents to shelter the weak and injured. "How," he finally stammered, "what makes you think that Cineon was involved?"

"The remains of the rescue team were returned to us. The precision and accuracy of their wounds leave me with little doubt. In possession of one of these soldiers was this," Greene handed something to Dak. "Everyone but Besen was among them."

Dak held a throwing star of Cineon's design. This one was dull; never sharpened, never used. All of the attacks lead by Cineon had a single star of this type left at the scene as a calling card. "If Besen were dead," Dak mused...

"Then we would know about it. Our top priority is the control of information, Captain. Evan may feel differently, but we must keep Cineon inside the Plains of Harvest by any and all means necessary. Any rescue attempts must come after that. I know you and the President are close, but Besen is still just one man. The propaganda The Lobby is preparing will only entice the Kramei people further."

"I understand, General," Dak replied. "I assure you that my personal stake in Besen's life will not compromise the operation abroad."

"Good," Greene replied. "Now if you'll excuse me, I will take my leave."

Dak jumped to his feet. "Wait! You aren't staying?"

"No. I'm heading to Moaschen to inspect the shipyard and to begin deployment of a blockade around the planet."

"With all due respect, General, you can't do that."

Greene, who had already begun to leave, halted upon hearing that. "No, I can't. Not on my own. President Gie is letting his emotions get the better of him by sending you here. A naval officer has no business leading this army. I'm better off here, but since my talents aren't appreciated, I'm going to go where you should be. I pray that you can keep Cineon contained, but I'm going to start on Plan B. This is the biggest challenge our country has ever faced. If you can't get the job done, I will."

"Parliament won't issue a proclamation of war. What makes you think they'll approve a blockade?"

"It will be a blockade in everything but name. The President can't declare war or sanction a blockade. But Evan isn't the only one who can work in gray areas. We can amass a majority of the fleet in orbit without declaring any official sanctions."

Dak, clearly frustrated, turned his back to General Greene. "Don't worry. Cineon won't escape. Not this time."

With his doubts in Dak made clear, Greene resumed his retreat. "If you get to him, make sure he pays for all the suffering he's caused."

There was a bitter taste left in Dak's mouth after speaking with Greene. The General was going to Moaschen and was going to attempt to convince the fleet to blockade the planet. Not only did this endorse the General's mistrust in Dak, but it could also entice more of the peoples of Kramei into joining The Lobby. Dak decided he would examine Advanced Tactics before returning to HFCC. Ensign Lea joined him as he briskly paced through the outpost. "Give me some good news, Ms. Lea."

"Yes sir," she squeaked as she nervously opened her report folder. Dak appointed her as his second-in-command. He would not have appointed her if he didn't feel she was ready for the task, but she hadn't yet fully adjusted. "Our reconnaissance teams have located the location of Sergeant Gie. He's being held captive at TAC-OPS. Recon states that Cineon has managed to compromise a hard-line to the Network, but he has been unable to decrypt it. We've briefed the DNC on the situation, and they have not yet reported a breach."

"Now we know why Cineon chose TAC-OPS. Hard-line access to the Network." Dak looked over to Ms. Lea. Her facial expression indicated she didn't follow his train of thought. "KILLER couldn't hack in over-the-air, so now they're trying to get in the old-fashioned way. That's why they invaded a Damos asset with no way to get back out; because there's only one way in. They could have attacked the Kramei Hub directly, but that's in the middle of a mile long open field. Cineon couldn't keep us from re-taking it."

Ms. Lea began to understand. "TAC-OPS has a hard-line to the hub as a fail-safe for Republic Security. So we don't get cut off from Damos. Any insurgency might be able to interfere with the Network Broadcast, but only a full-scale attack could take down a physical line."

"And unlike the hub itself, Cineon has time where is now. Surely the DNC has orphaned security exchanges with TAC-OPS as well as the central hub, but Cineon has fail-safe protocols he might be able to reverse-engineer. So far Cineon and Daben have gone a long way without committing an Act of War against Damos. Always managing to paint us as the bad guys to the people of Kramei. With TAC-OPS having a mountain at its back and a physical access point to the Network, Cineon will eventually gain access. They might gain enough support to declare war. We have to end this now."

The Ensign couldn't believe what she heard. "Sir, we can't attack. If word gets out we've led a direct assault they may build more support."

"The word's getting out already!" Dak shouted, frustration clear in his voice. "Greene lets Cineon walk in and take TAC-OPS on a whim. On a whim! He took it overnight! He then green lights an ill-fated attempt at taking down the Harvest Repulsor. Now we've lost our entire First Strike team."

"That's a bit harsh, sir. I understand that TAC-OPS is a strategic holding, but Greene placed the space elevator as a higher priority. He didn't want the Lobby getting off world. As for the corporal, it seems Veian will be fine." Her face squirmed upon the realization that she rhymed. "Those spec ops guys don't appear to go down easy."

Dak stopped his stride and looked her dead in the eye. "Great. Grebllyh is going to make it. And when exactly will he be able to be of any fucking use?" He stared her down waiting for her to answer, but she stood silent because she knew the answer wasn't good. "It's going to be weeks before he's combat-ready, much less be able to get another team assembled!"

Ms. Lea wasn't accustomed to this kind of hostility. "Sir, that doesn't mean we have to put all of our chips in now," she said, careful to avoid eye contact with her superior.

"No. Cineon might not have made his first move, but he's made it clear to me what he intends to do. If we sit around and wait, he's going to get into the Network and show everyone what is going on here. And when that happens we will be a nation divided. We will be facing anarchy in the streets. We might even see revolts at home. Daben won't stop until there's nothing left!"

"Sir, with all due respect, aren't you being a little hasty? The Lobby is fighting for Kramei's rights. There's little indication from their actions that they'll invade Damos next."

Dak took a deep breath. "Maybe, maybe not, but this isn't up to us. We need to present the President with the facts. Tell him what's happening on the ground and convince him that we can't wait much longer. Cineon is getting ready to make his move. We need to act first.

# 13. CALM BEFORE THE STORM

B alconies were few and far between on Kramei. Senjek closed his eyes and tried to recall a time he ever as much as saw a balcony on his homeworld. His eyes squinted shut as the morning sprinkling of rain dotted his face. He allowed himself to see out into the morning dawn as the soft drizzle shouted at his instincts to do the opposite. The rain landed on his bare chest as well, but the fresh breeze that took it away made him cold. He buttoned up his black shirt (the very one he was wearing the night before). He didn't sleep with a shirt on; he had only grabbed it to protect himself from the morning wind, now forced to wear it properly.

He was just a man alone with his thoughts right now. His outward appearance might not have suggested it, but he constantly thought about Ljero and what he had said.

Would he be prepared for whatever the Lobby had in store for him? Senjek pondered over this all night. Ljero was playing a dangerous game. Senjek had two distinct goals: protect Treistina and stop Daben once and for all. Herein lied his dilemma; was it possible to do both? Treistina would only get in the way of his mission to defeat his nemesis. If he left her behind to stop Daben, Senjek might lose the only thing left to him that he held dear. One more thing Daben would take away, even in defeat.

She would need to know. Senjek had always intended to tell Treistina the full truth about his past if things became serious. The two of them had briefly discussed matters such as living together, getting married, whether or not they would have children. Senjek never really weighed the consequences of such things. He never had to. Such things were so far away in the future.

He preferred to live his life looking ahead; always one step ahead of everyone, even if it meant a level of dishonesty. From his grandiose romantic gestures to the elaborate ruse of life he portrayed to his co-workers – Senjek was always ready to reinforce one lie with an even suaver one.

He glanced at his watch, then back into the blackness of Treistina's bedroom. He was anxious for her to wake up. He was uneasy with staying in one place for so long right now.

Senjek knew this day would come. The day he would have to tell Treistina who he was. He had hoped, though, that the truth would come on his terms. He would have preferred that Daben didn't force him to it. That was his great foil, though. Daben was able to force Senjek to do terrible things that he may not do under normal circumstances.

Senjek looked back outside. The satellite had crept over the horizon, and the reflected daylight quickly galloped across the water to flood his senses. His eyes fought back against the assault on his vision. His skin felt a rush of warm relief from the cold rain. The sensation was like an epiphany for him. He felt totally consumed by it, brief though it was. It was as potent as his hatred for KILLER. Just like his love for Treistina. The feeling was gone, but two of the three passions remained.

Senjek felt a tap on his shoulder. He lost his composure and jumped. He rarely let himself be surprised. He quickly turned to see who had intruded on him.

"Sorry," Treistina giggled, "I was just coming to see what you were doing; I didn't mean to frighten you!"

Senjek laughed away his moment of lost control. "Well good," he insisted. "I'd hate to make you split costs this morning."

Treistina cocked her head; eyes widened in surprise. "Is Senjek Bohmet trying to pay for two dates in a row? Do you know something I don't?"

Senjek's smile faded. He walked past her into the apartment. He took off the wet shirt and placed it near her sink.

Treistina was quick to follow him. "I didn't mean anything by it," she pleaded. She walked up behind him and rested her hands on his shoulders.

He pried her hands away and turned to face her. He opened his mouth as if to say something, but he stopped. Something so serious was going on. She had no idea, and he didn't know where to begin. He had no idea how to explain things to her.

Treistina saw the pained look in Senjek's eyes. She put her right hand on his cheek and could tell that were he a lesser man he might have broken down into tears. "Hey, you," she whispered.

His smile tried to fight its way back upon hearing that. Unfortunately, there were other, more overwhelming emotions, in the way. "Hey, you," he simply replied.

"You know that whatever it is, you can tell me. You know that right?"

"I know," he answered. He felt that his eyes had started to swell. He put his hand over hers and held it over his face. He closed his eyes and took Treistina in. Her skin was soft and inviting. Everything he had left to live for personified by such a simple form. She only reminded him of how quickly he could lose everything. He couldn't bear to suffer such loss again. "I better get ready." He pulled her arms away from his waist and walked back into her bedroom. As abruptly as he left her embrace, he was in her walk-in closet. He had some of his clothes stowed here. Not much, but there were some. They didn't live together, but he spent enough time here to warrant keeping some spare clothes around.

He put on a dark gray polo that bore several runic symbols. Supposedly the iconography was used by the Tutors of old the monarchy. Few knew how to read what the symbols said; their arrangement was meant purely for aesthetics. Senjek had already changed his pants. He opted to continue wearing jeans. He pulled out an outfit for Treistina to wear next. She had picked out something already, but she had just gone to the shower (where her suggestion that he join her was less than subtle). He walked out of the closet and replaced her outfit with his choice. He needed her to wear something less constraining in case they had to move quickly. He tossed the clothes onto her bed and went into the living room. He heard talking. Treistina must have turned the on the television.

"... the sighting was documented by several people, but appeared as nothing more but a discharge of electrical energy in the atmosphere, due to the high interference in the rain clouds. We were lucky enough to get the sighting on tape, and we will show it to you again if you have just joined us."

Senjek didn't particularly care for the news, but this somehow caught his attention. There was a large crackle of electricity which flickered in the sky for about ten seconds. Senjek turned up the volume to hear better. The phenomenon did not look natural.

"Witnesses are speculating that given its general direction, that, if man-made, the anomaly is originating from Monarch Fall. The President's office has denied any such activity, as is the commissioner of the New Xenue Development Group. We will continue to bring updates to this story as they develop."

Senjek set the remote down, bewildered. "I wonder," he murmured to himself.

"Thank you, Lilith," the anchorman of the news broadcast said. "In other news, the governor of Kramei has scheduled a press conference this afternoon, and it will be his first public appearance in months. Rumors of his death or capture by the Kramei Lobby have been far and wide, and it finally appears that he has decided to dispel such rumors. President Gie believes that the local Krameian government will condemn the recent actions of the Kramei Lobby. Damos officials still insist that the local government attempt to suppress the activities of the group, but to-date Mayor Haeese has done little to curb the violence. We had a chance to –"

Senjek abruptly turned off the television. He didn't care to hear about what was happening on Kramei. Ordinarily he tried to keep track of what was going on there, but today was not the day to be concerned with that.

Treistina walked into the room. "Smooth, Bohmet. Very smooth."

Senjek looked up at his girlfriend, who was fresh from the shower. She was wearing the clothes he had left out for her. A pair of white khakis and a forest green sweater. The collar hung a little loose; it wasn't tight to the neck. The collar covered most of her throat. Along her waist was a brown cloth belt, which was only for show. The sash rested above her left hip and steadily dropped down to her right thigh, The belt joined near her belly button with two brass rings. She sported a pair of knee-high boots (which she apparently found herself, because Senjek couldn't).

"I was going to wear what you got me for my birthday last year! I thought you'd like that," she declared with disappointment in her tone.

Senjek stood up and walked straight to her. "Sweetie, I love how you have a special place for the things I get you. But you look so much better in the clothes I *didn't* get for you."

She put her arms around his shoulders and pulled herself up to her toes to see him eye-to-eye. "Never. They're my best clothes because you got them." She planted a wet kiss on his lips before recoiling again.

Senjek let out a long breath. He turned over to the door and put on his longcoat. "Why does it have to rain today?" he muttered to himself.

"Have you heard from Dan about that fight yet?"

Senjek turned his head toward Treistina. He hadn't thought about it. "It's *Dak*. And no, I don't believe so." He reached for his phone to see if he had any missed calls. "No," he reiterated, "he hasn't called. I hope he didn't get in any trouble."

"Trouble?" Treistina gulped.

Senjek chuckled. "Don't worry. Worst thing that would have happened is he spent a few hours getting chewed out by a superior. I doubt they'd throw a naval officer in jail for the night. It is odd that he hasn't tried getting a hold of me, though."

Treistina went to her vanity to finish her make-up. She decided on pink eye shadow and matching lip gloss. She looked into the background of her mirror and saw Senjek spying. "You know I spoil you, mister, with all this preparation for even the smallest things."

Senjek stepped out of the mirror's view. "You're beautiful without all that. Even wearing what I buy for you. I wouldn't change a thing."

Treistina smiled and looked at the stand by the door. She quickly finished with her lip gloss and put it away. "Do you know where my umbrella is?"

Senjek began to scope around the living room. "Hell, I'm sure it's here somewhere."

Treistina stood up and slyly began to walk toward the door. "Did I leave it by the door in the kitchen?"

Senjek looked into the kitchen and didn't see it. "If it's not by your coat rack I don't imagine you'd leave it in here." He looked over and saw her walk to the front door. He quickly realized what she was doing and tried to sprint in front of her, but he was too late.

"Ha! Too slow Bohmet," she teased as she flaunted his car keys in front of him. "You're getting soft."

Senjek scoffed. "Hardly."

Treistina flashed him a wide grin. "You coming?" She opened the door and stood next to it, waiting for him. "Lady's first," she teased.

Senjek popped his collar and zipped his coat shut. "Fine, you can drive, but I want my keys back when we get there."

"Deal!" She grabbed his coat by the lapel and pulled him down for another quick kiss. "Where are we going?"

# 14. SETTING THE BOARD

*The Palace in the Old City of Damos has been without a tenant for hundreds of years. There are laws written that make it illegal to even be in the city, much less even make it to the castle at the center of the land. I had hoped that my search for The Unknown Council of Moashei would end here, but I am still without success. I have one of their sons, a man I considered an ally before finding out about his heritage. I doubt a cast-out will be of any real help, but the fate of KILLER depends on this.*

The Master of the Kramei Independence and Liaison Lobby for Ending Radicalism sat arrogantly upon the throne of kings Se'har and Xen'que. History scholars had trouble agreeing on who was actually the last king of Damos. This, of course, mattered very little to the whims and ambitions of Daben Celt. He sat there and flipped through the pages of his journal with one hand. He wasn't reading the diary; he talked to someone on his mobile.

"That's no way to answer when I call. You know that," he growled. "I'm not working on your schedule. You're supposed to be checking in. Why so shy?"

He closed his journal. The man of his current obsession now stood before him. He motioned to his men to keep the man quiet with a finger to his lips. "That's outstanding to hear. It will all be over soon. I trust as long as you bring him in I can forgive you keeping me in the dark."

# The Kramei Insurrection

Daben's guards pushed the man's face into the ground. He could hear Daben's conversation, but it didn't sound like anything that could help him. Daben wrapped up the conversation and hung up the phone. "Nodo Haeese. Mayor of Kramei. I am sure rumors of your death are greatly exaggerated back home. Welcome to my humble abode," Daben exclaimed.

The guards threw Nodo to the ground. They promptly turned tail and evacuated the throne room. The man was bloodied and defeated. Not a warrior; he was a politician. Born on Damos, he moved to Kramei at an age that he could not remember. He held little hope for his life.

"Ever think that you might set foot inside this place, Nodo?" Daben asked aloud. "The architecture is timeless, classic beyond comprehension. This is the very room is where it all began. A revolution that forever changed the course of history. A revolution that was bridled and compromised. This time things will go as they should have before. You may even live to see it, Nodo, if you cooperate. If you tell me where The Unknown Council is."

Nodo just stood there. He wouldn't answer. Or maybe he couldn't. How could he? He probably knew less about The Unknown Council than Daben did.

Celt stood from the throne and approached the broken man. "Nodo, please. Don't be this way. You were born a 'son without sight,' and abandoned by your clan. Sent to Kramei where you could have a life. But a life they let you have. They entrusted some purpose for you to fulfill for their foolish visions. You are the key to finding them. If you don't help me, I assure you that you will share the fate they await. Now tell me!"

Nodo wearily looked up to Daben, who towered over his feeble shell. He took a deep breath. "Surely these not be the wasted days—"

Daben slapped Nodo in the face and knocked him to the ground. His nostrils flared, agitated by the taunting from his once ally. "Smart ass, huh? Well, I hope you lived your life without regrets, my friend. If you can't at least point me in the right direction, you've outlived your usefulness to me."

Nodo pulled himself up off the ground. His face was no longer on the cold floor, but he couldn't bring himself to stand. "I don't know how I didn't see it sooner, you snake. So many you have deceived with your lies.

112

Thousands of people believe that what you are doing is for the greater good. They think that you make Damos the enemy of Kramei for the good of Kramei. You want it all for yourself. I know who you are, Celt. You think that this place will be the arena for your triumph? You will only meet your ruin here."

Daben freed his pistol from its holster; the barrel pointed at Nodo's ear. Nodo slammed his eyes shut in fear of his imminent doom. Daben didn't pull the trigger, though. He pulled the gun back and regained his composure.

"I have one use left of you, Haeese. For that you are fortunate. Else you'd be bleeding on the floor right now. You were elected by our people to restore Kramei's honor. A fine place to call home and not some landfill for Damos. A place that was a peer to Damos and Iedin, not a hive for those Moaschen wouldn't take. You failed us. You can't be allowed to continue failing us."

Nodo closed his eyes, letting one short laugh escape as his breath did. "Listen to yourself, Celt. Trying to convince me further of your lies. The gospel according to the Master. You speak such fallacies as if you actually believed them yourself. Save your breath and save your rhetoric. Even if I knew where The Unknown Council was, I would not oust them to you. If so confident you are in your plan's success, what news could they possibly have for you that could stop you?"

An opening door shook Daben's gaze. He looked beyond Nodo and saw some of his men enter the throne room with camera equipment. He bit his lower lip and looked back down at Nodo. "Perhaps I just want to eliminate the competition."

Nodo's breathing became more labored. He knew what Daben was about to do. His part in this story would soon be over. "What about Senjek? Is he just more competition?"

Daben smiled. He motioned for his men to set up their equipment. "That's entirely up to him, Nodo. It's a shame, really. You've helped as much as he did, yet you won't see the promised land. Let us hope, for his sake, he chooses not to wander the desert."

# 15. THE PRAESAGE

"We have located Bohmet's vehicle on the highway. We have projected his trajectory to a local restaurant. Requesting permission to pursue." Ljero listened intently to his reconnaissance team's briefing. "There isn't a soul out here. Some woman, possibly his girlfriend, is driving the car. He may be navigating. They are going toward a sector outside of New Xenue. I don't think he knows; the area is practically empty." Ljero knew why. The area was cleared out for a press conference and a catering event later in the day. Something that his agents had coordinated.

"Acknowledged," Ljero replied over the radio. "Remember that the secrecy of our mission is paramount. Consider that when making your decision. Are we ready to move in, recon?" The radio had some static, but he was able to hear the answer he wanted. "Besides his girlfriend, is there anyone else in his car or on the road? Are you sure it's Bohmet?"

"Positive, sir."

Treistina turned the car onto the highway. She had never gone this way before, but she trusted Senjek's directions. She looked over to him as he blankly stared through the windshield. "Senjek? How long have we been dating?"

Senjek glanced at Treistina briefly before he returned his attention to the road. He didn't answer immediately. "Almost three years. Why?"

She refocused on the road. She tried her best to be subtle. "Do you know how long exactly?"

Senjek shrugged. "It's not so important how long it's been, only that it's happening."

She couldn't disagree with that statement, but she needed him to answer a question. "So, there's nothing special about today, then?"

Senjek thought about that. To what she was referring to, he didn't know. It wasn't any kind anniversary of theirs today. He flashed an annoyed look her way. "You're trying to trick me," he surmised.

Treistina shook her head, "No, it's not that at all. I'm just wondering why you've up and decided to take me out for a nice dinner then bring me out for breakfast the next morning."

Treistina slowed the car down to a stop at a red light. Much of this new road was designed to eliminate as much cross traffic as possible, but this was one of the few necessary intersections. Senjek looked around. "I don't even see any other cars. Don't these things have sensors?"

"Don't try to change the subject. What's happening? Is there something going on Senjek? Something you aren't telling me?"

"No, Treistina, I –," he began to say. Something else drew his attention. He saw something in the rear-view mirror. A car sped behind them as it approached the intersection.

Treistina turned around to see what Senjek was eying. "They're going awful fast, aren't they? Do they know the light is red?"

Senjek pointed at a round light around the bulb of the traffic signal. "You see that other light that's circling the red light? Once it gets full, it'll turn green again. The guy is probably trying to avoid stopping."

Senjek looked into his rear view mirror again. He spotted two more oncoming cars. They all competed to be ahead of the other as if they were racing. "The fuck?" he muttered under his breath. "Idiots. I hope they hit somebody going through the intersection."

The light turned green, and Treistina started to move again. Two of the cars whizzed past them. "Holy cow," Treistina exclaimed. "Those guys are gonna get somebody hurt, Senjek!"

Senjek turned to look out the back window. He saw two more cars speed toward them. "Not our problem. Nobody out here anyway, they'll probably end up hurting each other."

Treistina grabbed hold of the dashboard, obviously discomforted by the horseplay around them. "I hope you're right. I don't want to be eating my breakfast in a hospital bed."

Senjek chuckled. "Relax, baby, the safety features in cars these days are top notch."

Treistina briefly glared at Senjek and tried to keep an eye on the road at the same time. "That does not inspire confidence in me. Where do I turn off?"

Senjek shook his head. "Not yet, the exit isn't for a few more minutes. Just try to –"

"Holy shit!" Treistina shouted, cutting him off. Senjek turned around just in time to see one of the cars slam into their rear. Senjek impulsively grabbed the steering wheel to correct heir path. "They almost knocked us off the road!"

The vehicle that struck them lost some distance after the hit. It quickly regained speed and rammed them again. Senjek activated the cruise control. "Let me drive!"

A panicked Treistina looked over at Senjek, dumbfounded. "Do what?"

"Slide over and let me drive!" he shouted. He put his hand on the dash where it met the windshield and pulled himself up away from the seat. Treistina slid over into the passenger side, and he pulled himself into the driver's seat.

One of the other cars came up to his rear bumper, but Senjek quickly hit the brakes. The impact shook him and Treistina, but so was the passengers in the other car. He gained a considerable amount of space between them as a result of the stunt. Next, Senjek pulled up the handbrake and turned the wheel to the left as hard as he could.

His car spun around, and the front end was now facing the assailant. Senjek accelerated toward the other vehicle, who barely had time to react. The intruder tried to escape, but Senjek swung into the front left corner. The impact flipped the attacking car onto its side. Senjek pulled the handbrake again, and his car faced the original direction he was traveling.

Senjek was forced to stop almost just as quickly. Several cars were parked across the road to block his path. He could see even more approach from behind. "You want to play boys? Let's play," he muttered under his breath. He turned off to the side as much as he could and pressed the passenger side against the guard rail.

He checked his surroundings and his suspicions were confirmed. The assailants had them surrounded. He looked over to Treistina, who was near hysteria. "Senjek, what's going on? What do we do?"

Senjek grabbed Treistina firmly by the hand. He turned her face to focus on his own. "Look at me, Treistina. Look at me. We're going to be fine, OK?" She merely nodded. There were tears on the collar of her sweater. "I'm not going to let anything happen to you. I love you."

"I love you too, Senjek," she said, sniffling. "What are you going to do?" Senjek looked around, scoping out how many actual people were in all the cars. His mind was racing. He finally found himself a step behind. "Senjek? What are you going to do?"

Senjek regained his composure and looked Treistina dead in her emerald eyes. He clutched her hand tight. He tried to bury the guilt that rose in his throat. "Something I wished you never had to see. Do you trust me, Treistina?"

She didn't answer. Senjek couldn't wait any longer for her reply. Without warning, he opened his door and stepped out of the car. Treistina, instantly alarmed, crawled over to the driver's side and rolled down the window. "Senjek! Get back in the car! Call the police or something!"

"Treistina," he shouted back, "do you trust me?" Treistina just stared at him in horror. Senjek double checked his surroundings, to be sure no one started to advance. He looked back at her. "Treistina?"

There were tears in her eyes. She couldn't muster the strength to reply. "Senjek," she replied, but not loud enough for him to hear. "You don't have to do this." He walked away when he didn't hear a reply. She wiped the tears from her eyes and rolled up the window.

"It really is you!"

Senjek looked over to see a man approaching him. An imitator. "What's the matter?" Senjek taunted, "Ljero isn't up to the task himself?"

The man chuckled. "Sometimes the pawns can win without their bishops, sir." The man brandished a pair of weapons with a sinister origin. Forbidden even amongst the outlaws of Moaschen. Though formerly wielded by an exiled member of their ranks, the Lobby even denounced the weapon. Done so to improve their public image, but it was widely speculated Cineon and Daben both still carried one.

Instead of a handle, there was a pistol. Two long blades protruded from either side of the barrel. The two blades joined at the very end of their length to form a hook. Between the hook and the barrel were several braces; to ensure the aesthetic of the blade didn't compromise its practicality. The two blades were roughly half an inch apart and designed as such to inflict maximum damage.

The weapon's brutality was in the joining of gun and blade. The user would pull the trigger to discharge the firearm as they struck with the edge. This sent a violent tremor into the blade. When used correctly, one could kill a person with a single blow that might only injure otherwise.

When used improperly, or without proper training, the user could bring about significant personal harm. It was true even that one could accidentally kill themselves if not properly trained to handle the weapon. This particular version of the weapon bore the insignia of the Lobby; a circle with the letter K realized in the negative space. The emblem was placed tastefully above the trigger guard.

Senjek took in his surroundings. There was only one man in each car. There were just enough here to physically trap him here. This wasn't the main force; it was a reconnaissance team. "I thought I was falling behind, but your captain is a far cry from the Fury, isn't he? What do you call yourself?"

"You don't even know me," the man said in disbelief. There was evidence in his voice that he took offense. "My name is Victor Lowe. I was born and raised in Dola, Kramei. There isn't much left there, now. But you already know that, don't you Praesage?"

Senjek slowly – and cautiously – made his way toward the man. "Victor, I'm sorry for what happened to you in the pursuit of Daben's dream. I did bad things myself, even helped him get this far, but there is a chance for redemption. Just because you've done horrible things does not mean you need to keep sinning. A long time ago I saw what I was doing, and I shunned it. You don't have to stay with KILLER. You can fight them."

"No, Bohmet! I can fight *you*! You took everything from me. Left with only my life and my country. Since you left the Lobby, though, I've gotten something else! The chance to make you pay. My orders are to bring you in alive. I prefer to take you in barely as such."

Senjek sighed. "That is why you will fail. Ljero already fucked up by confronting me first. Now you are coming at me before you can get reinforcements. Just run away, Victor. You don't have to do this."

Victor lifted one of his gun-blades as if to admire the craftsmanship. "Almost perfect replicas of *Sola* and *Narth*, aren't they? Do you remember when you once wielded *Kilinus* and *Selna*?" The latter pair of names were in reference to the two weapons currently in his possession.

"No, I never used them. Too violent for my liking."

"LIAR!" Victor's face was red-hot with rage. "You used them when you burned Dola to the ground! I was there! I saw you! Don't say you didn't!"

Senjek took a step back. It would be futile to argue with the man. There was no telling who was responsible for starting the fire at Dola. Nor could Victor have physically seen Senjek. He wasn't there, but Senjek always wore a hood and cloak when he donned the Praesage persona. "Let me help you, Victor. We can put an end to all of this. We can put a stop to the violence and help our people another way."

Victor regained his composure. "No, there is no other way." He tossed a red scrap of cloth onto the ground, a piece of a flag or garment; it was hard to tell. "Funny that you say 'our people.' You haven't been one of us for a long time."

"Please, Victor, don't do this," Senjek pleaded.

"It is my duty to inform you that we will assimilate you into our own to build our ranks for the utter defeat of the oppressive Republic. As a member of Kramei's Independence and Liaison Lobby for Ending Radicalism, I say to you this: we will kill you if necessary. As a citizen of Kramei, do you understand our intentions, the intentions of The Lobby?"

The words cut through Senjek like a knife. There was a time when he delivered the KILLER Ultimatum. The creed was the last thing some people ever heard. He said it many times before he crippled entire villages. Victor was once a man who resisted joining the Lobby before his forced assimilation. He wasn't the only one; the Lobby drafted many of its members. These people were dedicated entirely to the cause, but few ever worked with Senjek.

# The Kramei Insurrection

Senjek's identity was kept a secret from almost everyone, save Daben and Cineon. This was to prevent his crimes in the name of Kramei from being linked to him (and later, other reasons). It was also kept a secret because many of KILLER's members resented and hated the Lobby's Omen. Every single person that would be coming after him would have undoubtedly personally volunteered for the mission. To hear this man offer him the Ultimatum was a stab to Senjek's soul. Spoken with such disdain from a man who claimed to have heard it from Senjek. Now this Victor had the chance to return the favor. Senjek remembered the response he received the last time he spoke the Ultimatum before falling out with Daben. A tear formed in his eye. "I accept death should I refuse to join you, if I am defeated," he replied, echoing the words of his final victim.

Victor swung at Senjek's waist with *Kilinus*; he left *Selna* holstered to his back. Senjek jumped back and dodged the strike. He prepared to disarm his adversary, but other members of the squad knocked him to the ground. Victor swung again, this time with the intent to maim.

Senjek would not go down so quickly, however. He managed to grab the man above his head and yanked him down. The errant edge found itself inside an ally. Senjek showed these boys how inexperienced they truly were. They were stunned by the inadvertent blow to their comrade and paused their assault to regroup.

Their brief stumble surrendered time they could not afford to lose. Senjek shoved his thumb into the eye of the man that held him down on his right. He kicked his leg upward and embedded *Kilinus* deeper into the dying man. He caught an uppercut that came from his left. Senjek wrapped the man's wrist around the exposed hook of the gun-blade. With a roll to the left, he pried the handle from Victor's hand. Mr. Lowe found himself on the pavement.

Senjek got to his feet. He parted his legs and lowered his center of gravity, ready for Victor's next move. Those who did not enter the fray raised their guns. Laser sights dotted Senjek's vulnerable points.

"Hold your fire!" Victor shouted. Their commander stumbled to his feet. "We need him alive!"

Senjek ripped *Kilinus* from the heap of fading life on the ground. He swung the blade quickly to his right. He just as abruptly stopped the motion, causing the majority of the blood to fly away. "Perhaps you should have asked nicely, as Ljero did." Senjek taunted.

Victor grabbed *Selna* from his back and engaged the asset. Senjek, the more experienced swordsman, easily parried every swing. Victor's assault was relentless. He tried to break through Senjek's defense, but the skill of the Praesage lived up to his reputation.

Senjek finally made an offensive strike and used his sheer strength to knock Victor down. He quickly jumped back to allow the man a chance to regain his footing. Senjek didn't want to kill him. "Victor, it doesn't have to be this way. I'm sorry for what I did to you, but don't let that destroy your life."

Victor ignored Senjek's pleas, drunk with thoughts of revenge. Even his impending doom wasn't enough to stay his hand. He got to his feet and continued his failed attempts to best his opponent. Senjek hadn't held this type of weapon in years, but his legendary handling of the gun-blade remained faithful to the stories. Victor was no threat to him; Senjek exerted hardly any effort.

Victor's next swing had a little something extra. He pulled the trigger with hope the tremor would give him the opening he needed. Unfortunately, Senjek was able to predict the foolhardy attempt and moved out of the way. Unable to handle the discharge, combined with missing his target entirely, Victor nearly fell on his face. He quickly regained himself physically, but his rage and embarrassment were at the boiling point. He swung one more time, but Senjek had enough of this squabble.

Senjek fired the handle of his gun-blade as the two put all of their force into a clash of metal-on-metal. The strength of the impact disarmed Victor, as *Selna* flew from his grip. Senjek kneed the man in the gut. He put the handle of his gun-blade on the bridge of Victor's nose and pulled the trigger. The leader of the recon team found himself blinded from the proximity of the blast. He scurried blindly away from his attacker. He shouted at his men to retreat. They were quick to pull Victor back.

The cars pulled away. Senjek had won for the moment. He knew this would only be the beginning of a long struggle. He looked down at the ground and stared at the pair of familiar weapons on the ground. Senjek walked over to *Selna* and picked it up. This foolish attack was unorganized and ill-fated, but KILLER would be back. They would retaliate with greater numbers and with better preparation. He had a decision to make. Would he leave these tools behind or use them in his battle?

# 16. AN UNKNOWN WARNING

*I will have my vengeance on these people, by the hand of my countrymen, and they shall suffer my fury. I will stretch mine hand upon Damos and cut off the rule of Gie from the Remnants of their own foundation. They will know my name when I lay their doom upon them. The hour of victory is nigh, and none can stop it.*

Daben Celt had false walls and lights arranged around him. The equipment was made to hide his true location. The lighting was poor, just good enough to showcase the scene. In one hand he held his gun. In the other, he grasped a black hood. "It doesn't have to be this way, Nodo. Your freedom I can't promise, but you can save your life. I won't ask again. Tell me. Where?"

Nodo Haeese was on his knees as he faced the camera. His face was bruised and bloody. Some of the blood wasn't even his. The unrelenting barrage broke the fists of his tormentor. "Surely these not be the wasted days. Please, someone, save us from our decrepit ways. And the hour too is drawing near, that our fates be decided 'ere. To ruin and to fear — the end of all things," he quietly murmured to himself.

"Insolent bastard," Daben cursed. "I'm sorry you feel this way, Nodo. I'm sorry you couldn't be of more use." He put the barrel of his gun against Nodo's temple and pulled back the hammer.

"Wait!" the broken man gasped. "Wait, I'll tell you what you want to know!"

Daben's grin was wide as he pulled his gun back to his side. "I'm glad you have to come to your senses, Nodo. Now, then, where is the Unknown Council?"

Nodo didn't want to say, but no one else could help him now. He knew that Daben would not hesitate to kill him if he didn't talk. "Their conclave is hidden from more than just the naked eye. An enchantment hangs over their dwelling that makes it invisible to your gaze. Makes it intangible to your touch. Makes it deaf to your ears."

Daben grew impatient. "Yes, I know all of this already. You waste my time. I don't need a lesson on them; I need to find them. Tell me how." Nodo felt a sharp pain shoot up his back. He turned his head away from Daben, defiant to the end. Daben paced around his hostage. "It doesn't have to be this way, Nodo. Just tell me how to break their enchantment."

Nodo grunted in pain. "You need not... break it... for you need not seek... the Unknown Council. We will send upon you the... bringer of death. We will speak... to you... here only. And only... now."

Daben, angry and confused, walked around to see Nodo's face. His eyes were rolled back into his skull, and his breath was shallow.

"What have we here, Nodo? Either you've crafted a clever ruse, or these witless worms intend to stay my hand. To whom am I speaking?"

Nodo's head fell limp. "There is no... name by which you can call us, for our clan is Unknown across... Time and Space. Identity and... Recognition struck from us. Ancestor's Past. And our Descendants. All Born with the Sight will suffer the wrath of *Narthalos*... until The End. Your plan to find The Council of Moashei will fail. Your plan to assimilate Bohmet... will fail. Your plan to conquer Damos will fail."

Daben pulled up a chair. He sat in it with the back against his chest. "You seem so confident, whoever you are. Though a mystery to me, I know you are not a member of the Unknown Council. They have the power of foresight. Their visions of any worth come from their combined diligence and never speak as individuals. They do not have the ability to present me with a glamor such as this. Now either break this spell and stop wasting my time or provide me with something useful."

Nodo's invaded head arose. His dead eyes stared into Daben's. "It is your great misfortune that you will not see the realization of your ill deeds.

124

You failed once before, so too shall you fail again. This great nation is not for you to rule. Not for any of you to rule."

Daben got to his feet and tossed his chair aside. He grabbed his gun and shot Nodo between the eyes. The lifeless form tumbled backward. Silence fell over the room as Daben followed through his shooting motion.

"You think you know the true reality," he finally muttered. "How could you betray us, brother? How could you give Damos a way into Harvest and let them slaughter so many of your own people?" He collapsed onto the floor, seemingly broken in front of Nodo's corpse.

"I know that The Lobby has done its fair share of evil deeds against our oppressors. We have had to make strong arguments to our own people to help us; not everyone understands the necessity of our actions. I have done horrible things… but I remained true to my country! It was supposed to be you! You who could lead us as a nation when The Lobby fulfilled its mission. But," he continued, his voice cracking, "you tried to give us up on Kramei. What Cineon has just shown us is your doing. The blood of all those deaths at Harvest is stuck on you now. We all would have followed you in our new country, but now we are without a leader for the future."

The entire room was bewildered. Daben was just moments ago ruthlessly interrogating this man before he fell under a spell of sorts. Daben was unprovoked in executing this man, who was very instrumental in Kramei's rebellion. One of those present in the room approached Daben.

"Sir, are you OK? What's going on?"

Daben looked up at the man, eyes puffy. "The Plains of Harvest. Damos invaded the Repulsor we were maintaining to deter violence and disabled it. We fought them off, but we couldn't put the facility back online before Damos could carpet bomb the whole area. It was just broadcast on the Network."

This member of KILLER, unaware that Daben was acting, received this news much as the rest of the Republic would. "No, that's impossible. We changed all of the security exchanges; they couldn't have gotten in!"

Daben looked up at Nodo. "That is mostly true. Nodo has been sabotaging us. I hope not from the beginning, but I don't know how for long now. He gave Damos the new codes, and we weren't prepared to defend the Repulsor. Get him out of here."

A handful of Lobby members that stood by slowly approached the body, unsure of what was going on.

Daben got to his feet and turned to face the camera, which was still running. "This treachery will not go unpunished, Evan Gie. We have had our differences and, yes, both sides outside of Harvest are armed, but what you've done... I can't ignore. I can't forgive. The people of Kramei cannot forgive! I was going to give you a chance to leave Kramei given this threat, but it's too late for peace now. I know now that you won't abandon Kramei willingly. Ever. If you are too much of a coward to do it, then I will."

Daben cleared his throat and wiped a tear from his eye. "In light of the heinous conspiracy orchestrated by President Gie and former Governor Nodo Haeese, I, Daben Celt, the sole representative of the Peoples of Kramei and General of Her Lobby, declare war on the State of Damos and any other provinces of the Republic that intervene. You wanted a fight? Well, now you have a fair one."

With a sniffle, Daben walked past the lens and approached the cameraman. He leaned in close so that only he could hear. "Cut."

The cameraman did as instructed and stopped filming.

Daben waltzed back into the center of the room. "Excellent. Blank out the audio from before I shot him, edit the video up a bit, and prepare it for Network upload."

The entire room was still unsure of what they had just witnessed. "Barring Nodo's little spell before his end, that was all a ruse. Propaganda to entice the rest of Kramei into joining our cause. Lies to make the people of Damos sympathize with us. Once Cineon prepares his video package of events on Kramei, all we need to do is wait until they have hacked into the Network."

"What is this 'Unknown Council' and why are we looking for it?"

Daben walked back over to the throne and sat on it. "The Unknown Council are the only men who a part of the coven of witches who taught the monarchy how to use magic. Collectively they create prophecies by combining their visions of the future. They then do what they can to persuade events toward their predicted outcome. They are dangerous to our plans if they decide to assist Damos. We must remove them."

"If they can see the future, wouldn't they see us coming?"

126

Daben laughed. "The Unknown Council is not The Council of Moashei of past millennia. Their visions are few and far between. Providing they are even capable at this point of foreseeing their demise; they have little resources on which to act on that knowledge. They live in secret, few knowing of their very existence."

"Sounds like we're chasing ghosts, sir," one woman spoke out.

Daben looked at her. "Is that so, Areka?"

"With all due respect, sir, if these people are as you describe them, then how have you come to know of their existence?"

"I have my sources, Areka. I understand from your standpoint, nay, many of you, that I'm speaking things of madness, but I promise you these people still exist, and you would be wise not to question me."

"How are we going to get our video to Harvest for upload," the cameraman asked, changing the subject.

"That will not be difficult, I assure you. I already have that plan in motion," Daben replied.

"And what about what Nodo said before he died? What about Bohmet?"

Daben turned his gaze to the bloody chair where Nodo met his demise. Daben merely clicked his tongue and said, "Things change."

# 17. AN UNFAVORABLE TRUTH

*Every great plan has its Masterstroke. Some of The Lobby have their ideas of what the Ace up my sleeve may be. Others, my closest lieutenants who witness my deception at the expense of Nodo Haeese's life, believe that they know. Even the Fury, the precise surgeon of this operation, is blind to my greatest advantage – though perhaps willingly so. It is Bohmet that I am after, for whether his aid or interference, he will have an impact on my endgame. However, it is my greatest safeguard that will prove to be the most ingenious.*

The actions on the highway were not addressed and seemed to loom over the whole room. The restaurant was alive and buzzing save for one table. A couple who just witnessed something that could forever change their lives. Silence dominated their morning meal. They hadn't spoken to one another since they arrived. They only said enough to be seated and awkwardly place their food orders. The long silence between the two finally broke. "How's your steak?"

Senjek stopped eating. He didn't even have an answer for that. He had hardly looked at Treistina since the ambush and had said nothing. He took another sip of his second glass of whiskey before replying, "It's good." He looked up at Treistina, who had apparently not taken her eyes off of him. The look on her face he had never seen before. Anger? Fear? He didn't know what it was he saw in her eyes. He looked down at his plate, pushing bits of food around with his fork. "How's your salad?" he whimpered.

"Senjek, what was that?"

He put down his fork and focused his attention on her again. "Treistina, I need you to trust me."

"People just don't pick up a pair of swords and do anything more than twirl them around like a jackass. They hurt themselves or get themselves killed. It's obvious you've used those before. Just tell me you're not... you can't be... him."

"Treistina, there's nothing sinister about me knowing how to use a pair of bladed pistols. As Repulsor technology was becoming a more feasible way of subduing protest, the weapon slowly came back into vogue. It's still dangerous to pull the trigger within the Radius Effect, especially if you're inside the reactor—"

"Senjek," she said, cutting him off, "I'm not one of Evan's soldiers you're prepping on how to survive the environment on Kramei. Just tell me the truth."

Senjek bit his lower lip. He was tempted to give her the short answer. "The truth. The truth isn't so simple."

"It's the easiest thing there is, Senjek. I've only seen one person use a weapon like that. Back on Kramei. He forced entire communities into submission. People were inhumanely injured. A man was brutally murdered during a live Network feed. Tell me that wasn't you."

Senjek looked down at his plate, unable to look her in the eye. "If you're talking about the hostage situation that was perpetuated by a copycat, he survived that attack."

Treistina could feel tears forming slowly in her eyes. "No. Bullshit. The Praesage was a feral dog. The man sitting in front of me isn't capable of doing those horrible things. The man I fell in love with isn't capable of murdering dozens of people for Daben Celt and the Lobby."

"With all the impersonators, officials are uncertain how many atrocities may have been carried out by the actual Praesage," he replied, his voice trailed off toward the end of the sentence.

Treistina grabbed her glass, which she had not touched yet, and drank nearly all of her wine in one gulp. "What do they want with you?" she asked, realizing he was dodging the question.

"Any number of reasons. Cineon is afraid I know things which might jeopardize their plans. They think since I've been living here I might be able to help them again. Daben holds a grudge. Maybe he just wants me dead for abandoning my country. No one just leaves KILLER."

"You must have been pretty high ranking if you knew anything or if Daben Celt would take your defection so personally," Treistina reasoned, already sold on the explanation in her head.

"You don't know how these people operate. Daben knew almost every person by name by the time I left. He made a point to. The way he absorbed people into their ranks; he had to. He became their friends. He would recruit entire towns and split them up. Put them in different divisions with separate assignments. He would destroy family ties. Uncharacteristically station two brothers together. Take one under his wing and snub the other. Divide them. Blood wasn't good enough. He made sure they trusted only him. And after being indoctrinated… what few people deserted, most cases tried to escape… it wasn't pretty."

"Senjek, this isn't what I signed up for, OK? I know we've been together a long time, but this is big. How can you never tell me about this?"

"How can I never…" he exclaimed, raising his voice. He looked around the restaurant, seeing if anyone noticed his abrupt statement. He leaned in toward the table. "How could I? Would you have stayed? Would you have given me a chance? How could this not be the only way you'd ever find out? I thought about it, whether or not to tell you. I realized that you could never know. Not because you would be horrified or ashamed knowing what I was a part of. Because every time I would look into your eyes after that the beauty and innocence I saw would be gone. I couldn't live with myself if you knew. I would be more ashamed of destroying what we have together now than anything I might have ever done in Daben Celt's name. Treistina, I never told you because I love you."

Treistina was about to finish her wine until he said that. She turned her eyes toward him and away from the glass which hung in front of her mouth. A tear had started to slide down her cheek. "What?" she barely managed to squeak.

Senjek reached across the table to grab hold of her free hand. "I know you don't hear it often enough, but I do. You should hear it more often. Every day. Every time we see each other. It's just something I have a hard time saying because before I met you, I hadn't said it to anyone in a long

130

time. The truth is I've loved you since the day I met you. And even if I've destroyed what we have by keeping this secret and you want nothing to do with me, please stay. Until this is over. The Lobby won't stop until they get what they want from me. They will use you to get to me, and I can't bear the thought of anything happening to you. I have to see this through. I have to fight."

Treistina pulled her hand out from under Senjek's. She struggled for the right words to say. The thought of what he might have been responsible for doing as a member of KILLER was mind-boggling to her. "I love you too, Senjek, but I need you tell me the truth. Yes or no. Are you the Praesage?"

Senjek let out a sigh. "No, Treistina. I'm not the Praesage." A sudden wave of relief could be seen crashing over her. The solace she found was almost tangible, but she could see Senjek held back something. She covered her mouth with her hand and shook her head. "I'm not the Praesage... anymore."

Treistina pushed her chair back away from the table. Another tear came free before it splashed on her lap. "No," came a muffled reply. To call it disbelief in her eyes did not do her expression justice. "How long? How long have I been here for you? How could you not tell me?"

"Treistina, I'm sorry. I really am. But you need to understand the severity of the situation. Daben's men may come after you to get to me."

"This... this is too much." Her hands clutched her legs. Her eyes looked frantic but didn't move. "I need time to let this set in. Alone."

"Don't you understand what I'm telling you? You are not safe. Not as long as you can be used as a means to get to me."

"Senjek," she muttered, "I believe that your feelings for me are real. I'm not saying that I don't love you. I'm not even saying that I love you less. But this is too much. If you expect me to make sense of this right now... to just in the blink of an eye accept the past that you claim to have abandoned, then your love is stronger than any love I've ever known. I can't do this. Not now. I think I need to be away from you right now."

"It's not just love, Treistina. You're my angel. The way I feel about you goes above more than just sharing dinner or isolated walks on the outskirts of the Old City, or.. or the intimate moments that two people share with each other. I was lost before I met you. I saw the indecency of the way I

131

had been living my life. I was a man going nowhere. I was so lost. I was going on living just to live. You're not just my angel because of how much I love you. When I met you, you brought me back from a dark place. You saved my soul."

Treistina abruptly stood up. Tears were freely falling, tears that Senjek caught a glance of despite her turning away to hide it. "Senjek... I didn't know. I had no idea. I'm so sorry." She pushed herself away from the table and left abruptly.

Senjek now sat alone in the restaurant. Treistina was gone. The waiter walked up to him, check in hand. Sensing that the mood had changed, he didn't extend the bill just yet. "Can I get you a drink, sir?"

Senjek just simply placed his credit card on the table. The waiter picked up the card and awkwardly left. The former Praesage of KILLER was back where he once was. Alone. He selfishly held on to love at that person's expense. He destroyed something precious to him. It was hard last time because he lost it trying to keep who he was from those he cared about to protect them. He needed this time to be different. At first, he kept it secret, but this time he recognized he couldn't. He hoped that he could protect Treistina with the truth. The loss of his family was tragic, but he couldn't bear to lose Treistina.

Senjek's spiraling mind stirred with the placement of a fresh glass on the table. His eyes snapped to the sound. He saw his card lying next to a whiskey on the rocks. He reached for his card. "Thank you, but as I said, I don't want a drink."

"No, thank you, General Bohmet."

Senjek looked up, realizing that the man upon him was not his waiter.

"Yes, yes, I know, you were never regarded with such rank, and obviously not by your real name. But even if you weren't regarded as such with the title, you were a leader of The Lobby. And you will be lauded as such now that you are back. Kramei needs you, and now, more than ever, it seems that you need it."

Senjek shot to his feet. "Lowe!" he exclaimed in suppressed rage. "What have you done?"

"Please, General, call me Victor. And I haven't done anything. You took a gamble on truth. The truth, you hoped, would save the woman you love. But as you know all too well, love is not a luxury allowed for some

132

people of Kramei. Not while the Republic of Damos makes her citizens miserable. The veil that Gie draws over his subjects is impermeable to most. But you are one of the few that can cut down the lies and bring justice to those who have suffered most. Whatever grudge you hold against your brothers must be forgiven. If not for the sake of your people, then for yourself."

Senjek slapped away the glass on the table, shattering several feet away on the floor. The entire restaurant fell silent and drew eyes. Senjek got in Victor's face so only he could hear. "Daben's words spewing from a puppet's mouth."

"General, let's not make a scene here…"

"Quit calling me that!" Senjek shouted. He took a step back. He could feel his hate contort his face. "You don't know anything about me. You have no idea what I'm capable of. Just let it go. Leave me out of this."

Victor smiled, ignoring the attention Senjek's words attracted. "No, Senjek, I know all too well what you are capable of. But do you? What The Lobby is capable of?" Leaning in as to whisper, he finished by saying, "What Daben Celt is capable of?"

Senjek turned away and briskly approached the counter. He handed a large note to the manager and apologized for the broken glass and for disturbing his business. He didn't look back at Victor as he exited the restaurant.

"We won't stop, and you won't even try. How do you expect this all to end? You can't just run away. We will find you wherever you go." Senjek faced Victor, now both outside in the parking lot. "It is with the utmost regret, though. Daben had hoped that in your time away you could forget the turmoils of your past. He assured us that by allowing you to live a life of peace in the heart of our nemesis that you would be able to forgive yourself and return to us in the final hour."

Senjek punched Victor, who in his vigor, approached his target too closely. Senjek refrained from beating down the reeling adversary, the poison of his words blooming. "What are you saying? That Daben has known about me?"

Victor clutched at his stomach. Even in so-called retirement, Senjek could strike with powerful force. "Naivety, it is not becoming of you, Bohmet. You know him better than most. Certainly better than me. Did you really think that this perfect life of yours went unnoticed by the man you insist on demonizing? You can't be a step ahead of a man who is ten steps ahead of you. It's not that you won't stand idly by when he makes his war; it is the fact that you can't. You might not want to admit it, but you must choose a side. If you love this woman, you will let her go and finish what you started."

Senjek struck Victor in the face. The messenger's blood spattered the pavement. "You leave her out of this! 'If you're not with me, you're against me?' You make it sound simple, but it isn't! Leave me out of this. You can have your independence, and you can have your war! I want no part of it! I want what Daben never let anyone on an entire planet have: a life to live!"

Victor chuckled, delirious from his pain. "I wish I could believe that. I wish that Daben could believe that. I'm going to let you in on a little secret, Senjek. We can't trust you not to get involved. If you don't join us, we will push you over the edge. In any case, your life as you know it is over. Treistina's life, as she knows it, is over."

Senjek grew angry and punched Victor again. "You leave her out of this!"

"You put her in the middle of this," Victor replied as blood trickled from his mouth. "Even now, Ljero presses his advantage."

Ljero. Senjek had almost forgotten that he was here. He picked Victor up and shoved him up against the wall of the restaurant. "You listen! Tell Ljero that if I even as much as think that he's going to do anything to her that I will hunt you all down and put you in a deep hole! You understand me!"

Victor grabbed hold of Senjek's hand that was around his neck. "Therein lies the problem, General. Do you really think that he won't?" Senjek pulled his hand back to hit Victor again. "Wait! Please, listen to me Senjek. I'm trying to help you! For your people's sake, for your own sake, and for the sake of the woman you love; you must see it! You have the life you've always wanted, but to keep it there is a price that must be paid. To make her safe, to save the lives of so many innocent people that might otherwise perish... you must come back."

Senjek's fist remained drawn. He could see his hand moving forward and crushing this leech's head. He envisioned his knuckles sending this man unconscious to the pavement. All he could feel, though, was his fist shaking; hesitant to hit Victor again.

Daben's lieutenant fell to the ground. Senjek let him go, and he collapsed on his own. It wasn't pity or mercy that spared Victor; it was love. He wouldn't do it. No matter what he told Treistina, not matter what he said to himself; if Senjek killed this man in a rage he had lost. He would prove Daben right. He put his back to Victor and started to walk away.

"Wait," he gasped, "aren't you going to finish me off?"

Senjek went back over to him. "If you want to fall to my blade then you better put yourself in a position where it's you or me. I won't help you win this fight. I don't care if Damos can beat you back. I don't even hope to stand on the sidelines and let this whole thing play out. Treistina is all I care about now, and I will do whatever it takes to make sure she's safe. If she can accept me for who I am and what I've done in the past, I'll be the happiest man alive. If she wants nothing to do with me, then I'll make sure that she doesn't suffer for having known me." Senjek leaned over him and searched Victor's pockets, pulling the key to his car. "This should slow you down." He rushed to the far end of the parking lot where he parked. Senjek's car was missing. Treistina was gone. "Damn it!" he cursed at the sky. He had done so much to be with Treistina and more-so to ensure her safety to be involved with a man with his past. Now that was all in jeopardy. Daben's agents were out there, and Treistina was a target.

"Excuse me, sir, but might you help me?"

Senjek turned to see a young woman standing behind him. She wore a navy blouse with dark green pants. A brown cape and hood, secured with a gold chain around her neck, covered her face. Was she the enemy? How could he possibly react to her?

"I'm sorry, how rude of me. *naema es* Naieena." She extended her hand out to him, but given his heightened alarm, he did not take it. "*vella veyra.* I'm waiting for someone to arrive. *e Healdra, preecisa,* I was hoping if you could tell me if you've seen anyone… *enu'ualsa.*"

Senjek looked around to see if anyone was nearby that might be watching him. "I'm sorry," he replied, apparently distracted, "My Moaschen is a little rusty."

The Kramei Insurrection

She covered her face with her hand to stifle a quaint giggle. "*ma epoiesloha...* I mean, I'm sorry," she said more sternly. "My family doesn't normally let me travel into *Ca'alpita*, the big city. Not many people are fluent in *Moashei diuahva*. I'm guilty of mixing it in with the Damic tongue. I was just hoping you could tell me if you've seen anyone strange."

He had already decided to leave and was very much so about to until she said that. Having begun to walk away, he returned to face this girl. "Strange, you say? Strange like how?" he asked, quite suspicious.

"I'm not sure, exactly. I was instructed to come out to meet someone but wasn't told much. He would look foreign, I guess. Not from around here. Maybe a little light on people skills. I know this person is to be of one mind, unwavering in their pursuit. Selectively violent, but only specifically deadly. *eomda briernha*, as we might say."

She might have been describing Daben. Or Senjek, even, but neither of them was particularly lacking in their interpersonal traits. Then again, it would have appeared she knew hardly anything about the person she was seeking. "Wish I could help, but that's not a lot to go by. I could very well be the man you're looking for, for as little you know about this mystery person."

"Don't flatter yourself, Senjek. I know you think pretty highly of your skills, but even your blade couldn't bring down civilization as we know it," the girl responded crassly.

Senjek took a step back and dropped into a base stance. "How do you know my name? What is this?"

The girl rolled her eyes. "Please. More than just philosophers and prodigies speak Moaschen. The natives who spoke it still walk among you. And we see much."

"If you are who you say you are, and see so much, why do you need help from 'philosophers and prodigies'?"

"We have a common enemy. Daben Celt, as he chooses to call himself, is a threat to us. Though not directly. The *moashent* have seen glimpses of something terrible, which if Celt continues upon his current course of action, may ultimately bring to pass *fiana viosinas moaschent*. We cannot allow that to happen. He must be stopped at any cost. You must kill Daben Celt."

136

The last foreign phrase was something he recognized. "The Last Prophecy? You must be joking. That's just a story."

"Senjek, Daben Celt is preparing for war. He is seeking to finish what his namesake started five hundred years before him. The fighting men of this entire nation will be bled, and we will all of us be unprepared to defend ourselves from the coming storm."

Senjek was unconvinced. "If you truly are afraid of this fairy tale coming to life, then you should also know that your seers predicted the arrival of a champion to stop it."

"The Known Council foresaw this disaster! It was the Unknown Council that predicted salvation. Even if it were a risk we were willing to take, millions of lives will end!"

"I haven't decided Daben's fate," Senjek admitted. "I would find no remorse in killing him, but I want him to suffer for what he's done to me and so many others."

"Then you are a fool. You and Daben are playing a game. You don't even know the rules. We cannot allow this herald to be."

"I make my own decisions. I no longer let someone else chose my path for me. If I find this friend of yours, I can handle him, miss…?"

"Naieena. I wouldn't call this man a friend, only that I should not make him my enemy. That would be quality advice to follow yourself." Naieena handed him a small card with her contact information. "This man I'm looking for is unmistakable. You will know him if you see him. Without a doubt. If you do, get in touch with me. Do not engage him. And no matter what, *tu'irsthmo doounta*"

"I don't trust *you*. I make my own judgments."

Naieena smiled. "Perhaps I can earn your trust. I know where your lady friend went."

"Treistina? Where?"

"*teehra*, that way," she answered, a finger pointed toward the highway. "She left in a hurry. She was heading towards the Old City."

Senjek hastily turned away, pulling Victor's car keys from his pocket. He pressed the remote unlock button and saw one pair of lights across the parking lot light up. The door was barely open, and already he had one foot inside. He pulled up next to Naieena. "Daben will get his comeuppance; I can promise you that. But don't look to me as some knight."

"You would do well to kill him immediately. It would be a shame for one to mourn both your deaths."

"It would be a small group that would miss us both, I assure you. Right now Treistina is my priority; not Daben. Thank you for pointing me in the right direction."

With the gas pedal pressed to the floor, Senjek sped away in pursuit of Treistina. He hoped he would reach her before the Lobby could. He looked up into the rear-view mirror, for only a second, to see the girl watching his retreat.

You are welcome, Senjek Bohmet. I wish you the best of luck in finding your Treistina.

# 18. RULES OF ENGAGEMENT

Treistina had plenty of time to gain a considerable lead on Senjek. She didn't have the training or the capacity to disregard traffic laws like her pursuer. Senjek was capable of driving safely at breakneck speeds offroad. Pavement caused the car to behave differently, but his skill was still more than capable of alluding or catching most. It was dangerous to traverse the streets of Damos in a Lobby vehicle, but caution was a luxury he would not allow himself. Treistina may not have wanted to be around Senjek, but that didn't make her any less of a target.

Senjek caught up to her in a manner of minutes. Just as he pulled up alongside her, another car crashed into him and pushed him up against a guard rail. He took note of his surroundings and saw several different vehicles between himself and Treistina. The other vehicle drove into Senjek's back tire and sent his car careening out of control; both cars narrowly avoided impact with Treistina. Within seconds he regained traction, but his car faced the wrong direction.

He scoped out the surrounding vehicles. Lobby, the whole lot of them. Three urban assault vehicles supported about a dozen on motorcycles. Even in reverse, this car was quite fast. He quickly caught up to one of the motorcycles. He got ahead of the bike and threw open the driver's side door. The door ripped off violently, smashed into the cycle, and sent the rider to the pavement in a bloody mess.

Another of the bikes approached the vulnerable driver but did not anticipate what would happen next. Senjek turned hard to his left, the underside of his car slammed into the bike and sent its driver into the passenger seat of Victor's car. Now that he faced forward, Senjek changed gears. He took the man's sidearm, and with a single blow to the head, knocked him out.

Senjek tried to ram one of the belligerents, but his car bounced off a guard rail. The car he had acquired was too light and small to be of much use against the bigger vehicles.

He cocked the pistol now in his possession and opened fire on one of the motorcycles, but they had reinforced frames. Bullets seemed incapable of taking out the tires, and the riders wore bulletproof gear.

He tried to ram one of the bikes, but just as his car was too light and small to be aggressive to the UAVs, it was too slow to engage a motorcycle.

One of the bikes had nearly reached Treistina's car. Senjek continued to shoot the gun, if not to kill the driver, then to dissuade him from getting near Treistina. The biker grabbed hold of the car with his hand and pulled himself onto it and left the motorcycle to fall behind.

Senjek was quick to follow and used the hook of *Kilinus* to grab hold of the bumper of Treistina's car. He jumped from Victor's car and left it to crash and burn. After the jump, he slammed *Selna* into the car. His feet slid along the road as Treistina unwittingly pulled him along.

The Lobby agent looked over the car to assess what Senjek was up to but got his face slashed from chin to forehead for his trouble. Senjek had swung upward to make his strike and brought the hook of his blade back down onto the top of the car to pull himself up. He followed up with the second blade and sliced the wounded soldier across the chest. The soon to be corpse twisted from the strike and crashed to the pavement.

Senjek fell to his stomach and leaned over the windshield. "Treistina! Stop the -"

One of the UAVs slammed into the right side of the car and cut Senjek off. He was about to fall off himself, but he was able to lodge one of the hooks of his gun-blade into the car and found himself dangling on the side.

Treistina shrieked at this, the blade came through the canopy of the car and narrowly missed her right ear. She jerked the car to the right out of instinct, but she only managed to slam off the side of the hostile vehicle.

140

A Fatal Vendetta

Senjek was able to get back on top of Treistina's car before another UAV drove up to the other side of the car. A trio of bikes approached from behind to ensure that Treistina kept moving. The car on the left lowered the window of the passenger side. It was Ljero.

"Senjek! Are you sure you want to do this? Stop this now. Do this easy and quietly and you won't be harmed. Neither of you. We will make sure that Treistina is well taken care of."

Senjek searched for some part of the environment he could use to his advantage. It was just an empty highway. Every so often they would pass under power lines or pass mounds of gravel on the shoulders of the road.

He shot a cutting glare at Ljero. "Go to hell, Liachem. If you bring me in, I'll be broken or dead. Let's see what you're made of!"

With that ultimatum, Senjek swung *Kilinus* at Ljero, but the driver distanced the two with plenty of time to prevent the strike from landing.

"Board him," Ljero commanded via radio to his cyclists. He heard protest, ranging from the logistics of performing the task to compromising their formation that kept the asset boxed in. "Then knock him off the car! A few shattered bones will make it easier taking him into custody. Keep the secondary target moving until we have him, though. Daben wants any witnesses or persons usable as leverage to be detained as well."

One of the bikes in the rear steered to the right onto the shoulder. The driver used one of the gravel mounds as a ramp. Senjek fell flat onto the hood of the car as the bike grazed his back. The cyclist barely stuck his landing and nearly wiped out.

"Careful, men. He already took three of you out. He's a dangerous and capable man, let's not throw away our own game pieces," Ljero warned.

Senjek saw another cyclist make an approach for the next mound. He saw that there was a relatively low-hanging Network line a few feet behind the pile of gravel. He waited until the last second, once the enemy was committed to making the jump, before he acted. He flipped his gun-blades in his hands and grasped the handles upside-down. He jumped as high as he could and extended the blades upward. The hooks of his weapons caught the line. His forward momentum flipped him over the bike as it passed beneath him. The bike skidded across the top of the car and compromised the rider's control as he crashed to the pavement.

Senjek landed on the other bike behind Treistina and somehow managed to keep it upright as he tossed the rider aside. Before they had enough time to react, two more of the cyclists were cut down by Senjek. The remaining riders distanced themselves before Senjek could reach them. He got directly in front of one of them and ejected his gun-blade's clip. The rider didn't notice and ignited the clip as he ran over it. The front end of the bike slammed into the pavement and killed the driver.

Ljero looked on in horror as two-thirds of his cyclists were already dispatched. "Keep your distance!" he shouted into his radio. "Don't let him get too close to you! There's four of you and one of him. Control his position!"

Senjek wasn't focused on them anymore, however. He was soon on the tail of Ljero's assault vehicle. He leaned down to his right and emptied the remaining clip of his pistol into the UAV's exhaust. The driver soon lost control and inadvertently rammed Treistina's car, causing it to fishtail. Senjek rode straight for her and jumped off the bike onto the top of the car. He smashed the passenger side window and jumped inside.

"Treistina! Stop this car now!"

Though she may not have been willing to do so before, Treistina gladly obliged and pressed the brakes. The car continued to spin as another UAV slammed into the young couple and flipped the car over.

His vision was blurry. For a few moments, he was unsure if he was alive or dead. If it was a war they wanted, then it was a war they would get. The entire blade moved back as he cocked each gun in preparation. "You want me, Ljero? Come and get me!" Senjek shouted as enemy vehicles continued to circle the crash scene. Treistina was hurt, but not badly enough for him to give them both up to Daben Celt.

"Senjek," Ljero answered as he approached, seemingly unarmed. "Why do you keep fighting this? We're all in danger of being exposed the longer we draw this out. I'm already being followed by someone. You know I won't give up. Persistence is one of the better qualities you taught me."

"What else do you remember? Besides being paranoid."

"I know to be relentless; not to give up until my opponent ceases to resist. If there's a way to achieve a goal without violence to take that opportunity. Don't place your men in danger unnecessarily. If it's appropriate to do so, take prisoners."

"Exactly," Senjek whispered. He placed *Selna* behind his back and pointed *Kilinus* at Ljero. "I won't be a prisoner. That time is over."

Senjek's blade would have slit Ljero's throat if he didn't react in time to stop his approach. "For fuck's sake, Senjek! Think about Treistina! Think about your mother! Your brother! Do you want them all to die for nothing? Daben won't stop, and it's too late to defeat the Lobby! When the smoke clears, he'll kill everyone sitting on the sidelines! You can help make things better!"

Senjek swung at Ljero's head, but all his foe had to do was duck and roll back safely away. Ljero was thrown a flail to fend off his former mentor. He swung it above his head a few times to build momentum before he waved it toward Senjek's face.

He wildly missed as Senjek hit the mace with *Kilinus* and directed it into ground. He tried to strike again, this time he barely hit one of his own men circling the perimeter. He tried a third time. The head of the flail got caught inside the blades. Senjek pulled the triggers; the vibration and his arm movement were plenty enough to destroy the weapon.

"Impressive, Bohmet. Let's see if you're still as good as you think you are. As good as we were told you are." Ljero motioned for his men to stop circling the crashed car. "Get the girl. Try not getting sliced up on your way through him."

One of the men immediately decided to prove his worth. Senjek decided he was lucky in this regard. Better for a quick end than a drawn out one. He used the tip of one blade to toss the flail's head into the air. He swung the other blade, embedding Ljero's own weapon into the skull of his man.

"I can do this all day, Ljero."

"Fine. Mix it up a little, boys. Give him something he's not ready for. Something new. Something interesting."

Two of the UAV's tops blew off. The front ends became slightly elevated. The sides of the vehicles fell to the ground, revealing two motorcycles inside each. Senjek heard some kind of spinning mechanical noise. What he saw shortly afterward was a motorcycle being slingshot at him. That was certainly new to Senjek. He barely reacted fast enough to duck and roll underneath it. He quickly got to his feet. He had sufficient time to lift his twin blades to catch the second bike, which hit him dead-on.

Senjek had dropped *Selna* after the blow, but just as quickly recovered it. Liachem paced about like a bird of prey. He took pleasure in watching his target squirm. "Ouch. It looks like that hurt, sir. It doesn't have to be this way. Just throw down your arms, and it will be over. Treistina probably needs medical attention. Think of her."

Senjek looked up at his foe. He could taste blood in his mouth. He groggily made it to his feet, his left arm throbbed in pain. "I am thinking of her. I just want a normal life."

Ljero dropped his head into his hand. "Fine. Have it your way. The time for games is over. Take him down, boys."

There were six men left between the motorcycles and the urban assault vehicles. They were as smart and careful as they could be and surrounded him as best they could. A tactical advantage for them was Treistina, as he didn't make much distance between himself and her car.

Two charged his front but stopped just short of being sliced in half by gun-blades. Even though he appeared injured to some degree, they were afraid of the Praesage. Senjek turned around to see two more approach. He tried to cut them down, but they too backed off before getting too close. They were still toying with him.

The two remaining men who flanked his sides came at him next. One slid under his blade; the other jumped over it. They each revealed a sword upon returning to a vertical base. Senjek returned to his previous stance: One gun-blade behind, the other pointed at one of his assailants. The taller one came at him first with a curved blade.

He swung at *Kilinus*. Senjek loosened his grip and allowed the man to meet no resistance when he struck. The momentum of his sword sent

144

Senjek's blade from his hand into the chest of one of the men circling behind him. That was lucky for Senjek. Before the man had a chance to regain his footing, Senjek sliced *Selna* through the man's back. He turned quickly to block the next man's assault.

This man's swordplay was predictable. Senjek would parry and dodge and let the man think he was holding his own. He tried to put a little extra something into this next swing. He was dead before he hit the ground. Senjek turned his attention to one of the three goons remaining. What grabbed his attention, however, was another motorcycle hurled at him. He managed to avoid being crushed by this one. He got to his feet and saw Ljero hurtle toward him.

Ljero had retrieved *Kilinus* from his comrade. He pulled the trigger on the first swing. Unfortunately for him, he wasn't used to the weapon. The kickback from the charge sent the blade harmlessly away from Senjek's body. His opponent was not as fortunate. Ljero soon felt Senjek's gun-blade inside his stomach. Flesh ripped out as the hooked end of the blade was pulled free.

Senjek rolled across the pavement and cut two of the hostiles' legs out from under them. He flung *Selna* into the chest of the final target before he finished the recently maimed foes. Liachem tried to swing at Bohmet, but Senjek dodged the strike. He grabbed the handle and kicked Ljero in the chest. His skull made an audible cracking noise against the pavement. He lay helpless in the street, with both his hands pressed against his stomach. He tried, in vain, to stop his bleeding. "General... please..."

Senjek had already begun to pile the fallen onto the burning wreckage of one of the vehicles. He let Ljero lie in the street. The assailant gasped for breath as he desperately tried to cling to life. Senjek stepped back to watch the bodies catch fire. "Be at peace. *noelngro gaeva eneotenti.*"

"Don't leave me like this." The man once called the Praesage wouldn't even look at Ljero. Barely able to put words together, his hands pressed to the gaping hole in his gut, the fallen lieutenant knew he was going to die. It was only a matter of time. "Just toss me in with my men. No one wants Gie to discover the Lobby on Damos. Not even you."

Senjek walked over to the remains of another UAV, where Treistina sat unconscious. He wanted nothing to else to do with this man. He sat behind the wheel of the car and turned the engine over.

The Kramei Insurrection

"You can't win, Bohmet. You know that," Ljero muttered.

"I don't know. Maybe. Maybe I'll have to give myself up to Daben in the end. But I will fight it as long as I can. I'm no Cineon. I'm no von Breischa. But I imagine Daben thought you would have lasted longer against one man."

Senjek looked into Ljero's eyes. At that moment, both men could see the pain in each other. Ljero looked away, ashamed. "For what it's worth, General, I'm sorry. We both want the same thing, you know. For Kramei to be free. Maybe it can be. Maybe it can happen in a way you can live with. I never thought about the cost to one's soul. What it must have done to you; doing the things you did for the Lobby."

Senjek got back out of the car and knelt beside Ljero. "It's been so long since I've had something to fight for. Something that I believed in. I believe in Treistina. I believe that, with her, I can have a life again. A real life. I have to live with the things I've done, but that doesn't mean I can't try to make up for them. Maybe your life will be the last that I take, Ljero."

A tear trickled down the dying man's cheek. "I'm so sorry, Senjek. But we both know I'm not the last. Not unless you give yourself up to Daben. You know," his whole body shook as he gasped for breath. "You… know, that he won't stop. He has fallen further from a man than you could ever imagine. There are only two types of people who serve him. Those who are blind to his nature and…."

Senjek brought himself closer, Ljero's voice growing weaker with every word. Those who are blind to his nature. Those were his last words. Senjek saw no life left in his eyes. Even if he didn't say it, Senjek knew what he would have said next. There were only two different kinds of people who followed Daben Celt willingly. Those convinced of his charade and those who knew, but too afraid to stand against him.

Senjek made sure that Treistina was secure in her seat before he sped away from the scene. He looked into the rearview mirror to see the funeral pyre burn a little brighter.

He felt ashamed. Was he truly a different man than the one that fled Kramei? Or was he convinced by a charade of his own making? The way he let Ljero die was just as savage as any crime The Praesage committed. For the first time in a long time, he was afraid. He wasn't sure of what he ran from, and that frightened him. Was he trying to escape Daben? Or was he trying to escape his nature?

# 19. BREAKING GIE

There weren't many familiar with how Kramei came under Damos rule in the first place. It was quite a fascinating story to some. It went back to the Fall of the Moaschen Empire. The people of Kramei looked back upon this time as a pleasant period for them. The history books painted the Moashei, at their height, wise and benevolent leaders.

By the time Moaschen became space-faring, which was decades before Damos, half of the remaining planets in the system had established stable systems of government. The Moashei felt no need to force their ways onto those who had their own way. Even when Damos attempted to invade, in vain, they let them be.

Kramei and Brescha, however, were underdeveloped. Moashei came in and brought the two nations up. They raised future generations with the history of their magic and technological might. They instilled the fear of the Council unto the colonists and native peoples. They forged a flourishing ecosystem and created a legacy that would last for ages.

A calamity in the sky would forever change the history of the Moaschen Empire. One could see it from the deepest valleys of Iedenia to the highest peaks across Harvest to the densest skyline of the Old City. Many imagined going back in time to witness the Great Collision in person. What a sight it must have been. Even in the present day, there was no consensus as to what caused it. The prevalent theory, though not academically sound, was the Empire's own magic. The source of their might was ironically their bane.

# A Fatal Vendetta

Though they saw that Brescha had fallen into Moaschen's orbit in time to evacuate, it was too late to stop it. As the rogue planet neared, it caused tidal and seismic damage. The impact annihilated Brescha, whereas Moaschen barely survived.

The Council urged their leaders to seek asylum on Kramei. The empire would not accept this. Though resourceful, Kramei was strictly an agricultural resource. To abandon their home planet would have the empire fade into nothing. Damos had suitable natural resources to replace Moaschen's.

They made the mistake of attacking Damos first. Not only were they not ready for combat on the terrain, but they left their witches behind. The Damosi quickly repelled the invaders in the First War. In the time between, Damos secured Iedin as a strategic holding, denying Moaschen a port between Damos and Kramei.

The Empire constructed the Great Frame of Moaschen between the first two wars. Having noticed continued orbital instability in the system, the Council recommended restoring the planet's gravitational presence. The Frame was also instrumental in stretching the life of their artificial atmosphere. The Council foresaw that it would not last; they told the military and political leaders as much. Against the recommendation of the Council, the Empire planned to invade a second time.

A second time they were denied. The Council continued to explore options to make the planet stable. They were hasty in their ultimate solution. They gathered every Matriarch into their sanctum. They concentrated their power into something tangible. They would immediately recognize their mistake, but they could not foresee this thing's danger before it's birth. So powerful a thing this was.

Upon the creation of *Narthalos*, The Council had a vision. *fiana viosinas moaschent*, it would later be called. They immediately saw the danger it possessed, but the weapon could not be unmade. They would attempt to harness its power to restore Moaschen, but they could not wield it. They then decided *Narthalos* was too much a potential threat to be allowed to exist. So they tried to destroy it.

"Tried. This ordinary looking, yet powerful tool was imbued with the magic of Moaschen's witches and with the cognition of her seers. It fought back, you see. Their names and identities were stolen from them. Their visions of the future compromised. Forever doomed to suffer the wrath of *Narthalos*."

"Is there… a reason why you're telling me this story," a weak and faint voice finally interrupted.

"Besen," a voice replied. Still the same voice that had lectured the Damosi for hours. The voice of his captor: The Fury. "Besen, Besen, Besen. How rude are you to interject yourself? Here I thought we were two chums enjoying some quality together time. Do you find my stories boring?"

Besen and Cineon were alone in a small room. Besen was hooded and tied to a chair. Cineon patched him up a bit, but he was still allowed to bleed. No more physical harm came to him. Cineon only lectured Besen on various histories. He made no demands. Indulged Besen with no requests with food or water. He just kept talking.

"Please, just—"

Now, Besen! You are being quite the bore," Cineon exclaimed, cutting him off in kind. "Now where was I? Oh yes. The Council knew that the planet was doomed, and their Empire with it. They could never conquer Damos, so in the interest of their own survival, they betrayed the Empire. Neglecting to tell the government of Moaschen that their religious figures were severely crippled in their duties, the Fate of Moaschen was nigh unavoidable."

He went on to explain that not once in the first two wars did they send their entire military strength to Damos. There was always a garrison left at home. The Unknown Council, however, convinced the Empire to go all-in. They promised victory in their visions. Visions they never had. They pledged that the witches of their conclave would assist them in battle with their magic. They would not. They gave up their own kind to Damos. They had sought immunity with King Xen'bach'hou in exchange for everything they knew about the armies of Moashei.

"And so the Empire fell. Within a year the last remnants of this once great and powerful nation were wiped out. And Kramei became a Damosi colony. Quite a lovely story, wouldn't you agree?"

"Why don't you just kill me?" Besen wondered out loud.

"You would like to know, wouldn't you? I suppose there is no harm in saying. You are my last defense of TAC-OPS. Should your army succeed

150

in taking the Harvest Repulsor offline, you will be what keeps Damos from bombing the holy hell out of this place."

"Because of the Network hard-line…" Besen said, instantly aware of Cineon's meaning. "The ever-important Lobby Propaganda machine. Your cause depends on your lies."

"The truth, Besen, is what you make it. I hardly see it as propaganda. I see it as gospel. People pick their own truths; we are merely making sure that the people of Kramei see what is true for us. And Network access will not only strengthen domestic support but across the entire Republic. Perhaps you will answer for your crimes against Kramei in a live broadcast when the time comes."

"Veian will come back for me," Besen replied. It seemed he sought to convince himself as well as Cineon.

"Corporal Grebllyh is in infinitely worse shape than yourself. He's been sent back to Damos for medical attention. I'm sad to say he may miss the entire war. Hell, he may not live to see it. I don't doubt that a rescue mission is being planned, but it will take a back seat to keeping the happenings here at Harvest quiet."

"Why would you so easily tell me these things, when you killed your own man for saying less?"

Cineon tried his best to hide his grin. "Amon was a fool. Not just a fool, but undeserving in his pride. He had an officer of the Damos army cornered. Cornered in the middle of a Repulsor in between two opposing armies. Stroking his own ego, when none of the deeds were his fruit. Speaking up his own legend to a man he was about to kill. Do you not see how backward that is? You must see that!"

"Why, because he challenged the legend of the Fury?" Besen groggily taunted.

"No, sweet Besen. The glory of Amon would have been for the glory of The Lobby. He would have played his part for Kramei. But his arrogance put us all in jeopardy. First and foremost, he would have killed you. You, who are infinitely more useful to me alive. A good player can play and react to his opponent's every move. A great player anticipates his enemy before he acts. He prepares. He gathers his tools he needs first. He does not rush the board and make due once he's there."

The Kramei Insurrection

"And I'm just another tool for you gaining access to the Network? My life benefits you how in this task? Afraid you can't hold us off long enough to decrypt the hard-line. Is my presence supposed to stop Greene from burning this place to the ground?"

Cineon laughed. "Do not worry, Besen. That won't be happening. I've yet to unleash my first major offensive. Your generals will not be ready for my full onslaught. You aren't ready for my next move. Dak Johnsen won't know what hit him."

"Dak? What does he have to do with anything? He's not touring on Kramei."

"Poor child. Your uncle, the President, has relieved your General Greene as the commander of your armies: replaced him with his own man. A man with a history that is a bigger mystery to me than Greene. I'm sure that he's no General von Breischa, but I don't like playing a game when I don't know the players."

Besen did not speak. His pause was noticeably long. "You're lying," he finally spat in denial.

"The leader of Damos is acting quite queer, indeed. I might have lost to von Breischa if he wasn't MIA. I knew plenty about Greene to crush him, but I know nothing of Dak Johnsen. I've been telling you so many stories; I think it's time you told one of your own. Tell me all about Dak."

"There's only one thing you need to know about him. He'll stop you. He will," Besen panted. "You aren't as good as the Lobby says you are."

Cineon smiled. "No. No, I'm not." He ripped the mask off Evan's head to reveal the dank and dark surroundings. He gave him plenty of time to soak it in. Besen could look upon his mangled and injured body. His eyes were sore from the single light that lit the room. He could feel Cineon's ill-intentions.

The General of Kramei knelt down in front of Evan, to see him face-to-face. "I'm better. Now, then," he exclaimed as he jumped to his feet, "what do we do now? What story shall I tell you next? The Battle of Monarch Fall? The Last Prophecy? Perhaps I shall tell you how you're going to die."

There were many more stories. So many stories that Besen may or may not have known. The Dola Raid. The Birth of KILLER. But there was one story in particular that Cineon was about to tell, one that would change

152

Besen's understanding of this conflict. The legend of one man. A legend which had done so much to shape events. A man whose part in this tale could very well determine how the story ends.

# 20. MISSION PLANNING

Dak's war council sat at a table inside Forward Command and deliberated on the next course of action. The anticipation of attack was running high. They had to act first. Ideally, they would disable the Repulsor for good, but plans were being made to neutralize the hostiles with the Repulsor online. The lights dimmed and a holographic display projected from the center of the table detailing the following report:

"Reconnaissance reports that Lobby troops are beginning to mobilize. We are expecting an assault on Forward Command by 0900 hours, ahead of previous estimates," Ensign Lea announced. "Cineon, the General of the Krameian Army,"

"KILLER's army," Dak interrupted. "I don't care how many men of the proper military defect. I don't care if it's a majority. I don't care if it's every single man conscripted. If they fight for Cineon, they are fighting for The Lobby. Not a single person in that force fights for Kramei. They fight for Daben Celt."

"My apologies, Captain," Ensign Lea replied, slightly embarrassed. "Cineon, General of the Lobby, has all but emptied TAC-OPS, mobilizing his cavalry and infantry on a march straight for this facility. Initial reconnaissance suggested a much larger force, but their movement suggests they mean to abandon their building and overrun Forward Command. If we can punch through his lines during their march and retake TAC-OPS, we will have them boxed in."

"How can we be sure that this is the bulk of his men and not just a portion of the numbers suggested by earlier reports?" Evan asked, who was present via Network satellite.

Ensign Lea smiled. "I'm glad you asked, Mr. President. While the Repulsor was briefly offline, we conducted several scans of TAC-OPS. Combined with combat reports of men on the field that survived and scans carried out during the offline period, we estimate that Lobby forces occupying the facility are fifty percent fewer as previously reported."

*"Half?"* Dak blurted, dumbfounded. "General Greene overestimated enemy forces holding TAC-OPS by so much?"

"Foul play is suspected, sir," Lieutenant Abal responded, the only remaining member of the previous military council headed by General Greene. "One of the members of the reconnaissance team has since been outed as a Lobby mole. The new information we have is much more reliable."

Dak turned to face Abal, a disappointed look in his eyes. "A mole? Why was I not informed of this sooner? Where is this man?"

"Unfortunately," Ensign Lea interrupted, "he was found dead in his bunk when military police went to detain him. We suspect a suicide pill. He must have caught wind that his cover was blown."

"This changes nothing," Evan spoke out. "The Lobby cannot know we've realized their deception. Their inside man would have no way of relaying his capture to Cineon. Furthermore, Cineon cannot anticipate how we will act on the battlefield now that we have this knowledge."

"Agreed," Abal and Johnsen said in unison.

Ensign Lea turned changed the holographic display on the table to show the terrain between Mt. Fong and the Forward Command Center. "We expect Cineon to lead what we believe to be half his force in a direct assault against us. We have air support and cannons ready in case he disarms the Repulsor."

"A risky gamble, Ensign," Abal gawked. He made no attempt to hide his contempt that a second naval officer surpassed him in rank. "Early detection systems are not one-hundred percent accurate. If we fire cannons or attempt a bombing run with the Radius Effect active, it could be disastrous to our troops."

"The plan is not to fire first with heavy artillery," Dak interjected to defend his hand-picked executive officer. "We will be monitoring early warning systems, but only in conjunction with Lobby movement. Heavy artillery from their side will go a long way in taking this facility, but we can do more damage to TAC-OPS. I believe it unlikely for Cineon to attempt open war, but we will be prepared if he does."

"Any word on my nephew?" Evan asked. The entire room fell silent. No one present expected the President to ask that.

Dak looked up to Ensign Lea. She stood as solid as stone. He knew that she and Besen were close once as cadets. It was a lifetime ago, but her body language suggested that something continued to linger. Perhaps it was regret. Perhaps she viewed herself apart from Besen's conquests during that time.

"Ensign," Abal replied with a hint of anger. "Any reports regarding the state of Sergeant Gie?"

The young girl quickly regained most of her composure. The tone of her voice would have betrayed her, were it not for the source of her information.

"We have received some conflicting reports from recon, varying from his well-being to his execution. The only trustworthy information," she stopped speaking. She felt something horrible in her gut.

"We all care about Besen, Liz," Dak consoled, showing a rare display of emotion while in uniform. "We all want to get him back, alive and well, I promise you. Tell us what you found out."

She reluctantly nodded, "Yes, sir. Sorry, sir, but you won't like it."

Evan grew visibly aggravated. "Ms. Lea, I very much doubt reliable information regarding my nephew's status will displease me. Knowing he's alive or dead is better than the not knowing."

"Mr. President," she squeaked. Her voice cracked as a tear formed in her eye. The entire mood of the room sank. Besen was a part of few lives present, but he was an inspiration and symbol to all. "He's alive," she finally managed to report.

Relief swept over the rest of the room, but the President would not allow himself to hope. Not yet. "And what is the source of this information, Ms. Lea?"

She drew a deep breath and looked at the screen displaying the President. "The Fury sent us a sub-Network definition video, dated two hours ago, proving to us that he is still alive."

"Why would he show us that? He's bluffing with his numbers, why would he provoke us to invade TAC-OPS?" Dak wondered aloud.

"Maybe he wants Forward Command. Effectively exchange posts. We'd be against the wall at TAC-OPS, and he could cut us off from Damos. Wear us down," Abal suggested.

"No," Evan quickly disagreed. "Cineon needs TAC-OPS to upload to the Network. The Lobby's power lies in their message; not their military presence. His plan isn't to just give it up. If he's attacking with his entire force, he's putting in all his chips."

Lea made a suggestion, something she was rarely known to do. "Perhaps we should abandon the plan to take TAC-OPS? Just meet them head-on in battle? They're outnumbered and outgunned."

"They are outgunned as long as the Repulsor is online," Abal retorted. "As long as the Repulsor is in Lobby hands, every second our men are in the open field is a risk to their lives. If we root them out of TAC-OPS and keep Forward Command, we have them all but trapped."

"Mr. Abal is right," Dak said in agreement with the Lieutenant. "I don't know what Cineon's intentions are. His actions are consistent with our belief in his larger numbers. He thinks I'll give up Forward Command as easily as Greene let him take TAC-OPS. I'll be damned. He thinks he can outsmart us. But he's made a mistake, and it's time to act on it."

Evan spoke up. "Dak's right. Time to end this. Daben Celt has torn this nation apart for long enough. Let it be done. Take out his right-hand man and his army, and Daben fails. This can be over today. Justice can be done. Cineon will pay for his crimes, and Daben will give us his Omen. If he still lives. Dak, I've granted General Greene to begin organization of a blockade around Kramei, but only on my command. You send an emissary to Cineon. If he comes within two-hundred yards of Forward Command, it is an act of war."

That declaration came as a surprise to everyone in the room, not just Dak. "We're not talking about going to war, Mr. President," Abal argued.

"No, Mr. Abal, no one's talking about going to war. We've been at war for weeks. No one's had the balls to call it what it is, that's all. Today it's official. Dak, you are promoted from Acting General to Suzerain of Damos."

The entire room fell silent at this announcement.

"Sir, I'm honored of course, but there hasn't been a Suzerain for centuries." Dak protested.

"That's correct, Dak. However, I am only the president of our republic which rules from the seat of the crown. I am not the crown. I cannot declare war. Not without approval from parliament. However, there is a loophole. I do not need parliament's endorsement to appoint a Suzerain. In the times of the monarchy, the Suzerain could declare war during the King's absence. Parliament won't be happy about it, but it must be done. It's time we ended this."

"What about the Lobby's propaganda? Surely this will give more sympathy to their cause." Abal responded, also in protest against the President's decision.

"The Lobby's message has reached a plateau. The ball is in our court. Declaring war will do little to strengthen their cause at this point. It's time we stopped playing their game. It's time we stopped waiting for them to fail. Time to stop waiting for the citizens of Kramei to realize they have been misled. The Lobby has been using force against their own people for years to strengthen their message. It's time we fight fire with fire. It's time for war."

# 21. PARLEY

*Today is the day our plans finally begin to bear fruit. Today is the day we start to take away from our oppressors. Today is the end of the Damos occupation of Kramei. They may believe they have the advantage, but it is a lie. Cineon assures me that the President is playing right into our hand. He thinks he is in control. Today is the beginning of the end.*

Hundreds of soldiers marched toward Harvest from opposing sides. Some lagged and moaned, but they went onward anyway. Each group believed their cause to be noble; to be correct and just. Two separate groups were about to become one. A single display. Two armies would combine to battle and have war. The Lobby's advance started first, but Damos was ready. Undaunted. Unafraid. So much had been given up to Daben, out of fear. They feared action would make things worse. That point had passed. The situation could not get any worse, and there was no turning back from war. A member of the Lobby waved a flag to request an emissary. Finally, at this point, they wanted to talk. A single representative from each side to meet. To discuss surrender. To discuss a truce. To discuss Kramei's cessation. None of these things were possible. Dak knew this. He agreed to meet in the middle of the battlefield all the same. Even if it were for the sake of posturing. He expected someone to speak for Cineon's behalf, but he would have been wrong.

# The Kramei Insurrection

Being carried by what looked like a horse-carriage of yesteryear, but without the horse, Cineon himself approached the middle of the field to treat with Dak. He laughed when saw his enemy. "A horse? Motorcycles are more efficient in combat in almost every scenario. Horses are slow, harder to control... more difficult to put back together."

Dak sighed. How rude and arrogant this man was. Nevertheless, he would greet him. "I'm Captain Dakren Randal Johnsen, Suzerain and Commander of the Armed Forces of Damos. I am to deliver the Republic's terms to you. Your forces are to immediately disperse. We require you to hand over the criminals Daben Celt and The Praesage of KILLER; if he's still alive, and that you allow yourself to be taken into custody."

Cineon bore a wry smile. "Pleased to meet you Captain. I do not believe we have ever been formally introduced before now. I am Cineon Alexander Yahn, General of the Armies of Kramei. I have terms for you as well. Daben's terms. You must vacate these lands. Forever. The rebellion against the crown hundreds of years ago began with the freedom of Kramei. Kramei was content to be a part of this Republic. It was viewed preferable to the monarchy. Our compromise ends today. We led the people of Kramei to taking control of their own fate. We ask only for the same. Do this and we will deliver you Besen Gie. A token of our intentions. The intentions of the Lobby."

Dak could see that this was likely to deteriorate quickly. He had to try to reason with this man, though. Evan was already prepared for war, but Dak might still prevent it. If only these two could compromise. "As much as I may want Besen back, I am not authorized to give your state permission to secede from the Republic for the life of one man."

Cineon nodded. "Of course. What are you at liberty to authorize? Is there any room for compromise? If Daben and myself turn ourselves over to you, might Kramei be free? You favor yourselves better than your predecessor, but you tighten the noose just as tight as the crown ever did."

"You're wrong," Dak argued, "the people rule us. We're nothing like the monarchy."

"Nothing? Really? Is that why I see Xen'que's successor to Suzerain stand before me? Prepared to lead your army against those who have

160

spoken out against your regime. A regime that your enemy has infiltrated with informants. Does this story sound familiar to you yet?"

"Yeah, it sounds conveniently like the people's revolt against the crown five-hundred years ago. The poor oppressed citizens of Kramei rose against their tormentors. And you say you have one of your men on the inside. Ready to stab me in the back?"

Cineon chuckled. "No. Not you. Evan. Ironic, that one of the men responsible for overthrowing the monarchy would have his descendants oppress us. I wonder if the man with a pair of gun-blades has accomplished this task yet. He's never been far from your president."

Dak began to feel very tense. His horse began to mutter and whine lightly as the reigns tightened. "You're lying to me, Yahn. If your Omen were anywhere on the planet, I'd know about it."

"But you do! In fact, I do believe you are quite good friends. You even recently met his girlfriend, if my intelligence is to be believed."

Dak quickly put two and two together in his head. Cineon was suggesting Senjek to be The Praesage of KILLER. He was quick to reject this. He knew Senjek. He'd been in a fight with Senjek. Though he was a capable introductory instructor for counter-insurgency on the Kramei terrain, he himself wasn't very good at what he taught.

"I'm not going to fall for your lies and tricks. Let's just do what we're supposed to do. Negotiate a truce."

"Truce!?" Cineon shouted, visibly agitated. "Truce? Neither of us are here to negotiate peace. We each have an army to our back. We are each here to secure the surrender of the other. If you want Besen back - if you want hundreds of lives to be spared - you will vacate the planet. We will return Besen to the DNC Hub. We will allow you to occupy it and the surrounding area as a foreign embassy. From there you can assist with Lobby-sponsored restoration efforts to the planet and use us as a port to the Moashei Field and the Breischa Masses. We have no interest in the asteroids."

"Perhaps your demands would be viewed more generously if it weren't for the outstanding crimes the Lobby has committed against Damos. Our foreign interests, our embassies, our people. Wele Gie was executed on a live Network broadcast."

"His son may be facing the same fate if you don't wise up," Cineon threatened. "I plan to atone for my sins, but if Kramei is no longer a part of the Republic, it will perish without the Lobby. We cannot negotiate this. Our terms are as they are. Take them or leave them."

"I leave them."

Cineon broke eye contact. He looked at the ground. He was disappointed. Not for what was about to happen, but that Dak was so stubborn to allow it. "It was a pleasure to meet you, Captain Johnsen. It is a shame things had to come to this. I suppose there's nothing else left to say."

Cineon nonchalantly reached into a pocket on his shirt. The light of the satellite began to shine from the area. He looked up at Dak one more time. He had no idea what was about to happen. Cineon felt a wave of joy overcome him. It was finally going to start. And there was one thing left for him to say.

*"deecidehra boeura faeta. eomdo vella."*

Dak didn't even see the throwing star until it was already flying toward his throat.

*No one should ever become accustomed to killing. It certainly comes easier to some more than others. It comes so naturally to such a few that their exploits become the stuff of nightmares. Some men bring style to murder. To face such a nightmare yourself can be just as terrifying as facing death. To come face-to-face with such a terror can convince some people that they are dead already. Cineon is quite possible the greatest nightmare. He leaves a dulling throwing star at the scene every*

*atrocity he has ever committed. To let people know how deadly he is. A warrior who carries a weapon incapable of killing. That is how dangerous he is.*

Dak opened his eyes. He was still alive. Cineon's first projectile was harmless. So confident of his victory, he would begin this war with the token he left behind in his wake. "Dak Johnsen, let me be the first, perhaps the only, to congratulate you. You were the man who stood up against the Lobby. Valiantly. A brave soldier following his orders. I wish I could have the honor of fighting me." A visibly shaken Dak watched Cineon pull out a second throwing star. He wasn't done speaking, either. "The next one, should it find you, will do more than bounce off your throat. It will take your final breath."

Dak quickly jerked his head to the side, narrowly missing the second star. He was amazed by the man's arrogance. "You missed!"

"Did I?" The star circled back and hit one of Dak's escorts in the back, knocking him from his horse. Dak drew his sword, but he wasn't fast enough to catch Cineon off guard. Cineon was not without a sword of his own. The tip of Dak's blade was so close to piercing the skull of his target he thought he might have. "Frisky," Cineon taunted. "Tell me, the sword, do you like it?"

Dak examined the blade more carefully. He recognized it; it was Besen's. Before he had a chance to reply, Cineon's chariot flew backward. Dak's remaining escort had his crossbow ready and opened fire. The first arrow was deflected by Cineon as he simultaneously threw the sword into the ground. Subsequent shots were fruitless, as the chariot provided adequate cover. Dak motioned to fire on the escorts, but they were too agile and were able to evade their fire. Cineon fired first, in the arena of diplomacy, and got away without a scratch.

Dak checked his surroundings. The two bikers had flanked him. Though he was a safe distance away, Cineon was directly in front of him. He had only one escort left, and they were both on horseback. The two bikers drew their swords. Dak turned his horse around to face them. "This is where the fun begins."

"Do you think we'll make it, sir?"

"Yes, I do." He looked over to his escort. "For Besen."

His compatriot nodded in agreement. "For Besen."

They snapped their horses' reigns and began their movement toward the two Lobby escorts. Engines revved violently, waiting for the right moment to rush the enemy.

Cineon was taking a tremendous risk. Damosi soldiers could open fire at any time, but Cineon wasn't just arrogant; he was savvy. He knew they wouldn't. If Dak died in the crossfire, Cineon only had to withdraw back to TAC-OPS. It would be the Lobby's word against Damos. He would tell the whole Republic that Evan's Suzerain tried to kill him in cold blood. The Lobby's propaganda would reach a new height.

The pair of horses were nearly in range when the escorts drove forward. All four men raised their swords in anticipation of the collision. Steel collided, but Dak unexpectedly jumped off his horse moments before the strike. His blade was inches from claiming blood as he found himself straddled behind one of the Fury's escorts.

The driver had dropped his sword to grab Dak's. His gloves were thick enough to keep his hand in one piece, but the edge steadily sunk into the skin. Dak let himself fall off the back of the bike and took the rider's head with him. A flash of light caught the Suzerain's eye. It was Besen's sword. It was in arms-length from him. He reached for the handle, but a throwing star bounced off it, forcing him to recoil. He commandeered the motorcycle as his horse roamed free. He had to play on Cineon's arrogance. His best chance at surviving was to let his enemy toy with him.

"Another perfect shot," Cineon gloated. "Go on! Dance!" To the ignorant passerby, Dak was able to weave the bike back and forth effectively to narrowly miss Cineon's salvo of projectiles. Dak did not fool himself; Cineon could kill him whenever he wanted. He had to be careful not to get too close, though. Accurate as he was, he wasn't so good that he wouldn't accidentally kill his new plaything.

Cineon changed his tactics as Dak peeled away from his pursuit. With a bow hand, he shot an arrow at the remaining escort on horseback. A direct hit to the heart.

Dak directed his attention to the last remaining enemy escort, who was driving straight at him. He quickly lifted his sword to block the incoming strike. The man was driving so fast, that when they collided, the two bikes spun in circles while still moving in a definite direction.

A Fatal Vendetta

Dak let himself fall off, moments before he would have crashed into a rock. The two bikes engulfed into a ball of flame from the impact. His wits still with him, he was able to grab hold of his horse as it ran past him. He looked around for Cineon, but it didn't take him long to find his enemy. He found himself racing alongside the Fury.

"Crafty. Resourceful. You're good, Dak Johnsen. But it won't be enough to save you. Not when this is over."

"When it's over, Cineon, you'll see me again. Standing over your body as you and the rest of KILLER dies."

Cineon laughed. "What do you see when you look in my eyes? A monster? A prophet? A warrior? I hope I see you when this is over. When the glory of this world is saved, I will be here to claim it. The glory of the Lobby will come when your world falls."

Dak swung his sword, meaning to take another head, but Cineon's situational awareness was impossibly good. The pair had just passed Besen's sword on the ground and Cineon had brought it up just in time to block the death stroke.

Cineon distanced his carriage from Dak. He was overwhelmed with pride as he felt Dak's morale flee. The look of disbelief in the Suzerain's eyes brought the Fury great joy.

Dak turned his horse away and retreated to his troops. Cineon followed Dak's example and traveled back toward TAC-OPS.

Dak's horse had reached the safety of the Damosi army. He turned the beast toward the Lobby with his sword held high. Before he could properly give the command, his men charged forward. Catapults launched boulders ahead of their advance to squash some of the enemy cavalry. Clouds of dirt and dust filled the battlefield. The ground shook from the gallops of horses. Small pockets of water rippled from the feet of infantry sprinting forward. Engines of motorcycles growled as they advanced. All nearly drowned out by war cries from both sides.

The satellite was setting. The last of day's light signaled a single truth in the minds of every soul on the Plains of Harvest. The war had begun. The KILLER War had begun.

# 22. ON THE RUN

"Listen, I trust you, mister, all I'm saying is that she looks a little rough for someone who fainted. Are you sure you don't want to take her to the hospital?" The hotel clerk wasn't as naive as Senjek would have liked. He wanted to use a lie that wouldn't draw too much attention. Or cause him to call emergency services. He assured the employee that he would also check her blood sugar once they were set up in a room.

"I appreciate your concern, really, but she has these fainting spells every once in a while. Doctors aren't sure what it is. She just banged her head off the pavement this time. The doctor said I shouldn't move her too much and this hotel was the closest place."

Treistina kept her eyes closed as she listened to Senjek lie. She didn't know how to feel about it. He couldn't tell the truth about what happened without being arrested.

"Why. Why is this happening?" Treistina thought to herself. Everything seemed to be going the way she wanted. She didn't have a perfect life. Senjek's job wasn't perfect. In fact, many things weren't perfect. When she was with Senjek, though, all the world's troubles were invisible to her.

She tried to block out Senjek's conversation with the hotel staff. She racked her mind for something to think about instead of the Lobby. To her surprise, she recalled the time Senjek took her to the mountains of Iedin. She remembered a phone call she made after they came back to Damos.

"You know we aren't supposed to be talking. If my brother finds out,"

"I know, I know," Treistina said, "it's just that, I don't know who else to talk to, Eve. I know that Evan blames me for what happened, I still feel responsible myself, but you're the only real friend I have."

Eve was in the middle of an urban planning meeting for the construction of New Xenue. Not exactly a good time for a personal call, but this was the first time Treistina called her after Evan forbade the two to speak. "I'm a little busy right now, but I can talk for a bit. What's going on? Are you still stringing that guy along? What's his name again?"

"How do you know about Senjek?"

Eve chuckled. "Come on, honey. Evan might not be the president of the Treistina Yahn fan club, but even he couldn't keep quiet the fact that one of his contractors took you on a trip to Iedin on the government dime. Doesn't sound like your type of guy."

Treistina feigned a chuckle of her own. "No, I suppose no one would have thought so. That's why I'm calling."

"Listen, Treistina; you don't have to feel bad about letting him take you on a romantic getaway. It's not as if he paid for it."

"Such a playgirl. Now I know where your nephew gets that from."

"Funny," Eve chortled back, "Nothing wrong with getting pampered every once in a while. And Besen doesn't get that from me; I don't lie down with every pretty face like he does. I'm just saying you don't have to feel bad about having a little fun."

"I told him I loved him," Treistina blurted.

Eve was surprised by that. There was a noticeable pause on her end. After an uncomfortably long silence, she was able to muster a single worded response. "What?"

"I was surprised myself. I only met him by chance, and he pestered me a bit to get me to out with him in the first place. He's a good guy, and I didn't know how this whole thing would end, but I didn't think I'd end up telling him that I loved him."

"You keep saying that you told him you loved him," Eve prodded. "Do you?"

"I don't think I meant it, no," Treistina replied. "He brought me to this hot spring in the mountains of Iedin. Brought me down to this area where the rocks glowed. It was so beautiful. I didn't even think about it. It just came out."

"Treistina, you didn't answer me. Do you love him?"

That made Treistina a little agitated. "You aren't listening, Eve, I just said that it just slipped out."

"I'm not asking if you meant to say it," Eve continued, "I'm not asking if that's what you felt then. There's a reason you called me. You may not have known it when you picked up the phone, but it wasn't to tell me you told some guy you loved him. You called me because you don't know how to justify your feelings. You called because you are in love with him. And for whatever reason, you can't talk to your father about it."

"My dad can't know. He wouldn't exactly be thrilled if he found out. He has such high hopes for me on Damos. He would see this as a roadblock for me."

That comment did not move Eve. She even went as far as to chastise Treistina's father. "What kind of parent would presume to plan out their daughter's life to a design that didn't let his daughter find happiness?"

Eve clearly didn't know Treistina's father. Treistina responded by telling her as much. Eve wasn't convinced, though. She said that there was a difference between guiding a child's life and living it for them. Eve asked Treistina again to say aloud what she already knew. To admit the truth that she was fighting.

"Yes," Treistina said, as she fought back happy tears. "Yes, Eve. I love him. I've never felt this way about anyone in my life. I never thought that I would. And now that I do, I don't know what to do. What can I do?"

Eve told her that she had to figure that out on her own. "It's a journey," she said. "No one can tell you how to make it. No one can tell you how it's supposed to work. If you really love him, then it will work. Nothing else matters."

It didn't matter what she had done in the past. It didn't matter what future she saw for herself. If she truly loved him, Eve told her, then Senjek would fit into her life. No matter what.


"No matter what," Treistina whispered to herself. That was the moment she knew she truly loved this man. She knew that Eve was right. Nothing else mattered. Whatever happened in the past didn't matter.

"Treistina? Can you hear me?"

She opened her eyes. Senjek sat next to her on the bed. He leaned over her; his right hand firmly held her left arm. She reached up to him with her free hand and pulled his head down to her breast. She wrapped her arms around his neck and held him close. She didn't ever want him to leave. Never.

"Treistina? Are you OK? Are you hurt?" She shook her head but didn't say anything. "I'm sorry that I never told you about the Lobby. Who I was."

A few silent tears rolled down her cheeks. "I don't care who you were," she said, voice cracking. "You aren't that man anymore. People still search for The Praesage. But he's gone. He died the day he met me. That was the day you were reborn. The day you became the man I love."

She rolled over and pulled Senjek down to the bed with her. He didn't want to lie, but he wanted to say something to comfort her. "I know that things might not ever be the same, but I promise I'll find a way to make this right. I won't let you down, Treistina."

Senjek never felt a stronger embrace from her. "Forget about everything." Just for one night, she said. She wanted this one night. Just the two of them. No fighting. No running. No Lobby. "It might be the last night we have for a while," she said. She didn't want anything to ruin that. "I don't want to lose you, Senjek. I can't lose you."

# 23. PROCLAMATION OF WAR

"The threat from the Lobby is real. We have to begin preparations for a non-peaceful resolution to the events taking place on Harvest. The Lobby has already completely obliterated one of the main military bunkers at Setera. Half of the towns of Sector IV have already been burned to the ground during Cineon's campaign to deputize Kramei's civilians. Their forces are only growing stronger from our inaction. Do we stop them from seizing a Repulsor or do we allow them to keep the space elevator?"

The members of parliament sat in silence. They were quite content to let Evan speak his argument. A special session had been called to address his recent actions. There was a beep on the conference table's comm unit. Someone wanted to speak with the President. He told his secretary that he was in a meeting and was not to be disturbed.

"The Lobby would not have occupied the Repulsor without the intention of declaring war. They were quite keen to maintain control of it, as well. Lobby forces annihilated an entire Advanced Tactics Squadron. Corporal Grebllyh's debriefing mentions that Amon Veise is still alive."

"Representative Vincent von Breischa," the Speaker of Parliament, said first to identify himself for the record. "How dare you, Mr. President? Commodore Amon Veise was confirmed Killed in Action two years ago when he tried to stop The Praesage from converting the city of Eidolas."

"A friend of mine was from there, Mr. Speaker. Believe me when I tell you that I know full well about everything that happened that day. I saw the report, but I also trust Mr. Grebllyh. The man is as tough as they come and was squad mates with Amon during Basic. If he says Amon Veise is fighting for Cineon, then I reluctantly believe him."

"So, is this why you took it upon yourself to appoint Mr. Johnsen as Suzerain? To circumvent the authority of Parliament to declare war on Kramei? I doubt you even considered how furious Kaleb Vardos must be over this."

"I am not trying to make war with Kramei. I would have war with Daben Celt and Cineon. Our enemy is not our people a planet away. Our enemy is KILLER, the Kramei Independence and Liaison Lobby for Ending Radicalism. We need to mobilize our armed forces, as well as the Iedenian Guard. I appreciate Mr. Vardos' position in this and hope that any perceived slight against him will be forgiven. However, with all due respect, current events do not allow me to recognize any disrespect. I was elected to protect the people of Damos. I am acting accordingly. I hope that Kaleb can forgive me my passing of his favor."

"Stop right there, sir," Vincent cut in. "You may have made a Suzerain, but that doesn't give you the keys to this Republic. You're no king. You have no authority over the Iedenian Guard in any capacity."

"Iedin is a member of this Republic. It was a colony of the monarchy." Evan's head turned to his desk as his secretary had paged him again. He placed it on mute so there would be no further interruption.

"Yes, that is true. But perhaps you should have paid more attention in school. The Iedenian Guard was commissioned by King Xai'que after he succeeded his father, Xen'bach'hou. The Guard was born from paranoia following his older brother's death. It was formed to take commands from the King of Damos alone; a military force that does not take orders from the Suzerain. The Guard of Iedenia will not be raised without our endorsement. Or without Commandant Baena's consent. Period."

"And when, exactly, would you approve? When every single citizen of Kramei stands in revolt? Maybe when they find and capture Baron, if they haven't already done so. Perhaps you'll beg for the Guard to fight when The Praesage himself has cut the throats of every man in this room. Maybe you'll pledge yourself to a fake king again only to murder him."

"Careful, Mr. President," Vincent warned. "Don't be like this. No one in this room denies the threat that Daben Celt and his ilk represent. But war? Even if we were to believe that it has come to that, it is our duty to this country to stop it. As peacefully as possible. We are disappointed by your decision to appoint a Suzerain because you acted alone. This is a democracy. We serve the people; not the other way 'round. We do hope that Mr. Johnsen can stunt Cineon's movements with as little bloodshed as possible."

Evan nodded. "I may have acted alone, but I assure you that it was not to promote bloodshed. My actions are not for glory as the kings of old, but for the continued prosperity of our society. I honestly believe that Cineon is about to launch a major offensive against HFCC. We need to be ready."

"I think you're ready for Besen to be executed live on the Network like your brother was."

"How dare you-"

"No, Evan. What was done to Wele was horrible. And believe me, no one wants to see the same happen to your nephew. Don't you see? You are doing exactly what Daben wants. He's been targeting your family for years. And for what? You are one piece of this government, and you aren't all powerful. There are more damning things he could do to damage this country. But Daben Celt wants to see everything burn. Evelyn, Besen, Wele – he's tormented the people closest to the one man who can give him his war. The president. The throne's caretaker. You couldn't declare war, but you could give someone else the power to do so."

"Representative Clarissa Zophar," another member of parliament shouted. The room grew quiet. "Vincent, quiet down. The Gie family, as you've pointed out quite distastefully, has suffered enough. I will not stand for this persecution."

"Daben Celt has clearly engineered several attacks against Evan's family that can't be traced back to the Lobby. Don't you see that this must have been his plan all along? To further brainwash the people of Kramei into thinking us as villains. History will read that war was a direct result of Dak Johnsen's appointment."

"Enough," Evan bellowed. "You can continue to assassinate my character if you wish, sir. If you won't vote to raise the Iedenian Guard, then I will leave you all to your politics. Perhaps you'll feel differently about the threat of the Lobby when they are on our doorstep. Maybe you'll be forced to do what is necessary when Daben Celt decides to make your life a living hell. Maybe you'll react differently than I when someone tries to tear your world apart. Who knows? Maybe it'll take the Unknown Council to return from the dead to tell you to fight."

Evan stood from his seat and sent his chair crashing to the floor behind him. He turned away from the members of parliament and made his way toward the door. Words of protest from several representatives pleaded with him to return, but he would have none of it. They didn't have the constitution to do what had to be done. The door opened as he neared the exit and his secretary rushed into the room.

"I'm sorry, Mr. President, members of Parliament, but something is developing that you need to see."

Evan forced himself to smile, so he didn't yell at the poor girl. "This meeting is over. Leora, please cancel the rest of my appointments for today. Whatever it is, it can wait until morning."

He walked past her as members of Parliament continued to protest. The girl turned to face him. "Sir, it's about the Network. It's been compromised."

The president stopped dead in his tracks upon hearing that. He turned about and went back into the room. The members of parliament looked equally alarmed. "How do you mean, compromised?" Representative Zophar demanded. Evan pressed a few buttons, and a display appeared in the middle of the desk. It was an image of Daben Celt near a podium. Everyone in the room shared a look of pure dread.

"People of the Republic of Damos, my name is Daben Celt. A name I chose to echo the very same freedom fighter who fought to free us from the tyranny of the monarchy centuries ago. Many of you may know me as the political leader behind the Kramei Independence and Liaison Lobby for Ending Radicalism. Though the biased media of Damos has done their best to paint us as villains, we've grown as a result of what Damos has fed us. What started as a peaceful protest of Damosi treatment of our planet took a terrible turn for the worst five days ago.

"The Damos Network has been without report to recent developments. Your government has been lying to you. Perhaps not lied, but they have indeed withheld information, just as they neglected Kramei. Earlier in the week your president, Evander Gie, appointed his friend, Captain Dakren Randal Johnsen, as the General of the Armies of Damos. While no Baron von Breischa, Captain Johnsen's predecessor was a qualified and capable man for the job.

"It was an early indication of the man's true intentions. With a General he could influence to work toward his own ends, Evander Gie soon made his true plans apparent. Without the approval of you or your parliament, your president made his friend the Suzerain of Damos. If this position sounds foreign to you, be not alarmed. The last time you had a Suzerain you had a Prince of Damos.

"We have been prepared to defend ourselves from military action for almost a year now, of course. In fact, the Commander of our militia, a man by the name of Cineon Yahn, met with Captain Johnson on the Plains of Harvest five days ago. He had hoped to reason with this person. Cineon offered him a token of goodwill; a dull throwing star, to symbolize our reluctance to fight. Captain Johnsen raised his sword on Mr. Yahn, and regrettably, things fell apart quickly.

"This treachery and betrayal will not be allowed to pass. As I speak to you all, men beyond count lay strewn about the dunes of Kramei. Had we not liberated the main Repulsor in the province, the casualties would surely be exponentially higher.

"We are a vulnerable people, the citizens of Kramei. Mayor Haeese has been missing for weeks. Scandals have mired his stand-in. We are all but defenseless. And we are in need of defense. We will not stand idly by as Damos poisons our world. And the Republic will not idly stand by as we fight for our rights. Evan Gie has seen fit to force us into obedience.

"I ask the citizens of Damos, do not take up arms for this man. Every life that is lost in this madness is one too many. To the people of Kramei, I am not your Mayor. I am not your President. I am not your King. I am one who fights for many. I cannot order you to do anything. Nor would I make such a command if I could. I beg of you, please, do not let our people fall into obscurity. If you can fight, then please help us. Help yourselves. Contribute to making a Kramei that your grandchildren can live on.

"I promised myself that the Lobby's actions would not lead to this. I swore long ago that I would give Damos nothing more that it demanded from us. But like our lands and freedoms before, we have no choice. Hide if you must. Fight if you can. As no real authority is here to represent us, the burden falls, regrettably, to me. The People of Kramei declare war against the Republic of Damos."

The entirety of parliament sat in stunned silence. Their worst fear had come true. Damos and Kramei were at war. But that wasn't the only terrifying thing they witnessed in Daben's address.

"That was broadcast on the Network," Evan announced, breaking the silence. "Overridden across all live streams and on-demand viewership. Most of the population likely saw it. What I want to know is how."

"We're receiving reports from the DNC Hub on Kramei. The transmission appears to have valid credentials. No evidence suggests a hardline breach. Someone in TAC-OPS must have somehow superseded Network protocols to reverse the orphaned security exchanges."

"That's probably the best explanation we are going to get, Clarissa," Vincent replied, "but there is something more pressing we need to address."

"Daben Celt is still on Kramei," Evan thought out loud.

Vincent nodded. "Daben Celt is still on Kramei. The source of the transmission is confirmed to have come from Kramei. The recording is of Network definition quality. The transmission was pre-recorded and broadcast live."

"How do we know it was pre-recorded?" Clarissa asked.

"Daben Celt wouldn't be within a hundred miles of the war-zone. He wouldn't risk his death there. The Lobby is gaining more support, enough to go without him now, but losing him would be disastrous to their cause." Evan picked up a file of reports on Daben and tossed them in the trash. "Previous reports suggesting that he may have taken refuge on Iedin or even here on Damos must have been a result of misinformation from the Lobby."

"What is our next course of action, then?"

Evan and Vincent were both visibly annoyed with Clarissa's lack of contribution of ideas and only asking questions. "Our next course of action is to negotiate an armistice," Vincent explained. "Resolve this problem with diplomacy before Cineon disables the Repulsor."

"You can't honestly believe that he would dare do that," Evan argued.

"Reports suggest that Kramei has superior cavalry, but they are still outnumbered. Tactical use of the Repulsor will give them the advantage."

"The Lobby. The Lobby has superior cavalry. Our enemy is Cineon, not the people of Kramei."

"Evan, open your eyes!" Vincent roared. "Did you not see Daben's address? If he didn't have every able-bodied man on the planet deputized before he does now. People are calling our attempt at governance to be a failure. There are three of us in this room. President and two party leaders. The rest of parliament is discussing a resolution to grant Kramei independence."

"Maybe we should," Clarissa declared. "Maybe it's time. If they insist that they can govern themselves better, perhaps we should give them that chance."

"And how long do you think Daben convinces them independence isn't enough? If he withdraws from Kramei, what happens next? I'll tell you what happens," Evan reasoned, "domestic invasion."

"It pains me to admit it, but Evan is right," Vincent lamented. "Daben will continue to twist the minds of his people. The people of Kramei are ready to claim blood. Daben has an entire planet in the palm of his hand. He is bent on conquering. He won't stop at Kramei. Clarissa, what are we doing about the current situation?"

"All past attempts to contact Daben Celt have been in vain. We are currently trying to speak with Cineon at TAC-OPS to negotiate a cease-fire. We are using every type of communication possible, including restricted Network broadcasting, which he is sure to see."

"Great," Evan muttered. "Our best chance at peace right now is through a blood-thirsty maniac. I can't believe I'm saying this, but I'd rather negotiate with Daben."

176

# 24. BESEN'S HOMECOMING

"**W**here am I? Please. No more. I'll tell you anything you want. No more stories. No more of your tortures." Besen's pleas went unanswered. It seemed that he was muttering to himself. Cineon had broken his spirit. He couldn't believe the things the Fury told him. The horrors that the people of Damos had committed behind closed doors. The secrets the Lobby had learned. What actually happened at Monarch Fall. What happened to Baron von Breischa. The Last Prophecy of the Known Council. Could all the things Cineon told have been true?

He sat in his cell for days. Maybe it was weeks. He couldn't be sure. He had long since lost track of time. He hadn't been allowed to sleep much. Bright lights and sirens woke him the second his eyes closed. Or so it seemed. Maybe he was asleep all this time. Maybe it was all a horrible dream. Maybe Cineon killed him inside the Repulsor. He didn't know what to think.

"Wake up!"

Besen stirred from his slumber. He had been asleep, but he didn't know for how long. The light was dim. A woman leaned over him. He struggled to speak. "Who are you?"

"My name is Espera Rimeax. I am a member of the Lobby, but don't worry; I'm not here to harm you."

"What do you want?"

"I want this war to end. It's only been a few days, but we want it to end. And you are the key to making that happen."

Besen chuckled. "Days? We've been fighting for much longer than that."

"Poor Besen," Espera whispered. "The fighting has been going on for some time, yes. While you've been Cineon's prisoner, things have gotten worse. Kramei and Damos are officially at war. We're negotiating with your leaders for an armistice. Damos demands that you or your remains be returned to them. The Fury wants none of it, though."

"Then you are here to smuggle me out? Forgive me if I reject your help."

"This is not a trick. Cineon is not merely the commander of a militia as Daben has told the world. He is a monster without a leash. He is refusing to negotiate. The two armies are deadlocked in combat. If you are delivered to Forward Command, he will have no choice but to withdraw. He won't undermine Daben's message. Remember. We have to get you out of here!"

He shut his eyes. "Please, just let me die," he pleaded. "Just end this. I can't take anymore."

Besen couldn't stay awake. He felt that he hadn't slept in days. The sergeant felt like his body was floating. He dreamed that he was back on the field. He shouted out for Feathers and Deem, but they didn't answer. He looked around for Grebllyh, but he couldn't see his friend. He watched helplessly as the Lobby's army slaughtered Damos. He saw someone wield his sword against the enemy, but couldn't see the face. Besen thought it was Veian, but the man didn't respond to his shouts.

No one the battlefield paid him any mind. A woman shouted orders to the Lobby troops. She was ordering them to retreat. The Lobby seemed to have the battle won. He turned to look for an explanation. That's when he saw it. He felt a wave of joy flood through his body. The Iedenian Guard had finally arrived. Sand and dirt flew into the air as their motorcycles drove through the Plains of Harvest. He saw Kalus Baena lead the charge. Besen's relief slowly turned to dread. It did not appear that the Guard saw him. He waved his arms, hoping to get the Commandant's attention. The cavalry continued to build speed and would crush Besen in a few more seconds.

Moments before they struck, Besen opened his opened his eyes. Everything was a blur. He felt exhausted. He could still see the silhouette of a woman, sitting next to him. Her head was on his lap with her hand wrapped in his. He couldn't see much, but the sergeant knew he was in a different room. He looked around. He was in bed. Besen's mind continued to struggle with the trauma. He couldn't decide if he was alive or dead.

"Ma'am! We're getting something! He seems to be regaining consciousness! Inform Captain Johnsen! He's waking up!"

"Johnsen?" Besen muttered. "Dak?"

The woman's head stirred. She swept the hair from her eyes and looked at him. "Besen? Besen! Can you hear me? It's Liz! Can you hear me?"

A tear escaped his eye. "Margery Lea. What's a ship rat like you doing here?"

"I came for you, Besen. After Cineon had captured you, and Dak relieved Greene, I begged him to take me with him. I couldn't stay in orbit in some blockade knowing that you were down here somewhere."

"Dak is acting General? I must be dreaming."

"No, you're here with me. Whether you want me here or not, I'm staying. You may have left me, but I'm not leaving you. Not now. Not ever."

"Liz," he began to reply, but he was cut off by someone else that entered the room.

"Besen. You are a sight for sore eyes. After making me acting General, then Suzerain, I can only assume he'll make me President after this."

"Dak, what's going on?"

"Two weeks ago you were captured trying to retake the Harvest Repulsor. A few days later I found myself an arms-length away from Cineon himself. We were at war. Actual war. For a few days, actually. We're currently enjoying an armistice. You're safe."

"What's going on with me? I can barely move."

Dak looked over to Ensign Lea. She tightened her grip of Besen's hand. "You were hurt pretty bad. Cineon's medics treated you enough to keep you alive. They didn't do much actually to heal you."

"Liz. Give Dak and me a moment."

"No. I'm not leaving your side," she argued.

"I'm not going anywhere in the next few minutes, Liz. There are some things I need to tell Dak. It's classified. You can't be here."

Ensign Lea looked up at Dak; her eyes begged him to let her stay. He broke eye contact, unable to face her. "It's OK, Ms. Lea. We won't keep you long. Out you go."

Her eyes welled up with tears. She had only just got Besen back, and now she had to leave again. She kissed him on the forehead. She stood from her chair at his bedside. She backed away, reluctant to let go of his hand. As she let her grip slip, she could feel his hand try to keep hold. She looked at him in stunned disbelief. Even now, when he was like this, he would do that to her.

She quickly turned away and ran out of the room. Dak shook his head. "For fuck's sake, Besen. Why do you have to do that to her? Let her move on."

"I'm dying, Dak. She'll move on soon enough. I only wish I could before the end."

"You aren't dying, Besen! This might not be the best hospital Damos has to offer, or even on Kramei, but you are in good hands."

Besen chuckled. "Shit. You were always a bad liar. You know that, right? Even Senjek could see through your bullshit. Though I suppose that isn't so hard to believe now."

"What are you talking about?"

"Cineon. The things he told me. Crazy things. Crazy enough to be true. He told me about the Renaissance Watch. He said the Unknown Council still walk among us. He said The Praesage…"

"What about The Praesage? Did he confirm his death? Is he alive? Does he know where he is?"

"On Damos," Besen continued, "he told me Daben was on Damos. Said he's been there for some time. The things he said to me. Why would he ever let me go?"

"It's misinformation, Besen. We know Daben is still on Kramei. We have proof from the Network. Advanced catalog scanning has mapped the entire planet. The Unknown Council, if they ever existed, are long gone. It was all lies."

"I hope so, Dak. I'd hate to leave this world knowing what's to come."

"You aren't dying, Sergeant. You're going to be fine. You'll be back on Damos breaking girls' hearts before you know it."

"Thanks, I think. It's OK, just tell me. How much longer have I got?"

180

Dak looked at his feet. He couldn't bear to tell him and look him in the eye at once. "An hour. Maybe."

"Thank you. Do two things for me. And don't ask me why. You wouldn't understand. Can you do that for me?"

Dak looked up at Besen. It was a hard thing to agree to, but how could he deny a dying man's final wishes? "I can do that for you."

"Find Senjek Bohmet. Bring him into protective custody. He isn't safe. His girlfriend too, I'm sure she's in as much danger as he is. Go and do that. And send Liz back in here."

"Senjek? What's he have to do with anything?"

"Dak! Please! Just do it! Don't ask me why. You just have to. Trust me."

Dak hadn't been the trusting type for a long time. Besen was a good man, though. He never wronged him or asked for any favors. "Fine. I'll get it done. Goodbye, Besen."

Dak begrudgingly left the room, unsatisfied with the information Besen had given him. He had hoped to learn something useful from his capture. Something he could use against Cineon in battle should the cease-fire end. It was beyond his control, though. The Fury broke one of their best and brightest. All he could do was let him die in peace.

The ensign rushed back into the room once the Suzerain left. She knelt next to the bed and put her hand over his. "I'm here, Besen. It's Liz. I'm here."

"Liz," he said with a smile. He took her hand and pulled it to his chest. "Liz, I never said I was sorry."

"No," she hushed, "don't talk like that. Everything is going to be okay. You're going to be all better. I know it. You're too stubborn to die."

"Remember the day I left? Do you remember what I told you when my ship was pulling away from the dock? Do you remember?"

She nodded as she tried to hold back her tears. "You only said one thing. 'It was fun.' Did you mean the time we had?"

"No. I never told you about the time we had. I was talking about when we were holding the perimeter around the DNC hub. When those two madmen fought for the right to be called The Praesage, and one of them got away. It was rather fun. Even though you thought you were going to die."

181

"I don't regret it, Besen," she said, cutting him off. "I figured I was going to die, yes, but what happened, happened. I might have hoped that it became something more. Maybe I still hope that. But if I had to do it all over again, I would."

"I would do it differently," he revealed. "It's not going to be easy for you to hear now, but I have to tell you. I didn't want to leave that day."

"Stop it," she cried out. "Just stop. You don't have to do this."

He wrapped his other hand around her wrist. "Please, just listen," he plead, as his body shook and fought to hang on. "Cineon didn't do enough to keep me alive. He did nothing. I stayed alive so that I could see you again."

"Why?" she asked, unable to keep her tears back. "What's so special about me? I was just another girl to you."

"You were everything to me. The fight that day was fun. The time you and I had – that was the best. I remember the first day I saw you at the academy. Do you know who I was that day? Besen Gie. Playboy. The boy who would inherit control of the greatest family in the Republic. The family that brought down the tyranny of Se'har. Descendant of the man who single-handedly killed Xen'que. My life was mine to make."

"What does this have to do with me?"

He laughed. "You don't remember. You didn't know who I was yet. Introductory Repulse Theory. I said that a Radius Effect could never be reduced to a concentrated area. You shot that down before I finished talking. You postulated that it could one day provide coverage for a single person. You did your homework. Brought your equation to class."

She smiled. "That was you, wasn't it? I worked on that theory all week. The professor agreed with you, though. He said it was rubbish. Impossible."

"No one had ever disagreed with me before that day. No one had ever told me no. My upbringing imbued with the pride of my family. I was so convinced that I could take anything I wanted in life. You made me realize that I was wrong."

"You're still Besen Gie. Anything you could have wanted is still yours to take."

"Not you. I realized that day I wasn't my family. I recognized that my name granted me privileges, but they were all opportunity's afforded to countless people in my family. It gave me nothing that was important. Some things worth having can't be merely taken. You have to fight for them."

"I'm flattered you remembered that day in class all those years ago. But I'm not special. If I knew who you were, maybe I wouldn't have spoken out. Save me the embarrassment."

"No. I saw it in your eyes. Even if you knew who I was, you still would have stood up that day. I could talk my way into any girl's room, but I couldn't have you because I had to change. Evan and my dad never joined the military. I couldn't tell you the last member of my family who did. I had to prove my life was worth something. That I was someone worth having."

"So, that night, after the Old Hub was in ruin. When it was all over," she said, trying to piece things together.

"It wasn't because you were the closest girl. It wasn't just because we were both so grateful to be alive. Not because we wanted to feel alive after so much destruction. I found you, Liz. I looked for over an hour. Just to make sure, that if you were there, that you weren't hurt."

"Why are you telling me this now?" She asked, her every breath sudden as if she had suddenly learned how. "I would have stayed."

Besen began to produce tears of his own. "I wanted to stay. And I know you would have stayed. But I saw the look in your eyes. You knew all about me. You thought you were just the next girl. Hope in your eyes that maybe you'd be the last because you knew who I was. Perhaps in spite of who I was. And something happened. You wanted something more. But as I lied there, with you in my arms, I knew that I was so far past that."

"I always felt, knew, that I was somehow different. My heart sank when I learned that you were captured. I knew I shouldn't have felt the way I did. I tried to deny it, but I knew. We could have made it work! Why didn't you say something?"

"That's what I would have changed," he said. His voice continued to get weaker. "I said 'it was fun.' I had to leave that day. Nothing I would have said could have changed it. I only had a chance to say three words. Three words to tell you. And I chose the wrong ones."

"It's OK, Besen. I'm here now. I'm not letting you leave this time. You can tell me."

He smiled at her. She had seen him since that day a few times. He was every part of him a soldier. There was something he was holding on to, though. She never knew what it was, but every day since that day, he carried some weight. She had seen him many different days. She had never seen him happy. Not like he was now.

"Besen. I'm here. It's OK. You don't have to be afraid anymore. You can tell me." He meant to say three words. He said he chose the wrong ones. That's what he said. What would he have told her? "Besen!" she pleaded, her voice cracking. She had never seen happiness in someone's eyes. Not like Besen's eyes had. But now there was nothing. They were just eyes. "Besen!" she cried louder. The door to the room came open. She heard footsteps as others entered the room. "Besen!" she screamed as she felt hands take hold of her to pull her away. She grabbed his hands. She refused to let him go. He had something to tell her. He fought so long just to see her again. She couldn't leave before he told her.

# 25. ON THE LAM

Senjek and Treistina had been in hiding for days. Treistina tried to enjoy the time together, pretend that it was a little vacation. They couldn't stay in one place for too long, though. They were attacked twice by Lobby members when attempting to move. "Why can't we just go to Evan?" she would ask. "Let him protect us?" He would tell her they couldn't. If the Republic ever found out who he was, he would be locked away. They would never be together again. "There must be another way," she begged. He told her there wasn't. She could be safe or be with him. She couldn't choose both.

"There is one place we could hide. Somewhere no one would look for us. No one in the Republic, or the Lobby, would look for us there. We can wait for this whole thing to blow over."

Treistina had doubt all over her face. She refused to believe that Senjek was about to suggest what she suspected. "Senjek, please don't tell me that you're thinking of hiding inside Monarch Fall."

"Think about it, Treistina. Parliament hasn't lifted the property ban over the Poleb Estate. Now that there's open war on Kramei, they won't be pushing that agenda. Not until after Daben and Cineon are in custody. Or dead."

"I don't think we should hide there," Treistina cautioned, clearly afraid of the idea. "What if someone finds us there?"

"Trespassing isn't punishable by jail time; you would receive a fine at worst."

"Thanks, Senjek, that makes me feel much better," she replied sarcastically. "Couldn't we just go to Iedin? Maybe go into hiding on Moaschen."

"Moaschen is a lawless world, save for the Republic's occupation of the West Fork. Pirates and criminals overrun it. It's a brutal and dangerous life. I could never allow you to live like that."

"Live like what, Senjek? What's so horrible about a life with you?"

Senjek was surprised to hear this. He knew that she loved him, of course, but he never thought she'd throw her life away for him. Especially after recent events and that she now knew about his past.

"Treistina…"

"No, Senjek. Don't even. I know it's hard for you to imagine. I never expected you to tell me about your time with the Lobby. I could never imagine you'd expose me to that truth. But there is one thing that hasn't changed since you told me. I may have struggled about how to deal with your confession, but my feelings toward you haven't changed. I still love you. I will always love you."

"I love you too," he replied. "If we went to Moaschen, it would be a decision we'd be stuck with. We might not ever be able to leave, even when this is all over. You deserve more than that. I couldn't condemn you to live a life in a place like that."

"We'd have each other, Senjek. Isn't that enough for you?"

He smiled. "Of course it is. But I don't think you understand what it would be like. What you'd have to give up. I don't want you to grow old and regret me. Moaschen is a terrible place. I couldn't even promise that I could keep you safe there. Monarch Fall is the best place to lay low."

"You really think that is for the best?" she asked, still visibly upset with the idea.

"Once this is over, we can come back. Start a new chapter in our lives. Put all of this behind us. Start fresh. Live our lives like we were meant to."

Treistina put a hand on his cheek and stared into his eyes. She looked afraid. She looked at him like she might not ever see him again. She leaned toward him and kissed him. She lowered her head to rest against his chest.

"It's going to be OK, Treistina. I won't let anything happen to you," he reassured her.

"I'm worried about you," she replied, voice cracking. "I don't want to lose you. I don't want to miss out on you. You are the most important thing in my life. You know me better than anyone, yet you barely know me at all sometimes. I feel that if we go to this place, I might lose you."

He wrapped his arms around her to make her feel safe. "You don't have to worry. You aren't getting rid of me that easily. Maybe it was meant to be this way. We're finally moving in together. And we're going to live in a castle. That sounds nice, doesn't it?"

"It seems like a fairy tale. Too good to be true."

"Maybe. But you forget the best part about fairy tales," Senjek told her. She looked up at him, waiting for him to say something. Anything. Anything to make everything OK. "They always have a happy ending."

She grabbed his hand as she walked over to the cot they had been sleeping in for the last two days. She pulled him down to sit next to her. He wrapped his arms around her as she curled up next to him.

"Tomorrow," she said, voice weakened. "If you want to go, then we'll go. But not today."

"Treistina, every day we're out here is another day someone might find us."

He could feel her shake her head, her face buried in his chest. "Not today. Tomorrow."

"Treistina, it's not safe to stay here."

"Just one more day. Please. Give me this. If you really truly love me, please. We can pretend we're back in the mountains. Do you remember when you brought me there?"

He forced a laugh. "I remember you were disappointed we weren't going to the beach."

"No one ever did something like that for me. I've never been taken someplace that beautiful before. Tell me we can go there again someday. Just say that we can, and I'll believe it."

"Of course we'll go back. Not just to the caverns. We'll go to the top of the mountain. The view is fantastic. Going up, it seems that the snow goes on and on without end. Once you're at the peak, though, wow."

"Have you ever been to the top?" she asked.

"No," he replied. "But I've heard the tales. You look down, and all that frosted earth you climbed to get there looks so much smaller then it is.

You look down and see the snow melt. You witness the warmth come back to the ground. You can see where the grass starts to grow. It's so green and lush, twice as beautiful as the Plains of Harvest ever were. Then it gets too warm for grain. The ocean will be coming soon, and the grass gives way to sand."

"And you can see it all? All of that from a single place?"

"I hope so," he said as he stroked her hair. "They say that the kings of Damos formed the Iedenian Guard to make sure nothing came to destroy such beauty. If only they hadn't gotten things so wrong in the end. Maybe we'd be better off."

Treistina chuckled. "Kings and witches and the Unknown Council. Whatever made Javk Gie think there was a better way?"

"Yeah, if only Javk Gie hadn't acted. Then there wouldn't have been a Daben Celt in the annals of history. No mantle for a madman to take up to get an entire planet to revolt. Maybe we'd be better off with the monarchy."

"If it was up to you," Treistina asked with a quiet voice, "would you have done it? If you could go back, and the decision was yours, would you have acted against the kingdom?"

"No, I wouldn't," he replied.

"You really think things would be worse off?"

"No, I don't. I think that maybe if they were left in power, that most everything would be better off. But I wouldn't change anything. Five hundred years is a long time. To change something so big from so long ago, I couldn't live with myself."

"Really? You wouldn't?" She sounded amazed. "If you could stop all of this from happening, why wouldn't you?"

"I came to Damos because of Daben. The protests. The revolts. The Lobby. Things would never have gotten so bad to the point that I had to leave. If it weren't for Daben Celt, I would have never met you."

"Senjek…"

"It's alright, Treistina. Just something I have to accept. So much of my life I owe to Daben. Not just the bad. He brought some good to my life. The best thing to ever happen to me. He brought me you."

Treistina had gathered what little belongings she had with her. It wouldn't be long now. The satellite had already begun to set. They had moved under cover of darkness for some time now, but Senjek emphasized the importance of this action. They didn't just have to avoid the Lobby, but police as well. He promised her that he would make it up to her; the way she would need to live to be with him.

She pleaded with him that there must be another way. "Treistina, we've been over this. If you don't want to come, you'll have to go to Evan and tell him who I am. That way you can be protected. You won't be safe on your own as long as Daben is looking for me. If that's what you want, I understand. I can live with that. I can't have your blood on my hands. But you have to realize that you'll never see me again."

She tried to think of another way for hours. Each new idea was more ludicrous than the last. She even suggested trying to seek asylum with the Unknown Council. Growing up on Kramei, they both believed the seers to exist still. Senjek reminded her, though, that it was a long shot. They would be no guarantee of asylum, provided they could even find them. She then suggested taking refuge in the Breischa masses. He explained that they would be no better off there than on Moaschen. She even suggested they seek out the Renaissance Watch.

"That's a fairy tale, Treistina. Even if it were true, they surely died out a long time ago."

"Maybe we can leave the system altogether," she pleaded. "Go to the Tivrus System. Just start fresh. Not many people ever go there."

"Yeah, that's because people rarely survive the trip. The logistics of navigating through the interstellar medium is mathematically impossible. The only person confirmed to get through died trying to come back. Even if we made it, there's no way of knowing what we'd run into. Why are you so frightened?"

"Frightened? What you mean?"

"You're willing to try any and every alternative to hiding inside Monarch Fall. What's there that so terrifying to you? I know you love me, but you're eventually going to suggest suicide at the rate you're going."

"It's nothing."

It hardly seemed like nothing to Senjek. He could tell she was hiding something. Something that she didn't want to say. "Treistina, whatever it is, you can tell me."

"I'm not allowed to have secrets?" she defended.

He took a deep breath. "I know I kept things from you in the past. I'm sorry that I did, but keeping secrets now is only going to get someone killed. What is it?"

He could tell that she didn't want to say. Whatever it was, it scared her. She clearly had decided against ever telling him about it. He continued to pry. She knew he was right. "The night this all started. When I left the restaurant, I bumped into a girl outside. She was talking about spreading awareness. She was talking about parliament's attempt to lift the property ban on Monarch Fall."

"Just sounds like a political activist to me. What does that have to do with anything?"

She was hesitant to answer, but he reassured her; told her that he needed to know the whole story. "I was in such a hurry to get out of there, and I just kept going. But she kept trying to talk to me. I stressed to her that I was in a hurry. I told her I didn't have time. She handed me a pamphlet. 'Promise me you'll read it,' she said. I told her I would."

"I still don't understand. How does that make you afraid to go there? Is the government close to lifting the ban?"

"It wasn't about the legislation, Senjek."

He was very much confused now. "What do you mean? You said she was talking about the property ban on Monarch Fall. She didn't give you some information to make you afraid of going there?"

She nodded. "Yes, but it didn't concern anything about the law they're trying to supersede."

"Treistina, you aren't making any sense."

"It was a warning. Addressed to me personally. It said to stay away from Monarch Fall. At any cost. It said people would die if I went there."

"The letter," Senjek asked, "do you remember what it said exactly? Do you still have it?"

She nodded again. She reached into her purse and produced the piece of paper. She looked at Senjek for a few moments and contemplated whether or not to let him read it. She relented, however, and handed it to him. He moved closer to the lamp in the room to better read it:

*"My name is Naieena Haeese. It's most certainly been at least a day since you saw me. A day since I gave you this. Maybe weeks. It's so hard to foresee these things. After the events that have transpired, I would not be offended if you have forgotten me completely. I only hope that you read this. Events are in motion that must be averted. You may think that you are safe traveling together. Perhaps you think you can move on past The Praesage. Maybe you think you can deny Daben Celt his prize. None of this matters. The war that will begin on Kramei will spread. By design, the Republic will suffer much loss of life. The fighting men and women will perish. And far greater things will follow. If you value the lives of this country, then you will heed my warning. Do not enter the land where the monarchy fell. Just leave him to his fate. If you stay away, there is hope for everyone. More will die if you go. Please heed this warning. teehsa suyrla beonto daya vaest'i; sauv'romoi peelsa soemna vaya deicrep'i. da'aravinh'era beota mienuti, deecidehra boeura faeta. fiynalta exiestenci toiruna e toafera."*

Senjek looked away from the letter. Treistina was upset. "Naieena. I think met this woman too. I ran into her that night as well. She said strange things to me as well. Failed to mention this bit. She told me which way you went. She helped me find you, and for what? So you could let me go to my death?" He crumbled up the letter and threw it to the ground. "Bullshit. It's fucking bullshit. This is Daben. It has Daben written all over it. Cryptic and sometimes beyond me. This is how he always operated: two steps ahead."

"I don't understand, how can this be Daben?"

"Naieena Haeese? Name sound a little familiar? How about Nodo Haeese, the Mayor of Kramei. Lobby sympathizer. Daben must have gotten to him. Naieena must be a relative. Monarch Fall must fit into his plans somehow… his plans for me. He wants me to go there. He thinks there's something there that will change my mind. Make me align with him again. And whatever it is, he doesn't want you there when I see it."

"This seems a little complex, even for a man like Daben Celt."

"It's him. He even quoted the prophecy that led to Monarch Fall. Untranslated. Those were the words that guided Javk Gie. The words that forced his hand. The words that dismantled a kingdom. Daben believes that his cause is so similar. He even told me once that he was named after one of Javk's accomplices. Complex? The man is insane, Treistina. He probably has every single step planned out to victory. But I promise you. I won't let it happen. I'm not afraid of him. And I won't do as he wants. We're going, and we're going to wait this out. Are you with me?"

# 26. ALL IS FAIR

"Cause of death: intracranial hemorrhaging. The deceased was returned to our custody forty hours before his demise. Due to recent developments, he is to be recognized as a prisoner of war. The commander of the Krameian army is believed to have either caused these injuries or was willfully ignorant in treating them. As such, the continuation of this armistice will be dependent on his punishment for the mistreatment of an enemy combatant. Time of death, 1800 hours. Local time."

Dak stood in front of a gathering of troops, many of them distraught over the recent loss. The captain wore his dress uniform. One he never thought he'd actually wear, tailored after an old Suzerain uniform in a Damos museum.

"The president appointed me as Suzerain of Damos. I was given the position to ensure the freedom and safety of this Republic. Nothing more. I fully expected, still expect, to be relieved of this rank when this over. It's not a permanent position that's barely official. I never thought I would wear the uniform.

"But here I stand now, staining the promise and duty of the position. I stand here as the first Suzerain of the Republic of Damos. And I stand here in failure. I stand here to pay the final respects to Master Sergeant Landon Besen Gie. Deceased, with honors, in the line of duty. A leader to many. A hero to others. A friend to those privileged enough. Besen died in a conflict for the heart and soul of an entire nation.

The Kramei Insurrection

"Damos, neither the Kingdom nor the Republic, has existed without Kramei as her domain. Should we leave these people to their own devices? This is not for us to decide, even now. Should they pay for the lives they have cost? Of course. Should we seek vengeance for this one man who they made to suffer so much? No. Let it end with him. Let this tragedy open the eyes on both sides. Let this senseless loss unite us. Let this end."

Dak turned to his left. "Honor guard, present arms!" A detail of seven soldiers, commanded by Ensign Lea, lifted their rifles.

"Ready! Aim! Fire!"

The detail opened fire. They used ultra-low caliber, ultra-low velocity rounds. They didn't travel very far and did little to no damage, but any other ammunition would be caught in the Repulsor's Radius Effect, injuring anyone present. Dak gave the order to fire twice more. "Honor guard, order arms!" He looked across the field. Somewhere on the other side was the man responsible for this. And despite what he said, Dak wanted nothing more than to see him dead.

He was about to dismiss everyone when someone ran up to him. "Captain! We have a situation."

"Soldier," Dak snarled, "show some respect. We are in the middle of a funeral procession. Return to your post."

"Sir, I'm sorry, sir. It's the early detection systems! Cineon has deactivated the Repulsor."

Dak felt a lump in his throat. Eyes wide, he struggled to speak. "What? What do you mean, he deactivated the Repulsor?"

"The Radius Effect is gone! The Fury is advancing!"

Motorcyclists swarmed into the heart of Damosi uniforms. Lobby cavalry ran down multiple men for every one of them that fell. Dak quickly assessed that more than a dozen of his troops were already dead. Cineon had lured them into a false sense of security.

Dak pulled his sword from its sheath. "Go, everyone go!" The motorcyclists caused panic and chaos as they went further and further behind Forward Command. They weren't ready, and now the entirety of Cineon's cavalry was behind them.

He looked toward TAC-OPS. Cineon's infantry advanced quickly. Most of his men focused on the enemy behind them. It was a trap. The armistice was a trap.

194

"He really must fancy himself the god of war. I would call him the god of dishonor," he cursed. He put away his sword and grabbed a rifle. "Stay down! Take cover! Man the towers! Take out of those bikes! Everyone else move forward! Don't let their infantry reach this station!"

Ensign Lea ran up alongside Dak and provided a portable shield capable of stopping ballistic slugs. "Captain, if we push forward, what if they take Forward Command with their cavalry?"

"Then we keep moving forward to TAC-OPS. First order of business, though, is to call in a bombing run. Take that Repulsor down now!"

"But sir," she protested.

"Do it! I'm not letting Cineon control the pace of this conflict any longer. If it's war he wants, it's war he'll get!"

Cineon was flawless in the execution of his deception. If Daben were to say that he disliked fighting like that, he would have been lying. All throughout history there have been many wars. One thing always fascinated him: how the combatants insisted on being civil when they killed each other. The strategy was flawless. Torture one of their most beloved and talented leaders to the point of death. Then catch them unawares while they mourned. They never saw it coming.

Cineon stood idly aboard his chariot. He looked across the Plains of Harvest and marveled at his own handiwork. The entire Damos war machine was a convoluted disaster. He watched as Dak led a charge toward his position. As the majority of Forward Command emptied, his cavalry launched the second phase of their plan.

Only a few motorcycles maintained their position behind Forward Command. Little more than what was required to draw the fire of the fort's turrets. The rest of them advanced beyond and approached Dak's rear.

Cineon watched as his troops began to enter the trenches dug from earlier conflicts. His men had something to fall back to as well. Dak did not.

Dak and several troops with him jumped into a trench. His immediate plan was to trap one of the motorcycles. On his command, two of his men jumped out of the trench, swords extended and cut down the rider. The bike went over the ditch but landed close enough to retrieve. The two men who secured the bike, however, were both gunned down in the attempt.

195

Cineon looked on as Dak tried to commandeer or disable members of his cavalry. It was not going well for the Suzerain. "Stay steady, men," he announced, even though no one could possibly hear him. "We have them right where we want them. Just keep doing as I told you."

It would have been useful if his soldiers could hear him, though. Some of the citizens who took up arms became anxious. Recently joined members of the Lobby grew impatient. Cineon was trying to wear them down. He was playing it safe.

A younger man fighting for the Lobby picked up a grenade. His orders were clear, but war changed people. He was afraid. He wouldn't just hold his position. He wanted to kill anyone who would try to kill him. He lobbed the grenade toward the trenches. The explosive landed in the path of a motorcycle and blew it in half.

It succeeded in killing a few men, but it had cost Cineon one of his pieces. He searched the battlefield for the man who threw it. He saw the young man just as he tossed another. A throwing star was in his throat seconds later. "Idiot," Cineon cursed.

The grenade landed in the middle of Damosi troops, but Dak jumped toward it. He knocked it away with his sword. It flew into the air and exploded in the face of a biker, killing him instantly. Cineon watched as Dak obtained a few more bikes as a direct result.

He watched as Dak led a small group on a motorcycle. He watched as Dak started to eliminate his infantry slowly. He looked on as Forward Command put down road spikes to prevent the remainder of his infantry from rejoining the battle.

Cineon heard something. An air strike. He looked up as three ships jetted over the battlefield. The planes dropped a carpet bomb over the Repulsor. The shock of the explosion and resulting collapse killed a good number of Lobby soldiers. The facility suffered some cosmetic damage, but the bombardment failed to destroy the Repulsor.

"Looks like Evan did something right when he picked you," Cineon said. It was almost as if he admired his opponent. "That's what I get for being sentimental. Should have killed you when I had the chance."

Cineon saw Dak as a problem now. He wanted to toy with him for a bit, but he was becoming more trouble than what it was worth. He pulled a

196

star from his belt. It was time to cement his name in history. The first man to kill a Lord Suzerain in battle.

He threw his arm across his body, letting the star glide gracefully through the air. One of his own troops ran right in front of it, though. "Pity," he said without remorse. He released another. By the time it got close enough, it had veered away from the course Cineon intended for it.

He decided that he was too far away. He retrieved his bow and propped an arrow. He was careful with his aim and released the arrow. To his amazement, Dak saw the projectile and cut it down. Dak backpedaled. He knew that Cineon had taken an interest in his death and began his retreat.

"OK, if you insist, Mr. Johnsen," he growled. He looked on as Damos cavalry entered the battle. He received word that his remaining infantry behind Forward Command became overwhelmed and lost. He brought a radio to his lips. "Attention all troops. Discontinue stratagem one. It's time to shake things up a bit. Commence stratagem four. Commodore, you know what to do. Do please try to save Mr. Johnsen for me."

# 27. THE VON BREISCHA THAT DEFECTED

Daben sat arrogantly upon the throne inside the palace. He thumbed through the pages of his diary. Some of the entries were from before he acquired it. It had two previous owners, as best he could tell. The previous owner was a conspiracy theorist, obsessed with the events of Monarch Fall. He apparently felt that some of the details in the history books didn't add up. Acquiring the diary vindicated him to a degree.

The man who wrote it was the current owner's namesake. Written by the man who led the revolution against the kingdom. His family, in the many years following, grew more and more into obscurity. This slowly gave the majority of the credit to Javk Gie, as his family was prominent figures of society even to this day.

The previous entries fascinated Daben. At first, they inspired. Eventually, the words inside brought him to his current mindset of anarchy. On some nights he wondered how much this book had influenced him. He continued to skim over the contents. It had been some time since he had written anything himself. Surely there were things worth writing, he thought to himself, but this wasn't a diary for him. He hoped that this journal would become a bible for his new world order. The vision of a world that he and his predecessor had envisioned for the world. Perhaps it was time to write again. He was about to reach for a pen when he heard someone enter the throne room.

## A Fatal Vendetta

A shorter than average woman with black hair all but shaved from her head. She had been with Celt for some time now. Always kept nearby, Daben kept her on a short leash. Never quite able to trust her entirely. "You wanted to see me, sir?"

"Yes, I did," Daben answered. He locked the diary and put it out of sight. "Events are proceeding at an exceptional rate. All except, of course, the delivery of The Praesage. Ljero is dead. The escalation of events on Kramei keeps Cineon there. It is too late to pull him out to handle this. As you know, you weren't even my third choice; Espera is also too entrenched inside TAC-OPS to transfer. I had no choice but to exploit your talents, Areka. At last. You've had a couple of days to fulfill your task. Report."

Areka von Breischa. Her service to the Lobby was a continued embarrassment to her family. Once a noble family during the days of the monarchy, the von Breischa continued to thrive in military service. Some gave credit to exceptional tutoring at a young age. Others said it was in their blood. Daben wasn't concerned about hows or whys. All he needed to know was that members of this family were great military minds. And even more important to Daben, was the fact that he had one.

"I'm continuing to monitor his movements. He doesn't stay still for long. I sporadically engage him with a small team when he moves. I allow him to evade this team, but I keep a reconnaissance team on him at all teams. At a distant, of course, so he doesn't know that he's under constant surveillance. It shouldn't be long before I have him."

Daben stared at her, dumbfounded. "That's it? That's your plan? Does any part of that strategy do anything to accomplish your assignment? If you always know where he is, why not take him? He has to sleep, you know. I doubt the woman is much good at keeping watch."

"I made early attempts at doing that, yes," Areka explained, "but, with all due respect sir, perhaps you shouldn't doubt. I managed to avoid detection, but both targets are keeping watch. Both are doing an exceptional job of it. Perhaps you underestimate this woman's convictions."

"I think that I'm quite a good judge of character, Ms. von Breischa."

"Well, my observations contradict your judgment, sir," she boasted. "If I wanted to, yes, I could breach while he's asleep and she's keeping watch. But I won't. Not if I can avoid it."

"Areka, please don't tell me that you aren't prepared to do all that is necessary for the pursuit of this goal," Daben hissed in agitation.

She scoffed at the veiled threat in Daben's words. "Don't misunderstand me. You will have Senjek Bohmet inside these walls. One way or the other. I've been observing him for some time. He is afraid of anyone finding him. I think Ljero must have told him that you'd blow the whistle on him if he didn't play ball. It is for this reason that I'm confident he won't flee the planet, even if he suspects that he's been outed. Now that we are at war, security is on high alert. Even trying to get to Moaschen would be a risk. So he has to stay on Damos."

"That, of course, is a relief. Bohmet is safest on Damos, which is where I would have his aid. Or his detainment. Things cannot proceed here without him in custody. You need to be more aggressive. Take some risks."

"I don't plan on ending up like Ljero. I will eventually attack him at his various hideouts if it comes to that, but only to scare him. I'm not losing any more men for a single asset. Once I convince him that he can't run or hide, there will be only one place left for him to go. Here."

"Here? You expect him to come straight to us?"

"Not us," Areka explained, "to Monarch Fall. The one place the Republic won't look for him. He won't suspect that we've made camp here based on the same assumption."

Daben's eyes gleamed with excitement. "Oh. That is just brilliant. Very good! Using his paranoia to drive him straight to the one place he should avoid most. If Baron could see you now."

"I would do without the comparisons to my brother, if that is fine by you, sir."

"Fair enough," Daben replied. He stood from the throne and walked toward his agent. "I assume that you are taking all the necessary preparations? How does the parameter fair?"

"Everything is secure, I assure you. I have all angles of approach under constant surveillance. We've only had one person come anywhere close in the last week. My teams suggested that he was scouting the area."

That news worried Daben. "Does someone know that we're here? Was it a local?"

"It would appear so, yes," she confirmed. "Most likely a criminal or vagrant. According to my agents, he wasn't around long enough to gather any useful information. Even if he had noticed a presence, he wouldn't have been able to discern who we are."

"When was this, exactly?"

"The beginning of the week, there's been no sign of anyone since." Daben was about to speak, but Areka opened her mouth first. "We are continuing to monitor for activity. I'll let you know if something changes."

Daben had slowly made his way over to the bar he had brought in. He retrieved himself a cigar. He held a second out, extended toward Areka. She declined. Daben cut the bottom off before lighting. "So tell me, in your professional opinion, when do you think we should expect Senjek to arrive?"

"Well, I believe you have time to finish your cigar," she replied. Daben thought that was particularly amusing. Areka had never heard the man laugh so sincerely. He stopped, though, when he noticed Areka wasn't laughing. "Don't linger, though. The final preparations are being made. You will have the Praesage soon."

"Very good, Ms. von Breischa. I won't hold you from your designs. You may leave me."

Areka found herself inside the observation tower. She ran her fingers through the only hair she hadn't shaved off. She was waiting for her prey to arrive and considered all possibilities. She hoped that he would surrender upon realizing he had fallen into a trap. Hopefully, he would recognize the Lobby presence for some time. Today would be the first time he stepped foot inside the royal estate. Areka was confident that no one knew this place better than her. She had explored and studied the building for weeks. In fact, she was almost eager to meet anyone who knew it better.

"Ma'am, I'm sorry to bother you," an approaching voice said. She turned to see a member of her team charged with harassing Senjek. "We have a situation."

"Is that so, Mr. Vall? I hope you have good news. The expression on his face suggested otherwise. The color as well, she had never seen the man so pale. She turned back to look over Monarch Fall. "Go on then, out with it."

"There's a caveat to this, but we may have a security breach." She quickly turned back to look at him, now concerned. "Yesterday we found a woman in the road as we came back from a raid. Her physical traits matched those of people Mr. Celt asked us to keep watch for, so we grabbed her. We've been asking her questions, but she hasn't cooperated until just now. She said she was knocked out by a man who was asking her a lot of strange questions. Questions about Mr. Celt. Questions about the palace."

"Is it Bohmet?" she asked, excitement in her voice. "Does he suspect that we're here? Heavens, would that be so thrilling."

"She didn't say exactly, though she talked about him. She has also told us that her name is Naieena. When we brought up her physical traits, she neither confirmed nor denied affiliation with The Unknown Council. I thought you might like to know first before we told Mr. Celt."

She smiled as she approached the soldier. She put her hand on his shoulder and leaned in toward him. "That won't be necessary, Mr. Vall. Daben doesn't need to know about this. Not yet, anyway. Tell no one else. Bring this woman to me."

He grew anxious with her proximity. "Ma'am, information of this kind is fascinating to Mr. Celt. We are under explicit orders to report this immediately."

"I'm aware of Daben's desires to neutralize the Unknown Council," she whispered into his ear. She walked around behind him, to whisper to the other. "But the last lead he found is now the guest of the kings of Damos. I don't want to bury another lead due to Daben's... zealousness." She backed away from Mr. Vall. "What did she say of Bohmet?"

"She is under the impression that he will indeed come here, as you've predicted. She then told us to flee. She said that we disrespect the dead. She said we might join them if we stay."

"So cryptic. I think I'll enjoy her very much," Areka said with glee. She looked out toward the perimeter, as she noticed activity. She bit her her bottom lip as she grinned. She turned back to Mr. Vall. "Keep her quiet. Keep her hidden. I think this little reunion is about to begin!"

She ran past the man and down the stairs. She quickly made her way through the various hallways toward the throne room. Daben would be thrilled. So relieved he put his trust in her. So ecstatic that she brought him The Praesage. She ran and ran as quick as her legs could carry her. Daben saw her run as she passed statue after statue of former kings. He stood to receive her, his heart racing. Was this the time? He begged her to tell him what he wanted to hear.

"He is coming! Senjek Bohmet is on your doorstep!"

# 28. BATTLE OF HARVEST

The Kramei army re-aligned their troops to become more tightly-knit. Each row of men held a shield with Repulsor-like properties. The technology in the shields was simple in comparison to the massive facilities that produced the Radius Effect. They were comparable to using a regular shield against arrows. If wielded wisely it could halt a single bullet at a time. There was no guarantee that a skilled marksman couldn't get past it. It offered simple protection, but it was better than standing in an open field. The shields provided some safety against gunfire so that other resources could be used to neutralize mortar attacks.

Dak was immediately alerted to this action by Lieutenant Abal. "Sir, the enemy has entered a *Natraps* formation. I suggest we cease-fire and engage them with close combat weapons."

"The main Repulsor is back online. I applaud Cineon for his caution, though it is unnecessary. There's not a chance of a single round making it anywhere near one of those shields as long as the Radius Effect is active."

"Maybe Cineon knows something we don't. Maybe he plans on disabling the Repulsor himself."

Dak was worried by that notion. "We've already tried to take it down once ourselves. We outnumber Lobby forces in men and munitions. Cineon knows that. He knows we know that. I don't think he'd be bold enough to throw away the one thing that gives him equal footing. Even if he were to offline the Repulsor on his own accord, he wouldn't be able to out-gun us. It's advantageous to the Lobby that the equipment continues to run. Cineon is not the type of man to discard an advantage."

Lobby troops continued to advance toward the Forward Command Center. Dak tried to conceive a scenario in his head where a Repulsor-less situation would work against his favor.

"Permission to come aboard, sir." Dak turned to address the voice, surprised to see the speaker. "I'll hardly be of any use locked away mourning over Besen. I can help."

Dak wore his best fake smile. "Ensign, of course. No one was thinking anything of the sort."

"I'm not stupid, Dak," Liz berated. "I haven't received any orders since Besen got back. Anyone hardly even speaks to me. I'm an officer in the Damos military being treated like a widow. You brought me along for a reason. I'd like to think that it was because of my skills and not due to Besen's posting."

Dak turned away from her. Her words insulted him. He couldn't help but feel that people felt the same way about his position. He had become good friends with Evan himself. There were whispers about that friendship influencing Dak's standing. A small part of him even admitted it. "Ms. Lea, if you ever accuse me of playing favorites again I will strip you of your rank and send you to the West Fork. You wouldn't be here if I didn't feel you were the best person available for the job. If you don't wish to be treated like a woman in mourning, then stop acting like it. Do you have anything?"

It was impossible to hide the embarrassment on her face. She nearly lashed back at the Captain, but quickly realized she would have proven right everything he just said. She swallowed her pride and stepped up to his side. "We have been monitoring the Radius Effect, sir. It appears to be cycling down."

Preposterous was the word that came to mind. There could be no possible reason for Cineon to do that. The Republic army outnumbered Lobby forces in every significant resource. Cineon was outgunned, outmanned, and above all, trapped. His possession of the Repulsor was the only thing standing in the way of his utter defeat. "Bullshit," he finally muttered. "We have troop movement on his side. His forces would be decimated without the Repulsor."

"It is cycling down, sir, but not a rate that suggests terminating the Radius Effect," Liz explained. "It appears that the range is merely shrinking. We're trying to analyze the rate of decay and how the coverage will vary. We can only assume that he intends to keep his own terrain covered while compromising our safety."

"Can he do that? Is it even possible to do that?"

"I'm not an expert sir, but I can tell you that the Repulsor is designed to cover a specific range. Said range has to be maintained for the field to stay in harmony. In theory, you could reduce or expand the range of the Radius Effect, but not without compromising its integrity. The Effect would become erratic; it would be impossible to predict how it will behave."

Dak made orders to assemble ground forces. It was clear that an attack was imminent. He armed troops with pikes, swords, and other edged weapons. The Suzerain would leave nothing to chance; they also carried firearms. There were snipers assembled on the roof as well as a precaution in case the Repulsor failed. They were advised to hold their fire until ordered to do so. Having a shot on Cineon was to be an exception. If they believed they had a clear shot they were authorized to fire at will.

"Lieutenant Abal, inform General Greene and Admiral Kinem that the Lobby is advancing," Dak quickly made his way to the battlements as the ground started to tremble. He could see the chariot in the distance. A sniper bullet impacted against the air, mere inches Cineon's face. The shields must have been worth the price. That or the Radius Effect retained some integrity. "Keep trying to take him down. Ensign, take the battlements. I'm going back down there."

"Sir, I must protest. I am not qualified to coordinate our defense."

Dak ignored her plea. He continued back the way he came, Liz pleaded with him the entire time. Lieutenant Abal intercepted him. He did not agree with Dak's decision either. "Sir, I must agree with Ms. Lea. She's not fit for the job. You would not have been my first choice, but I trust the president put you here for a reason. I implore you to stay here."

Dak made a dead stop and turned to face them both. "The both of you! I am your commanding officer, and you will do as I say! We need to keep our forces from being intertwined. It will be a blood bath. Furthermore, our use of the Repulsor will be utterly useless. Cineon is a cold-hearted killer. I'm not about to throw away the lives of all these men and women here today."

"Cineon may be ruthless," Liz cautioned, "but you surely don't think he would fire on his own troops?"

"I wouldn't bet my life on it," Abal interjected. "We outnumber Cineon. One of his for five of ours? I think that's a loss he could accept. Having said that I must insist you stay here! I know she is my superior, but she is not qualified for this."

Dak struggled not to act irrational, but he felt more useful leading from the front. Liz continued to argue her assignment. He ripped her rank from her collar and pinned it on Abal. "Ensign Lea you are relieved as my executive officer. Mr. Abal, get your ass up to the battlements and coordinate our efforts from the rear. I swear to all that is holy that if I hear one more word of protest, you will spend the rest of your career patrolling the Brescha Masses!"

Abal rubbed his throat where the pin of rank clung to his uniform. He could see there was no use arguing with this man. He offered a brief glance of condolence to Liz as he reluctantly made his way up to the battlements. The ensign stood dumbfounded from her unceremonious demotion. She barely listened as Dak instructed her to monitor the Radius Effect. She fought back a tear and nodded. "Yes, sir. If there is any significant change in the field, you'll be the first to know."

Dak called for a rifle as he made his way to the door. He caught the flying weapon and slammed his back against the wall. He checked the magazine and loaded the first round. "Fuck you, Baron," he muttered to himself. "Fuck you for not being here. Wherever you are and whatever you're doing, I hope it's worth it."

He made his way outside to see another sniper shell fail to kill Cineon. He suspected the shields guarding his chariot were perhaps more sophisticated than the regular foot soldier. Cineon was in plain view and couldn't be touched. He was essentially baiting the Damos snipers. Still, Dak would not re-purpose those men. If he could get a lucky shot and kill him, it would be worth it.

"Hold them back!" His words were futile. They wouldn't risk firing their weapons. The Repulsor was still running. They were holding up pikes to discourage the siege, but their ranged weaponry was severely handicapped. They could do little but hold their ground as the Krameian army came bearing down on them. Dak used his rifle's sling to strap the gun across his chest. He pulled out his sword and kept his pistol in reach as the two armies collided. "Stay tight! Don't let them through!"

The Damos line spread kept themselves spread horizontally across the field. They still outnumbered the Lobby. The opposing troops were making little progress of penetrating the front lines. Dak commanded to push forward. If Cineon were trying to take Forward Command out of the Repulsor's range, he would drive the conflict toward TAC-OPS.

Some of the more inexperienced soldiers fired their rifles. Fortunately for them, they didn't hit any of their own. They didn't hit any hostiles, either. The Radius Effect was becoming somewhat diminished, but the forest of physical shields did not allow the rounds to travel very far. Another Kramei soldier hurled a grenade, but it bounced into the air, exploding safely away from the target. Damosi soldiers pushed against the Lobby's front line to allow room for them. With some safe space granted to them, the next row of men followed up with a coordinated thrust of spears.

Cineon fired an arrow at an exposed spear-bearer and hit him in the forehead. "It's always a strange thing, watching a man turn into a vegetable," he mused. He fixed his bow on his back and reached for his radio. "Espera, what would you say are the odds of successfully flanking enemy forces?" There was silence. "Ms. Rimeax? Answer me."

"Sorry, sir," she finally answered. "The question caught me off guard. Quite frankly, I don't understand how we could achieve that. The Repulsor is still in operation, and we're too close to their base. They've also commandeered some of our motorcycles which doesn't help matters."

"Espera, I did not ask you for intel. I want your opinion on trying to flank Johnsen. Do you think we could do it?"

There was a reason Cineon was known as the Fury of KILLER. Daben was certainly the leading mind in the Lobby for a reason. She couldn't imagine Daben even considering such a wild notion. She didn't think him reckless to consider such a measure, though. Their current strategy to slowly cut down every last man was more in line with the Praesage's methods. "Several factors would hinder such an attempt. The re-purposed vehicles in their possession will provide the nearest obstacle. The further outside we go improves our chances, but it offers us less protection from the Repulsor. Any flanking group would be noticed and obliterated. I think there may be better approaches than our current course. Do I think attempting to flank them is viable? No."

"I think we are qualified for the task. Our front lines are slowly being ripped apart. Dak Johnsen is ready to fight like a big boy." He pulled a throwing star from his pocket and played with it, spinning it through his fingers. "If we can't shore up our front line they will push our backs against TAC-OPS. Undoubtedly the reduction of the Radius Effect has pressed Dak to this strategy."

"I don't understand, sir," she said, confused. "Isn't that what you want? Draw their forces away from Forward Command?"

"I want to keep them guessing. I don't want him to figure out what we're planning. Dak Johnsen doesn't seem qualified to engage in Repulsor warfare. I'm grateful that they aren't commanded by von Breischa. I believe he would be able to see far enough ahead to realize what's happening. Damosi forces are pressing. They're winning. Baron would consider that. Think twice about continuing his press. Anticipate what's about to happen. Suspect we're trying to look desperate."

Espera didn't like what she was hearing. They had already lost enough people. She dreaded to accept her intuition. Cineon insisted on spreading their forces outside relative safety. His manipulation of the Radius Effect forced the enemy closer to them, as planned. The Lobby had done well to conceal their true numbers from the Republic, but the longer they waited, the smaller their advantage. "How many lives are you willing to throw away to win this battle? You wouldn't dare try this against a proven general. What would you do if Baron were here? What then?"

"We would fall," he said with a grin. Amazingly, he seemed to be genuinely amused. The integrity of the Radius Effect was faltering. Enemy snipers were periodically shooting into their ranks. Every shot out of ten made it close enough to hit a shield. Cineon issued the orders he had revealed to Espera. "Take as long as necessary to make it look convincing. Get out on the edge, try to mow out their spears. We will provide what suppressing fire we can. Those shields are infants compared to the Repulsor, but they'll be your best friends out there."

No sooner had he said that when a sniper round navigated through the shield wells, finding a home in a man's neck. Cineon's eyes were like daggers as he stared at the radio. "I'll be sure we hurry, sir. Our men will be in position before the Radius Effect collapses." She replied as if she could see his gaze.

Cineon gathered his escort and prepared to make his move. Dak continued to press. Lobby troops fortified their front line and established enough space to leverage their spears. There was no decided advantage in swordplay, both armies having soldiers fall victim to blades that grew redder as the battle progressed. The physical integrity of Lobby shields faltered to the constant barrage of Damosi spears. Cineon moved his chariot forward and approached where the Repulsor's effectiveness was growing weak. Two pairs of bikes flanked him as he approached the action. Each bike had a passenger carrying large shields.

There were several loud bangs as sniper shells impacted against the more efficient shields protecting the Lobby general. Some Damosi soldiers tried to attack the bikes directly, as they left themselves relatively exposed to protect Cineon. It was too late, though. Cineon's entourage got past his side and plowed through Dak's front line. Several spear-bearers were run over by the chariot alone. Abal called off the ranged assault. Cineon was inside enemy territory and snipers would risk killing friendlies.

Damosi bikes approached the chariot, but Cineon's escorts tossed their shields to their general; the passengers retook bikes they had lost. Cineon swiveled his craft and opened fire from his mounted machine guns. Dak watched helplessly as Cineon made short work of the inside lines. His front line became compromised as they doubled back after Cineon. The two armies came closer and closer entwined. The scene looked more like a collection of brawls rather than a single battle.

210

A Fatal Vendetta

The chariot stalled as static shot away from it in all directions. Cineon had detonated an electromagnetic charge, shorting out all surrounding equipment. His cavalry had distanced themselves, so most of the damage was done to Damosi troops. Almost all of the forward batteries malfunctioned. So many died so quickly as the chariot's driver dismounted, throwing knives into the hearts of the scattering forces.

Dak tried to get into the fray, hoping to end it himself. So many of his men fell as they tried to rip out the heart of the Kramei offensive. He had gotten close enough when he was sent crashing to the dirt. An enemy mortar had struck the men behind him, wasting scores of them. There was a ringing in his ears from the blast. He instinctively raised his rifle just in time to parry an enemy blade. He cut the legs from under the attacker. Poor soul overexerted himself expecting an easy kill.

Abal tried to alert his general to what had happened, but to no avail. Cineon's attack had disabled radios on the ground. The pulse had also signaled Espera to deactivate the Repulsor completely. Lobby troops were flanking on either side. Though many fell in the beginning, it wasn't a significant number lost. Bikes raced around the outside, moving too fast for snipers to hit. Abal commanded men to pursue Dak to bring him back to safety. Ensign Lea had elected to lead the group herself.

Dak watched bodies collapse with each pull of his trigger. Friendly faces were too rare for his liking. His troops steadily recoiled to escape the batteries of TAC-OPS, but their formation snapped. Even as they escaped mortar range, enemy soldiers were quick on their heels. The Lobby laid waste to Damosi trenches and took them for their own. Cineon took residence with his men inside.

"Here is the plan," he shouted to his brothers. "We will hold this position. Try to keep enemy forces divided for as long as possible. Don't push them too far away or they'll rain hell on us. We will wait for reinforcements to replenish what equipment I've crippled. We will dismantle as many enemy turrets as possible so we can dispatch air raid vehicles. Keep an eye out for Damosi birds in the air. I'll signal TAC-OPS from here."

Espera looked on as a blue flare shot up from the trenches. She could hardly believe it. Cineon's plan had worked. She retreated to the inside of TAC-OPS to forward news of the development. "It's time to let Daben know of our progress. Prepare the video package for upload to the Network," she said with a sense of pride. "We only have one chance to get this right. They might disallow all Network traffic coming from the entire planet after this. Doctor the footage as much as realistically possible. We're going to need the continued sympathy from the mainland."

Espera removed her breastplate and let it bounce off the pavement beneath her. She instructed a portion of the reserve troops to make for the Repulsor. The intention was to keep it offline, but they would not dare relinquish it. She grabbed a cup of water and poured it on her head as if to wash away the savagery from outside. She looked over to see a man watching her as the water soaked into her shirt. "I want our batteries to focus on any ships fleeing for the atmosphere. I don't want a single Damosi returning to their fleet."

# 29. AN ONCOMING FRONT

*For years, I have waited for this day. Nothing will be the same after today. I can feel it. So close now. I can taste it. The Praesage of KILLER is again within my grasp. Too long has he alluded me. I finally put my faith in the right woman. The hand of a von Breischa will bring the fall of Damos. How poetic. The excitement overwhelms me. I can hardly stand it. This is the day it truly begins.*

Senjek tried to avoid major streets as he made his way toward Monarch Fall. When he first arrived on Damos, he had scoped out most of the city. The old royal estate was the one place he never explored. He learned every back-road and most of the topography. If he needed to get somewhere quickly or discreetly, he knew the best route. His only concern was that he would have to go back to the New Xenue highway to get to Monarch Fall.

Senjek had difficulty coping with his actions from that day. He spent every day since trying to convince himself that he did the right thing. His battle with the Lobby stirred old memories. His thoughts flooded with past deeds: crippling a man at the DNC hub, foiling the attempt on Daben's life, and his many raids. He thought his identity as the Praesage died after the Eidolas raid. For the first time, he began to think of how many other lives he must have ruined.

He looked over to Treistina. She fell asleep shortly after getting into the car. She hadn't been sleeping well, and he woke her up early before the sun rose. He remembered the face she made when she realized who he used to be. She was surprised, angry, and heartbroken all at once. He hoped she wouldn't react that way, but he wasn't shocked. What bothered him was how quickly she trusted him again. Was she fearful for her life? Or was his paranoia growing?

He looked back to the road and noticed he had drifted into the other lane. He quickly corrected, but it was too late. He saw flashing lights behind him. He was close to the end of the highway and reaching the edge of Monarch Fall. He looked back and saw two squad cars in pursuit. There was no way of losing them. He had no choice but to pull over.

"Treistina," he said, as he firmly shook her shoulder. "Time to wake-up."

She quickly came to, fear immediate in her eyes. "Is it the Lobby?"

"Shh! No, it's just the cops. I swerved a little, that's all. I'll talk my way out of this… I hope. Things could get ugly, though. I don't know. Try to be ready for anything." He opened the door and stepped out of the car. He lifted his hands so the police could see. "Morning, officers. What seems to be the problem?

Two of the cops cautiously walked toward him. The one that took the lead seemed more confident, but the other looked anxious. Senjek immediately noticed that the officer in the back had her right hand on her sidearm. "We saw your car swerve. You corrected in a reasonable amount of time. Thought about letting it go. Then I realized where we are. Do you know where you're going?"

"I'm trying to get home. My first night of midnight rotation and I'm not used to driving at night."

"Not many residences require you get on the New Xenue highway," the second officer replied. "Just the military housing, if I'm not mistaken."

Senjek nodded. "Yup, that's me. Well, not proper military. I'm a private contractor hired by the Office of Naval Intelligence."

The first officer placed his hand on his right hip. His fingers brushed his gun as he did so. "That so? Do you have your papers? Who do you report to?"

"Captain Dak Johnsen. My name is Senjek Bohmet. I'm an introductory course instructor for Krameian counter-insurgency. My credentials are in the car."

214

A Fatal Vendetta

"Get them. I want to see. Wykurt, get on the Network Line and run his name."

The second officer complied with her instructions. Senjek leaned into his car and grabbed his ID badge. He slowly reached his arm out with it as he handed it to the policeman. "Still adjusting to the new sleep schedule. I guess I must have started to doze off. I'm really sorry, Officer...?"

"Dillin. I'll be the one asking the questions, thank you." He inspected Senjek's credentials. He handed them back. "Looks to be in order. You realize the housing units are in the other direction, don't you?"

Senjek was so relieved that he almost didn't respond. He feigned annoyance. "Shit. Really?" He looked up to the sky. "Are you sure? The housing is to the East."

The officer chuckled. "Yes, they are. And you aren't on Kramei. You were driving West. Your navigation must be better suited to the Krameian landscape."

Senjek looked dumbfounded. "Damn it. I'm an idiot. The stars are positioned differently."

Officer Dillin nodded. "Guess you must have grown up on Kramei. Some of those provinces don't even have roads. Navigating by the using the heavens must be a hard habit to break." The officer smiled. "Hey. Maybe you can help us. I'm sure you know about the Lobby. If you drive this road to get to and from work, did you happen to see any of that scuffle?"

Senjek feigned ignorance. "Scuffle? What do you mean?"

"We're not sure, actually. Only a few people saw bits and pieces of it. We don't know if it was local gangs or a race that went bad or what. One eye-witness said someone with a gun-blade wasted the whole lot of them. Emergency services didn't get to the scene as quickly as we would have liked. A lot was destroyed in the fire. We think they might have been Lobby or Lobby sympathizers."

Senjek nodded. "Oh. That. I wish I could help, but like I told Captain Johnsen, I wasn't in the area when that happened."

The policeman bit his lip and looked down at the ground. "Shame. Thought maybe I'd get lucky. And, uh, has Captain Johnsen uncovered anything with ONI?"

ﾂ215

Senjek shrugged. "Haven't heard anything. I'm a private contractor, though. I doubt he'd tell me anything about it. Besides, I haven't seen the Captain since I started the midnight rotation."

The officer nodded. "I see. I won't hold you up much longer, just want to follow up with my deputy. Just hang tight for a minute." Dillin walked back to his car and leaned through the window. "Contact the station. I think he might be under duress."

"Sir, I can't reach the station," Wykurt replied.

"I think he's legit; you can stop running his name. He might have seen something. I believe he's trying to tip me off. He told me he talked to Captain Dak Johnsen about that Lobby incident, but he hasn't been on Damos for over a week. Tell them to send backup."

"Sir, you don't understand, I can't contact them. There's interference in the Network signal. It's like someone is jamming us."

Senjek had put his credentials away and turned back toward the cops. He felt something strike him in the temple and fell to the ground. Officer Dillin rushed toward the car and pulled out his pistol, but he fell to the ground with a bullet in his head. Officer Wykurt tried to escape, but her car backed into her colleague's. She changed gears, but it was too late. The assailant emptied the clip of her gun into the second officer.

"Ms. Yahn?" a voice called out. "We know you're in there. Don't get any smart ideas. Get out of the car."

The rest of the Lobby's party surrounded the vehicle. Treistina reluctantly exited the vehicle. She knew the woman that stood in front of her. Most citizens did. "Areka von Breischa. How did you find us?"

Areka did not look pleased. "Please. Your family might be enjoying political relevance now, but it's in my blood. You're just as arrogant as your brother. Coming to our doorstep wasn't that bright, either." Areka looked to her team. "Restrain her. Escort them to the palace. Dispose of the law enforcement. No one can know we're here."

"Restrain her? Ms. von Breischa," one protested.

"You take your orders from me! Not Daben. Not Ljero. Cuff them both and get them out of here!"

216

# A Fatal Vendetta

Senjek felt disoriented. He tried to get to his feet, but his legs crumbled beneath him. He leaned forward on his knees. He attempted to take note of his surroundings but found it difficult to think. "Hush darling," a woman's voice coyly whispered. "Don't fight it. Just a simple sedative. Nothing too romantic. It's not every day a girl meets the great and terrible Senjek Bohmet. I'd rather not rush things."

Senjek tried to look at who was speaking to him, but he felt a hard kick to his abdomen that put him on his back. The woman sat on top of him. His vision was still blurry. He couldn't make out who it was. "Who are you? Where am I?"

"She's pretty; I'll give you that. Such a famous warrior, running around with a normal girl." He felt her hands roam across his chest. "I'm pretty famous too, you know. Beyond my name, even. The von Breischa that defected." She slowly rubbed herself up and down against him. He felt her cold hands reach up inside his shirt. "She wouldn't have to find out, you know. Unless you think she'd like to join us. Have a little fun. So boring, being with the same girl. I tried it once, a relationship, I mean. Women understand me better, but they are insane."

Senjek tried to push her off him, but she grabbed his wrist and flipped him over. She straddled his back and grabbed him. "Maybe I was wrong. Naughty, aren't we?" she said, teasing him. She nibbled his ear and whispered to him. "I would fuck your brains out if you didn't break me in half first.

"That's enough, Areka!" Daben's voice echoed. It didn't matter how long it had been since they last met. Senjek could never forget that voice. "I applaud you for your work, but Senjek is my prize. I have plans for him. I won't have you jeopardizing those plans. Now get off him."

She giggled. "Sounds like daddy doesn't want us to play. Your loss," she teased again. She got to her feet and lifted him to his. She made sure he could stand on her own before letting go. "You boys play nice, now."

Daben's eyes didn't leave her until she exited the room. "Sorry. She was behaving so well before now. I guess you can only bottle up what's inside for so long. Of course, I don't have to tell you that, do I Senjek?"

Senjek blinked rapidly to get his head right. "Where are we?"

"Ah yes, the most important of information must be delivered," Daben declared. "Quite the survivalist. Unfortunately for you, we are in a place where you have no intimate knowledge of the grounds. Already, I see the wheels spinning in your mind. The quickest way to escape. No, you can't be lethal in your escape, you have a companion. You must account for her well-being. No, can't risk bringing her harm. Do you know the terrain? How far away is the forest? Could you evade law enforcement during your escape? Where are the roads? Is it day or night? The sewers, maybe? I know! Go up. You could go up as far as you can and take to the rooftops. But can Treistina make the jumps? Does she have the courage? It's so much harder to plan an escape when you know neither your location nor how far your dead weight will push herself to get away—"

"Enough!" Senjek shouted. His vision returned and the struggle to stand was fleeting. He closed his eyes. "This is a dream. This isn't happening! You would never come here."

Daben signaled his men to target Senjek. Laser sights covered his chest. "Rest assured, my friend. Your instincts, your skills, your knowledge; they can't help you this time. Enjoy the moment. Take a look around." Daben removed his holster and tossed it away. "Did you ever imagine you'd see this place? Say what you will about them," Daben smirked, "but you can't deny the Poleb family's taste."

Senjek started to pace back and forth, still fighting off the effects of the sedative. "I always thought you were the superstitious type, Daben. I never thought you'd look for me here."

"I hope you come to your senses and return to the Lobby. You clearly lack the mind to best me. I was waiting for you. After Ljero's tactics had failed, I found someone who would not fail me. Sure, her approach took more time, but this revolution is years in the making. What're a few days in the grand scheme?"

"I may lack your brilliance, yes," Senjek admitted, "but even you suspected I'd leave one day. The great Daben Celt, ready for anything. How long have you obsessed over finding me? How many nights did you dream of correcting your one mistake?"

"I had no control over Cineon's decision to let you go. My error was sending you to Eidolas that day. Stupid idea. Even though you grew into the man you were, it should have occurred to me they might not resist."

"Resist? They surrendered immediately, Daben! I had it under control, but you already had plans for Eidolas, didn't you? You were never going to spare them! We both regret that day, but I think your regret is that I didn't do it myself."

"You know very little, Senjek," Daben replied. "You think you are so smart and so wise to the world around you. You know so little, even of those around you. Those you trust, those you love. Dak, Evan, Treistina, all those you have befriended here. Do you really think their commitment to you, their friendship and love, outweighs that which the Lobby holds for you?"

"Is this your plan?" Senjek asked in disbelief. "All this time trying to get me back and that's all you have? Do you honestly think I would just choose the Lobby? You ask me to abandon my life as if I had merely forgotten about KILLER. As if I could forgive you for what you did. You just expect me to return after what happened?"

Daben walked back over to the throne and sat down. "Give Mr. Bohmet his weapons," he ordered. A Lobby member walked in and did as Daben said. Senjek watched as Selna and Kilinus fell to his feet. "Now that you have your weapons back, you must surely be plotting an escape in that mind of yours. You hold your infamy in your hands not to get away, but so you know I still trust you. I know you won't escape. You came here to hide." He smiled. "I trust you not to expose us here. I know you won't destroy your own life, even to spite me. I sincerely suggest, as a friend, that you reconsider."

Senjek nodded. "Always two steps ahead, Daben. Too bad it only took falling one step behind to lose me."

Daben's smile disappeared. "You make it seem as if you're the only member of the Lobby to have experienced loss. Do you still blame Cineon for what happened?"

"I blame you!" Senjek shouted.

Daben chuckled. "How can you blame me? Tell me how I made you weak."

Senjek shook his head. "No, you turned me into something I wasn't. It wasn't a moment of weakness; it was a flash of clarity. My eyes were finally open. For the first time in years. I was ashamed of what I had become."

Daben got to his feet. "Your eyes were opened? Is that why you fled to Damos? Why you abandoned your countrymen? You had forsaken everything we've done, everything you fought for and began helping our enemy! You betrayed your friends! Eidolas had to be taken care of. I did it so you could finally be the man the Lobby needed. And you left, making their sacrifice worthless! You disrespected the memory of your family every day you fought against me."

Senjek was about to say something, but he noticed Daben was still talking. At least it seemed that he was. Daben's lips continued to move, but Senjek heard nothing. He got the strangest feeling that someone was watching him. He knew something was wrong, but couldn't put his finger on it. He shook his head, and just like that; he was all right.

"What was that?" Daben asked. Senjek looked up at him, able to hear him again.

"I don't…"

Areka rushed into the room, much to Daben's distaste. He was about to reprimand her, but she spoke first. "We have a situation, sir! We have to move!"

Just as she finished speaking, all the windows in the room shattered. Daben jumped off the chair, covering his head as shards of glass littered the throne room. He pulled a pistol from his waistband. "Senjek, you idiot! You were followed!" He got to his feet and turned to face the center of the room. A wooden staff slammed into his forehead and instantly knocked him back down.

Senjek looked up to see a man standing over Daben. A man with hair longer and darker than any hair he'd ever seen in his life. The man looked around to observe the room. He appeared to be disgusted. His beard reached down to his stomach. His clothes were dark and raggedy. It appeared that he hadn't changed clothes in years. He spun his weapon

220

around a bit, positioning it above his head. The look of disgust turned to pure rage. With arms flexed and hands clinched, he brought the end of his staff down to crush Daben's throat.

That was his intent, at least. Areka had recovered and tackled him. She quickly got to her feet and made some distance from the intruder. "It's you, isn't it? Our little spy from a few weeks ago. How did you know that I love surprises?" Despite the fact that she was flirting with the man, she pulled a knife from her boot. "Daben is boring. Wouldn't you rather play with me?"

The man didn't respond. In fact, he ignored her and turned his attention back to Daben. Areka tried to slash his arm, but he was able to dodge her strike. He was faster than anyone she had ever seen. Even quicker than Cineon or Kalus Baena. She saw the staff fly toward her head, but her body just couldn't react in time. Senjek watched her collapse to the ground.

Senjek made eye-contact with the man. There was nothing but hatred in those gray eyes. He knew what this intruder must have been thinking. He tried to decide if Senjek was a threat and if he needed to stop him. He looked up to the balcony where every gun previously focused at Senjek now pointed to him. They looked too shocked to shoot. "That is probably for the best," he muttered. He resumed his approach on Daben, ready to strike again.

He was interrupted again, though. He turned to the sound of a gun cock behind him. One, two, three, four, five shots aimed right at his chest. They flew harmlessly away from the target. Some harmlessly into the walls and ceiling, others into the snipers positioned above. Senjek turned to see who was shooting. It was Treistina. He got to his feet to stop her, but Daben's would-be killer leaped the distance toward her. He watched as the intruder kicked her in the chest and knocked her through the damaged wall to the outside.

Senjek picked up his weapons on pure instinct. Daben must have had a Repulsor installed somewhere inside. That wouldn't stop him, though. Senjek had forgotten that this man was seemingly here to execute Daben. What he had just done to Treistina was all he needed to witness to act.

Senjek swung his gun-blades repeatedly at the intruder, in a fluid and graceful movement. The man strafed, turned, and ducked to dodge

Senjek's attacks. Senjek got frustrated at his inability to hit the man. He was so fast. He was barely missing with every attempt. He suspected the man was letting him get close to frustrate him. He didn't even try to use his staff to attack back. He was toying with Senjek. This only made the former Praesage angry; his swings became less graceful and erratic. He overextended himself with one swing, and that was enough. The man grabbed Senjek's arm and quickly pulled it down so that one blade blocked the other. He now held both Senjek's arms. He drove Senjek's weapons into the ground and head-butted him.

Senjek dropped his gun-blades as he fell. He had never been hit so hard in his life. He reached out, but the man kicked both gun-blades out of reach. Senjek got to his feet, but quickly felt the staff against his stomach. He dropped to one knee and gasped for breath.

One of the snipers finally gave the order to shoot. They all looked at him, in awe. "That man just took down a von Breischa, the Praesage, and Daben single-handedly! Kill him!"

They took aim and fired, but just as Treistina failed earlier, the bullets didn't get anywhere near to the target. He looked up at them. "I have no quarrel with you lot. You can't save him. I'll lay waste to every last one of you before Daben Celt lives."

Daben shouted out. "Archers!" The man turned to face his prey. "He must have some portable Repulsor of some kind. Don't shoot him! Get your bows!"

Trained to fight with or without a Repulsor present, the snipers put their rifles down and grabbed their crossbows. The man didn't even flinch. To the amazement of all, however, the arrows flew harmlessly away from him, just as the bullets had done.

Senjek crawled over to Areka. He rattled her arm to wake her up. More members of the Lobby entered the room, but Senjek feared what good it would do. He was amazed at how skilled this madman was. He clearly had no love for the Lobby, Daben in particular.

Areka seemed to be waking, but Senjek couldn't linger. The man had just reached the snipers via a series of jumps. He had taken one of the rifles from the ground. Senjek quickly ran up the stairs as each member of the Lobby was dispatched, one by one. The gun somehow behaved differently. The Radius Effect didn't grab the bullets. Every time he pulled the trigger a bullet found a home in someone's skull. The last sniper had reached for his gun. He tried to shoot, but still, the bullet flew in another direction. Senjek watched in disbelief as the gunman's neck snapped.

Senjek lifted Selna to attack, but the man jumped over the rail and landed on the first level. This man was bold, but Senjek knew he couldn't allow this rampage to continue. He stepped onto the rail and jumped toward the man. Weapons held above his head, he brought them down on his descent, hoping he could at least knock the man down.

His blades made contact with the staff. The wood splintered and gave way, and the gun-blades sank into the floor. Senjek suddenly realized his error. The man wanted Senjek to do that. He didn't realize it quickly enough, unfortunately.

With a hand on the outer edge of each end of the staff, he let go and moved his hands inward, grabbed hold of where it snapped, facing his palms toward him as he did it. He brought his arms together and struck Senjek on each temple with a broken half in one fluid motion. Senjek opened his eyes and saw that more bodies had entered the room. He suspected he briefly lost consciousness. Every blow was stronger than the last. The intruder used his whole body to throw one-half of his staff into the generator. The machine sputtered and whined before shutting down.

He pivoted on his foot, throwing his weight into his throw, and launched the other end of the bo at Areka. It struck her in the throat with such force that it crushed her throat, rendering her unable to scream from the pain of the blow as she was knocked unconscious from the strength of the blow.

Kilinus flew toward the man, who caught it in his hand. Senjek reached for Selna and pulled it close. He knew he couldn't stop this man. He was going to kill Daben and had given no thought to killing anyone that tried to stop him. He crawled away from the battle to look for Treistina.

Daben had twisted the barrel to fire his custom slugs. Slugs that had been developed to work within the Radius Effect. But like all other projectiles before, the bullet didn't reach the target. Daben pulled the trigger again, but all the shells exploded simultaneously. The gun shattered, and Daben cried out from the pain, lucky to survive. The man continued his approach, though. He inspected Senjek's weapon as he did so, amazed at the design.

Daben shuttered as he felt his own mortality. "Who are you?" he pleaded. "What do you want? What did I ever do to you?"

"My name is Devian Strife." He spoke his name loud enough for everyone to hear. Daben clutched his hand in pain and tried to back away, but found himself unable to move. The gray-eyed assailant showed the faintest of grins. "I know it has been such a long time, but I would have thought you would remember me. Perhaps not in name, but surely my face. You would have to have forgotten what you had done to forget me."


"Treistina! Treistina, are you OK?" Senjek cried. He pulled her into his arms. "Are you hurt?" She weakly nodded, but she didn't say anything. She was terrified. Tears of pain and fright ran down her face as she sobbed. "I'm coming back. I'm going to get us out of this. But you can't move like this. I'll find something. Just wait here."

Senjek cautiously made his way back into the room, Selna in hand. Strife had noticed. "You are most resilient, boy. And I applaud your courage. I know your mind. You are alone here. You are not like the others. You do not serve Daben Celt. Just walk away."

"That's it?" Senjek asked in disbelief. "You'll just let us go?"

"I'll let you go, yes," Devian responded. "I only came here for one man. And I thank you for your weapon. I want him to suffer in his demise." He continued to inspect the weapon. He looked utterly fascinated as if he had never seen one before. "The craftsmanship, it's unique. It's quite beautiful, yet bizarre." He leaned in closer to examine it. "The hilt is so strange. Almost like a gun. This even looks like a trigger."

That was the last thing he said before the Kilinus violently shook as he pulled the trigger. He clearly hadn't expected that to happen. It was so close to his face that it jumped up and gashed his face. He growled out in pain. He dropped the weapon to clutch his face.

Senjek saw Daben reloading as he got to his feet. Senjek ran over and tackled Daben before he could fire. "Look, just get out of here!" He turned to face the man, but he wasn't there. The intruder was gone.

# 30. TRUTHS REVEALED

Members of the Lobby flooded the throne room, guns drawn. Some searched the room for the intruder. Some took aim at Senjek and demanded the weapon that he was now holding. During the confusion, he had acquired a pistol. A single blade holstered to his back, the other left abandoned on the ground by the invader. Senjek had the gun cocked and ready to fire. He demanded an explanation as to what happened. He inched closer to Daben and demanded answers. Lobby members aiming at Senjek increased, demanding that he put the gun down.

"No, I don't think so," he muttered to himself.

"I'm done keeping secrets from you, Senjek," Daben cautioned. "Put the gun down, and my men will do the same. I swear it. I'll even go first. Men, lower your weapons." Daben's words were made to look like a lie. His people neglected his command and continued to take aim on Senjek. "I said to lower your weapons!" he shouted. After a few shared looks, they finally complied. "Good, thank you. Senjek, will you do the same? Do you want to hear what I have to say?"

"No. I don't want to listen to what you have to say. What I want is the truth. I want Treistina left out of this, and I want my safety guaranteed."

"Treistina is in my custody," Daben argued. "Our little party crasher is gone. I have complete control of this little hideout of mine. You have nothing to bargain with. The only play you have is to alert your friend Evan. If you try to call for help, however, I will sell you out as the wanted criminal you are."

Senjek reset the hammer on the pistol and placed it inside his waistband. He didn't trust Daben enough to throw the gun, or his blade, away. "I understand that you have an unprecedented need to be in control. At the very least promise me that she will be kept safe."

Daben stepped away from Senjek and walked behind the throne. He appeared to be inspecting some objects. "You aren't in a strong negotiating position. You must know this. I obviously have a personal stake in the girl's safety, especially in regards to yourself. You don't have to worry about her."

"And what about this Devian person?"

Daben looked to be relatively calm regarding the situation. He lifted up a bottle. Upon closer inspection, he smiled. He removed the cork and lowered it. Next, he grabbed a glass and placed a single ice cube inside before pouring a drink. "I'm not sure. Could have been any number of things." He grabbed a cigar and quickly made it ready to be lit. "It may come as a shock, but I am as surprised as you are."

"You said no more secrets," Senjek warned, resisting the urge to grab a weapon.

Daben sat on the throne again. It was at this moment that Senjek noticed Daben's shaken state. "Of course. My apologies. Not any number of things. Only two possibilities that I can surmise." The cigar shrunk rapidly with each puff. Dark gray smoke rose to the ceiling. The smell was pleasing and putrid at the same time. "I don't know for certain. That much is true. I can only guess that he was either a member of The Renaissance Watch or an agent at the disposal of The Unknown Council."

"What is The Renaissance Watch?"

Daben took another drag from his cigar. "I'm still not entirely sure. I've only gotten bits and pieces of information concerning the group. I know enough that they play against Lobby interests. Some of the more ridiculous rumors would put the Republic proper to worry as well. The Unknown Council is apparently also interested in them, but I don't know to what end. Nodo didn't provide me with any proof to substantiate his claims. May have just been spinning me a story."

Senjek sat down on a bench facing Daben. "Perhaps Nodo didn't, but what about Naieena?"

Daben continued to smoke his cigar. "Naieena? Who's that?"

226

"Don't play stupid with me, Daben," Senjek replied, agitated. "Naieena Haeese. I suspect she's related to Nodo somehow."

Daben dropped his cigar. His expression quickly turned to anger. "What? Did you say Haeese?"

"Yes, she approached me a few weeks ago. I assume you got to her through Nodo."

Daben stood up and slammed his glass to the ground. The dark amber fluid spread across the floor, carrying the shattered remains of the chalice even further out. "You stupid, fucking idiot!"

Senjek quickly got to his feet, surprised by Daben's reaction. "What? What's wrong with you?"

Daben buried his face in his hands. "So close," he whispered to himself. He pulled his hands away to look at Senjek again. He could tell immediately that his former omen was unaware of what he had encountered. Daben tried to stay as calm as he possibly could. "This Naieena that you met is not in league with Nodo or the Lobby. Haeese is one of the five houses of Moashei."

Senjek felt a knot in his stomach. Could it be true? Could they still exist? "No," he said, immediately dismissing the idea. "That's bullshit. The Unknown Council, if they ever existed, have been gone for centuries. We would know about them. No way hey could keep their existence a secret for so long."

"If they ever existed. Listen to you. A few years on Damos and you think like them now. You would deny the beliefs we hold true. Besides, secrets are easy if you tell few enough people. I've kept you, The Praesage, a secret," Daben countered. "I've spoken to them, through Nodo as an intermediary. The Unknown Council still walk among us, I promise you. And you were contacted by one of their agents. And you let her slip through your fingers."

"Fuck you, Daben," Senjek said. "If I let this person escape me, it's because I was running from your attack dogs."

"You think you are safe in Evan's world?" Daben shouted. "Whose ears do you think they whisper into now? The Unknown Council betrayed their own people. They betrayed the monarchy. They won't stop until this entire system is under their control. They will lead us all to ruin with the Republic's own hand! They've already begun with the degradation of

Kramei. Our entire way of life is in peril, and no one but me can see it! You saw it once, Senjek. Then you abandoned us. Make up for that. Return to the Lobby. Become the Praesage once more. Fight for the freedom of everyone. Fight for a new government that isn't influenced by ghosts!"

"Wow," Senjek gasped. He couldn't believe what he was hearing. "You've gone mad. You are totally, irrevocably insane. You would use fairy tales and myths and magic to justify your actions. And you are diluted enough to believe them yourself. You're a tyrant in the making."

"Explain this Devian person, then! You think yourself to be so wise. You think that you see the world as it truly is. You tell me. Were you not here? Did you not see what he did? How else would you explain what's happening?"

"He kicked my ass; I saw that. I saw him handle Areka and me like we were children. He had one mark, and he only killed those who tried to get in his way. And you let all those men die for you. Your training is embedded deep in your followers' minds. Even I was trying to stop him, purely on instinct. Trying to protect the man I despise."

"You are in denial, Bohmet! Guns didn't work on him. Arrows did not work on him! He fired freely on my men, and they couldn't shoot back. It wasn't a Repulsor keeping him safe; he was using magic."

Senjek chuckled. It suddenly occurred to him what was going on. "This is another one of your tricks, isn't it? Daben Celt at his finest. The foremost expert in manipulating the minds of others. He makes people turn on each other. Then he turns around and asks you to be so thankful for everything he's given you. He takes away so much, and in the end, you're happy for it. It's a gift."

"Spare me your misguided self-righteousness. You stand there thinking yourself so much better than me. Everyone knows about what the Lobby did on Eidolas. Everyone knows that the Praesage just stood by and watched. Let it happen. You made a choice that day, and you chose Cineon. You picked the Lobby. For a short time, you believed in our message more than anyone, even me."

The words cut through Senjek's heart like a knife. He demanded the truth from Daben. He was speaking it now. He felt like he was somewhere else. Back on Kramei. Saddled on a horse next to the Fury. Cineon gave

228

one command. Senjek gave out another. They didn't obey the Praesage. Cineon offered him a way out. A way to end it. "I couldn't. I lie awake every night regretting what I did. What I didn't do. Telling myself over and over, that if it happened all over again, that I would have stopped it. My soul would be tarnished one way or the other. I know better now, but the price of ending it wasn't greater than letting it continue."

"Perhaps the conflict of mind is what swayed Cineon," Daben replied, coming to a realization of his own. "He saw what you let him do and he couldn't bear to look you in the eye knowing that he destroyed the Praesage. You are a shell of a man. A shadow of what you were when you woke up that day. Perhaps I am to blame after all."

Senjek turned away from Daben. He would have liked to strangle the man if he weren't grief-stricken. For the first time since that day, he saw the reason. He understood why Daben had done it. He had cursed his name every day in between. "What should have become your greatest accomplishment became your biggest defeat. You took everything from me that wasn't the Lobby. Is today the day you ask me to thank you?"

Daben felt that he was near to breaking Senjek. "What would you thank me for? You let Cineon live and sacrificed your conscious for nothing. Would you thank me for your lavish estate in the capital? Your home that is paid for with the suffering of the people you once fought to liberate? Certainly don't thank me for the fate of every man, woman, and child at Eidolas that day. You let them die for Kramei, only to leave us all to perish. You would even thank me for Treistina until you thought better of it."

"Don't speak about her as a consequence of my actions. She's not the result of your grand scheme."

"Senjek Bohmet. You insult me. There are indeed consequences for blade and gun. Many things are the product of my schemes. Treistina Yahn is neither. I made sure that her passport credentials were invalid when you tried to bring her for that ever so romantic outing. Had to make sure that people didn't ask the right questions about Hotel Iedenia. Of course, the only thing I ever questioned was how Eve Gie managed to survive."

Senjek struggled with what he had just heard. In his unconscious mind, he already knew what Daben was suggesting. The thought never surfaced, though. He wouldn't let himself even think it. He merely stood there. Giving Daben a stare that demanded the meaning to his words.

"Every piece on the board is mine to play, General Bohmet. It was only your own ignorance to think that I lacked the vision to anticipate how you reacted. Did you truly believe that I would let you go so easily? All that time with her. You never, even once, suspected that I was watching you? I call myself Daben Celt to evoke the freedom fighters that brought this palace to ruin. It wasn't mistrust for the Yahn name."

Senjek turned to face Daben again. He had to look into his eyes to know if he was lying. He could always tell when he was lying. He made a promise on Eidolas to never let Daben Celt hurt him again. He gave Daben the satisfaction of his tears. Hot, wet, stupid tears. How could he have manufactured such a thing? Why would he? "This is low," he bellowed, voice cracking. "This is lower than anything I thought you might be capable of doing."

"It's alright, Senjek. You're home now. You are with your brothers and sisters. I have done nothing to harm you. I've only opened your eyes to see what matters most. And it is the most important thing in your life."

"Just another lie," Senjek gasped, short of breath.

"I didn't intend for the two of you to become what you are now. It wasn't my intent to give you such a thing, I admit. In fact, it's so much the one thing I tried to take away from you. And I was wrong for it. Taking your family away is what destroyed the Praesage. It was your passion that made you great. And I delivered it back to you, albeit unintentionally. And your resolve is so much stronger now. More powerful than it ever was."

Senjek fell to his knees. "It's just another trick. I saw straight through your plan to rid me of my humanity. I thought you made a great error. Daben Celt fell a step behind. But you never did. You were still two steps ahead. How could you do this to me?"

"Do what? The plan was to observe you from afar. There were rules, Senjek. Rules that I made very clear that were ultimately ignored. The result was the same. It goes against my plans for you, but this story is not written by me alone. It has ideas of its own. Don't think less of you or herself. I assure you that it is real. You have always been like a second son to me. Don't be ashamed if that one day becomes a reality."

230

# 31. CHANGING THE GAME

No one would dare cross the border. Perhaps even with orders to do so. Police surrounded the estate. Almost the entire Damosi military was in conflict on Kramei, blockading the planet, or held hostage on the West Fork of Moaschen. Veian Grebllyh was one of the few battle-hardened in attendance. There were those who questioned his competence following his failure at the Plains of Harvest, but local law enforcement was hardly qualified to lead such an assault. There was no reply to the many warnings issued. Many whispers spread across the ranks in regards to the situation. All three were inside. The triumvirate of the Lobby. The Master, Daben Celt. The Fury, Cineon Yahn. The Praesage, Senjek Bohmet.

His anonymity relinquished when he refused to play ball with his former allies. Many had returned after the incident concerning an other after he intervened with affairs. Daben had planned ahead for much, but his fallibility was exposed. A plan for every possible situation. Even without a plan, the presence of himself, the Praesage, and a von Breischa were barely enough to stop his assault. Many pawns fell to this knight. Daben always tried to be a step ahead, but he wasn't the only one making plans for this new wild card.

Treistina opened her eyes. She stood amongst a battle field. She saw the castle ablaze. She felt her heart drop. Her initial fear of Senjek being inside, or worse, responsible, quickly subsided. The landscape somehow looked much different. She couldn't see the new roads paved in the distance. She felt like a ghost standing among some event which happened long ago. Her senses refused to believe her surroundings. She saw things going up in flames. People and objects being thrown about with no apparent outside force causing it. Few had guns, but as odd as that was, there was no evidence of a Repulsor nearby to make a man think twice about pulling the trigger.

It was then that she saw him. He looked almost familiar to her, though he was as strange as everything else. He was different. He walked among the chaos as if it were not real. She could feel a cold stare fixed upon her and she knew it was the same man. She was doing everything she could to keep both worlds apart, though they were inherently the same. She could have never had one without the other. And yet this stranger persisted. Why was here? He had no business getting involved. He continued his pursuit, and she felt powerless. Could not flee. Could not hide. Who was he? Why was he approaching her?

"Who are you!" she screamed.

He continued toward her, seemingly ignorant to her words. His eyes were dead as if you could not show them a single thing they hadn't yet seen. She felt vulnerable. She reached for a gun, a spear, a club, anything. There was nothing at hand. She trembled as he continued toward her. Helpless. As helpless as she felt on Iedin. The day she knew she could not do her duty. Those caves that were so hypnotizing, yet so liberating and enlightening. Treistina remembered that day when she discovered she had a choice in how she lived her life. That beautiful day with Senjek when he took her to Jade Peak. She closed her eyes to escape to that day. That perfect day. She never wanted to leave that place. She knew then that her past would catch up with her. She lived in denial for so long after that day. She enjoyed the lie as long as she possibly could. She always hoped the dream wouldn't end.

And so she stood there. In strange surroundings, eyes squeezed shut. She was afraid of many things: Senjek dying, going back or finding out. None of those things brought her the level of dread she experienced now. She felt something right above her. Something dark. Something judging. She wanted to open her eyes and face it, but she was too frightened. This was something else. Something no one expected.

# A Fatal Vendetta

She shuddered as she heard an explosion nearby, but still kept her eyes shut. She didn't want to know what was going on around her. She heard men shouting. They were ecstatic. It sounded as though some great victory happened. What was going on? She knew that she must be dreaming, but of what? She almost opened her eyes, but she was too scared. Too frightened of what she might see. She was worried she would see Senjek. Was he captured? Was he dead? Was he leading the Lobby to victory? She couldn't bear the thought of any of those things being true.

Treistina knew it was only a dream. She only had to open her eyes, and it would all be over. All over. It was simple enough, she thought to herself. Just open your eyes. It would be OK. Senjek would be there, and that would be enough. Her and Senjek together despite it all. There was so much she would have to explain to him, but as long as he would be with her, that was enough. It was time to be brave. Time to open her eyes and be with Senjek.

And then she did. Her eyes suddenly pried open. She saw what she had convinced herself not to expect. The ruin of the monarchy. The palace ravaged by a battle so long ago that history could not agree on what happened. Her mind had wandered. She was where she had been the entire time. A relic of older days, Monarch Fall was the perfect place for Daben to hide; a place which local law prohibited admittance. There were none that surrounded the area, too scared and superstitious to enter. It was all in her head. It was all guilt. Guilt in not being forward and honest with Senjek about who she really was. It was all just a nightmare. She could almost hear his voice. "Treistina? Treistina, are you OK?"

"No. I'm not," she wanted to shout, but she didn't. Somehow couldn't.

"I'm coming back. Just wait here. You are not like the others. Just walk away."

She opened her eyes. There was nothing. She stood in the old palace and didn't see a single soul. She was beginning to think that perhaps she had died. Maybe dreams went on after the dreamer was gone.

"No."

She quickly turned around. She saw the castle burning, though much more majestic in flames did it look now than what it did in ruin as she knew it. None if it made sense. She tried to run away from it all, but she was stuck there. It had to be a dream. It had to be.

"And it is," a strange voice said. "I would tell you to choose, but I know that you cannot make a true choice. You will do as you have always done. What you've been instructed to do."

Treistina was frantic. She turned 'round and 'round looking for the man who was speaking. "Who are you? Why are you doing this?" she pleaded.

"I made a promise to you, Treistina. I promised that I would never do anything to hurt you. I promised that I would look after you. I can't ever take back what I did, but I promise that I can keep you safe. Please believe me. Please trust me. Please, just wake up. Please. Are you OK? Are you hurt?"

She opened her eyes, almost uncertain of what she would see, but she had hoped. Her hope had rewarded her. He was there and cradled her in his arms. It was him; it was Senjek. She nodded weakly, unable to speak. She felt strange. Something was wrong.

"I did what I could. Please remember that I didn't want this. This isn't what I wanted. I wanted for you not to know this hardship. Forgive me, Treistina. I wanted better for us, better for you."

"Why are you saying this," she wearily asked. "You aren't going anywhere. You aren't leaving now. Not after all of this."

"Poor child," a strained voice replied. "He's not here. I'm sorry to say that I don't know when you will be reunited."

Treistina's senses finally returned to her. She sat up on a bed, but too quickly. She immediately fell on her back, caught by the soft bed beneath her. Had she dreamed the whole thing?

"You have been a very bad girl, Ms. Yahn," the strained voice teased. She knew it could only be one person. "Rest assured that Daben will use you for your worth. And I hope that I can see that invader again. Repay him for what he has done."

"Areka," Treistina gasped. She was frightened. More frightened than she might have thought she could be. She opened her eyes and saw the woman behind the stories. "What did you do to me? Was I drugged?"

The suggestion brought a chuckle to her captor's lips. "Do you mean those dreams you were having?" Treistina tried to feign ignorance, but Areka saw straight through it. "I could hear some of your mumblings; I couldn't help but overhear. Alas, I did nothing. You can thank my friend for that."

234

"I'm no friend of yours, von Breischa," replied the girl. Treistina had felt like she had seen her before. The gray eyes were familiar. "Do not use me as some pawn. You haven't told Daben about me, and for that I'm grateful, but don't use me to leverage your own agenda."

"The von Breischa that defected," Areka retorted. "Isn't that what you said the first time you saw me?"

The girl didn't answer.

"My apologies, Treistina. People have been having some strange dreams ever since I detained Naieena here. Some may even call them prophetic."

"Naieena?" Treistina replied, alarmed. "You're the one that gave me that note! You're the one who told me to stay away from here!"

"A warning you certainly took very seriously," Areka replied out of turn. "Naieena, my darling. Have you not been forthcoming with me? You told me you had no idea who our attacker was and yet you warned Treistina not to come here. Almost as if you knew what was about to happen. How very interesting." She paced around the girl as she sat, tied to a chair. There was no reply. "All the same, I'm glad I kept you hidden away. I can always tell when someone is hiding something."

"How can you expect me to have known what this Devian was about to do? I'm not what you think I am."

"No, you are," Areka replied, unconvinced. "Still, the bastard has no idea what he's done. He's ruined everything. Everything has changed. And not for the better, as he might have hoped, I'm sure. You performed wonderfully, though."

Treistina looked up when she realized the last comment was for her. "I'd take it back if I could."

Areka sat at the edge of Treistina's bed and placed a hand on her leg. "You can't, though, can you?" Areka grabbed Treistina by her hair and yanked her out of bed and onto the ground. "I should kill you right now! You know that, right?" Treistina tried to reply, but there was a forearm pressed too tightly too her throat. "I nearly died because of you. I'm only trying to do what is right, and you almost got me killed for it. You are very important to a lot of important men, Treistina. But I'm no man. I have plans of my own. Give me one reason why I should keep you alive."

"I fell in love with him, Areka."

Areka let her go. She seemed to find some satisfaction in Treistina gasping for air. "Pathetic. You almost disappoint me, Treistina. You were given such a small and simple assignment. I cannot fault you for your heart, though. I would give anything for a man to look at you the way that Senjek does. Or a woman. But that doesn't matter now. I am resigned to my fate. I chose my path a long time ago. You could even say that it was chosen for me. I won't deny you that which I never had. You can stay here, a trading token, or you can leave and seek asylum with the Damosi. I understand that neither choice is preferable, but you have a choice. Know that if you stay here, you will not be allowed to be by his side. Not unless he cooperates. Even then, Daben won't let you be together unless his goals come to fruition. You know what he once was. Will you stand by him if he decides to be the Praesage again? Be the Praesage again for you?"

"Why would you just let me run away to the enemy? Is this part of Daben's scheme? To bring Senjek back down to his primal instinct? Remove everything he fights for, and he will lapse back to what he once was?"

Areka helped Treistina to her feet. She was surprised by this. Everything she knew of Areka von Breischa clashed with the woman's current actions. "I am not entirely without pity. Apparently not without stupidity, either. I must be half out of my mind to even give you this choice. Everyone has to sleep at night, though. I won't have you on my conscious. Tell me what your choice is, and I will either see to it or chose not see it. Ask me anymore about it, and you will continue to be a pawn to your father's ambition."

Treistina soon found herself sitting in the back of an unmarked vehicle. She didn't know where she was going. Her only company was a person of less-than-savory qualities. How this traitor climbed the ranks of her father's movement was unfathomable. Her talents were many, and she held a beauty that was unlike other women. Treistina thought her as a person of good looks but could see how others might think otherwise. Every part of her said not to trust this woman. But what choice did she have? This was her only way out. Her only hope of having a future with Senjek. At least she hoped so.

Areka von Breischa had a promising life as a citizen of the Republic. Not just citizenship, but a military career. Her family had a long tradition

236

of service. Dating back to the monarchy, the von Breischa were famous for having minds wired for war. When she thought about it, Areka's actions should have been surprising. "What game are you playing?"

Areka focused on an old book. It was a history of the Second Damosi Patrician Regiment. A group that often contained at least one member of her family. She seemed confused by the question. "Game? I gave you a choice, girl. Nothing more. If you don't appreciate my help, I can turn this car around and bring you back to your father."

"And when you explain why you took me away from Monarch Fall in the first place?"

"I'm sorry, did you not see what that man did in there? He was clearly after Daben for a reason. I don't think he's an enemy of the Lobby as much as an enemy of Daben. He would have killed Daben and left. He could ransom you to get to Daben. You need protecting. You aren't safe at Monarch Fall. Just creating distance until we know it's safe to return. Simple as that."

Good enough an answer for her father. Areka's reputation proceeded her. She wasn't without pity like she said. If there were any chance of this backfiring on her, though, she wouldn't have acted. "And what happens when you return without me? What do you tell my father then? What do you tell Senjek?"

"I won't be returning without you. I'm not long for this world. My destination is Kramei."

"Kramei? How do you expect to do that? With all that's going on you think you can just fly off world?"

"Hostility with the Republic has been going on for a long time. Daben was able to bring a large group of us to the belly of the beast. Even before war broke out, Daben was a wanted criminal. If he could infiltrate the Capitol, I can get out. Your brother is leading the attack. I'll not allow Espera Rimeax to be responsible for our army. It should have been me in charge from the start."

Cineon was a quality commander in his own right, but Areka would have been more qualified. "I suppose you should only expect so much trust shown to a turncoat."

Areka closed her book. "My loyalty has never wavered. Never. My commitment evolves, just as yours. You were sent to Damos to monitor

Senjek. You had a clear mission to assist in a cause that you believed in. And what did you do? You actively sought to evade us. You fought against us as we tried to acquire him. You once owed your allegiance to the Lobby. Now you serve your own interests. Don't speak about my affiliation with KILLER as if you have the moral high ground."

"And where does your loyalty lie, Areka? I fell in love with Senjek. Something that would have never happened if I wasn't sent to keep him out of trouble. How exactly did being a member of the Republic's greatest military family lead you to rise against it?"

Areka was irritated. She was doing a favor to Treistina. She could understand her skepticism, but it exhausted her. Even if she explained her intentions (she wasn't going to), this girl would never know. Already so blind to so much in the world. "I suppose one would have to be, to fall in love with him. Knowing what he was," she muttered under her breath.

Treistina strained to listen, but she couldn't make sense of what was said. Maybe it was the injuries to her throat. Her thoughts focused on what happened back at the palace. None of it made any sense. The things she saw. Such impossible things. If Areka wouldn't talk about herself, maybe she would talk about what had befallen them. "Who was that? What was that?"

Areka suddenly looked more reserved than usual. You could always tell that she knew more than what she said, but not now. She didn't seem to know anything, but she never knew nothing. If she did, she looked like she knew something. There was nothing in her eyes. A look of obliviousness. She had something to hide. "Did you ever hear the story of Kal-Vass the False?"

"I'm not interested in your stories, Areka. I want answers. Who was that?"

Areka bit her lip. "You ask for more than what you're entitled to know." She cracked the window of the car to let in a breeze. "I'm not sure. No one who's meant to be. Someone who shouldn't exist."

"Is it so hard to believe that Senjek is the only person that spurred Daben?"

"Senjek never launched a one-manned assault against a Lobby outpost that no one knew about." Treistina was about to respond, but Areka knew what she was going to say. "Senjek finding Daben was a fluke. You two were going there to hide. Never in your wildest dreams did you expect to find him there. This man was looking for Daben. Not only that, but my guess, he was looking for a ghost."

"You aren't making any sense."

"None of this make sense. That wasn't a Repulsor. I don't care how advanced or compact the technology becomes, it can't do that to arrows. They're too primitive. Too slow. Let yourself be fooled like all the rest. I know what I saw."

"And what did you see?"

Areka reached into her shirt through the collar. She pulled out a small medallion hanging around her neck and let it rest on her chest so Treistina could see it. It bore a symbol resembling an X. An old symbol or crest most likely. Areka ran a finger over the design, caressing it. "Do you recognize it?"

Treistina had leaned forward as much as she dared in order to inspect it. She had an idea, but couldn't be sure. "No, I don't think so."

"You're either lying, or Kramei schools need more funding. Though I suppose it's history is further removed from such things." She tugged on the medallion with a quick jerk, snapping the chain loose from her neck. She gently tossed the necklace into Treistina's lap. While she inspected it, Areka continued. "It dates back to the old Moaschen Empire. When the monarchy rose to prominence during the empire's collapse, this was one of a few like it that survived. I'm not sure how many survive to this day, but I know there are two in my family. My brother Baron has the other one. Or he did, at least, if he's still alive."

She continued to explain the significance of the medallion. There were as many as seven during the height of the Damic Kingdom. In those days there were an elite group of seven individuals. Each member wore the medallion as a sign of their rank. Initially charged with the preservation of their colony, this group evolved to be the protectors of their king. Of course, these people ultimately failed in that charge the day the Republic came to be. These medallions were nothing more than heirlooms in the present day.

"Why are you telling me all this? What does it have to do with anything?"

"That medallion is a reminder of our past. As great and powerful as the old Moashei were, they still fell. In their hour of need, when they relied on their protectors for salvation, they fell. The monarchy relied on them, and they fell. The Republic has chosen to depend on them, and they too will fall."

Treistina tried to think of who these protectors were that Areka referred too. She looked over to Naieena, who had remained quiet next to her. She thought about asking what her excuse would be if Daben discovered this witch had been smuggled away as well. Something compelled her not to ask; there would be no point. Even if Areka gave her some type of answer, she couldn't trust the reply. Her thoughts returned to the medallion and fallen dynasties. Her eyes met with Naieena, and somehow the answer was in her mind. Areka, like so many others, had recently begun to do so, was talking about ghosts.

# 32. A NEW ASSIGNMENT

Evan sat in his office and reviewed reports from Harvest as they arrived. He hadn't received any raw Network footage; most of it was news reports that a positive spin on events. There was a knock at the door, but he ignored it. He told his secretary that he didn't want to be disturbed. "How did everything get so fucked?" he asked himself.

He stood up from his desk and walked over to the window. The view of the city was nearly unrivaled. He could see the new road under construction. The DNC building towered over the entire landscape, even the presidential estate. Most of the major commercial channels were broadcast directly from the building.

The majority of all information passed through the central hub underground. Evan had just signed an executive order to limit all traffic from the Kramei hub to go through that hub. The government was a big part of the consortium, but a business decision forced by law would anger shareholders. It was necessary, in Evan's mind. He would not be convinced otherwise. Not by anyone.

There was another knock at the door. The president's irritation was growing. He had made it known that he did not want to be bothered. He leaned over his desk and pushed the small red button on the intercom. "I said to cancel all my appointments, Svetlana. Why is someone at my door?"

"I'm sorry, Mr. President. It's Corporal Grebllyh. He insisted, said it would be okay."

# The Kramei Insurrection

The man was unwavering in all his pursuits. He never knew when to quit. There could be only one reason why he had come. There would be no point in sending him away. He would only delay the inevitable confrontation. "Send him in," Evan said. He watched the marine walk into the room. Evan could see the physical toll the Corporal took when he failed to retake the Repulsor. The mental weight he carried for the men left behind. "It wasn't your fault, Veian."

Veian ignored the words. "Besen shouldn't have been there, Evan. I should have never let him be a part of the mission."

"Let him? He was in charge of the mission, Veian. You need to stop blaming yourself." Veian's guilt only angered him. Veian was a soldier on a battlefield. Soldiers falter. Soldiers die. Soldiers didn't put Besen in that situation. Evan did.

The wounded soldier was evidently unmoved by the president's absolution. He hadn't come for forgiveness. He wanted something more. "I know you and Dak are friends. I also know that you wouldn't let that friendship place a man in a role he isn't qualified for. When you proposed the naval raid of the Moashei Field, Mr. Johnsen was one of the few who supported it. He was able to gather enough support to overwhelm parliament's objections. And in the end, a clear and present threat to our society was neutralized."

"I'm sensing a point coming soon."

Veian smiled to himself. Evan wasn't one to succumb easily to flattery. It was a quality attribute lacking in most politicians. "Of course, sir. I understand your guilt, and with all due respect, as the man who failed to save him, I choose to shoulder my share of the blame. I also wish to carry my weight in making his loss worth something. The doctors say I am in good health. I'm here to request my post be restored. I want to go back to Harvest and finish what we started. Dak will need real soldiers to defeat Cineon."

Evan pulled a piece of paper from his desk. He carefully examined the words. "You are a good and loyal soldier, Mr. Grebllyh." Veian might have left at that, knowing his request was about to be denied, but he would not disrespect the man. Not after all that he had lost. He was given the piece of paper to read himself. He was nearly at a loss for words when he finished reading it.

"I don't understand."

"You are a good and loyal soldier, Mr. Grebllyh. I could think of no man better for the task."

Veian should have felt honored. There would have been many who would have been honored by the assignment. He felt as though this was an insult to his skillset. "By your own admission, if I may, sir... I am a soldier. Not a bodyguard."

Evan did not appear as though he would be swayed. "Would you call yourself a friend, Veian? As I am friends with Dak and Senjek? Would you not look out for my family and me as they have done? How many people with the name Gie are you willing to see buried? You would simultaneously commend Dak for his skill and condemn him for being my friend. Your military career stands on its own merits. I'm sure it didn't hurt that she always thought you were cute."

"Evelyn has a small army guarding her. The best soldiers Iedin has to offer. I would be almost useless among their ranks." He received another letter. This one signed by Kaleb Vardos. He withdrew the personal detachment afforded to Eve by the Iedenian Guard. "Are they insane? They can't do that. It's treason!"

Evan shook his head, "No, it's retaliation. Every member of the Guard shares varying degrees of outrage over Dak being appointed Suzerain. None more than General Vardos. I can't say I fault him. Historically the General of the Guard should hold this position. My decision to name a Suzerain might have been met with less rage if I gave it to one of them. I trust Dak. I don't trust Vardos. Even if had appointed one of their own, I believe his reaction would have been the same. Sure I might still have some friends on Iedin had I selected Kalus Baena, but that would have been risky. If the Guard were willing to commit, I wouldn't need a Suzerain. Least of all one under Vardos' thumb."

Veian was dumbfounded. To think Kaleb Vardos would behave that childishly was baffling. Even so, the Lobby crossed a line. Even if you could look past previous hostilities, Cineon had committed an act of war. If they would not take arms now, when would they? There were already rumors that the Lobby had committed acts of violence in the streets of Damos. Would a full invasion of the homeland need to happen before they assisted?

The Kramei Insurrection

"Sir, it breaks my heart what happened to Wele and Besen. I don't want anything to happen to Eve, either. I believe that my service to this country is better served on the ground. On Kramei." He had to think about what he would say next. He didn't want to defy the President openly, but he could hardly be blamed for side-stepping protocol when Evan did it without a second thought.

"My mind is made up. My sister is as safe here as she would be on Iedin. You will command the personal guard for the chamberlain's estate; with her safety being your primary focus. I have already chartered a ship, and she is on her way home. I want you to vet candidates personally. I expect a list this time tomorrow."

Veian had no choice. He knew his worth. He would willfully relegate himself to this role. "I don't think this is the best use for me, sir. If I have to, I will contact Dak Johnsen and request that he draft me back into combat. Against Cineon and the Lobby."

Evan was less than thrilled. He walked over to Veian and got close. Somewhat uncomfortably so. "You do what you have to, Corporal. Things are getting dicey on Kramei. I wouldn't expect an immediate reply from Captain Johnsen. Even if the answer is to your liking, I know you will do your duty. I trust that you will do what I have asked in the mean time. Can I trust you to do that, soldier?"

Veian took a step back and presented arms. "Sir, yes sir, Mr. President. I will begin vetting candidates for the presidential guard after I submit my request to Captain Johnsen."

The president nonchalantly returned the salute. When he lowered his hand, it was motioning toward the chair. "Have a seat, Commander of the Guard. There is more I wish to discuss with you, now that you're here." Veian straightened his shirt as he sat down. His dress blues would have been more appropriate in this setting, but he wore his fatigues. The uniform was designed to blend in with the sands that now covered a great deal of Kramei's surface. "I think a new uniform may be in order. Something befitting of your new post. Maybe it's time to form the Fourth Damosi Patrician Regiment."

Veian couldn't help but laugh at the antiquated term. Not because it wasn't fitting, but because the idea was absurd. Perhaps not as ridiculous as compared to Evan's recent decisions, but crazy nonetheless. He

244

received a cold stare from Evan as he sat down, unamused. "My apologies, Mr. President. You've appointed a Suzerain already. Reforming the DPR? What's next?" He leaned in close as if to whisper. "Are you about to declare yourself king?"

"Droll, commander. Very droll," Evan replied. "This country needs to be prepared for what's coming. Daben Celt will stop at nothing. I was hoping, sincerely hoping, the people of Kramei could be placated before it came to war. We will need every man when the time comes. I had hopes to appeal to Cineon. I thought perhaps he would lay down his arms, but I failed to give him the proper incentive. Apparently."

Veian was surprised to hear that. He was unaware of any negotiations with the Lobby. "You contacted Cineon? When? How? The DNC has quarantined communication with the Kramei hub. You made it very clear that the Republic views them as terrorists. We don't negotiate with terrorists. Does Parliament know about this?"

The look on Evan's face was all the answer that was needed. The President was playing a much bigger game than anyone had realized. He circumvented Parliament wherever possible. This much was clear to Veian. Senjek, a relative nobody, was being used in military training. Dak Johnsen, while a capable naval officer, was appointed Acting General of the Armies of Damos. Now that man was Suzerain. He was going to reform the DPR, even if in name only. What else was Evan hiding?

Evan opened a biometric safe, tuned to his fingerprint. He pulled out a dark green folder marked as eyes only. "What I am about to tell you is beyond confidential. A secret executive order written after most of the surviving members of the Third Damosi Patrician Regiment died under mysterious circumstances. To disclose any of this information to any unauthorized person is punishable by death."

"Your majesty," Veian said sarcastically, "you do know that the Republic Charter prohibits capital punishment, right?"

"I don't appreciate your tone, Mr. Grebllyh. I know the laws of this nation. The thought of executing a man abhors me, but I am bound to the duties of my office."

Veian stood up from his chair. "I can't believe what I'm hearing. No agency in this Republic would give you this authority. Your office is that of stewardship. Your actions, if I may say, sir, are appalling. I think

Parliament is right to doubt you. And Kaleb Vardos is right to take the Guard from you."

Evan stood as well, somehow more agitated than the hot-headed marine. "You're talking about things that you don't understand, Corporal! Don't throw a tantrum because I won't let you play soldier. You have a much bigger responsibility ahead of you! You will play the role you are given!"

"And what is that, playing babysitter to your sister?"

"Eve is crucial to our work. I want you to be a part of this too. Someone has to replace Amon Veise."

Veian's mouth opened, as though he were about to speak. Instead, he stood there for a moment. He turned his head to look behind him. The room was still empty. He turned to look at Evan again. For once he had nothing to say. He sat down.

# 33. AFTER THE FLOOD

Senjek dared to sit upon the throne inside the castle. He looked down at the scene below him. The room before him was once full of life. This was the cradle of modern civilization, the foundation of the Republic of Damos. He struggled to recall the number of how many had died in this room so many hundreds of years ago. The last time this room made history of any significance, there was another man called Daben Celt. He and Javk Gie, an ancestor of Evan's, had made a grand plot to overthrow the ruling class. One made himself known as a villain to the crown; the other gained confidence before betraying it.

The details, in fact, had become lost to time. The spirit of what happened was not a mystery. Were it not for what his namesake so many years ago, Daben might not have accomplished what he had done so far. Would he have stood by helpless that day at Eidolas? Would he have acted? He carefully eyed a pair of guards walk across the grand hall. One made a passing glance; the other refrained from looking. Was it shame or fear that averted his gaze?

Senjek wouldn't trouble himself with the opinion of a puppet. It was hard to judge the man objectively. He didn't care if the man joined the Lobby against his will. Everyone had a choice, he had decided. He had a choice once, and he chose wrong. He had forgiven Cineon. He may not have done it without Daben's insistence, but he couldn't hold the Fury solely responsible.

"Still no update on the intruder, sir," a voice said behind him.

He turned to see a low-ranking officer of the Lobby. Senjek gave her a polite smile. "Ms. Vytautos, isn't it? Has Daben set you to taunt me now that von Breischa is gone?" Senjek didn't count a woman out in a fight, but it alarmed him how many officers were female. Apart from Areka, he couldn't recall a single woman associated with the Lobby during his time as the Praesage. To Daben's credit, he knew nothing of Treistina's affiliation.

"Please, call me Cratania," she replied, unphased. "I would not blame you after Areka and Treistina, but don't fool yourself to believe all the women of the Lobby exist to tempt you." Senjek was about to rebuke but wasn't allowed. "Spare me your apologies. Or your scolding, for that matter."

"Excuse me if I don't trust a woman named after one of the more devious of the old Krameian pantheon."

"There's a lot of words and names derived from those tribal days, sir. We can't all be named after the goddess of love and beauty," she fired back. She let her long bangs cover the right side of her face. Her hair was red like Senjek's, but it looked an inferno when the light caught it right. Her eyes were a bright brown, but amidst the waves of her fiery hair, the right seemed especially menacing. "Let's not quarrel; that's not why I'm here. Areka has left on assignment, and I'm to assist you now, where appropriate."

"Would helping me escape Monarch Fall with Treistina be appropriate?"

"Ms. Yahn has been exported to a secure location off site to avoid any," she paused to think of the correct phrase. "Let's just say, conflict of interest. You are here because you are wanted here, General. You've lived amongst people who fear you as a criminal. Would you rather not be loved and respected as a hero? Why are you so eager to leave and hide who you are?"

At that moment Senjek wished he was who many thought he was. All he had to do was pick up his blade and strike her down. No one would bat an eye. It wouldn't be as if he killed Cineon or Daben. She was nothing compared to them. Daben could be upset by it. Surely she had friends who would be enraged, but they would turn a blind eye and welcome him back

248

all the same. "I wouldn't expect you to understand my reasons for wanting no part of the Lobby."

She leaned up against a crate nearby, but still maintained a comfortable distance away. "I know why you left." She waited for him to look at her. The look in his eyes and awaited some lie or story. "You spared Cineon. You let him live... and you can't live with that decision."

"You make it sound simple. It wasn't that I didn't kill him." He cut himself off. He took a step back. He never expected to hear anyone say that. Did people know the truth? Would Daben be so bold to tell? He turned his back from her to shelter his expression. "What did you say?"

"You think we don't know what happened? You've seemed to have forgiven Cineon, but you can't forgive Daben. Have you forgiven yourself?"

"I'm not talking to you about this," he replied to change the subject. "What do you know about the man who attacked us?"

"I told you, there's no update."

He stood up from the throne and took a few steps away. "I don't care so much of his whereabouts. What do you know about him?"

She went on at great length about what they discovered from the assault. Nothing that Senjek hadn't been able to figure out himself. It wasn't Repulsor technology used to defend against the Lobby's ranged attacks. Many suspected the truth, but no one was prepared to accept it. Hardly anyone even spoke of it. What had happened inside the throne room was frightening to behold, but the thought of who or what he was, that was infinitely more terrifying. She addressed the most pressing concern with her next question. "What if he comes back?"

Senjek guffawed. "So what if he does? Let him take what comes for. You heard about what happened. Even I couldn't stop him."

"Could not? Or would not?"

He would have made the argument that he was Daben's hostage, but that wasn't an excuse to spare him. There were very few reasons to let Daben live. Treistina was one of them. Daben always planned ahead; his death would not free Treistina from his grip. There would be back up plans. The endgame was control. Was Senjek's love for Treistina real and natural or engineered as another means to influence him? Whether or not he could believe the woman he loved was capable of carrying out this ruse was another question. One could reason or negotiate with Daben. His words after his death might not be. "This man is dangerous. If he manages to kill Daben what happens next? Does he target Daben's lieutenants? Maybe Evan Gie is next. We don't know anything about him or what his plans are."

"His plan is to destroy us. Mr. Celt may have a variety of contingency plans, but he's irreplaceable. The Lobby would be in a dire state if he were assassinated. And much harder to reason with."

He said that he agreed, but he didn't. In Daben's entire campaign against the mainland, he had never once compromised. The thought of reasoning with him was almost laughable. If he wanted to beat Daben, he would have to play his game. He looked to his weapons. It was strange to him how comfortable he still was using them. If he wanted to rid himself of the blades, he would have to use them again. "Get me a team." He turned his attention back to Cratania. "I'm going after Strife."

"Would you like me to fetch *Sola* and *Narth*? I see you've been working with knock-offs. Daben was thoughtful enough to bring the real deal."

Senjek shook his head. "That's all right. *Selna* and *Kilinus* will do."

It was easy to tell by the look on Cratania's face that she was pleased with his decision to pursue Devian Strife. She pulled out a cloth from her bag and handed it to him. It was something from his past. He was reluctant to take it from her, but he knew he had to sell his deception. His prolonged gaze was uninterrupted as he looked into her eyes. He merely shook his head. She giggled. "I appreciate your newly found morals, sir. But your anonymity is paramount. You've already attacked several of our people in the streets. We don't believe anyone witnessed your actions, but if they did, they would have been too far away to see your face. Suspicions may have already been aroused. Wear it."

There was a slight chime as he unfolded the cloth. The sound came from the ring of chains attached to the edge, which gave it quite a bit of weight. It was a plain black hood, and the chains were meant to keep it from flying off the head unintentionally. It was simple in its design. He could see out of it from the inside, but it obscured his facial features. His signature blades were only part of the Praesage's image; the mask made him look like a reaper. If Evan weren't sure of the Lobby's presence on Damos already, this display would erase all doubt. He didn't want to become this person again, but he could slyly alert the President of the enemy at his door. "I'll need backup. Can I expect your assistance, Ms. Vytautos?"

She wouldn't answer until he put the hood on. He hesitated but donned the article all the same. He was free to drop his visage of reluctance as she couldn't see his face. She was undeniably gleeful, though. "Oh, my. I never thought I'd get to see this image. Thank you, sir."

"Don't be too excited, Ms. Vytautos," he warned. "Seldom have those who have witnessed this guise lived to speak of it."

That strangely amused her. After a brief outburst of laughter, she was able to contain herself. "My apologies, of course, sir. Best then not to further endanger any more Krameian lives. Let the face of death be the last thing this Devian Strife ever sees. You'll be going alone."

# 34. THE PRESIDENT'S SISTER

Veian deftly pierced through the reports presented to him. He had discovered there were may ways he could subvert his assignment. He first made an appeal to parliament. He wrongfully assumed they would overturn an executive decision. They refused to intervene even in spite. The entire body had enough of Evan's erratic behavior, but they agreed that Eve needed protection from the state's enemies. They also knew that Veian was one of the few purposefully deployed to Kramei to provoke a war. They agreed to undo his assignment on only one condition: get the Iedenian Guard to reverse their decision and return the personal outfit they arranged for the Presidential Estate. That had so far proved to be an even more challenging task. He had met Kalus Baena on a number of occasions and hoped to appeal to him.

The corporal looked at a report from the commandant's office that he could hardly describe as desirable. Mr. Baena stated that he was not in a position to deliver upon the request. He was not the one who passed the order; it was General Vardos. He did not want to be any more involved in the tension between the Guard and the Republic than he already was. Kalus was also unwilling to contravene a direct order from a superior. Veian had hoped that Baena might grant a stay on the withdrawal of troops. He insisted that he needed time to arrange his own secret service; the vice president still needed protection until the formation of such a force.

Baena denied that request as well. He also made it clear he didn't want to be bothered with further requests regarding the matter. He was directed to appeal to General Vardos directly if he decided to discuss the issue further. He would have had a better chance of becoming the General of the Guard himself before he could get Vardos to change his position. He had sent a request to Dak to conscript him, but he had not yet heard an answer. Forward Command had apparently received the request, but Suzerain Johnsen did not have the opportunity to review it. The lack of response from Dak was troublesome and only made Veian more eager to return to Kramei.

He set all correspondence regarding his possible reassignment aside. He turned his attention next to prospective candidates for the Fourth Damosi Patrician Regiment. Veian was hesitant to operate under the DPR moniker and was publicly referring to the group as the Damosi Secret Service. He requested that Kalus be loaned off as a member of the team, but he had yet to receive an answer to that question. He believed that the commandant was sympathetic to his position, given his hands-off denial of his requests regarding the Iedenian Guard. He wouldn't hold his breath given the fact General Vardos would need to approve the request. He had another candidate who was unlikely to arrive anytime soon, if at all. He felt somewhat hypocritical to ask, but he asked Ensign Lea be pulled from Kramei to shore up his troops. Given Evan's paranoia, he wanted to have as many people loyal to the Gie family as possible in the fold.

He had a few other prospects, but he didn't have time to review their qualifications at the moment. Eve's ship had landed an hour ago, and she was on her way. He had expected her to have arrived by now. He had sent a message to her chauffeur but hadn't received a response in several minutes. He was beginning to fear that something had gone wrong. If he didn't get a response in a few more minutes, he would have to go out after her himself. Despite being in a position of such authority, Eve was still quite irresponsible. He had thought of her as inconsiderate on many different occasions. The corporal had lost count of the times she was either in danger or allowed everyone to believe she was in peril. He knew Evan was still furious over the incident during her holiday on Iedin a few years ago. He always thought it was a bit hypocritical that the president had forbidden his sister's friendship with Treistina Yahn, especially since Evan became friendly with her boyfriend.

He had the pleasure of meeting Senjek once. There was something Evan never quite trusted about that man. Seemingly worthless in a fight, but yet Bohmet was somehow qualified to teach people in guerrilla tactics for survival on Kramei. To be so qualified to teach something he could not do himself made Veian somewhat suspicious. Maybe that was what led him to his current predicament. He had scouted Senjek for some time to see if he was hiding something as a favor to Evan. He monitored the man for weeks and found nothing out of the ordinary. Many more favors would be asked of him by Evan after that. The President always trusted Veian with the safety of the Gie family. He was posted to Kramei with Besen for that very reason; to keep him safe. His failure to do that somehow did not shake Evan's trust in him, though. Veian wished nothing more than to get back to Kramei to make amends for that failure. There could be redemption in protecting Eve, but it would not quiet Veian's demons. He feared what may happen to him if he failed again. The death of another Gie on his watch was something he couldn't bear.

Enough time had passed. The corporal stood from his desk and put on his coat. It was a dark blue with bronze buttons. The asymmetrical design had the buttons placed off-center toward the left of his body. He fastened five of the eight buttons, leaving the bottom and top two undone. He placed his cover upon his head, a beret modeled off those worn by the old regiment that protected the Poleb family centuries ago. Faded gold with a thick black band around the bottom. A pin that resembled the silhouette of the Gie family spear adorned the right side. There was a cape that went along with his uniform as well. Brown in color with a gray spear on the background. He didn't care for such extravagances, but Evan insisted he wore it. What the president didn't know wouldn't hurt. It didn't clash with the uniform so much since his slacks were the same brown with a gray stripe on the right hip. He felt paying homage to Damosi history was one thing, but costuming himself as princes once did was over the top.

He moved to the door and reached his hand out toward the knob. It turned before he could grasp it, though, and the door pulled away from him. Agitation seeped from his eyes. Eve had expected him to be pleased to see her. He could see the resemblance to her brother, but it brought

254

some pain to him. Besen always had more features in common with his aunt. Maybe it was because the two were much closer in age. He wore his expression to hide his sorrow, but he was also genuinely annoyed. Eve wasn't alone. Treistina Yahn was with her. He had seen the woman in reports and, on occasion, from afar. Veian had never recalled seeing her distressed, though. He stepped aside to let the two in his office before closing the door behind them.

He turned from the door to see that Eve had quickly taken a seat at his desk. Eve smiled at him. He merely stood there, stoic. Her strained grin didn't hold as she spoke. "At ease, corporal." He loosened up a bit but remained standing. He kept Treistina in the corner of his eye. She would also not sit. "Mr. Grebllyh, you take orders from me now, do you not?"

"Yes, ma'am."

He was clearly uneasy with Treistina in the room, but that would not deter Eve. "I have a simple question for you, Veian. Who comes first in your loyalty? Mine or my brother's?" He didn't answer. The question vexed him. The question seemed to imply that the two would be at odds. Evan's actions had become exceedingly erratic as of late. Would Eve be more level-headed in her actions? Would she favor her brother's course or act more in accordance with parliament's wishes? He didn't know how to answer her question. "I'm going to trust you with some information that, if Evan were to find out, could jeopardize this country. His goals are short-sighted and absolute. He isn't willing to do the wrong things for the right reason. I need to know if you would be able to withhold information from our president in the name of both my safety and the longevity of our democracy."

He walked up to the edge of his desk and looked deep into her eyes. If there was any mischief or naivety in her intentions, he didn't see it. She asked that she see his sidearm for inspection. Though annoyed, he did as she asked. She unloaded the clip and ejected the round in the chamber. She began to ask some strange questions. She asked what he knew about Areka von Breischa. He knew enough about the traitor. Not nearly enough, it would have seemed. She had more than a few shocking revelations for the corporal.

"If Areka von Breischa were a double agent, Evan would have told me." As soon as the words left his lips, he remembered what the President said about Amon Veise. If the siblings were truthful in their words, that would make two agents embedded deep inside the Lobby. The two people claimed to be in deep cover didn't make sense, though. If Amon and Areka were both playing for Republic interests, how had the Lobby grown to the monster it was? Amon Veise was second to Cineon in command of Lobby troops on Kramei. He didn't know what role Areka was playing, but such a gifted military mind must have ranked high amongst Daben's lieutenants. There were two distinct differences, though. Amon had been declared dead over two years ago, despite that clearly not being true. Areka was publicly declared a traitor. Something else was wrong with this, though. He didn't know if it was his place to ask, but he had to know. "You've been under lock and key for months. You're the acting vice president in name only. You've been removed from this conflict more than most civilians. How could you possibly know that Areka is deceiving Daben Celt?"

"There's no other explanation," Treistina declared. He looked over to her. He hadn't expected her to have anything to say regarding this. He looked back over to Eve. She had inserted the clip back into his pistol and loaded a round. He turned his attention back to Treistina and demanded an answer. Treistina made contact with Eve and received a reassuring nod. "This doesn't leave this room, Mr. Grebllyh," she insisted. He would have scoffed at the order, but he noticed Eve pointed his gun at him. They weren't playing. He assured Eve that he was loyal to her and keeping her safe. "Eve didn't know about Areka. I'm not sure anyone knew, outside maybe her brother. Areka is playing against Lobby interests, which places her on your side. She would have never allowed me to enter Damosi custody if she weren't."

Veian didn't understand. He looked to Eve for answers but wasn't sure if he could trust someone that had him at gunpoint. "Veian, I'm going to tell you something, and I need you to be cool about it. Actually, I don't know if you can do that, but you can't tell my brother."

"This is about Treistina, isn't it? Are you going to tell me that incident on Iedin wasn't an accident? Did she have something to do with it? Government officials are rarely granted the luxury of staying in that hotel. I always thought that contest she won was a bit suspicious."

256

"I didn't know what was going to happen, Veian," she pleaded. "You have to trust me. Even though you would be right not to once you know the truth."

Veian knew there was about to be a bomb dropped on him. He'd never seen Eve touch a firearm, much less have a target in the sights. She was afraid of how he might react. He could see it in her eyes. He took a deep breath. Against his better judgment, he would listen. He assured the both of them he wouldn't act in haste, regardless of what he heard. Eve was clearly not convinced. She kept the gun trained on him. "Say what you have to say."

Treistina walked behind the desk behind Eve as if to use the vice president as a shield. "We don't have anything official to prove her deep cover. We don't even have her word, but I don't think you'd accept that anyway. Trust her actions. We have an idea behind her intent given her actions. If she truly were loyal to Daben Celt, she would have never allowed me to be standing here right now."

"Don't start defending something you haven't said yet. Just say it."

Eve sighed. There was no easy way of saying it. She tightened her hold on the grip of the pistol. "Treistina used to be a member of the Lobby." Veian instantly felt the urge to get up range of the gun and detain the both of them, but he didn't. He surprised himself by staying composed. He did a poorer job of hiding his emotions, though. He was clearly enraged, but he insisted that she continue. So she did. She explained the details of Treistina's assignment; that Daben had sent her here to keep tabs on a Lobby deserter. Someone of great importance to their cause who had turned his back on them.

He didn't wait for a name. It suddenly all became clear to him. It didn't make sense, but it somehow did. Outside of Eve, Treistina was only seen associating with one person. An individual who was a mystery to him. "Bohmet. She is here to watch Senjek Bohmet."

"That was the idea, but I don't report to him any longer," she said to defend herself.

"Who is he? Who is he to Daben and the Lobby?" He hoped she would deny his newly found suspicion. Treistina replied by saying that he was the man she loved. That did not satisfy him. Daben and Cineon were only two of the three top figures of the Lobby. There had been no report of the third for years. As ridiculous as it was, it somehow made sense to him. "Is he the Praesage?"

"Senjek Bohmet is just a man," Eve replied. It was clear that she held her friendship with Treistina in high regard.

"Is he the Praesage!?" he shouted.

There was a brief, but painfully obvious pause in the room. Treistina searched for the right way to phrase her response. "The Praesage is not a man, but an idea."

He had heard enough. He knew what that meant. His face was suddenly red hot. "Evan and Dak have been harboring a fugitive for years. Not only hiding him but paying him."

"Senjek Bohmet knows how the Lobby operates. He's been training our troops for months the techniques that are needed to defeat Cineon and his troops on Kramei." Eve's quick and sudden defense of the man troubled Veian. He suspected if she somehow knew. He was not shy about asking her how long she knew about him. "Not long," she admitted. "He and Treistina were trying to hide from Lobby forces when they unwittingly went straight to their base of operations."

"Why do I feel that you are about to admit to being complacent in more than one crime?" He made no attempts to hide his disdain. He took a few steps back and sat in a chair across from Eve. He had hoped to prove that he wouldn't act out. Treistina would be someone Evan would want to know about, but he knew if he said anything it would endanger Eve. Maybe that was part of the pair's plan. "What else don't I know? Cineon has made it no secret to us that he's on Kramei. You said they were hiding from members of the Lobby and walked into their arms. There's a force planetside, isn't there? Where is he?"

"Veian," Treistina said with a tremble in her voice, "we're telling you all this because I want to trust you. I want this to end as badly as you. I need to know that I'm not spending the rest of my life in a cell."

"I don't give a shit about what happens to you, Yahn. If it means taking down Daben, I don't care about what happens to Bohmet, either. If you give me information that leads to the collapse of the Lobby, I'll be the best man in your fucking wedding. Where the fuck is he?" Eve very loudly placed the gun down on the desk. Veian broke eye contact with Treistina and looked at the woman Evan charged him with protecting. She knew.

Yahn had already told her. "Evelyn," he said, "if you know where Daben Celt is, I need to know."

Eve agreed to tell him everything she knew. She had some rather strong conditions, though. The Vice President demanded his silence regarding certain matters. She would not prohibit him from alerting the president to a clear and present danger to the government, but she insisted on withholding certain details. She wanted Treistina, and Senjek's name kept out of it. He had strong reservations about one of the two. He demanded to know why Senjek deserved a pardon for his past actions.

"Senjek has forsaken the Lobby and what they are doing," Treistina reasoned. "I've been conditioned since birth to obey my... orders. Since I've been freed of Daben's influence, I have done the same. At some point, Senjek saw the evil that is the Lobby's agenda. Not only has he stopped helping them, but he's also been actively trying to make up for his wrongs. He has been helping prepare your soldiers to combat Cineon on his home field. We can all agree that Evan won't be able to forgive Senjek for what he helped build. Senjek has never murdered anyone, including Damosi lives. What he has done is try to help them survive and win this war. That has to count for something."

"I don't care about that. You know where Daben Celt is. Tell me where."

"Somewhere we can't follow," Eve declared with disdain. She explained that he had taken refuge at Monarch Fall. Even if Evan knew this, he could do nothing to apprehend the criminal. Troops would not be allowed to step foot on the grounds. The location was a nationally protected landmark. Anyone who went there would be subjected to criminal charges, even if they were there to capture an enemy of the state. Daben had long used the laws and sympathies of the Republic to his advantage, but this was a new low. Monarch Fall was the only remaining remnant of the oppressive family who once ruled the planet with an iron fist. It stood as evidence to the revolution that brought democracy to the land. It was also a monument to all the lives lost in that conflict. Daben could just as well be held up in a mausoleum. His disrespect for the dead disgusted Veian. Even more troubling was the admission that Senjek and Treistina both deliberately sought refuge there themselves. Even if it were in an attempt to hide from Daben, Veian would have a hard time ignoring the fact.

"Why are you telling me this if there's nothing to be done to challenge him?"

These past few minutes were probably the longest Veian had spent with Eve without seeing her smile It was clear that there was more bad news to come. "Evan is the president. As you know, the Republic is nothing more than a stand-in for a king. There were many loyalists to the Poleb family after the revolution. To establish a brand new political paradigm would have been chaos. Even in the past hundred years, any attempt to create a true democracy free of the monarchy's shackles have been unsuccessful. We may have lost control over the Iedenian Guard completely. The current state of Kramei would have only happened sooner. Evan treats his position as that of a caretaker of the throne. And he has been pushing the boundaries of his authority. I have no doubt my brother is only doing what he feels is right. He has taken every liberty, used every loophole to bypass the bureaucracy of parliament. Evan can discover or manufacture a legal means to send troops to Monarch Fall. Of that, I have no doubt."

"If he hopes to use Suzerain Johnsen to provide legal passage to the castle, I should have you know that he's not so easy to reach these days."

"Dak is easily the obvious workaround," Treistina agreed, "but his presence on Kramei is too important. Even given the current state of affairs, if he is not present, parliament would surely remove all Damosi troops from Kramei. Even if Evan tried, by the time Dak could get here, Daben may escape before we could attack the palace. Evan would find a way."

"Even at his own peril?" Veian demanded to know.

"If that is what necessary? Yes, I think so," Eve answered. "I don't like this any more than you do, Veian. But Areka brought Treistina to us for a reason. Daben may think he's a step ahead, but he's not as clever as he thinks. The von Breischa have been a loyal family for years. As shocking as her supposed betrayal was, it makes more sense that she's deceiving Daben in the long game."

"And there's absolutely no reason to think Areka might be playing us?"

Treistina tried her best to convince Veian. She admitted that Areka might have had an ulterior motive, but there was no way of knowing for certain. "I want our names kept out of this. Or at the least be granted amnesty. I don't want to spend the rest of my life in prison."

Veian chuckled in exasperation. He looked over to Eve and saw the look in her eye. He knew what she was thinking. "I'm grateful that you've stepped forward, Treistina. I truly am. If I can, then I will. Evan will want to know where this information comes from. I'll tell him I got it from a Lobby deserter, but if he presses for a name I will not lie to the man."

"One more thing. Daben Celt will stand trial for his crimes. He is to be taken alive." Eve sounded very insistent. "The lives lost through his actions deserve justice. Also, if he were to be executed he would become a martyr to the Lobby."

# 35. *EOMDA BRIERNHA*

The man who called himself Devian Strife made a bull-rushed assault on the palace single-handedly and failed. Only one of his dark eyes was spying the grounds. He had wrapped half of his face in a cloth that was closer to gray than the yellow it once was. He had to conceal the mistake he made in picking up that weapon. A weapon that contained components of a gun. The weapon wasn't designed to fire a bullet from along the blade. It was intended to harness the recoil of a firearm to achieve maximum damage with each strike. He had been in exile for too long. He could have never imagined such a tool. Perhaps the girl was right.

The girl had discovered him when he had returned. He knew what she was immediately, but didn't know her name. His arrival didn't go unnoticed. She had tried to follow him, but the hunter quickly became the hunted. The Unknown Council didn't properly brief her before she had been sent to spy on him. Either that or their visions had become even weaker. He quickly had her up against a wall with a knife at her throat. He thought back on what had happened.

She did a good job of feigning ignorance. She pleaded Devian to take her money and not to hurt her. There was a gold chain around her neck securing her hood and cape. He grabbed hold of it and used it to pull out the medallion tucked under her shirt. He let the crest of her family dangle freely in front of her chest. There would be no denying who she was. He asked her why she was following him. She insisted that she wasn't. He pulled the blade away from her throat and lifted her off the ground. She stared at him with a look of disbelief as he took a few steps away from her. She kicked her legs back and forth. She wouldn't be able to free herself, though. He would try to disguise his power to those inside the palace, but she already knew what he was capable of doing. She had done a good job of pretending otherwise, though. She was suspended a few feet above the ground now. He tucked the knife away and asked her again. He wanted to know why she was following him.

"*fiana viosinas moaschent*," she replied. It was immediately apparent that her answer did not satisfy her interrogator. She instantly felt a sharp tug at her throat from an invisible hand.

"I don't care about the Known Council of Moashei's final vision. I want to know why you are watching me."

She grabbed at her throat as if to free herself from the grasp that was digging into her windpipe. There was nothing to pull away, though. She felt as though Devian's eyes pierced directly into her soul. "You shouldn't be here," she croaked. He relaxed his grip around her neck. She understood that he ceased choking her because she was finally honest. He wanted to know more. "You should be dead. Long dead. How can you possibly... be?"

"I'm the one asking the questions," he replied bluntly. "Some of them you will have answers to. Others you may not. I will expect your best guess. You're an Observer, that much is obvious. How many others? Who else is with you?" She claimed to be the only one in the quadrant. He believed her. She felt herself slowly drift back toward the ground. "Where is Daben Celt? Are you working with him?" She claimed to know nothing of his whereabouts. She didn't immediately deny working with him. He chuckled under his breath. "And I thought we were just beginning to trust each other."

"I don't know where he is! We are not a part of his design. He's hunting us. He thinks we are a threat to his plans." She pleaded with him to let her go, but he wouldn't. Not until he had the information he needed. His mission was too important. He pressed her. He found it hard to believe that she didn't know of his whereabouts. "The Unknown Council may, but I don't know. I'm meant to monitor. I'm not given many details, and

Daben Celt is not my mission. They foresaw your return and wanted to make sure that you didn't take any drastic actions."

She felt invisible fingers clawing into her neck again after saying that. That only angered Devian. "Drastic? Did they tell you, before they sent you, did they tell you? Did they tell you what they did to me? What Daben did to me?" He had his own theories about how he had survived. Daben would have survived by some other means. He suspected he had benefited from outside intervention. He had already convinced himself that the Unknown Council played a part. "If I find out that you are helping him," he said, voice cracking. "If you were anything more than complacent in what he did. I will burn your society to the ground. Your marble floors won't flash in green and orange, but with every shade of red. I will hang every seer in some town square. Unhooded, where no one will ever notice them. You know who and what I am. You know what was done to me. Do not think that anything I do qualifies as drastic!"

As quickly as the grasp around her throat lifted she felt her back crash into the wall behind her. She soon fell to the ground. Devian shouted at her to look at him. She did as he demanded. There was nothing she could do to defend herself from his rage. He demanded that she say his name out loud. She was hesitant. He could have been one of two people wronged by Daben. She remembered her instructions to guess if she wasn't sure. She said the name she believed to be right. He lowered his hand. She guessed right. She was alarmed to see that he had come to know such rage. This was behavior unlike him. Daben's actions had changed him for the worst. He continued to demand Celt's whereabouts. She didn't know, but she would provide her best guess.

"We have been so far unable to monitor him. If he is planet-side, I would put him at Monarch Fall. The Damosi don't maintain any premise there. Only the desperate and criminal ever venture there. Please don't kill me."

He lowered his head in shame. He wasn't proud of what he had done so far, but he knew it was necessary. He would not find aid without forcing the hands of others. "Yours is not a life I wish to claim." He used his unworldly gift to lift her to her feet. "I only want to silence one voice forever. I know that times change. Dynasties fall. I don't seek vengeance for your people's inaction. I only aim to deliver justice for those who wronged me directly. Daben Celt is the only one left. Do not get me in my way. If you speak to your superiors, what will you say of me?"

"I will say nothing."

"Good. I will hold you to that. Tell me your name, child." She obliged him. She was called Naieena Haeese. He somehow even doubted that. Her name seemed to enrage him as much as anything else that she said. She swore to him that she was not lying. She gave him her true name. He quickly approached her again. She feared that he would hurt her again, but he didn't. He dropped something on the ground. A silver band with a single stone embedded inside. "I'm sorry it came to this. I wish things were different. I would have never considered myself a vengeful man, but we surprise ourselves, don't we? You should return to your people. Go to your mother if she's still alive. Seek her wisdom and ask forgiveness."

He let her go after that. He believed that she would remain faithful to her word. She didn't confirm his return to the Unknown Council. He suspected she might have said something to someone else, another enemy of Daben Celt. Senjek Bohmet clearly held a grudge against a common enemy. He was a skilled warrior in his own right. Bohmet's exotic weaponry was the only thing that had defeated him. Devian wouldn't suffer from the same mistake twice. He had witnessed multiple people leave Monarch Fall since his assault. He would no longer have the element of surprise. He doubted his ability to reproduce the extreme display of power he had employed in his first strike. Years of anger had built inside of him, and he used much of that in his failed assassination. There were allies to be made. Some of his rage had subsided, but he would not deny himself vengeance. The sound of a loaded round in the chamber of a gun was unmistakable. He knew someone would come for him, but he was surprised by the choice.

"I don't know who you are or why you're after Celt. I have no desire in aiding him, but we have to be smart. Killing him may do more harm than good in the long run." Senjek had tried to recall what happened in the last encounter with this man. He had shot himself in the face, but he didn't seem to be suffering from the wound. Devian was no longer armed after Senjek cut his bo staff in half. His fancy footwork and quick hands wouldn't beat Senjek with two gun-blades.

"Senjek Bohmet, isn't it?" Devian said aloud.

The answer came quickly enough. Strife could feel the blade swing toward him. He ducked underneath the attack. He turned to face the one once known as the Praesage. He wore a hood now, but his dress remained the same. The twin gun-blades still in tow. Another strike. Devian dodged the blade again, as he prepared for the encounter. Another attack came toward his neck. He merely leaned backward and pushed the blade away with his hand against the blunt edge. He followed the momentum of his arm and jumped into the air. He spun in the same direction and kicked Senjek in the jaw to send him reeling. Senjek pulled out the second gun-blade. He swung at the head and the torso simultaneously. Devian back-flipped through the strike without so much as a scratch. Senjek tried to hurl a blade at the man, but it was impressively knocked down with a boot heel. Devian moved about as if there was no danger to him. This frustrated Senjek.

Senjek rolled through a swinging kick and picked up his other gun-blade. This time he swung them both at the midsection. Devian jumped over this attack and landed behind Senjek. Bohmet wasn't fast enough to react and soon felt a kick in the back of his neck. He was quick enough to regain his balance and put his forward momentum into his next swing. Devian angled the edge of his hand perfectly to make contact with the blunt side of the blade and knocked it to the ground. Senjek was surprised. How he could still be surprised after the assault on the palace was a mystery to even himself.

Senjek felt a sharp pain in his chest as he was sent flying across the roof. He grabbed hold of the ledge to keep himself from falling to the ground below. He pulled himself back up to see Strife had a new weapon. It was a blend of red of black. Senjek took the initiative and brought his blade down on the center of the bo. He had hoped to snap it in half like before. He threw himself too hard into his swing, though. He felt a sharp sting in his hand as the staff remained whole. Made of metal, not wood, the bo absorbed the blow. Strife pulled the staff toward the sky, catching it in the hook at the end of Senjek's blade. With the edge of the bo trapped in the hook of the blade, Devian lifted himself and shoved both feet into Senjek's stomach. He dropped to his back and used his momentum to flip Senjek over his head.

Devian rolled up onto his shoulders. He put the tip of his bo on the ground to support his weight. His shoulders came off the ground and would have stood on his head if it were a few inches closer to the roof. He used the bo to dig into Senjek's body and throw himself to his feet, all in one fluid motion.

Senjek knew he wasn't defeated yet. He lost his gun-blade during the last assault, but it was within reach. He picked it up as he got to his feet. He brought the blade behind his back so he could swing it around his head. He hoped the added momentum in the downward swing would be enough to do something. He was wrong. He felt a great deal of resistance as he tried to drag the blade over his head. It quickly came to a stop as it neared the target's head. He put all his strength into the swing. He struggled to bring it down on Devian but to no avail. A swinging fist knocked the second handle from Senjek's hand. Bohmet quickly felt himself flying backward and landed hard on his back.

Senjek noticed that there was a gash in his waist. He saw his blood dotted across the roof. He tried to get to his feet, but Devian hit him hard in the forehead, flooring him again. He placed his staff between Senjek's body and right arm. He lifted Senjek up by the armpit and threw him several feet into the sky. He raised his hand up, flared his fingers, and brought his fist down quickly. Senjek briefly lost consciousness during that strike. He wasn't sure what happened, but he suddenly was looking through a hole in a ceiling. He soon realized that he was forcibly knocked through the roof and landed on the floor below.

"I warned you, boy," Devian shouted from above. Senjek tried to roll over onto his side, but his strength was leaving him. He saw Devian slowly float to the ground from the broken ceiling. Senjek pleaded to know how he was able to do that. There was no answer. Senjek asked him who he really was. "A man who has lost his patience with you."

Senjek felt the rounded tip of the staff pressed against his throat. Devian claimed to be a man of reason. He offered some choices to Bohmet. He could choose to die right there. He could step away and let Strife do what he came to do. The third option was to help assassinate Daben. He felt it was better to capture Daben alive, but he wouldn't give his life in an attempt to bring Celt to justice. Senjek struggled to speak with the staff pressed to his throat. "I won't commit to helping you, but I won't get in your way."

"Good." Devian took the staff away from Senjek's throat. "I was hoping you would see things my way. I would have hated to carry out an execution for Daben."

Senjek rubbed his throat. He was grateful to be alive, so he didn't immediately pay attention to what he just heard. He got to his knees and ripped the sleeves off his shirt. He removed his hood and used it to apply pressure to his wound. He tied the sleeves around his waist to keep the hood in place. Then it hit him. He looked up at Devian. "What do you mean? What execution?"

Devian laughed. "You were sent after me alone. Everyone in that palace knows what I'm capable of now, even if they don't understand how I'm capable of it. Daben sent you here to eliminate a wild card in the game. He sent you to your death."

"You're a dangerous man. I volunteered to take you down. Daben didn't send me."

Strife had made his way to a window. He looked around to see if anyone else was coming. "Did you volunteer to take me down on your own?"

Senjek was about to lie and say that he did. He shook his head instead. Devian was right. He asked someone else for help, but that person was loyal to Daben. Strife and himself were both threats to Daben. It was in his best interest to get rid of them both, but one was better than none. "I have my reasons for wanting Daben brought to justice. What did he do to you? Why do you want him dead?"

"All you need to know is my goal. To see Daben Celt hung by his entrails. You clearly have no love for the man. You think killing him will do more harm than good in bringing down his whole regime. Even if I agreed with that point, it wouldn't matter. If I thought for one second you were man enough to the job yourself, I might have approached you before Naieena had the chance."

There would be no way to hide the shock in his eyes. "You! You're the herald she warned me about! She said you were a bringer of death. She said not to engage you, that I should tell her about you."

"Daben isn't the only one who should be frightened of me," he revealed. "The Unknown Council fears that my rage will fall to them next once I deal with Celt."

"There's no such thing as The Unknown Council! If there ever was such a thing they don't exist now. I'd sooner believe there was a surviving prince to take residence at Monarch Fall. I would be less shocked if Treistina chose her father over me."

Devian lifted his hand above his head. Senjek's gun-blades quickly flew in through the hole in the ceiling. They spun in opposite directions before the points slammed into the ground. "Look upon me as your savior, Bohmet. I can dismantle everything Daben has built. I can make the threat of the Praesage a distant memory. You have a life. Purpose. Treistina. You may have lost much, but you still have plenty. Daben Celt took everything from me. My home. My love. My daughter. My whole damn life. He has manipulated the people of Kramei and is trying to destroy order. I've seen him do it before and I won't let him do it again. You let yourself believe that you escaped him. Once Celt enters your life there's only one way to be rid of him. That's with one of you dying."

Devian holstered his staff to his back. He knelt down and placed his hand on Senjek's waist. Senjek groaned in agony as he a felt a burning sensation against his skin. Devian was using his power to excite the air around his wound rapidly. Senjek grit his teeth as he felt his wound cauterize. He saw something in Strife's eyes. He took no joy in bringing Senjek pain, but something brought him glee. Senjek knew that look. It was the look of a man who would soon kill another man.

# 36. SUZERAIN'S CHOICE

Dak looked on as enemy troops continued to hold their ground. The Repulsor was cycling at a dangerously high rate. He found himself outside of the Radius Effect, but he couldn't take advantage. His own men were too entangled with enemy combatants. He could call in air strikes, but at the cost of friendly lives. The Lobby had gradually gained the upper hand. He knew there was only one reason to remove the Radius Effect. That would be to keep Damosi reinforcements from entering from the air. Any reinforcements would have to land a safe distance away, outside enemy battery range. If he couldn't turn the tide quickly, he would have to abandon Forward Command. He feared that Greene's actions might have held merit. HFCC was the last major outpost between TAC-OPS and the space conveyor. There were a few smaller outposts that he could fall back to, but none of them were ideal to make a stand. Forward Command itself wasn't important outside of defending the elevator. If the Lobby hoped to gain control of the planet, they would need to take the elevator. Moving troops on and off world without access would be difficult.

He knew Greene had good intentions in driving Cineon away from the DNC hub, but it had proved unwise. Initial intelligence had shown that Cineon had too small of a force to be a serious military threat. The primary concern was keeping the Lobby from cracking the Network and uploading propaganda. By focusing so heavily on routing the Lobby from the hub they left TAC-OPS vulnerable. He planned to send a request to Admiral Kinem to bring additional troops down the elevator to bolster defenses. He believed that Kinem would have no problem with that, but the problem was parliament. They continued to drag their feet in support of the war effort. At this point, it seemed out of spite. They were unsupportive at every turn. They were clearly still furious over the fact that Evan appointed a Suzerain to undermine them. Kinem had tried to be objective. He wasn't necessarily taking a side, but he understood the severity of the stakes. He would probably agree that the Lobby's ultimate goal was to take the elevator. Their taking of the DNC hub was a ruse to conceal their ultimate goal. The elevator was a strategic advantage to whoever held it. It would be harder to supply Damosi forces on the planet. He didn't believe the Lobby would ever try, but an invading force to Damos would be more feasible if they controlled the lift.

Dak hoped that he would be able to repel the Lobby with the troops he had. He couldn't count on additional forces coming from home. He wished more of his men had benefited from the training Senjek provided. Cineon and his men were better suited to fight in the current terrain. The Damos army made up for their lack of numbers with their better training. Lobby troops had excellent training, but most of the Kramei army weren't members of the Lobby proper. There was something odd about the Lobby's current tactics. They appeared more engaged in keeping the two forces from separating than actually killing their enemy.

He tried to signal to Lea or Abal but soon found that his comm unit wasn't working. Something caught his eye. A blue flare shot into the sky. Cineon had sent a signal of some sort to his troops. Dak didn't know what it meant but knew it was nothing good for him. He spotted several projectiles launched from TAC-OPS. When they detonated, they exuded a dark and dense gas. Continued fire helped to accelerate the gas enough to achieve entrance velocity. Dak had never seen someone take advantage of the Repulsor in such a way. Cineon covered the entire battlefield in a fog that blotted out the satellite. With communications down and visibility compromised it would be tough to track enemy troops.

Dak began to shout to his men. "Fall back! Fall back!" The Radius Effect would soon collapse with it's continued erratic wave. With no visual clarity, Cineon could easily commence a bombing run that would obliterate anyone on the ground. He pulled his trigger and heard only a click. He ejected the clip of his rifle and loaded a fresh magazine. He fired four shots toward an attacker, but only one stayed straight and struck its target. He slowly inched his way backward toward Forward Command, pleading with his soldiers to do the same.

"Captain!" Dak turned to see who shouted at him. Jeol Abal desperately rushed toward him. Dak fired the rest of the bullets in his clip before he turned to intercept. "Captain," his lieutenant gasped, "we have to get back to Forward Command immediately. Lobby troops are flanking us."

"Damn it," Dak cursed. "Move your asses! Back to Forward Command! Double time!"

Dak could hear men dying as he ran. He quickly looked back and saw a fair number in pursuit of him. Not everyone would make it back home, though. He slowed his pace and motioned his arm for his men to keep running. He pulled a grenade from his backpack and pulled the pin. He counted to the three in his head before hurling it back toward Lobby pursuers. He felt himself being shoved aside to the ground just before a Lobby explosive detonated near him. He quickly got to his feet despite the ringing in his ears. He looked around and saw a familiar face lay motionless nearby. He slipped onto his stomach as he tried to get close. He quickly dragged himself to his fallen comrade and grabbed hold of his collar.

"Get up, Abal! That's an order soldier!" Abal didn't move. His eyes were wide open with fear and stared blankly at the dark sky. Dak put his fingers to Jeol's throat to check for a pulse but felt a tug on his shirt. He ripped himself away and went back to Abal. His soldiers pulled him away and prevented him from checking for vital signs. "No! We can't leave him! Let go of me, damn it!" His soldiers weren't that loyal that they would abandon their commanding officer. He continued to scream in vain. "Jeol! No! We can't leave him!"

"He's dead, sir! If we don't get out of here, we'll all be dead too!"

Dak stopped resisting. Denying the truth wouldn't make it untrue. The Suzerain got to his feet and followed the rest of his troops inside of Forward Command. He shouted for Ensign Lea. She came running, expecting to see Lieutenant Abal as well. Dak didn't have to say anything, she could tell by the look on his face. Another friend lost. "We had to warn you, sir. I'm sorry, but he insisted on going himself. We couldn't stop him."

Dak dropped his rifle to the ground. He walked past her. "Man the battlements, Ensign. I don't want a word of protest, this time." He refused to let the Republic down. Evan put him here because he believed in him. He wouldn't betray that trust. "Get our heavy airships ready for patrol. Take no quarter. If anyone from KILLER or the Kramei Army moves for the elevator shoot them dead."

"We can't get them airborne, sir," Lea explained. "The Fury already has his ships mobile. They're shooting our ships down before we can get them off the ground." Johnsen ordered her to point all batteries toward the elevator. "Sir, the Radius Effect is expected to collapse any minute now. We'll need the batteries to defend this station."

"Margery, if we lose the elevator we lose the planet." It was a lose-lose situation. The Lobby would overrun the station in minutes if the batteries weren't used to fend off their cavalry. If he used the batteries to hold the station, the Lobby would be able to coordinate action from both sides. Heavy gear from TAC-OPS and supplies from the lift. The latter option would only buy them a few more hours. The elevator itself was not a defensible position, but it was possible to launch attacks from it. He could see it in his Ensign's eyes. She knew it too. They all knew it. No one wanted to say it out loud.

She nodded in compliance. She turned from Dak to see some soldiers standing behind her. There were many at their posts frantic to contain the situation, but just as many seemed lost. "Suzerain Johnsen is right. We can't lose the planet." She saw fear. They all knew the gravity of the situation. No one was particularly willing to die. The idea of maybe seeing Besen in the next life was almost appealing. There was more at stake than just their lives, though. "There's nothing we can do to stop that, though," she said as she turned back toward Dak. "We can only delay the inevitable."

Dak chuckled to himself. She was right. He would seem mad if he argued that. "What else can we do? We can't inform the fleet of our situation. There's no help coming. We're the last defense."

"We can slow them down. We can go down swinging. Maybe even buy ourselves enough time for Admiral Kinem to bring a ship into orbit."

A radical idea, that was. There would only be one reason to have a destroyer enter the atmosphere. "Parliament has expected us to stop this madness with two arms tied behind our backs. Even with the DNC hub and TAC-OPS compromised they refused to make a declaration of war. I never asked for my appointment, but I believe President Gie did what he had to do. It should have been General von Breischa. It should have been Kaleb Vardos or Kalus Baena. We're making due with what we have. Our leaders have dragged their feet and bickered back and forth while this whole thing has unfolded. It's time to take serious action. We are a democratic people, yes, but I am in a position to take the action that's needed. Not everyone back home may agree with it. Parliament won't like it. The Network Consortium won't like it. But if we can't defend this planet, if we can't hold this planet, I'll make damn sure they can't take the homeland."

Lea knew what that meant. They could use their arsenal for more than just shooting down Lobby troops en route to the elevator. "There's no way to signal an evacuation, sir. We'll suffer causalities. If we survive this, we may be charged with war crimes."

Dak was unmoved. "No. I take full responsibility for what needs to be done. They have eyes in the sky. The men and women stationed there would have some time to retreat to orbit. Keep our birds on stand-by. If they see a chance to get airborne, they are to take it. We will do anything we can to defend this station as long as it does not interfere with the defense of the Republic." He didn't see any other option at this point. There was a generator at the base of the elevator which provided power to the ground team. It also assisted in the transport of personnel and supplies to and from orbit. There was some inherent risk to the space station, as well as the counter-weight, but they would have enough time to react accordingly.

Ensign Lea wouldn't let him act alone, though. She gave the order. "Take aim at the anchor and open fire."

# 37. A PLEA TO PARLIAMENT

E van Gie carefully studied the face of the two members of parliament who were present. He could see shock, disbelief, and rage. His report contained everything. There were eye-witness reports of the activity as well as testimony from an escaped captive. Veian had compiled the report per Eve's instructions. The corporal was made to be present, and he wasn't happy about that. Public enemy number one was right under their noses. Daben Celt was within reach. With the refusal to fully commit to the ground on Kramei there was no shortage of local soldiers. He hoped that they would agree to take immediate action. He was prepared, though, that his hope would not translate to reality.

"How did you come across this information, Mr. President?"

Evan lowered his head to break the gaze of Vincent von Breischa and sorted the different pages of the report. "Mr. Grebllyh has presented me with reliable sources." He took a few select pages and passed them to Clarissa Zophar first.

Ms. Zophar straightened the papers in her lap. "I'm surprised to say, but it seems Vincent is too," she paused while she thought of the word she wanted to use. "Restrained. So I'll ask. Why did you invite us to your office to discuss such a matter? This is something that should be brought before all members of parliament." Evan motioned his hand to the report, prompting her to read it. She quickly skimmed through the selected pages. "Treistina Yahn and Senjek Bohmet? Who are they, exactly?"

The Speaker of Parliament knew the answer to that. "Senjek Bohmet is a native of Kramei. He was hired as a private contractor to help our troops survive and battle in the Krameian environment. Treistina Yahn, also from Kramei, is his lover. What does it say about them?"

Clarissa explained that the Lobby apparently took Senjek and Treistina captive. An assassin attempted to take Daben Celt's life, and in the chaos, Treistina was able to escape. Senjek was still missing, likely still in the Lobby's custody. Treistina's account of events identified the assailant as Devian Strife. She passed the papers to Vincent. "It also says that he launched a one-man assault against Lobby troops to get to Celt. I don't see any more information on this Strife person. Who is he?"

Evan placed the rest of the report near the edge of his desk so his guests could look at it if they so desired. "We don't know. There's no other information on the man outside of Yahn's report."

"This man single-handedly led a coordinated assault against a foreign occupation of Monarch Fall." Vincent thumbed through the pages and pieced everything together. "He had some type of miniature Repulsor which is what caught the Lobby off guard. Your report states he failed in his mark because he accidentally struck himself in the face with a gun-blade? Do you honestly expect us to believe this shit?"

Clarissa turned in her chair to face von Breischa. "We have been able to corroborate the reports. There is indeed an occupation at Monarch Fall. We don't have any proof outside of Yahn's account, but our intelligence points to the Lobby."

Vincent didn't accept that. "You don't think it's convenient the way Evan has come about this information? It's no secret that he has a friendship with Senjek Bohmet. He's using his personal relationships to engender his own agenda. Let's not forget that if he hadn't appointed Dak Johnsen as Suzerain, we might still have the support of the Iedenian Guard."

"Vincent, mind your tongue," Clarissa warned.

"It wasn't enough that he had to create a war on Kramei? Now he wants to bring it here? And at that, he wants to do so by desecrating this country's longest standing monument? If you bring this to the rest of parliament, I promise I will see that it's shut down."

# A Fatal Vendetta

Evan leaped from his chair and loomed over the Speaker. "Even with the legitimacy of my source in question, you would allow Daben Celt to possibly have an occupation of the mainland? He is the one that is desecrating Monarch Fall!"

"I don't care if the Praesage is there with Celt. Parliament will never approve of a task force to step foot on the royal estate. I suppose you'll find some way to get what you want, though. It's clear that you are blinded by the many tragedies in your family at the hands of the Lobby that you'll fabricate any story to justify your revenge."

Evan quickly found himself punching Vincent in the face. Vincent fell out of his chair from the force of the strike. Evan knelt over him before punching him again. Clarissa and Veian pulled him off the Speaker. Vincent rose to his feet spouting curses. He did nothing to hide his rage. "I hope your sister is a more reasonable president. Mark my words, Evander: you are unfit for office. I'll make sure that the rest of parliament votes to have you impeached."

"Get out of my office! All of you!" Evan shouted. Zophar escorted von Breischa out of the office. Grebllyh began to follow them out, but the President stopped him. "Not you."

Veian stopped at the door and hung his head in frustration. He began to see the truth of Vincent's words. Evan was truly out of control. He would not abandon his duty, though. He closed the door and turned to face his president. "Yes, sir?"

Evan sat in his chair and rubbed his knuckles. They were red and began to swell from the force of his strike. "There will be no help from parliament. My sister was quite the optimist to think they might agree to act."

"I don't mean to sound out of my position, but Vincent von Breischa is only the Speaker of Parliament. He is not himself parliament."

"He might as well be," Evan lamented. "The von Breischa name stills holds a great deal of weight, despite the fact that one of their own is a traitor."

"Do you mean to discredit Vincent because his cousin Areka joined the Lobby?"

Evan shook his head. There would be no use in trying. Vincent had done and said enough so far to seed doubt in the minds of the government.

The speaker had convinced everyone that their president was losing his mind in vengeful rage. "I cannot say that I don't hold a vendetta toward Celt. But I'm not wrong. You know that. Celt has occupied Monarch Fall. I don't know Treistina very well, but she has no reason to make it up."

"But without Vincent's help, you will never get the legal support to send anyone to Monarch Fall."

President Gie pursed his lip. There was a way, but if he did it, his legacy might be forever stained. Evan would legitimize everything that so many had said about him. He trusted what Treistina and Eve had told Veian and hoped that with the gift of hindsight he might be absolved. Even if not, he believed his cause was righteous. "My office is that of stewardship. Our government is a stand-in for a king. I'm the caretaker of the throne. I have a legal right to enter the grounds."

Veian laughed. "Are you going to go after Daben Celt on your own?"

"No," he replied. "The presidential guard will escort me." He could see Veian's tone change for the worst. "I don't trust parliament to do the right thing, but they will keep her safe. Take Eve and Treistina to parliament. They will be safe enough there until this blows over. Get your people ready for mobilization. I intend to move on the palace by sunset. Bring them in."

Veian made his way to the door as if to block Evan's way. "I maybe have a dozen men committed. It's not a force I'm comfortable with defending your sister, much less capable of storming a fucking castle."

"Then deputize whoever you can find. Vincent is dragging his feet in supporting our democracy, but he'll send the hounds after me. Assure anyone that commits to our cause will not be held accountable for any wrong-doing. With any luck, parliament will send additional troops after us to arrest me. Daben Celt will have nowhere else to run." He walked over to the wall next to his desk. There was a family heirloom placed inside of a display box. A spear. A weapon once used by his ancestor that toppled the monarchy. He elbowed the glass that protected it. His late brother Wele trained him how to use such a weapon. His ancestor conspired once with a man named Daben Celt. He would use the same tool against a man who used the same name. "I'll kill him myself."

278

# 38. RETURN TO MONARCH FALL

Senjek Bohmet stood beneath of an overpass of the new highway. He was as close to Monarch Fall as legally allowed. He used a pair of binoculars to spy on the palace. Daben's security was superb. There was no evidence of any movement, but he knew the Lobby still occupied the castle. There were a few vehicles visible from the outside. None of them contained the Lobby logo, but they did show the worn insignia of King Xen'que. They were older cars, of course. They were still capable of doing their job, but none of the models parked were in production before the Poleb dynasty fell. Old enough to fool almost anyone, but new enough to still be effective. Daben wouldn't stay for long, though. The longer Senjek didn't come back the more likely his failure was. His assailant no longer had the element of surprise, but Daben would be lucky to survive another attack. He wouldn't stay put for long.

Devian silently dropped to the ground nearby. Senjek wouldn't have known or noticed if he wasn't expecting it. Senjek turned to see the man approach. The metal staff was in two separate parts. There was a thin metal wire connecting each half. He must have used it to abseil from the support leg of the bridge. The wire coiled in on itself as he brought the bo staff together. The one half had a thread inside which allowed the other half to screw inside of it. He placed the staff on his back, held in place by a magnetic holster, similar to what Senjek used for *Selna* and *Kilinus*. He was curious as to where he got the holster, though. The man was unfamiliar enough with a gun-blade to strike himself in the face with it. The holster seemed a little advanced for a man who fought with a stick.

279

# The Kramei Insurrection

Devian spread out his fingers and stretched his hand out in front of him. A flurry of earth erupted from the ground. The wind took the dirt eastward. Senjek dropped to one knee as he collapsed the binoculars. He saw another drift of soil fly toward the sky. Devian measured the strength of the wind. Senjek picked up the barrel of his blade to finish cleaning it. This man made him nervous. He displayed a talent that he didn't understand. He would be lying if he didn't say it frightened him at some level. He had to know.

"How do you that? How is it possible?"

Devian lowered his hand to his thigh and pulled a pair of gloves out of his back pocket. "Surely I'm not the first person you've seen to display abilities that seem... unworldly."

Senjek shook his head. "No, I've never seen anything like it. There are stories, of course. Fables. People who could move things with their mind, like you do. More insane powers like command over fire and ice. There are stories that the last king of Damos had such power. Propaganda spread by the monarchy to ensure their control, I'm sure. The stories are consistent with the entire Poleb family. Some of the more outlandish tales say they were gifted with such powers by the remaining natives of Moaschen. A gift in exchange for their continued asylum."

Devian pulled the fitted gloves over his fingers. His gray eyes were strangely calm, yet somehow filled with fury. It was unsettling. "There are truths to every story ever told. Some aspects or details may be exaggerated over time, of course. No story is ever created solely in the mind, though. Maybe the legends of the disposed royalty have more truth than what you're willing to accept. Do you doubt that Xen-Que could conjure flames from the tips of his fingers?"

Senjek began to reassemble his weapon. "Maybe not as much as I doubt the whispers of this Unknown Council. But yeah, I find it hard to believe."

"You should broaden your horizons. Don't be so quick to dismiss that which you can't comprehend." Devian knelt down next to Senjek. He produced a small vial of liquid from his pocket. Strife weaved the vial in and out through his fingers. "I hope you are prepared to pay whatever cost, Bohmet."

Senjek was slightly shocked to hear that. He wasn't sure how to take the meaning. Was that a threat? Were his motives being questioned? He thought he had made it more than clear on how he felt about Daben Celt. "Not whatever cost, no. I won't do anything that might endanger myself or Treistina. Don't be shocked if I choose her over him."

Devian smiled. "You may yet have a life without Daben Celt," he said as if he would not. He extended the vial toward Senjek. He was hesitant at first, but he took it. He took a moment to inspect it. The liquid inside was an unremarkable shade of blue. The glass was very thick. He wasn't sure if he could break it with his bare hands or not. The bottom of the vial was curved, and the top sealed with a rough feeling metal. It had rusted considerably. Senjek could break it open with a reasonable effort. The bottom of the vial was heavier, even if placed upside down it couldn't be set upright.

"This is ancient. What is it? Where did you get it?"

Devian's smile disappeared. "I wouldn't say ancient, but I can't be sure of how old it might be. I retrieved it from the stables across from the castle. I'm surprised it was still there."

"But what is it?" Senjek insisted.

"Insurance," Devian said. He was committed to ending Daben Celt's life, even at the cost of his own. If for some reason he did not survive, Senjek was to keep this vial safe. He was instructed to trust no one else with it. Not his government, not the Iedenian Guard, no one. Except for The Unknown Council.

"How many times do I have to tell you. I don't believe in that nonsense," he explained.

"And I hope that you never find yourself in a place where you do. The Unknown Council may not want me interfering, but there may be worse than me one day. This vial may prove to one day be the salvation of your whole world."

Senjek scoffed at the grandiose statement. He placed the jar inside his coat pocket anyway. He pulled a small box out of another pocket. It was black with a rounded top and a hinge in the middle. "I suppose it's important to have trust amongst ourselves in this mission. Hold onto this in case something happens to me."

Devian took the box and opened it. The afternoon sky reflected off the object inside. The band was simple, thin, and bronze in color. There were three gems set on top. Two smaller diamonds flanked by a larger one in the center. An engagement ring. Devian closed the box. "Shouldn't you give this to Treistina?"

Senjek shook his head. "Not yet, no. Not until after this is settled. I don't know if she would accept it if I killed Daben."

"I hear you've taken lives before. Why should a snake like Celt make a difference to her?"

"A week ago I would have agreed with you. I've learned a lot of horrible truths in the past few days. I want to spend the rest of my life with her. Of that, I have no doubt. I can't bear the thought of her regretting it should Daben, or I, end up dead."

Devian didn't press any further. It seemed strange to him that Treistina might mourn Daben Celt, but there were so many truths he held himself that were odd to Senjek. He agreed to keep it safe until after the day's deed was complete.

They began their trek toward the palace. Senjek took point while Devian watched the rear. There was a ship patrolling the sky. Its flight pattern went inside Monarch Fall's airspace, which surprised Senjek. He had never seen a ship fly this close toward the monument. They both agreed that the Republic would be sending troops soon. Whether it was for them or if they knew about the Lobby was unknown.

The two passed through the high grass and dead vegetation that surrounded the edge of the land. The prohibitive laws were absolute; the government didn't even landscape it. As they approached the stables, the ground shed itself of any foliage. Nothing had grown on this land for ages. The laws that forbade occupation of the land were led with fear as much as they were respected. Early members of Parliament feared that the ghosts of the royal family would come back to enact vengeance against the Republic. Such superstition was fading, of course. The New Xenue project planned to annex much of the estate. There were even controversial plans to utilize the castle itself.

Senjek saw a flash of light out of the corner of his eye. He suddenly found himself on his back. He saw a wave of fire pass around the pair of them. As the flame disappeared, he saw Devian standing firm with his hand outstretched to his side. They were under attack. He got to his feet and saw four women in their path. One flicked her wrist, and a ball of fire

282

came from the palm of her hand. Devian also deflected this. They were mostly strangers to Senjek, though he recognized one.

Naieena Haeese stepped in front of the other three women. At first, all he could see was the blackened stick in her hands. Upon further inspection, he noticed a crescent-shaped blade attached to one end. It was obvious that she didn't use the scythe to tend the land. She intended to wield it as a weapon. She seemed not to notice Senjek; her gaze fixated on Strife.

"I warned you to stay out of this," Devian replied.

The trio of complete strangers all began to laugh. They all had white eyes. All save Naieena, whose gray eyes did not flinch. "We can't let you do this, Hou-Jo."

Senjek took *Selna* from his back. He switched off the safety and loaded a bullet into the chamber. "Who the hell is Hou-Jo?"

"He has many names," said the one who had thrown the fire from her hand. "The Unknown Council has dubbed him the Herald Which Brings Death."

"No doubt the Iedenian Guard would call him Majesty or Highness," said one who held a long sword in her left hand.

The third of them bore a pair of long daggers. "He has chosen the name of Devian Strife, no doubt to avoid unwanted attention."

Naieena lifted the blade of her scythe from the ground and rested it on her shoulder. "The name he was born with as he entered this world still suits him. I prefer him as he truly is. Hou-Jo Poleb, The Prince of Damos."

Senjek took *Kilinus* into his grasp. His eyes widened and looked to Devian in disbelief. "What? Hou-Jo… Poleb?"

"Leave it, Bohmet," Devian replied. "We don't have time for this."

"I disagree, Hou-Jo," Naieena replied. "We can't let you go on with your plan. Your actions have consequences. The Unknown Council cannot allow you to carry on with your plan. I know I agreed to let you be, to not tell the Council of you. That was prior to the spectacle you unleashed on these sacred grounds."

"This is my HOME!" He replied. He threw both palms forward and sent a concussive wave that knocked all four women to the ground. "You let it be taken from me once before. It will not end well for you if you bar my way back."

Senjek suddenly doubted so many things. Magic, the Unknown Council, the Renaissance Watch. There were so many times, during the early days of the Lobby, where Daben would speak of these things. At first, he took them for fairy tales. Later, Senjek decided they were proof of Daben's madness. He had convinced himself a long time ago that Daben would use anything to justify his deeds. At this moment he feared the righteousness of Daben's scheme. There were so many things he wanted to know, but he could only muster a single question. "Is it true? Are you really called Hou-Jo Poleb?"

Devian took the staff from his back. The four women in front of him were getting to their feet. It was clear that neither side would back down. "I told you, there's no time. Daben will be alerted to our actions. We can't let him prepare anymore than he may have already. His followers are still weak and scattered after my last attack. You can handle yourself. Leave them to me."

"No," he replied, as he cocked his second gun-blade. "We're in this mission together. We do this together."

Naieena was also eager for Senjek to depart. "If you seek Daben's head, go and take it. You may do as you like. This is none of your concern, Bohmet."

Senjek laughed. "He's not allowed to kill Daben, but I am? What bullshit is this?"

"No, it's not just that," Devian replied. "They don't want me to interfere with this world in any way. I'm no longer welcome here. I will go when I have my revenge."

The one holding the daggers offered her words to the conversation next. "This will prove to be a fatal vendetta. You can't foresee the consequences of your actions. *koonto waoht'o.*"

"I know exactly what I'm doing. Your prophets are not their predecessors; crippled in fear of the last prophecy of the Known Council. I hold zero confidence in their visions. This is your last warning. Let me pass."

Naieena shook her head. "I can't let you do that, your majesty."

Senjek pointed *Kilinus* toward the young women in front of him. He placed his other arm behind his back and rested *Selna* on the ground to his rear. "If we work together we can dispatch them quicker. We have a better chance of storming the castle together, Devian."

"My name is Hou-Jo." He twisted the bo staff in his hands. He did not seem pleased to admit to that. "This is not your fight, Senjek. You can disorient them. If they have a chance to fortify the palace for siege the battle is lost. I need you inside."

Senjek exited his attack pose. "Fine. I hope you know what you're doing."

Hou-Jo soon stood alone in front of those who would seek to hinder him. He only knew the one by name, but through somewhat playful banter, he soon learned the rest. The pyromancer was Yadira of House Daroes. She had long, flowing red hair. She had no physical weapons like the others, but she wore a pair of thick gauntlets. She had a short black skirt that only covered some of her thighs. She wore a simple white shirt with a leather coat zipped up to her bust. The one with the long sword was Crasanya from House Soeren. Her brown hair looked like a tail from the back of her head as she had it tied up to stay clear from her eyes. She wore a tight blue dress that went to her calf. Saunia of House Valenti was the last. Her daggers curved back and forth like bolts of lightning. Her hair was blacker than a starless night, darker even than the leggings and vest that covered her form. Her eyes were white as snow, just like most of her sisters. Only Naieena had eyes of a different shade, the gray before a storm.

He knew what Naieena was capable of, and Yadira had already openly displayed her skills in front of Senjek. He didn't have to guess what the other two might be capable of doing. Saunia could manipulate the earth and ground beneath her, but Hou-Jo was confident she would do nothing to disturb the grounds in which they stood. He never knew what House Soeren's major was, but it was quickly revealed to him once Senjek had made distance between them. With a flick of her sword, the five of them were surrounded by a wall of ice. No doubt to deter Senjek from coming back to partake in the conflict.

He gave them one final warning that fell on deaf ears. He was firm in his belief that they would not withdraw, but he hoped they might anyway. If nothing else he wanted to have a clear conscious. He did not blame them for the crimes of their forebears. If they insisted on carrying out their mandate, though, he would convict them of their families' sins. Naieena did not have any magic that would assist in this fight, but it was clear that her charge was to bring him in. She would see that mission through. The four of them were capable of assassinating Daben if they so wished, though he knew they wouldn't. The surviving families of Moaschen rarely took any direct actions. He was almost flattered that they were intervening because of him.

Naieena was the first to advance. She immediately went for a blow that might maim him. He easily stepped back, sparing his intestines a new home in the dirt. His staff easily found itself holding back a long sword. He used his bo to push the sword into the ground, using the other end to block one of Saunia's daggers. The other quickly followed, but he used the thick heel of his boot to knock it from her hand. He left his chest exposed and instantly felt a fist crash against his sternum. The physical force combined with the blast of fire knocked him back into the ice wall.

He quickly reacted to the scythe swinging at his feet. He leaped high into the air and used his power to levitate above the battlefield. Another ball of fire flew toward him, but he deflected into the ice wall. Regular ice would have absorbed the heat and turn in a veil of water. This ice was different. It caught on fire. The sight of the inferno in this place distracted him. He remembered the last time he witnessed a wall of fire in this area.

The distraction proved costly. Naieena used her scythe to launch Yadira into him. This time her fist found its home in his abdomen, supplemented with a blast of fire. He crashed into a wall that was still only ice, knocking it over. He got to his feet just in time for a flurry of follow-up strikes. He had lost grip of his staff when he crashed through wall, so he had no choice but to absorb the blows. Luckily, Yadira was unable to sustain the flame that accentuated the strikes. She clearly wasn't accustomed to battle (he suspected none of them were). She fatigued quickly. He immediately began to block her attacks and began to land some fists of his own.

His staff came flying toward him. No one threw it to him; he summoned it himself. He reached behind him with his right hand to grab it. As he swung it forward, Yadira jumped back, and the bo clashed with Crasanya's sword. A stream of ice protruded from the tip as she swung at him. Each swing left behind a block of ice suspended in the air where the blade had traveled. As he retreated from her advance, Naieena used the blunt end of her scythe to knock the ice toward him at an alarming velocity. He was able to avoid contact with each projectile, though.

Hou-Jo clenched his fist and swung it across his chest. The remaining ice wall that surrounded them shattered and flew toward each of his assailants. The attack knocked most of them back, but Yadira used a wall of flame to disintegrate the chunk of ice that was intended for her. She was unprepared for him to be right on top of her, though. A swift blow to the side of her head put her on the ground. Crasanya was on him next. The exchanged between them almost resembled a sword duel. Each strike was intended to make a non-lethal injury, but they were all parried with ease.

Naieena joined her sister. Her scythe was a unique weapon that most would not be trained to counter. Hou-Jo was not most people. He defended against the both of them seemingly as effortlessly as he would against one of them individually. Saunia was the next to recover and had soon entered the brawl. Still, even with the three of them, they could not wear down Hou-Jo's defense. He could see the doubt in their eyes. They began to understand the reality of their plight. He also knew they would not back down; they would continue as long as they kept him occupied.

He pushed the three of them away with another concussive wave of force. Yadira would have been the first to her feet if he didn't drive the butt of his staff into her stomach. She collapsed to one knee and tried to catch her breath. Saunia threw a dagger at him, but he caught it in his hand. He slid the blade through his belt and pushed her through the wall of the stable. Crasanya and Naieena both launched their knives at him, but he caught them both with his stave. He twisted apart his bo and used the metal wire inside to wrap up their weapons. He pulled them high into the sky as they struggled to free themselves. He was a few stories above the ground when he released himself from their blades, letting them crash to the ground.

They were able to compose themselves relatively quickly. These women were more worthy competitors than those who had guarded Daben. He levitated closer toward the field but kept a respectable distance from them. He placed his staff on his back. He had gotten a feel of these girls. He knew they didn't have what it took to beat him. Their misguided righteousness would not deny him of his vengeance.

Crasanya had created a spike made of ice as large as a person. Saunia used her command over the earth to shoot a rock into the ice. Hou-Jo allowed himself to drop to the ground, avoiding the projectiles. He soon had his staff in one hand and a dagger in the other. As he landed on the ground, he used the two weapons in his grasp to block two blades. Naieena leaped toward them and made a swinging motion for his chest. He ducked, and Naieena harmlessly flew past him. He carried the momentum to flip backward. As his feet went into the air, his heel caught the hilt of Crasanya's sword and launched it into the air. Yadira threw all her force into a haymaker. He made her regret that. With a flick of his wrist, he pushed her into Saunia, which knocked the lone dagger in her possession free.

Naieena tried to return to the fray. Hou-Jo launched the knife he held toward her, which caused her to alter course. He caught the sword as it fell back toward the ground. Yadira tried to punch him again but regretted that she tried. The sword was very sharp. With a single swing, he cut off her arm below the elbow. Saunia moved in next, but without any daggers to parry the blow, Hou-Jo left the sword in her stomach. He pushed himself away into the air as Naieena tried to swing at him. Crasanya and Naieena took a defensive position in front of their injured sisters.

Naieena and Crasanya looked at each other. Naieena wanted to keep fighting. She still hoped they might be able to detain him. Crasanya knew the truth of it, though. She shook her head. Their sisters were hurt. They could survive their injuries if they abandoned their mission. The odds of defeating him had proven slim at full strength. They would all be dead if he wanted it. She pulled her sword from Saunia and put pressure on the wound. She sheathed the blade. Naieena begrudgingly followed suit and holstered her scythe.

"Please, Hou-Jo," Naieena pleaded, "let Daben Celt go. You don't have to do this."

He walked past them as they dressed Yadira's arm. "If you truly know who I am and what I've been through, you would not ask me that. No matter the consequences of blade and gun, Daben Celt will die tonight. Tell your prophets you failed them. Just like they failed me."

Yadira and Saunia were helped to their feet and slowly made their retreat. Hou-Jo followed after Senjek. He hoped Bohmet hadn't reached the mark first.

# 39. TREISTINA'S VERDICT

Treistina learned more about the developing situation. She and Eve would soon make for the parliament building for safe keeping. Treistina was not happy with the idea of being on the sidelines, but she wasn't in a position to protest. She wanted to be with Senjek. She wanted the chance to tell him her side of the story. Everything began to spiral out of control. She feared that she might not have the opportunity. Evan was going to walk straight into the Lobby's den. He was going to force the presidential guard to follow him. If the President hadn't appointed Dak Johnsen as Suzerain, members of the Iedenian Guard would accompany him. Instead, he was with the best Veian Grebllyh could find on short notice. She feared what might happen at Monarch Fall.

Afforded the luxury of a hot bath to wash away the grime of the last few days, Treistina tied her hair up into a bun. She declined to apply any make-up. Her lips only showed their natural light pink shade. Her face was paler than Eve had ever seen it before. The paleness only made her emerald eyes more piercing. She wore a plain gray shirt and black leggings.

She currently sat alone in a small room. It was the room she had slept in the previous night. It had a bed, a chair, a sink, and a mirror. There was a small table near the door. It wasn't a room made to punish her; it was merely the only accommodations available. There were two lights. One above the mirror and one in the ceiling. The light above the mirror was the only thing illuminating the room. A room deep inside the building, there were no windows to the outside. She thought the room was oddly poetic. This room was like her life with the Lobby. There were only two lights in that life: her brother and father. Without any concept of what may lie outside the walls of the room, the light would be most precious. Something worth protecting.

Like the Lobby, there was a way outside of this room. The door. But why would you leave behind the only thing that you knew to hold dear? Someone wouldn't leave unless another opened the door. Senjek was the one that opened that door. When she first met Senjek, she was still very much resigned to her room. She had only allowed him to enter. After spending enough time with him, she had learned there was much more to life. She allowed herself to leave the room behind.

She stared at the door for nearly an hour. She hoped and prayed that Senjek would open this door as well. She hoped that somehow he had gotten away from the palace. He wanted her to run through that door and somehow had forgiven her for what she had done. "Let's go back to Iedin," she would say. "Let's go back to the Jade Peak and never leave." She rubbed at her eyes, fearing that tears may have formed. She didn't have any tears left it would seem. She feared that she truly was what Daben made her to be. She had spent the whole night thinking about what had happened, the Lobby coming after them in the streets. Seeking safety at Monarch Fall. What she had done when the assassin had come for Daben. She did things that she should not have done. Was she a slave to the Lobby?

The doorknob creaked. Treistina quickly got to her feet. Had Senjek come back for her? Did he find a way to escape? Veian Grebllyh immediately dashed her hopes. He was wearing the same uniform as before with a key exception. She couldn't help but smile. It amused her. The flowing brown cloth had nearly caught itself in the door as he closed it behind him. "I see Evan has made you wear the cape, Corporal."

Veian did not find the humor in the situation. "As the commanding officer of the Presidential Guard I am now afforded the title of captain," he began to explain before he was cut off.

"I see Evan has made you wear the cape, Captain," she said with a growing smile. She was faking it now.

"But please, call me Veian," he finished, clearly irritated. It was then Treistina noticed that he was holding something. He placed it on the table next to him. "For your protection, I insist you put it on."

It was a bulletproof vest. More than likely it would be better served to protect from a knife or other bladed weapon; parliament was well inside of Repulsor range. She let her smile fall away. "Expecting problems on the way to the state building?"

Veian shook his head. "Do I? No. I don't expect there would be any issues going from here to there."

Treistina nodded. "I see. Evan's idea."

"That's the President to you," Veian fired back, strangely annoyed. "You may be friends with Eve, but don't think you can be that formal. And no, it was not the President's idea. It's mine. Put it on."

She walked over to the table and picked up the vest. She pulled it over her arms and strapped herself into the protective garment. "No helmet?"

"We're not in a war zone, Ms. Yahn," he replied coldly. "You and the Vice President will be escorted in two separate vehicles." He explained that the Lobby had a stronghold at Monarch Fall, but there would no doubt be Lobby members spread out throughout the city. He didn't want Eve's life endangered by traveling with a member of the Lobby. He would take some measures to aid in Treistina's safety, though.

"I told you, I'm not part of the Lobby anymore," she argued.

"And I wasn't born yesterday," he retorted. "Parliament won't consent to send a military force after the Lobby stronghold. We're legally bound to protect Evan, and we're merely following him. When you and Eve walked into my office, she said that she wants Celt brought in alive."

Treistina shrugged. "So? With how diplomatic Parliament has insisted on being, I'm sure they want the same thing."

Veian smiled. "No, they don't. I've spoken with Representatives Zophar and von Breischa. Daben Celt is a menace. He's also the head of the snake. Without him, the Lobby dies. I've spoken with Vincent. He is, of course, furious that Evan continues to circumvent our democracy, but he recognizes this situation is beyond repair. He may not have had a military career like Areka or Baron, but he's still a von Breischa. Vincent isn't stupid. He does not condone what we are doing, but he wants it done right.

No restraint. He even told me to kill his own kin if I come across Areka. I can only imagine General von Breischa would tell me to do the same."

Treistina began to feel uncomfortable with where this conversation was going. "OK. So he's killed on site. I'm sure Eve will get over it."

Veian shook his head. "But it wasn't Eve that wanted him taken alive, was it?" There was no use in trying to hide her reaction, so she made no attempt to do so. He nodded to himself. "That's what I thought. Tell me why we shouldn't kill the Praesage as well."

"No, you can't! He's changed. He's been helping you!"

"Then tell me the truth. For once in your pathetic life." Everything that she had said to him before was true. She was raised on Kramei and conditioned from an early age for the Lobby; never assimilated like so many others. Veian wanted more than that, though. He wanted to know everything she didn't tell Eve. "Since you were a child, which means before the Lobby was ever conceived. Why don't you want Daben Celt to be killed if you don't follow him any longer?"

Veian was remarkably wise for a soldier. He knew the questions to ask that Eve seemingly didn't. Maybe she didn't want to know. "He's brilliant. He's been planning this for decades. He used to read about the rebellion against the crown from hundreds of years ago. He even has a copy of the original Daben Celt's journal. He took on the persona. Twisted it. My father, Demarcus Yahn, he died years before Cineon or I were born. He gave us the name he was born with so we could be anonymous."

Veian was shocked. Her own father. He finally saw the whole picture. Cineon was raised to be a blunt instrument. Treistina was his ace in the hole. If he ever needed someone to go deep undercover. She was a sleeper agent. She was able to resist, but she couldn't entirely ignore her programming. He couldn't think of a better way to describe it. "You've been programmed since birth to serve him. The Praesage, Senjek, grew a conscious. He deserted. That's where you came in. You had to get close, though, and you underestimated him."

"I love him."

"No, I don't think you do," Veian countered. That's why they went to Monarch Fall to hide. She was subconsciously bringing Senjek back to Daben. She denied that, insisted that she didn't know Daben was there. He didn't accept that. He didn't think she was lying. He believed that she genuinely believed it herself. He chuckled to himself. Evan was right. Right about everything. He never trusted Treistina. Not once. Senjek he trusted. The man who committed atrocities. Maybe Senjek was better in deceiving others, but he didn't think that was it. "Senjek freed himself of Celt. You never did. You never could. You might love Senjek, sure. I don't think you can help yourself."

He pulled a piece of cloth from under his cape. It was Treistina's sweater. He threw it to her. She was told to put it on over the vest. She looked at the garment in her hands and then back to Veian again. "You're not taking me to parliament, are you?"

"Maybe you escaped my custody. Evan would be none the wiser. I'm sure even if he suspected something I could come up with something."

"And what about Eve?"

He responded with the fact that he did not report to Eve. Evan was the president, and that was to whom he answered. "Be frank with me. Be honest with yourself for once. Would you rather be tucked away in parliament or be in the action?" The expression on her face was the only answer he needed. "I know a soldier when I see one. Once a soldier, always a soldier."

She didn't want to be locked away in parliament, and Veian was giving her the option to get out. Now that she had the chance to get away she doubted herself. What if he was right? What if she couldn't help herself? What if she found her father in danger and found herself trying to help him? She had already done it once. She picked up a gun and tried to kill Devian Strife when he attacked. She couldn't stop herself. Devian Strife was a man who meant nothing to her. Would she choose Daben over Veian or Evan? Would she choose her father over Senjek if it came to it? She didn't care what Veian said. She had some measure of control. She would choose Senjek. She had already chosen Senjek.

# 40. STORMING THE PALACE

Senjek arrived at the palace entrance. He was unconscious when the Lobby brought him there before. He never had a chance to marvel at the sheer size of the building. He stared up at the sky. The palace was quite tall despite its age. The outer section was three floors high. There were four guard towers toward the center of the palace that pushed further toward the heavens. The tallest was twelve stories high. It was used to survey any attacks that came from the south. The south base of the castle was on the edge of a cliff. As a result, one could scan a considerable amount of land in that direction.

Cratania Vytautos greeted him. She seemed surprised to see him. Hou-Jo was right; she sent him to his death. He was a liability to the Lobby. She saw the blood stain on his shirt. He noticed that she had seen. He dropped down to one knee and grabbed at the blood stain. Cratania quickly ran up to him and kept him from falling over. "General!" She shouted. She helped him get to his feet. He tried to push her away, seemingly not wanting her help.

"It's all right," he said. "Bastard put up one hell of a fight, though. I think I might need a medical dressing." She had the door opened and escorted him inside. She called for someone to get some bandages to wrap him up. Several members of the Lobby rushed to the scene to see the Praesage. Many of them had never seen the man before. "Where is Daben?"

# The Kramei Insurrection

"He's in the south guard tower waiting for Ms. von Breischa," he heard someone blurt out. Cratania's rage was tangible. She didn't want him to know that. Maybe not where Daben was, but the fact that Areka was expected to be back. That meant Treistina wasn't in the castle either. Treistina was the only bargaining chip they had. Without her, they couldn't buy his loyalty.

Senjek made eye contact with Cratania. He saw fear in her eyes. The rest of her face betrayed nothing, but terror filled her blue eyes. She asked what he did with the body. She was referring to Hou-Jo. He smiled. "You won't see his face again. I guarantee that. Is the medic far off?"

She tried to relax, but she couldn't shake the feeling in her bones. "I've sent someone to get him. We'll get you patched up soon. May I see?"

He nodded. Cratania was very suspicious. He wouldn't pull up his shirt. He made her do it. The dried blood on his shirt stuck to his skin, so she gently tugged it free. She pulled up his shirt to investigate the wound to discover someone already treated it. "I do have one question. If I had failed to kill Hou-Jo and you hadn't heard back from me yet, why is Daben waiting for Areka to return?"

She took a few steps backward. Her words had abandoned her. Senjek repeated his question, this time louder. She stumbled over her words. She was thinking of a lie to tell him. "You were gone for much longer than what we anticipated. Daben wanted Areka to be here to help defend against a future attack." She paused for a few moments. "Who's Hou-Jo?"

The other members of the Lobby that circled them had become intrigued as well. Some of them began to make their distance. Something was clearly not right.

Senjek rolled his shoulders a few times to stretch his muscles. "Hou-Jo Poleb. The man came in here and tried to kill Celt."

Cratania shook her head. She took another step back, but she wasn't far enough away. "No, he said his name was Strife. Devian Strife."

Senjek frowned. He looked around. Everyone wanted answers. Many of those around him weren't present during the attack. They probably weren't told the name of the attacker. To hear Senjek and Cratania confused on the name of the attacker was most odd. He closed his eyes and smiled as if he had an epiphany. "Oh. Right, of course. Well, at least the medic will be busy."

296

# A Fatal Vendetta

Cratania reached for the gun at her hip. She didn't move fast enough. She should have backed up further away. Senjek instantly had *Selna* and *Kilinus* in hand. They wanted the Praesage back. They, unfortunately, got what they sought. Cratania tried to back further away as she reached for her gun, but she bumped into someone behind her. She tried to pull the pistol from its holster, but she didn't unsnap the guard, and her hand pulled away with nothing. She reached for her gun again, but it was too late. She felt the cold metal of Senjek's blade dig into her throat. She gasped for breath as the edge dragged across her neck. She abandoned the gun and reached toward the wound. She tried to scream, but her severed vocal cords couldn't make a sound.

Near two dozen Lobby members circled them. Five of them quickly followed Cratania to the ground. They never had time to process what happened before Senjek cut them down as well. Only six of the remaining men alive had weapons with which to defend themselves. Due to his injuries at the hand of Hou-Jo, Senjek couldn't dispatch them as quickly as he thought he would. It was still no contest to him, though.

Two of them had spears; the other four wielded broad swords. He parried their strikes and moved past them. He slashed through the backs of those who tried to flee. After cutting down five more, he turned to meet the advance of those who were armed. They didn't attack with any honor. Nor did he expect them to. It wasn't two or three going after him. They all attacked at once. He made quick work of the two in front. They tried to stab him, but this wasn't war, it was a duel. They weren't accustomed to fighting like that.

He used both blades to attack one person. There was so much force in the strike he knocked the sword from the man's hands. His gun-blade found a new home inside the man's stomach. He left if there and engaged another with just a single blade. His opponents parried some of his strikes, but he quickly wore down their defense. He slashed one in the face and another in the arm. He didn't go for the kill yet; he had to defend against a spear. They both thrust their weapons at him and they both missed. He cut through both of their abdomens and took a spear in his free hand. He launched it at someone who reached for a rifle.

He shoved *Selna* in the leg of the last sword-wielder left. He grabbed the other spear and used the tip of the spear to cut the throat of the man.

He then threw that spear to someone else who was moments away from having Senjek in the sights of a firearm. He followed after the two stragglers, pulling his gun-blades from the bodies that had held them. He sliced down the remaining members of the Lobby, but one of them managed to fire a bullet from their gun. The slug hit the wall, but the shot would have alerted the rest of the castle.

Hou-Jo had given him the floor plan to the palace. He didn't have any maps; he apparently recited it from memory. Senjek didn't know what was harder to believe; that there was a living heir to the Poleb family or that he knew the layout of Monarch Fall as if he'd grown up there. He decided that it was possible that he may have had time to get inside the castle to explore. The Republic had no idea the Lobby was here, so why not Hou-Jo? That raised another question, though. If he had been on Damos long enough to explore the castle, why had he only now appeared to the world? He also questioned what Hou-Jo's vendetta was against Daben. He seemed to know the leader of the Lobby, but Daben acted like he had genuinely never seen the man before.

He shook the thoughts from his mind. It didn't matter why. The man was an ally against the Lobby. He just hoped that Hou-Jo would soon follow. The remaining members of the Lobby were few by comparison, but maybe too many for him to handle alone. He quickly made his way past the throne room and toward the base of the south guard tower. He holstered his gun-blades to his back and grabbed a rifle from the wall. He switched off the safety and loaded a round from the magazine. He looked down the scope and waited for anyone to enter the cross-hairs.

A few Lobby members entered the range of Senjek's rifle and quickly fell. He could tell that there more in the throne room now, but they stayed under cover. He could hear the rush of footsteps above him. More were coming down the tower. He fired a few suppressing shots toward those in the throne room. He propped the gun to point at them. He took a handgun from the arsenal on the wall. He stepped into the corner and tried to conceal himself behind a crate. He cut into the first two that came down the stairs with his blade. There were four more that had followed. He emptied the clip of the pistol into their chests. He relieved a revolver from one of the dead men and placed it in his waistband. He could hear a commotion above him. Daben had a sizable group in the tower with him.

298

He picked up another rifle and ran toward the throne. There was a blitz of bullets that followed him. He dived behind the chair to protect himself from the gunfire. He was surprised with the care the Lobby were taking not to damage the property too severely. He blindly fired a few rounds to keep them at bay. He needed to get up the tower, but he couldn't defend himself on a staircase. If a Radius Effect covered the palace, the scene would have been completely different. He heard shouts from near the entrance. Someone else was there.

He couldn't see it, but he felt the force of a man crash into the throne itself. Then gunfire. "It's him!" he heard someone cry. Senjek felt a sudden wave of relief. He peaked around the cover of the throne and saw that Hou-Jo had made it. He watched in awe as the so-called prince calmly walked toward the throne. Bullets approached him but never got made contact.

"Senjek! Where is he?"

He pointed his rifle south. "In the tower. More men are coming down that way!" Hou-Jo was clearly not discouraged. He immediately made for the tower. It was immediately obvious that he had no intention to clear the throne room. "A little help with these guys, maybe?"

"Sorry, Bohmet. I'm only here for one man. I'll send him your regards. Tell your president 'you're welcome'."

Senjek watched Hou-Jo abandon him, helpless to stop him. Member of the Lobby followed after him. Senjek used that opportunity to gun as many down as he could. Some made it to the entrance of the tower. Others made it back behind cover. The rest were dead. He heard pleas from the remaining Lobby members to give up his assault. They claimed that he could still make things right. He could finish what he and Daben had started.

"No," he said to himself. He didn't start this. What Daben had made the Lobby into was not what Senjek wanted. Daben was foolish to think that he would be the Praesage again. "Daben has killed enough loyal Krameians in his pursuit to assimilate me," he shouted out to them. "He would have been better off assassinating me. If you value your lives, you'll have to either kill me or retreat. This doesn't end with us on the same side."

He heard gunfire after that, but not from those who surrounded him. It came from outside. He remembered the drone that had patrolled the area earlier. Republic had arrived.

# 41. HARD STOP

Blood had stained the ground. The dark sky did its best to conceal it, but it was still there. Cineon looked on amongst his men as they tried to pull the wounded to safety. Reinforcements had made their way to him. He looked at the sky to see how the thick fog reacted. When it launched into the air, it spun like a tornado. It slowly began to stop. The mechanisms of the Repulsor had run off track. The Radius Effect was gone. He wrapped his bow across his torso. "To the Praesage," he shouted.

That was the signal to alert his men that the Radius Effect was down and to open fire. The Damosi troops did not have time to react. Cineon looked on in pure satisfaction that his scheme had succeeded. Soon the Republic would lose any strategic military holdings on the Kramei surface. He was handed a new radio from his reinforcements. This one had not been affected by the electromagnetic attack from earlier. "Give me the good news, Espera."

She first explained that the Radius Effect had collapsed completely. The Repulsor itself maintained integrity. No visible damage to the outer shell, but they could only guess to the state of the interior. Ships were in the sky to keep the Republic army from getting airborne. The order had been given to maintain a safe distance from the Harvest Forward Command Center. Two of their ships had already been shot down by the camp's heavy batteries.

"Excellent," he replied. He declared Operation Zerexei to be a success. "All troops proceed with Operation Kraimos." A force would be left behind to defend TAC-OPS. The remaining Lobby members would fan out and advance past Forward Command. There would be little to stop him from taking the space elevator. From there he could begin his plans to break the blockade around the planet.

The Lobby managed to repair most of the motorcycles used during the previous engagement. Some were too damaged in the fight to get running, though. "Lock and load," he announced to the men surrounding him. "All weapons are free. Keep in mind that Republic soldiers will also be using weapons capable of achieving entrance velocity. We know they have snipers. Stay low and fast. Keep yourselves covered. No matter what—"

Cineon's instructions were cut short. He felt a tremor in the ground. Something had happened. Something that he hadn't anticipated. He turned to face Forward Command. The turrets were all pointed south and had already opened fire. They continued to fire south. He felt the soil beneath him shake again. "No," he whispered to himself. "He wouldn't dare." His fears were quickly and unquestionably confirmed. He saw two large cables fall toward the ground that were as large as a tree. "Take cover!"

The cables hit the ground before anyone could react to his instruction. The cable crashed into a dozen of his comrades. He pulled out his radio. "Operation Kraimos is compromised. Abandon the mission! Retreat to TAC-OPS!" He took one of the operational motorcycles for himself and quickly made his way back to his base. Some of his troops hesitated. They had no concept of what was about to happen. Many did, though. They frantically followed their general. Those on foot that acted immediately had a slim chance of getting to safety. Shouts of terror quickly died down as he escaped the battlefield. He underestimated how quickly the elevator would fall.

A tremor in the ground threw him from his vehicle. The elevator impacted the ground with such force that dirt and dust flew high into the air. He opened his eyes and saw the sky wheel above him. He felt a strange sensation in his legs. His eyes regained their focus. His men tried to drag him back to TAC-OPS. The force of the impact knocked him out. He ordered the men to stop. He got to his feet and stumbled toward the entrance. He didn't know if he made more distance on his bike or by being dragged.

# A Fatal Vendetta

There was panic inside the base. The lights that still worked were flickering. Espera quickly greeted him. He hadn't seen such despair in her face in years. He made his way to the battlements, but she followed him. "Sir, the Suzerain opened fire on the space elevator's anchor. Those in orbit acted quickly and detached. The entire shaft isn't lost, but the impact of what fell has knocked out all but two of our generators."

He reached the battlements and observed the damage. The tip of the shaft struck the east side of the building. Further out he could see a fire. The Damosi who manned the counterweight couldn't act in time to salvage the cables. The heat of reentry ignited the dead foliage half a mile away. He turned back to Espera. "Divert all manpower to getting full power back. I want defensive batteries online as soon as possible."

Espera was bewildered by that. "Excuse me, sir. Shouldn't we continue to evacuate our troops out there? Forward Command—"

"Is closer to the equator than we are! The impact would not have been as intense there. They'll have full power restored before we do. That's if they haven't recovered already. Did any of our birds get knocked out of the sky?"

She replied that communications were down. The only ships they knew to still be in flight were the ones they could see from TAC-OPS. "I will instruct all hands to assist in the restoration of the generators. But after that, I will resume rescue ops."

"Fine. Make it so. Once communications are back up, I want you to mobilize a team to the Repulsor as well. We'll need to restore the Radius Effect." He left the battlements and made his way to his personal quarters. He was amazed at Dak Johnsen's actions. He wondered if General von Breischa would have done the same thing. General Greene certainly wouldn't have done it. President Gie had proven wise in his selection of Suzerain. This changed the entire game.

He entered his quarters and poured himself a drink. He quickly swallowed the contents and refilled the glass. He tried to determine how the fleet in orbit would react. The priority would be to secure the counterweight of the elevator. It would be months before they could repair the elevator. The Fury would need to resolve the conflict on the ground first. They would have to keep the dock for the elevator in orbit. They would have to adjust the orbits of their ships to compensate. Those were actions he knew would have to be taken.

He made a third drink for himself. He left his quarters and went to find Ms. Rimeax. What would they do next, though? His first concern was capital ships entering the atmosphere. He would have to get the Repulsor functioning again before that happened. The time it would take to secure the remains of the space elevator would buy him enough time for that. He met his right-hand woman in the hallway on his way back to the battlements.

"We have two generators back up and running. The other four have cracked casings from the shock wave that need repairing first."

"What about communications?"

"The radio transmitter was shattered. I'm sorry to say we can't fix it. We'll have to rely on over-the-air Network channels to communicate."

"Get someone to monitor Network transmissions to the DNC satellite. If the signal bandwidth degrades at all, it may indicate a ship is entering low orbit." He hoped the Republic fleet would be unable to coordinate an attack from orbit yet. "A single attacking ship from orbit will level TAC-OPS."

"You don't think their naval brass would take such drastic action?" She asked. General Greene seemed committed to losing the fight before Johnsen took over. "If the fleet were willing to fire from space, wouldn't they have done it by now?"

"Dak Johnsen would have to issue the command. I don't know if anyone in orbit has the authority to authorize such an attack. They certainly don't have the balls." Espera argued that Dak was the acting General of the Armies of Damos; his authority didn't extend to the Navy. "As Suzerain, he controls the Damosi Navy as well. Unless Evan Gie crowned him king, he commands everything but the Iedenian Guard."

Ms. Rimeax pleaded to divert some personnel to rescue operations. With two generators back online, they had a surplus of people committed to repairs. He granted her request. He instructed that if Network bandwidth had any noticeable change to declare Mauve Alert. He stepped up to the battlements and looked south toward HFCC. The sky had started to clear. They had taken considerable damage as well. It wasn't as strong as TAC-OPS. At best they suffered half the damage as he had. He hoped that Mr. Johnsen was more committed to his people than he was to the cause. Cineon's father would be furious at this major setback. No one person was above their cause, though. This was a war they couldn't afford to lose. The entire system would bleed if the Lobby failed.

# 42. FOURTH DAMOSI PATRICIAN REGIMENT

Evan Gie wiped blood from the tip of his spear. He thought it was poetic to bring the heirloom with him. It was valuable to his family because his ancestor used it in the Battle of Monarch Fall. The monarchy made it for Javk Gie, who was the personal aide to the Crown Prince. The spear helped topple the old regime. He would use it to bring an end to the Lobby.

"It's not entirely poetic," Mr. Grebllyh argued. "I don't remember Gie killing Celt during the revolution."

"The von Breischa fought against the rebels back then," he replied. "It's not a one-to-one comparison, Captain."

Veian shrugged. "Areka von Breischa is fighting for the new revolution."

"Enough," Evan moaned. "In any case, it feels good to get my hands dirty again. I forgot what it felt like to be part of the action."

Veian conceded to that. They had secured the throne room easily enough. Lobby troops were focused on something else and weren't guarding the entrance. There were four guard towers, though. It was possible that the Lobby had outposts in all four. Daben Celt had to be in one of them. The presidential escort had wiped out most of the Lobby members. There was less than a dozen left, detained in the throne room. Evan demanded that they be arrested and sent back to parliament.

"Not him," Evan said as the last one passed him. He noticed the gun-blades holstered to the man's back. He looked over to Veian who didn't look surprised. Evan's eyes widened. "You knew?"

"Evan…"

He didn't let another word pass his lips. He punched Senjek in the face as hard as he could. Bohmet dropped down to one knee. Evan took a step back. "Where did you get those? Trespassing on Monarch Fall and possessing two gun-blades. You know this is enough to put you in jail for the rest of your life?"

Veian personally accepted responsibility for Senjek's custody. The soldier who had detained him was sent to investigate the northern guard tower. He removed the restraints from Senjek's wrists. "You gave yourself up to our troops soon enough; I'm guessing I don't have to worry about you attacking us, General?" The look on Senjek's face was that of feigned ignorance. "Don't bother. Treistina told me."

"Treistina and I were taken captive by Daben Celt." Senjek refused to believe Veian. The corporal must have been bluffing. Senjek could talk his way out of this. "Daben knew Evan and I were close. He's been making Evan's life miserable for years. He's been goading him at him at every turn. I didn't think you valued our friendship this much, though."

Veian bit his lip. "I'm sorry. To both of you. Senjek, I promised Treistina and Eve I wouldn't say anything. I also told them I wouldn't lie to a superior. You didn't get those gun-blades here to defend yourself. You certainly didn't find a magnetic holster for a pair of them that fit you. Mr. President, one of your closest friends is an enemy of the state. Senjek Bohmet is the Praesage."

Evan was dumbfounded. He shook his head. "No," he cried out. "No. I don't believe that. Senjek tell me this isn't true." He waited for a reply, but he realized he wasn't going to get one. He punched Senjek again, this time knocking him on his back. "I trusted you! You were my friend! How could you lie to me like this?"

Senjek rubbed his jaw. Evan had quite the right hook. "When should I have told you? Would you have reacted less violently if I told you sooner?"

Evan had a tight grip on his spear now. His face was red with rage. "I doubt it. Tell me why I shouldn't just kill you?"

Senjek explained that he had abandoned KILLER. What the Lobby was today was not what it was initially set out to be. "The entire time I've been here on Damos I've been working to help stop the Lobby any way I can. I'm here now to kill Daben Celt."

Evan didn't like that response. He announced that he would be the one to take Daben's life, not Senjek. He had reservations about whatever hardship Senjek may have endured at the hands of the Lobby, but he had serious doubts that they were greater than his own personal strife. The Lobby attacked his sister. His brother and nephew were both killed. Two of his most trusted and valued military minds defected to the Lobby. Senjek insisted that he had more reason to go after Daben. Evan responded by saying that he could only go after Daben if he allowed it. "I won't kill you, but give me one good reason why I should release you from my custody?"

Veian saw an opportunity to kill two birds with one stone. "I have accepted responsibility for Mr. Bohmet, sir. He says he truly wants to help dismantle the Lobby. I'm sure he intends to receive a pardon for his past crimes. What better way to prove it on Kramei? Once we are done here, I can personally escort him to Kramei and he can assist Suzerain Johnsen's campaign to eliminate Cineon and the KILLER army."

Evan nodded in agreement, somehow oblivious that this benefited Veian as well. Veian had tried everything in his power to get transferred back to Forward Command on Kramei. "I'm going to check with the rest of the team. Figure out what our next move is here. Mr. Grebllyh, I trust you to hammer out the details with Mr. Bohmet."

Senjek watched Evan walk over toward the south tower. He was eager to follow because he knew Daben was at the top of that tower. He felt Veian's hand on his shoulder. He turned to face the corporal who punched in the face. He was surprised, but he shouldn't have been. Veian rubbed his knuckles. "I don't know you as well as Evan, but I think you deserve it. Let's just say that one's for Dak."

Senjek got to his feet. "I suppose Dak is probably owed two hits like Evan."

Veian shrugged. "I can punch you again if you'd like."

Senjek took a step back and raised his hands. "No, that's all right. I'm no glutton for punishment."

"All right," Veian relented. "Let's talk about the good work we can do together on Kramei. I trust you've kept up to date with current developments."

Senjek looked surprised. "I know what the administration has approved for the Network to display. I'm sure I could be briefed on a few things. Also, consider the fact I've either been on the run or held captive for some time."

Veian chuckled. "Dak once told me you were funny." He had Senjek tell him what he knew about the state of affairs on Kramei. He then updated him with everything they knew since Dak's last update. "Admittedly we haven't heard from Captain Johnsen for some time. The last communication we received stated that he had gone into the Plains of Harvest himself."

"Daben is here because of me, Veian," Senjek explained. "He believed I was the difference the Lobby needed to meet his endgame. But one man won't make a difference on the battlefield."

Veian considered that statement for a few moments. He nodded. "Maybe he was right. Maybe you are the key to stopping all of this. I guess you'd be handy in a fight, but you can do more. You can convince the people of Kramei to denounce the Lobby. Once Daben is out of the picture that will leave you and Cineon. He's proven a capable field commander, but he doesn't have what it takes to lead the Lobby."

"You might be onto something. I don't want to spend the rest of my life in a cage, but I have reservations. I want Treistina kept safe. If and when I would get back from Kramei I hope to have a life with her."

Veian smiled. "Of course. I've spoken with Treistina. I had doubts about what she had said, but speaking with you here now, I believe it. I'll make sure that she's kept safe." He felt a lump in his throat. Maybe it was some part of his conscious. Though it seemed to come naturally to him, Veian was never much of a liar. He didn't necessarily question their motives or intentions. The facts were undeniable, and he had already made up his mind. Maybe Treistina wasn't beyond saving, but what good could Bohmet possibly do to make up for all of his wrongs? Any moment Treistina was going to enter the palace. He could then arrest her and further coerce Senjek. If Daben had used Treistina as a means to control the mighty Praesage, why couldn't he?

Senjek offered his hand. "Sounds like a plan to me." Veian reached out and shook his hand. "I'll need to keep the gun-blades, though. Most of the Krameian people never saw my face. These weapons are one of my few identifying features."

Veian couldn't have agreed more. "Good thinking. There would be no place for those things here anyway. But leave them on Kramei. Let the Praesage die with the Lobby." Senjek seemed strangely relieved to hear that. The thought of being rid of that title seemed to uplift him. "Well, maybe not completely dead. I might have to call in a favor someday."

Senjek politely laughed. He wasn't sure if that was a threat or not, but he had few cards left to play. He heard a loud crashing noise come from above them. He looked around for Gie. He didn't see him anywhere. "Where's Evan? I don't seem him anywhere." He saw two soldiers standing at the entrance to the south tower. He didn't see anyone else, either. "Has anyone seen the president?"

One of the soldiers nodded. "We've cleared most of the towers. There were a few stragglers, but most of them gave up without incident. The southern guard tower showed clear signs of conflict. It seems the remaining bulk of Lobby members have pulled back to this outpost. We believe Daben Celt is holding out there. President Gie took the remaining escort with him to detain him."

"Son of a bitch went on alone." Veian reloaded his shotgun and pumped a round into the chamber. "You two continue to guard this exit. Keep an eye on Mr. Bohmet as well. He is not to leave without me."

Veian ran past the two guards in pursuit of his president. Senjek made no signs of doing the same. He would not stand idly by in this. He would wait for the opportune moment to knock out the guards and go after Daben as well. "Assuming Hou-Jo hasn't killed him yet," he said to himself.

# 43. THE HERALD

*My plans to re-purpose Senjek Bohmet to our cause has seemingly failed. All the pieces were in place. Then a new player joined the game. I don't know who this Devian Strife person is, but he clearly knows me. I made hard decisions and carried out harsh actions to lift the people of Kramei to a better life. I'm willing to admit that some lives were negatively impacted. I do not believe him to be from Kramei. Given the power he wields, my only conclusion that he was sent by the Unknown Council to assassinate me. If you see no further entries in this journal know it's because he succeeded. If you are reading this, I hope you are a supporter of Kramei and continue the fight. We must be ready for the days to come.*

Daben closed his journal. He stood on the top floor of the southern guard tower. One could see so much of the land from here. There was no construction like this on Kramei. He walked over to the southern wall and looked over the edge. A scaffolding built along the side of the tower obstructed his view of the cliff. It wasn't part of the original construction, built after the Battle of Monarch Fall. He tucked his journal into a crevice in the wall for safe keeping. He hoped that he could use Treistina to control Senjek. It was clear that either Bohmet called his bluff or he failed to kill Strife.

He had heard much commotion beneath him. Someone was climbing the tower and climbed it fast. It was possible that Senjek had come back for him. As skilled as Senjek was he wouldn't have been able to advance up the tower so quickly. He listened to the pattern of sustained gunfire. Just one side fired against another. It was Strife. Daben was ready this time.

He heard a loud crash a few feet beneath him. It sounded liked a part of the building came apart. His team had blown explosive charges to collapse part of the stairwell. He hoped that might stop Strife, but he feared it would only slow him down. Daben quickly realized his fears. He saw the man who called himself Devian Strife walk into the room. He had a new stick, one not made of wood. He was entirely confident in his stride; convinced that he had already won.

"I see Senjek failed to complete the task he was set out to complete," Daben said. "A shame. He was really quite good, if not insolent."

The assassin chuckled. "I let Bohmet live. It seems he would defy you until the day he dies. Or the day you die. Do you know what today is?"

Daben pulled his pistols from his waist. He pulled the triggers in rapid succession, hoping one might find its target. It was futile. Each bullet had come to a stop in the air before they made an impact. His enemy flicked his wrist and sent the slugs back, each one barely grazing Daben. No serious injury, but it did hurt. He dropped to one knee and clutched his left arm. "Playing with your food, huh? Before I die, tell me one thing. I truly don't know who you are. What did I do to deserve your rage?"

His target took a few steps forward. Just a few more was all he needed. He shook his head. "You really don't recognize me? It's been a long time, I'll admit. I forgot your face many years ago. But your name. Your name never left me."

That genuinely confused Daben. "Who the fuck are you?"

"My name is Hou-Jo Poleb!" He pushed his hand out in front of him, and Daben found himself against a wall. "You took my home from me. You killed my family. You sent me to the worst hell possible. My brother was King Xen'que. Your accomplice Javk Gie stabbed him in the back. Starting to ring any bells?"

The magic that held Daben released him. The man was insane. The Unknown Council made an assassin that thought he was a survivor of the monarchy. He thought about telling him his true name but decided that would do nothing. At worst it would probably enrage him more. Just a few more steps. "Not ringing any bells, sorry. Maybe you need to jog my memory."

Hou-Jo quickened his advanced. He stepped on a pressure plate and felt his foot noticeably sink a few inches. He paused. He never spent much time in the guard towers, but he didn't recall anything like that being there. He suddenly found himself on his knees. He pressed his hands to his ears. Some sort of cannon that fired sound waves. He tried to pull Daben closer to him, but his power had failed him. The sound waves were too intense. He couldn't focus or concentrate. It was a trap.

Daben cut the power to the sound cannon. Before Hou-Jo could retaliate, there was a needle in his neck. "It's a sort of nerve agent. It did wonders on Nodo Haeese. Made his mind very palpable. My guess is it will stunt those incredible powers of yours." He punched Hou-Jo in the throat. "That's for what you did to Areka." Hou-Jo got to his feet but quickly stumbled. The contents of the syringe took effect immediately. Daben reloaded a pistol with a fresh round. "Goodbye."

Hou-Jo wasn't able to use his power, but his physical prowess hadn't completely abandoned him. He grabbed his staff and knocked the gun from Daben's hand. Nothing would deny his vengeance. Not when he waited for so long. He swung his stave toward his target multiple times and landed a majority of his strikes. Daben managed to knock the weapon from his hands. Hou-Jo felt Daben's fist in his jaw.

Daben followed up with multiple other strikes. "You will not ruin this for me! You think you're the Prince of Damos reborn? Then follow the rest of your kin to the grave!" He continued to punch Hou-Jo. His face recoiled to the side with each strike. With each punch, though, Hou-Jo's head moved less and less. Finally, his punches didn't seem to affect him at all. It was if the serum had already worn off. "No. That's not possible," Daben cried out.

Hou-Jo pushed Daben backward with his mind. Daben reached for his other gun and tried to reload it. He wasn't fast enough. Hou-Jo summoned his staff to his grasp again and struck Daben in the chest. Celt found himself tumbling over the ledge. Hou-Jo fell to one knee and dropped his staff. He smiled. The southern tower was a poor choice for Daben to seek refuge. There would be no way to survive the fall. He got to his feet and picked up the pistol that he had knocked free from Celt's grip. He wouldn't get careless now. He had to confirm the kill.

He took off his longcoat and let it fall to the ground. He held the gun out to his side as he slowly walked toward the edge. He suddenly felt a sharp pain in his back. He fell to his knees and dropped the gun. He could hear the sound of a rifle reload behind him. "It's over Celt! There's nowhere left for you to hide!"

Hou-Jo chuckled. He was confused for Daben. He reached behind his back and grabbed hold of the stick protruding from his back. He pulled the weapon from his skin and brought it into his gaze. He recognized the spear. "Gie?"

"That's right, you son of a bitch. I bet you never thought it would end like this, did you?"

Hou-Jo got to his feet; his eyes never broke contact with the spear. He felt his rage return to him. "Gie!" He turned to face Evan. He didn't remember Javk's face, but he recalled the name. He remembered the spear as well. "GIE!"

Evan raised his rifle. Hou-Jo clearly wasn't affiliated with the Lobby, but he seemed to have no love for the president, either. "I'm sorry, I thought you were Celt. Just take it easy. I don't want to hurt you!"

Hou-Jo flipped the spear in his hand and drew it behind his back. Evan began to fire his gun but found that his bullets strayed off course. His eye widened as he saw his own spear fly toward him. It hit him right in the chest. The force knocked him off his feet and pinned him against the wall. Evan grabbed hold of the handle and tried to tug it loose. The pain increased with each tug, so he let it be. Hou-Jo walked up to him. "You and Celt both lived to this day. I'm glad for the people. Happy that they have found a way to rule themselves. But the Poleb family deserves justice."

The president didn't understand. He lost feeling in his extremities. "The Poleb family? Are you mad? They've been dead for centuries."

Hou-Jo twisted the spear. Evan cried out in agony. "Don't play games with me, Javk! It's too late to beg for your life!"

Evan grimaced. "Javk? Javk Gie has been long dead too. Do you not know who I am?

314

Hou-Jo's mind began to race. "Centuries?" He took a step back. There were many things that he had witnessed that did not make sense to him. Senjek's weapons. The advancement of the world in his absence. Anyone he spoke with that thought the Unknown Council was some tale. He looked down at Evan in horror. "How long ago has it been since the monarchy was overthrown? Exactly how long?"

Evan struggled to stay conscious. "I don't know exactly. Five-hundred years?"

Hou-Jo stepped further back toward the ledge. "No. It can't be." He looked out the tower and saw the landscape of the city. So many buildings were so much higher than the castle. He looked back to Evan. "What have I done?"

"Evan!" a voice cried out. Veian ran up to the president. He dropped his shotgun to the ground as he ran up to his commander in chief. "What happened? Medic!"

Evan's voice was weak. "I thought... I thought he was Dab... thought he was Da—" his let out a final breath. His eyes went blank. He was dead.

Veian didn't know what to do at first. He was handpicked to lead the presidential guard. Evan trusted him. He couldn't save him, not even from himself. The members of Evan's escort had cleared the blockage after detaining the rest of the Lobby in the tower below. Veian looked over at Hou-Jo. Most of the squad had him in their sights. Veian shook with rage. "That man just executed our president. Put him down!"

They opened fire, but Hou-Jo moved quicker. He leaped backward out of the tower. Veian got to his feet and ran to the edge. Hou-Jo was already on the ground and moved south. Veian jumped down onto the scaffolding and attached a wire to it. "Abseil after him! Don't let him get away!"

# 44. A FATAL VENDETTA

Treistina had tried her best to stay hidden as she made her way into Monarch Fall. There were visible signs of a conflict on the outskirts. There were a few puddles of blood scattered across the ground. She also noticed shards of ice dotting the landscape as well. She was curious as to what had happened here. It wasn't like this a few days ago. Veian had her in the trunk of one of the vehicles that escorted the president to the outskirts of the estate. After they had left, she was able to climb into the back seat of the car and let herself out. The bullet-proof vest was the only protection she received; she was given no weapons to defend herself.

She kept her hair in a bun as she walked through the royal estate. She approached the horse stables and hid there for a few minutes. She watched as Evan led the presidential escort into the palace. There was a single lookout guarding the door. The president chucked his spear into the guard's neck. She waited several more minutes to let the situation calm down. She crouched low to the ground as she made her to the palace entrance. She couldn't hear much of anything inside. She thought she heard Senjek's voice. She cautiously leaned inside. She saw four people standing several yards away.

"Son of a bitch went on alone. You two continue to guard this exit. Keep an eye on Mr. Bohmet as well. He is not to leave without me." She watched as Veian ran up the stairs. She slowly walked along the edge of the wall. She didn't want to be seen by the Damosi guards. Part of her wanted Senjek to stay where he was and not do anything. Another part of her waited for him to act as she knew he would.

Senjek had paced back and forth a number of times. The guards let their guard down and peered up the stairs of the tower. Senjek was there in an instant. He grabbed their skulls and bashed them together. The two guards fell unconscious. He made for the base of the stairs and stared straight up.

"Senjek!"

He climbed the first few steps when he came to a stop. He doubled back and ran into the throne room. Treistina had walked out to the center of the room and just stood there. He had learned quite a few unfavorable truths since she had last seen him. She didn't know if he would be happy to see her or not. He started to walk toward her. He was slow at first, but his pace quickened. She began to close the distance as well. Before she knew it, they were an arm's length apart.

He wrapped his arms around her. She had never been held so firmly in her entire life. He finally let her go. He kissed her. It wasn't a lustful kiss; he embraced her in unconditional love. He pulled away and looked into her emerald eyes. There was a tear in his eye. "Treistina," he said with a cracking voice. "I wasn't sure if I'd ever see you again."

"I'm sorry," is all that she could manage. "I'm sorry about everything."

Senjek cupped her chin in his hand. "No. You have nothing to be sorry for. Daben Celt has done his best to give us lives that are suited to only serve his designs. He made us things we never wanted to be. Together we found a life worth living, a life with meaning. I confessed to you about my past with the Lobby. And you sat there as if you had no idea."

She shook her head. "I had no idea you were the Praesage."

"Whatever. You didn't confess to your past the same reason I never did. Out of fear of losing what we have. If the Lobby never came after me, I probably would have never told you the truth. I can't blame you for intending to do the same."

She felt as if she wanted to cry, but again, no tears came. "Can we have a life together? Has your cover been blown?"

"It has. Evan knows the truth. Veian told him." He could see Treistina became angry with hearing that. "It's going to be okay." He explained to her that he had the opportunity to earn a pardon. Once Daben was dealt with on Damos, he would be sent to Kramei to dismantle what remained of the Lobby.

She nodded. "That's why you weren't sure if you'd see me again. Evan is sending you to your death." Senjek explained why he needed to act. She hated how much sense he made. They couldn't hide from both the Lobby and the Republic forever. If they just ran away someone would find them eventually, even inside the caves of Jade Peak. "What are you going to do now?"

He explained that he was going after Daben. "Evan went up the tower without us. Veian followed after him. Daben may very well already be dead, but I need to see this through. I can't let him get away this time."

Treistina shook her head. "No, please. Don't. Just come back to the city with me. Let us be together, even if it's for one more night. I love you."

Senjek wrapped her in his arms again. He ran his fingers through her hair. He took in her perfume. He didn't want to forget anything about this woman. No matter what. He wiped a tear from his eye using his upper arm. "I love you too. I'm sorry." He tightened his grip and restricted her airflow. She realized what he was doing, but it was too late. By the time her hand reached his bicep, she had gone limp. He gently propped her up against the wall. He kissed her on the forehead. "I'll see you again before the end. I promise."

He cautiously began to make his way up the stairs of the tower. He held *Kilinus* in both hands. He didn't want to be taken off guard and lose both weapons. Each gun-blade had two separate blades attached to the gun-barrel. They joined near the tip, which had a hook that came back up toward the blade. The gap was necessary to let the force of the gunshot out. Some braces held the blades together, so it didn't come apart from the recoil. There were about five floors left when he noticed a problem. A partially collapsed floor blocked the top two levels. The debris went into the stairwell. It would take time for him to get past the rubble, time he didn't have. He decided he would have to scale up the outside of the tower to get to the top in time. He went up a few more stairs and entered the next available observation deck.

"Hello, Bohmet," said an angry voice. Senjek was shocked to see Daben standing in front of him. There was a gash on his forehead. "You were sent to kill the intruder, and instead you lead him back. He launched me from the top of the tower toward the cliff. If it weren't for the scaffolding, I would have fallen to my demise. Is this the thanks I get for everything I've done for you?"

Senjek wasn't going to let Daben talk himself out of his fate. He rushed toward his former partner. He dragged the tip of his blade along the ground and threw sparks and shards at Celt. Daben had produced his pistol and started to fire at his former ally. Senjek managed to dodge most of the shots, but one of the slugs pierced his shoulder. Senjek quickly relieved Daben of his gun. He tried to bring his gun-blade through Celt's skull next. Daben had a sword to defend himself, though, and blocked the blow. Senjek switched off the safety of his weapon before the next strike. He pulled the trigger with the following swing. Daben managed to deflect a few of the strikes, but ultimately lost control of his sword and dropped it.

Senjek tried to stab Daben directly in his chest, but he missed. Daben grabbed the barrel of the gun and tried to pry it free of Senjek's grip. He twisted Senjek's wrist and pulled the trigger. The recoil knocked *Kilinus* loose and landed on the ground. Senjek pulled *Selna* from his back and tried to kill his enemy with that. Daben was quicker than he looked. He dropped to one knee, picked up the other gun-blade from the ground and blocked the assault.

Daben rolled away toward his sword. He got to his feet and twirled the hilt in his hand. "You disappoint me, Bohmet. You've chosen Damos over your own people. You know how they've wronged our people. Why fight for them? It's not too late to make this right. Does this Hou-Jo person not validate everything I've said?"

He didn't want to play Daben's game, but he wanted to say his peace. "You turned me into something I wasn't. We started the Lobby as a peaceful protest. You slowly convinced us that violence was needed. You convinced me that some people needed to die for us to be freed from the Republic. Then you put me in a position to let people I care about die. I can't believe you thought I'd look past what happened on Eidolas."

"You've said all of this before, Senjek. What I did was to make you strong. Sacrifices need to be made to save our world!"

Senjek advanced again. Daben was more of a marksman than a swordsman, but he held his own. Senjek had started to feel the pain in his shoulder. He could push through the pain, but his shoulder was less willing to cooperate. The wound to his stomach also held him back. He continued to swing his blade, hoping that his skill would overcome his enemy. He emptied the clip in his gun-blade amongst his strikes, but Daben was still armed. He ejected the clip and tried to reload, but Daben pressed him. Daben caught his blade in the hook of Senjek's weapon. He slid *Kilinus* between the gap of *Selna's* blades. He pushed the edge all the way through until the gun barrel hit one of the braces of Senjek's. Senjek was able to avoid being stabbed. Daben twisted his gun-blade as much as he could and pulled the trigger.

Senjek's blade could handle the recoil. Daben's assault had the opposite effect that he had intended. The blade Daben was holding shattered from the impact. They both backed away from the other. Daben tossed the broken weapon away. The blade broke right above the brace closest to the gun muzzle. Senjek attacked from the left next. Daben was able to parry the strike. Senjek wasn't able to put his full strength behind his strikes.

Daben backed away out of Senjek's striking distance. "What about Treistina? I have her tucked away. If I die, you'll never see her again."

Senjek picked up the broken gun-blade from the ground. He loosened the connection bolt that held the blade to the gun. Daben's newest lie humored him. He wouldn't show his own hand, however. "Don't you worry. I'm sure I'll find whatever hole you put her in." He advanced again. He mostly used the gun-blade that was still in one piece. The broken one didn't have the length to break Celt's defense. It would be good for one thing, though. He put what was left of his strength to push away Daben's sword. He lifted the broken weapon in his other hand and pulled the trigger. The blade flew off, and the final brace came off. Two small shards of metal landed in Daben's chest.

Daben dropped his sword and fell to his back. He sat up and pushed himself back against the wall. "Senjek," he muttered, "don't do this."

Senjek had enough. He lifted *Selna* above his head. He wouldn't give Daben the privilege of any final words. As he pulled the trigger, he heard the boom of the barrel as the blade dug into Daben's face.

# EPILOGUE

The commotion that embroiled the castle had all but subsided. It had returned to the tranquility that it had endured for so many centuries. It did not have its current name when a king ruled Damos. The palace and the surrounding grounds had been officially dubbed Monarch Fall around three-hundred years ago. It served as a monument to the people of the Republic to never forget from where they came. Other monuments were present in the Republic that paid tribute to the advancement of society. Every Repulsor was a monument to Baron von Breischa's bravery and military skill (many would attribute them to the genius of Braeden Almasy, though). The Moaschen Brace was the largest human-made wonder and was a tribute to the might of Old Moashei.

Senjek wondered if the Kramei Independence and Liaison Lobby for Ending Radicalism would have any memorials. During his brief captivity, he heard Lobby members saying that history would name the conflict The KILLER War. He mused on what his legacy would be. Would he be one of the men responsible for the Lobby's rise to power? Or would he be one of the people that brought it down? It was just as possible he'd be listed as both. Or perhaps not mentioned at all.

He hoped that the entire ordeal would merely be a footnote to history. With a single strike of his blade, he cut off the head of the snake. He struggled to catch his breath while Daben breathed his last. Blood poured from the wound in Celt's face. The gun-blade made contact above the right eye and dragged down across the nose and cheek. The cut resumed in the chest and shoulder area on the left. Senjek cut deep enough to rupture many blood vessels. Daben bled out in seconds. Just like that, it was over.

Senjek thought killing the man would grant him peace. He could forgive himself for his past deeds. Something didn't feel right to him. He could feel his chest on fire. He imagined it was a fraction of the rage Hou-Jo felt. He didn't understand Poleb's hatred toward Daben and the Lobby, but it clearly exceeded his own. With Daben dead and Hou-Jo gone, he was sure he'd never find out. He pushed the tip of his blade into the ground and leaned against it. He could feel the adrenaline wearing off. His pains had begun to return to him.

The pain in his stomach had returned. He could also feel the pain of the gunshot wound in his shoulder. He felt a sharp pain in his back as well. He didn't realize he was injured. Between his battle against the Lobby members, Hou-Jo and Daben; it was hard to tell when it happened. He put his second hand on the handle of the gun handle. He felt his knees get weak. He noticed something that he shouldn't have noticed, but he did. There was something wrong with his gun-blade. Something was missing.

He gathered his strength and stopped using *Selna* to brace himself. He lifted the weapon to his face. The slide was locked in the discharge position. He tilted it to look at the bottom of the grip. No magazine. He never reloaded the weapon. He nearly stumbled, but he pressed his free hand against the wall in front of him. He had a feeling why he felt pain in his back. If his weapon didn't have any ammunition, what caused the gunshot as he executed Daben?

He gingerly turned to see what was behind him. He thought maybe it was an undetained member of the Lobby. He hoped it was one of the presidential guards that had regained consciousness. It was the former. Daben had indoctrinated many to follow him. Even with the fight clearly over, his followers would not stop fighting. The war on Kramei would continue until every last rebel was either dead or captured. There was only one reason he was still alive.

He tried to walk toward Treistina, but his strength finally left him. He drove his blade into the ground to keep his balance, but it wasn't enough. It slid out away from him, and he collapsed to both knees. Her only movement was that of her breathing. Since she pulled the trigger, she hadn't moved a muscle. She stood in shock with the gun still pointed at where Senjek stood over Daben. She regained her wits as she saw him fall to the ground. She looked around the room as if she didn't know how she had gotten there. Then she realized she was holding the gun. Daben fell to a cut, not a bullet. The horrible truth soon came to her.

"No," she whispered as she dropped the gun. Senjek struggled to get to his feet, but he lacked the strength. The blood from his back had soaked his shirt and now dripped freely to the ground. She briskly walked over to him. She pulled off her sweater, exposing the bullet-proof vest she wore underneath. She helped Senjek onto his back. She hoped that if she could press him into the floor against her sweater, she could stop the bleeding. She was never trained to save a life, though. She had no idea if it was enough to halt the bleeding.

He reached into his pocket. There was something he wanted to give Treistina. The box was missing from his pocket, though. He pulled out a small glass vial instead. "Right," he cursed. He had forgotten that he had given the ring to Hou-Jo in case something happened to him. He regretted that he had such foresight.

Treistina saw the vial fall to the ground as it slipped from his grasp. She picked it up but was more focused on Senjek's well-being now. "Senjek, I didn't mean to. I couldn't stop myself."

He felt his mouth get dry. "Something Hou-Jo gave me to look after." He could see the confusion on her face. He placed his hand over hers. He tightened his grip so she could feel the vial in her fist. "I don't know if he's dead or not. If he survived he'll seek you out. If not, you must find Naieena. If there's a way to find the Unknown Council, it's through her."

She felt as though she was going to sob. She brought her free hand to her eyes to wipe away tears, but there were still none. She placed her other hand on top of his. "You can give it to him yourself." Her voice began to crack. "I'm going to go to the base of the tower and revive the soldiers down there. They can patch you up."

Senjek shook his head. "It's too late for that now."

"No," she protested. "You're not going to be some hero that died defending what was right. Evan will paint you as a terrorist. Everyone will only ever know you as the Praesage. You're not the man everyone thinks you are. I know who you really are and I'm not giving him up."

"I want you to be happy, Treistina," he murmured.

"So hang in there! One of Evan's guards will happen upon us any second, I know it. Don't leave me!"

Senjek smiled. There was no one else he'd rather be with at the end. He would have never known her if Daben hadn't sent her to keep an eye on him. She was sent to drag him back to hell when the time was right, but she saved his soul. She made him the man he was today. If she had known he was the Praesage from the beginning, she might have never fallen in love with him. The pain he felt was intense. Something hurt more. The knowledge that she would live on with her guilt and her grief.

"You have nothing to repent for." He stared blankly into the distance. She looked back and saw nothing. He had become delirious. "I know you blame yourself for what happened today. Don't. It was always going to end like this."

"Don't talk like that," Treistina pleaded. "I'm sorry. I didn't want this. I love you."

Senjek's gaze refocused on her face. He wrapped his other hand around hers. "I love you too. I know you didn't mean for this to happen. There's a lot of things that happened that I didn't intend too. The Lobby has been dealt a severe blow, but they won't stop. Not while Cineon and Areka still live. You have to continue the fight. You're free of Daben's control. Do something worthwhile with your life. Stop the fighting. This is far from over. Make my life worth something."

"Stop it, Senjek. Just stop." Her heart knew the truth even if her mind wouldn't accept it. "I need you. You're all I have left. You can't leave me. I love you. I love you!"

Senjek grunted. An apparent muscle spasm caused his back to arch; his chest pushed toward the ceiling. He took a deep breath. She felt his grip loosen. He let out a gasp. His back fell back to the floor, and his head dropped to the ground. She could hear footsteps rushing behind her. "The room is clear!"

Treistina wrestled her hands free and placed them on his chest. She felt something on her cheeks. Tears. Real tears. She shook him gently. "Senjek? Senjek, don't do this." She felt a pair of hands grab each of her arms. She didn't have the strength to get free, but that didn't stop her from trying. "No," she croaked. It was Republic soldiers. They had finally found them. "No! Senjek!" She saw others rush in front of her who immediately tended to her lover. She hoped they could revive him, but part of her knew it was too late. "Senjek!" she cried again.

*Today I met a remarkable man. His name is Senjek Bohmet. I wouldn't call him a violent man, but he definitely knows how to defend himself. His passion for the well-being of Kramei rivals my own. He has quite the unique armament. I don't know many men who are skilled in wielding such a weapon, but he does so with grace. He's been protesting the Republic's treatment of our countrymen for months. I think he and I will do quite well together. The future and prosperity of Kramei look bright indeed.*

Veian Grebllyh had lost track of time as he gazed out the window. There was quite the sizable crowd gathered outside the parliament building. His shotgun was loaded and strapped to his back. There might have been protests and outrage over bringing a loaded weapon into parliament just a day ago. No one had the nerve to say anything to him. Part of him was enraged with parliament's actions. Evan's body wasn't even cold yet, but he knew they did what they had to.

"I, Evelyn Lysa Gie, do solemnly swear to serve and protect the Valabrei Republic." She repeated the official words as Vincent von Breischa read them to her. Not once since the founding of the Republic was the verbiage ever updated. "To honor the legacy of the Old Moashei Empire. To lift the Kingdom of Damos to prosperity. To ensure the rights and protection of the Krameian colony and Iedenia. I vow to maintain the peace and justice of the Zerexei system. From the Medium to the Brescha Masses."

Vincent handed Eve the sheath of *Aldring*, the sword itself lost during the Battle of Monarch Fall. The crown and all other treasures of the Poleb family were kept locked away. It was tradition to hand the sheath of *Aldring* to the president when being sworn in to demonstrate the original charter of the Republic. "The Houses of Parliament, in the absence of our King, hereby declare Evelyn Lysa Gie our head of state. Steward of our society, Commander-In-Chief of His Majesty's Army, and President of Damos." He stepped down away from the podium and smiled at her. "Madam President."

Eve swore to heal the relations between Damos and Kramei. She vowed to succeed where her predecessor had failed. Evan was her brother. It clearly pained her as much as it did Veian to refer to him as merely her predecessor. She announced the assassination of Daben Celt by one of his own. Damosi intelligence had discovered the Lobby inside Monarch Fall. Celt's assassin apparently hoped to gain asylum. The man, unfortunately, perished during the raid that detained the fugitives. The same attack also resulted in the demise of President Evan Gie.

"Got some truth in there at least," Veian mumbled to himself. "Even if some details are lacking." He followed close behind her as she left the parliament chamber to a round of applause. He escorted her into the elevator. She asked her other aides to leave her alone. She buried her face in her hands. She wanted to look strong and confident in front of the onlookers, but she couldn't maintain the facade in private. "It's going to be OK, Eve," he said in an attempt to comfort her.

She lifted her head and inhaled loudly. She exhaled just as audibly. "Thank you, Captain. How are you holding up?"

He was touched that she had taken the time to think of his well-being. She had to be strong for the entire nation. He would be strong for her. He smiled. "Veian is fine."

She couldn't help but giggle at that. "What is that, your catchphrase?"

He continued to wear his smile. "Something like that." He put a key into the top floor button and turned it. "You know you don't have to do this now."

"No, I do. I made her a promise. I owe her at least this."

The elevator doors opened. The light of the sky was momentarily blinding. Veian followed Eve across the roof. Treistina Yahn sat on the edge of the roof, waiting. She got to her feet to meet Eve halfway and

326

embraced her. Eve was genuinely sorry for what had happened to her. "How are you holding up?"

"As well as you, I think," she replied candidly. There were no guards on Treistina. There was no way to use the elevator without a key, so she had no way to escape. "What's going to happen to me?"

Veian knew what he would do if the decision were his. He bit his tongue, though. It wasn't his place. Eve put her hands on Treistina's shoulders. "You are my friend. I promised to help you. I failed to live up to that promise. But I won't abandon you. My first act as President will be an executive order to pardon you for your Lobby affiliation. Your record will be sealed. The public will never know. You'll be safe."

"And what about the fighting on Kramei?"

"Eve will petition the Iedenian Guard for assistance," Veian revealed. "If they agree to pledge their support she will rescind Dak Johnsen's position as Suzerain. General Vardos will want to be named to the position, of course. To make up for Evan's sleight. If he insists on a replacement, she will nominate Commandant Baena. He'll be pissed, no doubt. But if he hadn't withdrawn his troops from Eve's security..."

Veian couldn't bring himself to finish that last sentence. If Kaleb Vardos hadn't revoked the squad allowed for the President's protection, Evan might still be alive. "General Vardos had every right to be enraged over Dak's appointment, but he will not be rewarded for his actions," Eve explained. "If he demands a new Suzerain, I will oblige him. And with a member of the Iedenian Guard. But I will not give control of our entire military into the hands of that bastard."

Treistina seemed uneasy over the proposal. "Do you think he'll accept those terms?"

Eve shrugged. "It's hard to know what that man will do. Baron is still missing. We need his help if we're going to put out the fire Daben Celt made."

"I think you might need his help regardless," Treistina retorted. "Don't put too much faith in one man; even if it is a man like Baron von Breischa."

Veian nodded. "I think I might agree with you there, Ms. Yahn." He pulled out a key for parliament's elevator and handed it to her. "You're a free woman. Eve has asked that you be her counselor for Krameian

Affairs. With Mr. Bohmet gone, you're the best viable candidate to coordinate further actions on the ground. Take some time to collect yourself. We'll expect to see you at the next cabinet meeting."

Treistina hugged Eve again before watching her leave with Grebllyh. She watched as the elevator doors closed. She quickly fell onto her bottom. She pulled the vial from her bra. Veian searched her at Monarch Fall, but she was allowed her modesty. She looked at the faint blue color of the liquid inside. She wondered what it was and why Hou-Jo gave it to Senjek. She feared she might never find out.

"I believe that belongs to me," said a voice.

She looked up and saw a man standing in front of her. "Devian Strife. Or should I call you Hou-Jo?"

She suddenly felt the vial fly from her grasp and saw it land in his hand. "Devian Strife was the acting Suzerain of the Second Damosi Patrician Regiment while the Crown Prince of Damos trained for the role. When he died, Xen-Que Poleb assumed the position before his father abdicated the crown to him. I had to use an alias to protect my identity. I don't know who may be watching. Haeese was foolish and reckless to reveal my true name. You would be wise to not make the same mistake."

"You're a wanted man. Half the Republic will be after you for killing Evan Gie."

The regret in his eyes was impossible to conceal. "That was a mistake, but he did attack first."

"You went out of your way to spare Daben's lackeys. What did Evan do to draw your wrath?"

"You wouldn't understand or believe me."

"I might," she replied.

Hou-Jo walked over to the edge of the building. He clambered up the ledge and looked at the lake below. "I hope for your sake and the sake of this whole world that you never do."

Treistina got to her feet. She was clearly upset. "So that's it, then? Daben is dead, and you're just going to leave?"

He turned his head back to face her. Her emerald eyes contrasted the redness of her cheeks. "I am sorry for your loss. I only came for Celt. It wasn't supposed to end like this. Maybe Naieena was right. Maybe I should turn myself over to the Unknown Council. Maybe I should just end my misery."

"Do us both a favor, then," she replied in disdain.

He nodded. "Maybe. Not yet, though. I need to make sure my actions haven't made things worse off. Senjek Bohmet was a good man. I failed him. I will do what I can to honor his memory. If you ever need my help, come back to this rooftop." He handed her a patch. He explained that it once adorned the uniforms of the Damosi Patrician Regiment. It looked just like Veian's, but much older. "Attach that to the flag pole. I'll be there."

She pushed the patch into her back pocket. "And why would I need your help?"

He faced the lake again. He took a deep breath. "I pray that you won't." He extended his arms and dove off the building. She looked over the edge and saw him land in the water. She watched for a few minutes, but he never resurfaced. She felt relieved that he was gone, but also felt a sense of dread. She never wanted to see him again, but part of her feared that she would. She watched the changing colors in the water. Her loss only became more real to her in the last several hours. The light of the sky turned to orange. It was the first satellite set that she had seen without Senjek.

"I'll finish what you started," she whispered. "I'll destroy the beast that you helped create. I promise." She stood at the top of parliament until the light had disappeared over the mountains. Tomorrow would be the first day of the rest of her life. If she had to spend her remaining days stopping the Kramei insurrection, she would.

# The Kramei Insurrection

Made in the USA
Middletown, DE
05 January 2019